Also by Catherine Alliott from Headline:

The Old-Girl Network
Going Too Far
The Real Thing
Rosie Meadows regrets . . .
Olivia's Luck
A Married Man

the wedding day

catherine alliott

First published in Great Britain in 2004
by HEADLINE BOOK PUBLISHING

First published in paperback in Great Britain in 2005
by HEADLINE BOOK PUBLISHING

A HEADLINE paperback

10 9 8 7 6 5 4 3

ISBN 0 7472 6723 5

Typeset in Palatino by
Letterpart Limited, Reigate, Surrey

Printed and bound in Great Britain by
Mackays of Chatham plc, Chatham, Kent

Headline's policy is to use papers that are natural, renewable
and recyclable products and made from wood grown in
sustainable forests. The logging and manufacturing processes
are expected to conform to the environmental regulations of
the country of origin.

HEADLINE BOOK PUBLISHING
A division of Hodder Headline
338 Euston Road
LONDON NW1 3BH

www.headline.co.uk
www.hodderheadline.com

This one's for my mate Sarah.

chapter one

'So you don't think she'll mind?' I asked again, coming back to the breakfast table with two slopping mugs of coffee. I handed him one.

'Annabel, for the last time, I *know* she won't mind.' David reached for a piece of kitchen towel and carefully wiped the bottom of his mug before setting it down. 'That house stands empty for months on end, for heaven's sake, except when she deigns to pop in for two weeks in September. She'll be delighted to have the place occupied; she always is.'

'And you won't mind? I mean, us going?' I perched on a chair opposite him in my threadbare blue dressing gown, cradled my mug in my hands and peered anxiously at him over his propped-up newspaper. 'You'll be here all on your own, David, for the whole summer. Well, most of it, anyway. Be awfully quiet.'

With a sigh, he folded *The Times* carefully into quarters, laid it aside and smiled. 'I'll cope.' He reached across my rickety old pine table, laid his

1

immaculate Hilditch & Key shirt sleeve in the crumbs and detritus of breakfast and squeezed my arm. 'I've coped on my own for the last thirty-odd years. What makes you think I'll forget how to boil a kettle now? Or go out with my underpants on back to front, perhaps? And with the best will in the world, Annie, it's not as if your culinary skills are keeping me from wasting away, either. I think I'll survive. Incidentally, speaking of things culinary, there is a terrible pong in this kitchen.' He dropped my arm and sniffed the air cautiously. 'Emanating, I think, from those Waitrose curry cartons you so lovingly decanted our supper from last night. They're not still lurking about somewhere, are they?' He looked around suspiciously.

'It *would* be rather marvellous,' I went on abstractedly, gazing at a small patch of sunlight on the wall above his left shoulder, dimly aware that my eyes were shining but that I couldn't help it. 'And just what I need right now. Nearly two months of peace and quiet to finish this wretched book, and by the sea, too. And without . . . well . . .'

'Shopping to do and beds to make and the telephone ringing constantly and your bloody sister popping round every five minutes, yes, yes, I agree. We've been through this a million times, Annie, *take* the house in Cornwall and *fin*ish the wretched book and get it over and done with.' He grinned and propped up his newspaper again. Gave it a vigorous shake. 'Go on, bog off.'

'And we'll get married the moment I get back,' I said, putting my mug down decisively.

'And we'll get married the moment you get back,' he repeated from the depths of the broadsheet.

'In the church at the bottom of Cadogan Street? You know, the one we were going to look at? Bully the vicar into letting us use it even though we don't live round there? Offer him, I don't know, money for the church roof or something?'

He ground his teeth, just perceptibly. 'In the church at the bottom of Cadogan Street, corruptible vicar permitting, yes.'

'And only because Mum was cheated out of the church bit the first time round and would love it so, and—'

'Look,' he interrupted, shaking his paper again irritably. 'We've been through this a hundred times, Annie. We've been through the unsatisfactory nature of your charmless wedding to your faithless first husband, and the not unreasonable demands of my future mother-in-law for church nuptials the second time around, and I've *said* yes. Please don't make me tread on hot coals again,' he implored plaintively.

'And Flora would love it too,' I mused, picking up my plate and drifting absently to the sink, stacking it high on top of an already tottering pagoda of dirty dishes. 'The wedding, I mean. Being a bridesmaid, all that sort of thing.'

He caught my wrist suddenly as I floated back and kissed the palm of my hand hard. In a swift movement he'd drawn me down on to his lap. 'Yes, she would,' he murmured, kissing me purposefully on the mouth. 'Now stop it. We've agreed. You go to Cornwall, you take my dippy aunt's house if it hasn't already been washed away by the sea, and you finish your book. Then you return, six weeks later, a woman of letters – and hopefully means, if they sock you the advance they've threatened – and in a matter of days you'll have a ring on your finger and all the bourgeois respectability that goes with being Mrs Palmer, the doctor's wife. Frankly, I think it's an admirable plan, and to be honest I don't really mind what you do so long as you stop burning the toast and making me drink coffee you can stand a spoon up in in Flora's chipped Groovy Chick mug.' He peered balefully into its pink depths.

'I'll have it back then, shall I? Since you're fussy?' Flora, having pounded downstairs, came through the door in her school uniform and plucked the mug from under his nose. She tasted it and made a face. 'Ugh, you're right, it's vile. Mum, pretending to make real coffee by putting in three spoonfuls of instant is not going to wash with your urbane, sophisticated boyfriend, you know.' She went to the sink and poured it away. 'And what are all these curry cartons doing in the sink?' She poked the precarious pile with an incredulous finger. 'No wonder it stinks in here. And stop hopping around,' she added as I hastily got off David's lap, blushing. 'You're sharing a bed together in this house, for

4

God's sake, I don't see that a cuddle at the breakfast table makes any difference.' She grinned conspiratorially at David, clearly relishing her role as the mature observer of impulsive love-birds. He winked good-naturedly back.

'Flora's right. Stop behaving as if we're just playing Scrabble up there and give her a little credit. And incidentally, where exactly does my new step-daughter fit into this great summer scheme of yours?'

I looked at him quickly, wondering for the first time if this was a veiled reproach, but his grey eyes were twinkling with amusement.

'What scheme?' demanded Flora. She threw back her head and gathered a sheet of silky dark hair into her hands, ready for the scrunchy poised between her teeth.

'Well, Flora, nothing's set in stone,' I began nervously, 'but you know this book I've been trying to—'

'Oh God, is it ten past?' Her eyes flew to the clock. 'My bus!' She seized a piece of burnt toast from the toaster and simultaneously stuffed books in a bag with the other. 'Yes, I know your book.'

'Well, Gertrude has a place by the sea, apparently.' I twisted my fingers anxiously, following her as she dashed around the kitchen gathering together gym kit, pencil case, trainers. 'You know, David's aunt—'

'Yes, of course I know Gertrude. Has she? I didn't know that.' She threw an enquiring glance over her shoulder at David as she reached behind the door for her lacrosse stick and shoes.

He nodded. 'She does.'

'And . . . well, I thought I might go there. Borrow it, just for the summer. Just for six weeks or so—'

'Six weeks!' She paused. Stopped her packing and gazed. 'What, you mean . . . and I'll stay here? With David?'

'Oh no! No, I didn't mean that. No, it'll be during the school holidays, so you'll come with me. I'll be working, obviously, but I could get a nanny or something . . .'

'A *nanny*. God, Mum, I'm twelve. I don't need a nanny.'

'Well, you know, a girl, a teenager or something. An Aussie girl perhaps. Just for you to play with, to keep an eye on you.'

'Play, Mother?' She regarded me witheringly. Shook her head and resumed her packing. 'I can amuse myself. And anyway, I think I'd rather be in London. All my friends are staying in London for the summer, and I could stay here with David, couldn't I?'

'Doesn't matter a jot to me,' said David equably, getting up from the table and reaching for his suit jacket on the back of a chair.

I looked at him gratefully, loving him for playing to her bravado. For not saying: 'What friends, Flora?' or: 'Flora, do me a favour, you can't even manage a *sleep*over without your mum, let alone six weeks.'

'You girls sort it out between yourselves,' he went

on. 'Frankly, I think you'll have a job persuading your mother to leave you behind, but on the other hand, I think Flora's right. I'm not convinced she needs nannying amongst the rock pools. Other than that' – he held up his hands to stem the flow of protests en route from both of us – 'not my problem. I ain't getting involved.' He grinned. 'One of the perks of marrying into a ready-made family, see. They get to sort out their own domestics.' He glanced at his watch. 'And I'm going to be late for surgery if I don't get a wiggle on, so I'll see you both later.' He kissed me again on the mouth and tweaked Flora's pony-tail on the way out. 'Bye, you.'

'Bye.' She grinned good-naturedly back.

When he'd disappeared down the front hall and the door had shut behind him, the stained-glass panes rattling in the frame, I turned anxiously to her.

'But you will come with me, won't you, Flora? I hadn't planned on doing this without you, you know.'

She munched her toast without looking at me. Brushed some crumbs from her mouth with the back of her hand.

'Hadn't talked to me about it though, had you?'

'Well, no.' I hesitated. 'Obviously I had to talk to David first.' I paused, letting this new level of hierarchy sink in, then lost my nerve. 'I mean,' I said quickly, 'he's the one being left behind, and anyway, apart from anything else, I haven't asked Gertrude yet. The house does belong to her, and I haven't even asked if I can borrow it yet.'

There was a silence as she fixed a silver grip carefully in the side of her hair.

'Where is this place, anyway?'

'Down on the north coast of Cornwall, near Rock. It's really pretty.'

'How do you know?'

'Well, apparently. And perched high up on the top of a cliff and – oh Flora, you can surf there and water-ski, sail dinghies, learn to ride, all that sort of thing. You'll have a terrific time! You'll meet people, make friends—'

'OK, OK, stop selling it. You'll be throwing in sing-songs around the campfire next. And what about David? Why isn't he coming?'

'He will, of course he will, for weekends. But he can't take all that time off, particularly if we want to have a honeymoon later on in the year.' I hesitated. 'Flora, you do realise we will *have* a honeymoon . . .'

'Oh God, I'm not coming on that!'

'No no,' I said quickly. 'Just checking you knew.'

'Mum, do me a favour.' She made a gormless face. 'Anyway, Granny will come and look after me, won't she?' She contrived to look nonchalant but her dark eyes were anxious and my heart lurched for her.

'Of course she will.'

Suddenly her face paled as she saw the sock she'd been looking for in the fruit bowl. She seized it.

'Oh Mum, my name tags! You didn't sew them on my games things and Miss Taylor said I'll get a debit

8

if they're not on by today!'

'Flora, it's quarter past already. Why didn't you remind me last night?'

'But I'll get a debit!' she wailed, pulling the whole kit out of her bag in a crumpled heap. 'And you never ironed it, and she said unless each piece is named, including the socks—'

'Here.' I snatched them up and ran to the kitchen drawer. The first biro nib disappeared up its plastic shaft, the second had no ink, so I seized a red felt pen and began to scrawl frenziedly.

'In pen?'

'So long as it's named, she won't mind,' I muttered. 'Tell her I'll do it properly tonight.'

As the red ink ran hideously into the cuff of her white socks I avoided her eyes which were round with horror. Poor Flora, always on the lookout for something new to fret about and always finding it in me. My daughter: so immaculate, so conscientious, so pristine, so fearful of incurring the potential anger of her teachers; a classroom helper and practically life-time holder of the manners badge, with shoes you could see your face in she shined them so assiduously at the kitchen table; and with a mother who tried hard to come up to her scrupulous standards, but failed miserably.

'Anyway, games today?' I stuffed it all back in hurriedly. 'I thought I wrote you a note? I thought you weren't doing games this week?'

'I tore it up,' she quaked. 'I know what she'll say.

9

It's no excuse. Lots of girls have periods, Mum. She won't let me off for that.'

I glanced up at my daughter's fearful face, but didn't comment. My petite, small-boned Flora, beautiful and dark with her huge brown eyes and her underdeveloped, childlike body, who, since the beginning of the year, had been brutally and systematically felled once a month with crippling tummy cramps and nausea. Doubled up with pain, her white face contorted with agony, she'd come home from school, drop her bags on the floor and collapse in a heap on the sofa whilst I hastened to get her a hot-water bottle to clutch to her stomach and a fistful of paracetamol.

'What is it, gym or netball?'

'Netball,' she said thankfully. 'At least I get to wear a skirt.'

I nodded, tight-lipped. 'OK. Now go. Go, darling, the bus will be at the corner any minute.'

We both glanced up as the familiar rattle heralded its approach and, through the kitchen window, saw the yellow school bus trundle around the corner.

'Go!' I yelled.

She went, snatching up her bags, flying down the passage and through the front door as I followed behind. But halfway down the garden path she turned. Ran back. Threw her arms around me.

'Bye, Mummy.'

'Bye.'

I hugged her hard. Kissed the top of her dark head

furiously to remind her how much I loved her. Then I turned her around by her shoulders, gave her a little push, and off she flew.

I stood at the door, shading my eyes against the low morning sun, watching as she boarded the bus. I saw her glance nervously over her shoulder as a couple of the older girls in short skirts bounded noisily up behind her. This morning they smiled as she turned, so she smiled back, then glanced quickly at me, to see if I'd noticed she'd been included. I held my smile, a lump in my throat.

'Four o'clock,' she mouthed, and I nodded. And not a moment later, she meant. Not a *mo*ment later.

The bus purred off and I stayed in the doorway, leaning on the frame and glancing up and down the quiet, tree-lined London street. The Victorian villas were more or less identical, give or take the window-box planting or the variety of white geraniums art-fully arranged around the front doors, and the sun, at this time in the morning, lit up our side of the street like a film set. Periodically, doors would open and spew out their occupants: schoolchildren followed by harassed mothers raking combs through their hair, jingling keys down to four-wheel-drives at the kerb, yelling enquiries to their offspring about vio-lins and book-bags; fathers, less crumpled – dapper even – in their dark suits, firmly shutting garden gates behind them (something the mothers never did) and forgetting, in that instant as it clanged behind them, the food-encrusted high chairs and

11

spilled Rice Krispies packets within, focusing only on the day ahead and the ebb and flow of the money markets as they headed purposefully for the City. Men who looked a whole lot like David, I reflected as I stood there, pleased, for once, to have a man who fitted in. Who conformed. Unlike Adam.

David was a GP, with salubrious premises in Sloane Street, which – if he'd caught his bus – he was doubtless striding towards even now. Off to heal the monied sick, off to the oak-panelled surgery where his late uncle, Hugh, Gertrude's husband, had practised before him, and Hugh's father before that; to the spacious second-floor consulting rooms which, lofty and sunlit, were flanked on either side by Gucci and Armani, ensuring, as I always quipped to David, that his patients arrived truly well heeled. But, as David always rather caustically quipped back, money couldn't cushion everything, and bum boils were bum boils no matter whose arse they were on. Neither the sheen on his mahogany desk nor the warmth of his Persian carpet, he maintained, could glamorise the lancing of them, however tasteful the underwear that had been dropped to reveal them.

So Belgravia was his given patch; and whilst it might be more uplifting, soul-wise, to serve the poor, to be shoving his way through a jam-packed, bug-ridden waiting room full of terminal coughers to get to his broom cupboard of a surgery in Peckham, people were still taken ill in his part of the world, and he was no less conscientious or hardworking than his colleagues on the other side of the city. Yes, he had chi-chi premises, but he still did everything in his power to save his patients from undue pain. And it was here, near to his Sloane Street surgery, that he'd saved me, too. In so many ways.

The first thing I'd noticed about David had been his eyes, huge with horror as he came towards me at a run, arms outstretched, ready to push me away.

'Look out!' he cried as a sheet of plate glass, the one in the window of Boots the Chemists, had been about to receive a mighty blow from a parcel of bricks swinging precariously from a rope as they were incompetently raised by distracted workmen to scaffolding on the roof above. As the bricks hovered, swayed, and then lurched perilously close to the window, David simultaneously launched himself at me and Flora – just as the glass smashed to smithereens. As we were flung across the pavement with David prone on top of us, he looked up and let loose a stream of abuse at the workmen, the first and last time I ever heard him swear.

Thankfully the glass had fallen pretty much vertically and hadn't injured us, but David wasn't satisfied. As he picked himself up from the pavement and helped us to our feet, he took one look at the two tremulous females before him – who for various reasons hadn't been in the best of health even before the glass had shattered – and insisted we accompany him back to his surgery so he could check us over. I protested, but he was adamant.

'I promise you,' he said, 'you're as white as a sheet.'

'No, really, I'm fine.'

'Then you won't mind if I take your pulse?'

'No . . . but I think – oh God . . .' I put a hesitant hand to my forehead.

'You might be about to pass out?'

I nodded and, as I crumpled, he helped me to sit in an undignified heap on the kerb again, this time with my head between my knees in the gutter.

He squatted beside me, one hand on my back, and made me stay like that for a good few minutes whilst making reassuring noises and reminding me to breathe. Flora, meanwhile, scratched her leg awkwardly and went very pink. An interested flow of people were rubber-necking past, and even as the nausea swelled within me I knew she was thinking: Oh, please God, please *God* don't let there be anyone from my school.

After that little bit of street theatre I didn't really have a leg to stand on – literally or figuratively – so, with Flora trailing behind us, David helped me around the corner to his rooms on Sloane Street. They were through an archway, off the main road, and above a shady courtyard, and shaken as I was, I do remember thinking that the little Italianate piazza complete with fountain and exotic palm plants we skirted around before going up the stone entrance steps and through the heavy oak door was all pretty damned swanky. Once inside, in the hushed, marble hall, David nodded to the uniformed concierge before shepherding us into an old-fashioned lift which concertinaed shut behind us like a gilded cage. We purred up in silence. On the second floor, the smooth blonde receptionist instantly abandoned Nigel Dempster and was all tea and sympathy at the sight of us, which Flora and I – completely overwhelmed now by the opulence of our surroundings – meekly lapped up. As we trooped into David's consulting room, the deep shine of the furniture, the pall of antiquity on the oils hanging from the panelling and the chesterfield sofa I was invited to sit upon all further contrived to render us mute and helpless. My daughter and I recognise social superiority when we see it.

David shone a torch in my eyes, and then carefully looked at my face.

'I'm checking for minuscule shards of glass . . .' he murmured, really very close up now, peering disconcertingly around. I could feel my cheeks reddening.

'But actually . . . you look . . . perfect.'

I flushed to my roots at this and, for a split second, he caught my eye. And that's where it all began, I think. In the eyes.

He cleared his throat and moved swiftly across to examine Flora, who was perched on an identical sofa on the opposite side of the room. This not only gave me an opportunity to breathe, but also to look at him.

God, he was handsome. Crouched as he was at my daughter's feet in his immaculate charcoal-grey suit

15

– oblivious of the fact that he might be kneeing his trousers on the oriental carpet – he made an attractive spectacle. His hair was fair and soft and swept back in a rather up-market way, and his narrow intelligent face, lightly tanned from a recent holiday, was concentrated into a look of deep concern. Flora sat before him, quiet as a mouse.

'You both look fine,' he declared suddenly, springing athletically to his feet. He snapped the torch back into a nifty little leather holster and went to perch on the edge of his desk, arms folded, elegant long legs stretched out before him, crossed at the ankles. He regarded us kindly. 'Though a little shaky. But if I were a betting man, I'd put your pallor down to exhaustion rather than the shock of that plate-glass window shattering. When did the pair of you last eat?'

I cleared my throat and tentatively admitted that we'd missed breakfast. Oh yes, and lunch too, on account of Flora being unable to face a thing with her appalling tummy cramps and me being too tired to contemplate food having been up all night trying to write. He frowned.

'I see. And you thought, having been up all night, that a little shopping spree in Knightsbridge might revive you?'

I smiled at his irony and gave him some of mine.

'Flora had set her heart on a pair of trousers. A crucial, must-have combat style that can't be found locally. Without them, her life would not be complete.

It had to be Knightsbridge.' I wasn't to know he wasn't a parent and that this would be lost on him.

He looked perplexed and said that he thought a decent breakfast a bit more important than a pair of trousers, and that since he'd been on his way to lunch when he'd literally bumped into us, why didn't we accompany him to Starbucks for coffee and sandwiches?

All of which, naturally, was above and beyond your average GP's call of duty, but as he explained to me later – much later, in bed in Fulham – behind the shock and fragility I was exhibiting that day he'd glimpsed something else. Something that made me an A1 example of the sort of woman – pale, gamine, ethereal and with long dark tresses – that he wasn't aware that he liked. And, whilst he didn't normally succumb to fey charms of this kind, he was suitably intrigued, not just to check me out for scratches, but to follow up the consultation with sustenance.

The hot chocolate and egg mayonnaise rolls in the window of the sunny café went down a treat and Flora and I guzzled greedily as dust motes gathered in shafts of light around us. Afterwards, equilibrium restored and swivelling restlessly on her high bar stool, my daughter announced that she was going down to Gap to secure the trousers. Promising to be no longer than twenty minutes, she disappeared, leaving the stage free for David to use those twenty minutes – impulsively I now realise, with the convenience of hindsight – to extract from me a promise to be allowed to restore my blood sugar levels further at a restaurant of his choice the following evening.

That next night, after dinner, he'd taken me to bed. To my bed, in Fulham, becoming the only man to occupy the slot on the left-hand side of the Heal's summer sale bargain since my ex-husband Adam had vacated it. All of which totally disproved a long-held theory of mine, which went that if I ever *did* meet someone I liked enough for that to happen, I'd let him dangle for months for fear of making the same mistake again. Yet after our very first date – only thirty-six hours after our very first encounter in fact – there he was beside me, and I knew it was no mistake. Sexual desire had been obvious – it had been clear and sudden for both of us, minutes after meeting – but as he'd taken my elbow outside the Italian restaurant that night and manoeuvred me across the rain-soaked street to a taxi, threading his way expertly through the traffic, I'd been surprised to find myself, not only with all nerve endings tingling, but also precipitously in love with a man I hardly knew. Happily, he'd known it too, and a year later – almost to the day – here we were, on the brink of a wedding and a future together.

David moved into my tiny, bijou Fulham house, full of folk art and scatter cushions and twee clutter and rickety pine furniture, and left behind his spacious, minimalist, double O seven flat in Islington. It made sense, practicably, Islington being too far for

Flora to travel to school; but nevertheless, in my eyes, it was another expression of his love. The plan was to marry in the autumn, to sell both the properties and to buy in leafy Hurlingham, where, David predicted, the garden would soon play host to a pram, a paddling pool and, later, a tricycle or two.

All of which, frankly, made me want to pinch myself. In fact, as I confided to my sister Clare a few weeks after the Sloane Street incident and the Italian dinner, and with David safely installed in my tiny Fulham house, it almost made me want to believe there was Someone Up There rooting for me after all. We were in her kitchen at the time, picking at a carrot cake she'd ostensibly made for the children.

'I mean honestly, Clare, considering.'

'Considering what?' she'd retorted, spraying crumbs everywhere.

'Well, considering there've been times over the last couple of years when I'd begun to wonder if my continued existence on this earth was to anyone's advantage – let alone my own – to find myself feeling like a contender for the happiest girl in the world is surely little short of miraculous, isn't it?'

Clare had made her famous face: mouth turned down at the sides, neck muscles taut, head bobbing dubiously from side to side. But in the end she'd conceded that actually, given my provenance, it probably was. She snapped the lid smartly on the cake tin. Little short of miraculous.

chapter two

It was to Clare's that I went now, having seen David and Flora off to work and school respectively, and having thrown the cereal bowls and spoons in the dishwasher. Admittedly I hadn't made it upstairs to turn lights off, open curtains or flush loos, but there was plenty of time for all that later, I decided as I hurried round to my sister's to share my news.

Clare lived three streets away from me, in a much taller, more elegant, cream town house – three storeys and a basement with a leafy walled garden – and where she'd been a lot longer. When I'd finally left Adam I'd flown geographically to her side, buying a place literally round the corner, unashamedly clinging to the small but strong residue of family I had in her: my big sister, my rock, who, from the moment she'd set eyes on Adam all those years ago, had folded her arms and declared, 'He's a shit of the first order, Annabel. Have nothing to do with him.'

Well, naturally I'd had everything to do with him and she'd had to moderate her tone.

'Well, no, OK,' she'd conceded warily, seeing me starry-eyed and with a heart-shaped locket containing his photo around my neck, for heaven's sake. 'He's not a *complete* shit, and gorgeous, I grant you, but a *boy*, Annie, who looks and behaves like a red setter puppy. He'll need regular meals and exercise, but the moment your back's turned, he'll go for a walk with anyone who jangles a lead.'

And I'd been proud to prove her wrong. I'd been proud to go out with him for three, glorious, monogamous years, and have him propose to me on a Hawaiian beach, and get married there, barefoot and with flowers in my hair, three days later. I'd returned home the proud owner of a dashing up-and-coming-actor husband, a dear little ring set with tiny seed pearls, a rented flat in Chiswick and a Peter Jones charge card. I also had a baby on the way, and all this before my sister – four years older than me, mind – had even got off the starting blocks.

Yet, as ever, her foresight had proved to be horribly accurate. He'd wavered when I was big with child, cast sheep's eyes at waitresses in my ninth month, and flirted outrageously with the assistant in Mothercare as we bought the changing mat. He'd balked at the breastfeeding and, having read an article which informed him he might be feeling excluded, instantly sought solace in candlelit restaurants with various supportive supporting actresses. He absented himself regularly on theatre tours during Flora's toddlerhood, and finally flitted off to Lyons on her first day at school with a nubile cycling enthusiast called Sandra, who was keen to introduce him to the joys of the Tour de France. He returned a week later – breezing brazenly through the back door and flicking on the kettle as if he'd just been to the paper shop – and confided to me in breathless tones that during the race competitors didn't stop to urinate, but peed in their spray-on shorts to avoid losing valuable seconds. Which pretty much summed him up, Clare and I decided later: can't stop now, late already, might be a pretty girl around the corner, better pee my pants just in case.

So what had attracted me to this man in the first place, you might wonder? Well, apart from fabulous dark good looks, Romany gypsy curls, and charm that would have the birds dive-bombing from the trees, there was also his strong gravitational pull. As if anything worth happening was happening around him. Charisma, I believe it's called, and to a nineteen-year-old farmer's daughter from Devon whose idea of a wild night out was a few drinks in the local with a group of friends I'd known all my life, his brand of London-based, theatre-world charisma was pretty irresistible.

Adam had originally arrived in our West Country market town in a production of *The Tempest*. He'd blown me away with his Ferdinand, his smouldering brown eyes, his declaiming speeches, his strutting on and off stage and his terribly tight doublet and hose.

'O brave new world,' I'd boggled with Miranda, 'that has such people in it.' After the performance I'd left my seat in a daze, hands sore from applauding, determined to go backstage to see him.

'You're going backstage?' Clare and my best friend Rosie had exclaimed, regarding me in horror. 'This isn't Drury Lane, you know. It's only a rep production in Tavistock, for God's sake. He'll think you're barking!'

Barking or not, I went, and they waited for me in the car, appalled at my lack of restraint, and giggling behind their hands as they watched me approach the stage door. But they hadn't accounted for Adam's ego, which was as big as the Ritz. He'd been neither derisive nor embarrassed by my stammering compliments, but merely taken them as his due as the next Olivier. I seem to remember him flushing initially with pleasure, then adjusting his tights and inviting me into the tiny dressing room. It was jam packed with other actors, but he introduced me to them all in a grand sweeping gesture, then without further ado, backed me into a corner, and flashed a look of unequivocal desire at me. As I basked in it, feeling his eyes literally frazzling my eyelashes, he'd swiftly followed through with a murmured invitation in my ear to join him for dinner that evening.

'But you don't know him!' Clare had gawped at me as she hurriedly wound down the fugged-up driver's window when I'd belted back to the car park to report. 'He could be anyone!'

'But he's not anyone, we know that. He's a brilliant young actor on his way to the top and—'

'Did he tell you that?' she demanded.

'Well, yes. And anyway, we're only going round the corner to La Cassata,' I added casually.

'La Cassata!' they shrieked in unison. Rosie's eyes over Clare's shoulder were huge and I could tell she was impressed. It was the only restaurant in town that had tablecloths.

'What'll I say to Mum?' hissed Clare.

'Tell her I was invited out, but *don't* tell her I picked him up,' I added quickly. 'Just say . . . Oh, say he spied me in the audience and – and sent me a note. Something like that.'

'Give me strength.' Clare rolled her eyes. 'He spotted her in the stalls and their eyes met over the conductor's baton.' She brusquely shifted the gears in our ancient Escort and lurched off down the road. 'You've seen too many films!' she yelled back.

I had, and Adam had too, particularly the one in which the leading man wines and dines his adoring fan and then she, heady with love, gives up her place at the local technical college and trails around the country with him, sitting in cold repertory theatres smoking Gitanes in black roll-neck jumpers and helping him learn his lines. There I'd be during every performance, always in the front row, always word perfect, and then, during the day, when I wasn't needed for prompting at rehearsals, waiting for him in some seedy bed-sit, writing short stories to pass the time. One or two were taken by *Woman's Realm*, which helped to pay the rent, and very occasionally I reached the dizzy heights of *Woman's Own*.

I suppose, in retrospect, that that was the one productive thing to come out of our union together, besides Flora. Those early years were conducive to writing, and I spent most of my time lying on candle-wick bedspreads in chilly bedrooms in seaside towns, penning my stories.

Despite my family's horror – my mother, alone at the farm now that Dad had died, felt she'd let me drift and that Dad wouldn't have – I truly believed, and still do believe, that Adam loved me. And Flora too. It was just that he was constitutionally unsuited for marriage. He simply couldn't help falling in love with other women.

Our coming unstuck was a gradual process. There was the first phase in our marriage when I knew about the infidelity and was heartbroken, but loved him so much I couldn't do anything about it. Then there was the second phase, when I confronted him, he broke down and said it would never happen again and I believed him. The next impasse we reached was when I knew it wouldn't stop, but was still too much in love to pack my bags. Finally though – and I'm talking an embarrassing number of years here – I mustered the strength to take Flora away and live elsewhere. I put down a deposit on the little house in Fulham with some money Dad had left me, and told Adam it was for ever. He didn't believe me, but I waited until he'd gone to rehearsals, then dragged the suitcases downstairs and, blinded by tears, sobbed my way to the car, with Flora trailing miserably behind me.

Adam visited us daily; in fact, he practically camped out in our front garden. Ostensibly he was there to see Flora, for which I was grateful, but principally it was to see me, to try to win me over and woo me back. He was honestly baffled by what he saw as a complete overreaction, and unable to understand why a few dalliances with other women had caused me to up sticks and file for divorce.

'But, Annie, you're my wife! You're literally the only person in the world apart from Flora that I really love, you must know that,' he'd cried, the decree nisi poised and awaiting his signature on my kitchen table. He was like a child standing there, wide-eyed and genuinely stricken. 'It's only *ever* been you, Annie. Don't do this to me!'

Me doing it to him, note. But by now I'd met David. Just. And I was slightly stronger, was eating properly, and sleeping a little bit more. My defences were not quite so low. I gave a tight smile.

'Sorry, Adam, it's me, I know. My fault. Call me old-fashioned, but I've got this thing about monogamy.'

He sighed and scratched his head. Shook it incredulously.

'Crazy. So middle class. So bourgeois, Annie, and highly irresponsible too, I might add. We have a daughter, in case you hadn't noticed, an impressionable, eleven-year-old child. What sort of message do you think this sends to her, walking out on our marriage? What sort of moral guidance are you giving her here, hm? And incidentally, how many married men d'you think are out there that *don't* stray occasionally? Not many, I can tell you,' he snorted, 'even if they may claim otherwise. At least I'm honest, for Christ's sake. At least I don't lie to you!'

'I wish you did,' I said wearily.

'Annie, men are different,' he explained patiently. 'Surely you know that by now? Different hormones, different biological make-up, different needs. Staying constant to one woman for the rest of our lives, however much we love her, is terribly, terribly difficult. But I do love you, Annie, I swear it, and it's only ever been you, despite my appalling record in the matrimonial stakes.' He paused. Scratched his head. 'All right if I borrow the lawnmower?'

I blinked. 'The lawnmower?'

'Francine's lawn needs mowing. She's playing Titania to my Oberon and I'm staying with her now that I've given up the flat. I couldn't face being there without you and Flora' – he shot me a bruised look – 'so I've gone over to her place. I said I'd help out a bit. You know, around the house. In lieu of rent.'

'Staying?' I folded my arms, eyebrows raised.

'Yes, just staying, Annie,' he said, affronted.

'Spare room?'

27

'Well, no . . .' He hesitated. 'She hasn't got one. But hell, it's nothing serious.'

I smiled. 'The lawnmower's in the shed, Adam. Help yourself.'

And so he went. In a huff. Really offended. Firmly convinced that I was the guilty party here. How *could* I leave him? How could I walk out on him and render him homeless? And what was he supposed to do, for God's sake, in his hour of need, aside from snuggle up with another human body for warmth and comfort?

And I knew, too, that a smidgen of what he'd said was true. That plenty of husbands did conduct themselves so, and none so honestly as Adam. And plenty of women accepted these marriages, right across the board: women in high-rise blocks, blankly staring at television screens awaiting the return of the father of five from the barmaid's arms; in the leafy stock-broker belt, staring at chintzy bedroom walls whilst the company director found his shoes in his secretary's bedroom; in classy Holland Park, pretending to read *Interiors* in the drawing room as the cabinet minister's footsteps came up the path, fresh from his young researcher's arms. And I didn't deride those wives either, because I knew how much easier it was to accept it, as I'd accepted it too, for a time. All right, for years. Eleven. Turned a blind eye. But when Flora was old enough to know what was going on too, and would turn not blind but astonished brown eyes on me when we heard his key in the lock way past ten o'clock as we sat watching the news together, and when, on one occasion, we even heard him outside the flat whispering goodnight to someone, I knew I had to escape with a few shreds of dignity intact. For her sake.

But it was hard. Bloody hard. Because I loved him. And just as I was wondering if dignity was such a big deal, or if being with the man I loved even if he did have the morals of an alley cat was more important, David stepped in. And saved us. Just in time. He arrived, as Clare often drily said, like the Seventh Cavalry, just as I was wavering. And just as my family were wondering, holding their breath in horror, if I'd bolt back to Adam.

As I opened Clare's black wrought-iron gate now and ducked under the magnolia tree in her front garden, I remembered her face as I'd shyly introduced her to David. Relief had flooded it. In fact, for a moment I'd thought she was going to drop to her knees and kiss his turn-ups.

I rang her bell and heard sharp high heels echoing down the passageway. A moment later the door opened and Clare stood before me, dark hair swept up in a chignon, fully made up and immaculate in a charcoal-grey Joseph suit. Her nose was in the air, but that was because her husband's glasses – a few sizes too big for her – were balanced on it. Handy, as she often crisply observed, to have compatible eyes, if nothing else.

'Oh, it's you.'

29

She turned and stalked quickly back to the kitchen. I wasn't affronted. A typical early morning greeting from a woman who's already got a husband off to work, two children to school, and is spooning Milupa into another whilst trying to get to the City herself.

'Bad moment?' I called, shutting the door behind me. 'I thought you didn't go in 'til later on Fridays?'

'Not this Friday,' she called back. 'There's a partners' meeting and I have to be there. I'm leaving in ten minutes.'

I followed her down to the kitchen where a wailing noise was emanating from, and where Henry, her toddler, was banging a spoon impatiently in his high chair, annoyed that the flow of nutrition had been interrupted. I boggled as Clare efficiently threw a white sheet over her head and stuck her arms through a couple of holes.

'What's that for?'

'I made it. Michael calls it my shroud. I use it to feed the children in.'

I giggled. 'Surprised you haven't got gloves and a surgical mask!'

'Oh, don't tempt me. I've resorted to Marigolds in the past, why not a mask as well?'

She dragged out a chair for me and perched on the edge of hers, resuming spooning duty as Henry opened, shut, swallowed, opened, shut, swallowed, faster than she could get it in.

'Eats well,' I hazarded, sitting down at the

immaculate breakfast table, cleared for action already save for a jar of tulips and Henry's bowl. How unlike mine, I thought, with its jumble of cereal packets, screwed-up tissues, dog-eared paperbacks and piles of bills and junk mail still mouldering peacefully.

'He has to,' she replied darkly. 'Poor little devil. He knows it might be the only square meal he'll get today. If Donna can bear to tear herself away from her mobile phone and *Countdown* to throw him a rusk he'll be lucky, so he gets it down his neck while he can.'

'Now you know that's not true,' I soothed. 'Donna does a brilliant job. Michael was only telling me the other day what an asset she's been.'

'Oh yes, an unbelievably effing marvellous asset, particularly from his point of view. If you had someone hanging on to your every word and laughing at your jokes and asking if they could possibly iron your underpants, you'd consider them an asset too.'

'You're making it up as you go along,' I said coolly. 'Donna doesn't give two hoots for Michael, and vice versa. You're just oversensitive.'

'Oversensitive, am I? Ah. And why might that be, I wonder?'

'Clare . . .' I sighed.

'Because my husband was caught fumbling up his fund manager's dress at the Christmas party while the rest of his department tittered and watched? In full view of everyone on the dance floor, and then behind the coat rack while people reached for their

31

pashminas? That, according to one of my more recent, reliable sources, was where they finally ended up. On the sticky carpet.' Her eyes widened. 'But surely that wouldn't render me oversensitive, Annie?'

'He wasn't caught,' I said patiently, 'he admitted it, and the only reason people are embellishing the story is because you invite it. You keep telling people you know, and that you don't mind and think it's refreshing to have it out in the open, and so they give you a bit more. And the only reason *he* told you was because the guilt was killing him. Anyway, he was drunk and it was a one-off snog and it was *months* ago, and you've belly-ached about it ever since. When are you going to let him off the hook, Clare?'

I got up impatiently and filled the kettle.

She put the spoon down. 'Oh, you think I should, do you? Like you did all those years with Adam. Turn a blind eye and say: Hey, who cares? Screw who you like, darling, I'll always be here?'

Henry yelled indignantly and waved his arms. She picked up the spoon again.

'No,' I said evenly, 'I don't. And if this is what this is all about, Clare, about not turning into me, then I have to tell you there's little chance of that. You're much too tough and not nearly as stupid.'

I turned and faced her defiantly. She gazed at me, two pink spots appearing in her cheeks. Suddenly her shoulders sagged and she sighed.

'OK,' she caved in. 'Sorry. I didn't mean that.

Didn't mean you were stupid. It's just . . . well, it eats away at me, Annie. I imagine him – them together. You know. Every time he touches me. And I don't think about it all the time, it's just when he wants sex. Like this morning, for instance. We both woke up early, and with our busy schedules and our increasingly savvy children who usually blunder in at inopportune moments for once still fast asleep, it should have been an ideal opportunity. But somehow – I just couldn't do it. I see his arms round her. Picture him kissing her, and—'

'So walk out,' I interrupted, sharply.

She stared. Gave a short bark of a laugh. 'Oh, don't be silly. I can't do that.'

'Why not?'

'Well, because there're the kids and the house and everything, and—'

'Exactly, so forget it.' I banged a coffee cup down in front of her, spilling half of it. 'Hell, Clare, a one-night stand. *Half* a one-night stand, a quarter even, a fumble that was going nowhere except to the back of the coat closet. Don't wreck the rest of your married life together just because of it!'

'You see,' she said gloomily, instantly reaching for some kitchen paper to wipe the coffee I'd spilled, 'that's the trouble. That's the difference between you and me. I can't forgive. Can't forget. And there's nothing going on between Michael and Donna incidentally. No hot looks on her part and meaningful glances on his. Michael's not even remotely interested. God, he's so terrified of me at the moment he even leaves the room so as not to be accused of flirting with the girl. It's just . . . well, it's me. I'm paranoid now, and I can't help feeling it'll happen again. And be more serious next time. And that I'll be left with four children under twelve because I took my eye off the ball and was always in meetings. Never there for my husband. Never having my nails done, or getting trim at the gym, or having my hair cut at Michaeljohn.'

'Oh, you mean like the rest of us stay-at-home mothers,' I said acidly.

'No, I didn't mean that either. I know you're not.' She swept a hand over her perfect chignon. 'It's just – well I do wonder whether it was my fault. Michael and that girl. Because I do too much, take on too much, and don't notice everything coming apart at the seams. That office party was a year after Henry was born, you know, Annie, and I was still breast-feeding at night for God's sake. But why? Why was I doing that? What was I trying to prove as I shimmied out of my Armani jacket and gave my toddler the breast? And why was I even *having* a fourth child at my age? What was I thinking of? I'm too old, too tired and too ratty. God, in a few years' time I could be menopausal, and yet I insisted on having him. Insisted on proving I was so flipping fecund as well as being a sensational investment banker and . . . well, to be honest, *Flora* would be a better mother than me. She's menstruating, isn't she? And she's young and energetic? That's what Dame Nature had in mind, not a desiccated old witch like me.'

'You're just tired,' I said firmly, lifting Henry out of his chair and setting him down. 'And who can blame you? You've got so much on your plate.' I wiped Henry's mouth with the bottom of his T-shirt and saw Clare blanch. 'Listen,' I went on quickly. 'I can have the children for you tonight. Why don't you and Michael go out? Flora and I will baby-sit.'

She gave me a weak smile and propped her face up on her elbow with her hand. 'Thanks. And you're right, I do need a break, but not tonight. Tonight Becky's in a school play and I've got to go and be a supporting mother. She's a rat, apparently, and really pissed off because Amanda Reid's the Pied Piper. She says it's because she doesn't play the recorder so can't pipe, which naturally is my fault because, being a pushy mother, I don't regard it as a real instrument. No, no, my daughter has to play the cello which is so huge she can hardly get the bloody thing between her legs to scratch it. My fault again,' she said gloomily.

'Yes, well, you can beat yourself with that guilt stick too if you like,' I said cheerfully, stroking Henry's fair head. 'I see you're adding to their social skills though.' I nodded over to the corner where a set of child's croquet mallets was propped neatly behind the door. 'What's this, then? In case Little Lord Many-Acres pops by and leaves his calling card?'

'Be nice, wouldn't it?' she said wistfully. 'Then Becky wouldn't have to get an education at all.

Could just sit in her rambling acres and paint water-colours all day. No, Becky and Luke turn those mallets upside down, stick them under their arms and use them as crutches. Cripples is their favourite game.'

I giggled. 'Imaginative.'

'Very, and they've even got a begging bowl. They're collecting for CD-ROMs though, not the deserving poor.' She sighed. 'But enough of me and my dysfunctional family. You didn't come to my door at this hour in the morning to hear about my marital disharmony and my grasping children. What gives? More doctors-in-love-true-romances? More blissful evenings in Battersea Park holding hands and sharing tender moments? Tell me again about how he bought you all those heavenly roses and lit candles in the bathroom, the lovely, lovely man, and tell him Michael's only ever lit a candle in a power cut. Go on, make me drool.'

'No,' I said, 'not candles, but – oh Clare, I'm so thrilled.' I couldn't suppress a beam. 'You know his aunt, the one who brought him up?'

'Gertrude in Onslow Gardens? I've formed a mental picture of the woman, got her swathed in fur stoles with those yucky fox heads on the end with tiny veiled hats, but no, I've never met her. Why?'

'Well, she's got this fabulous house in Cornwall, near Rock. It's that one right on the coast, up an inlet, all sort of Frenchman's Creekish – near where Dad used to take us when we were little. Remember we used to take the boat past?'

Clare shook her head abstractedly, reaching for her briefcase. 'No.'

'Well you did see it once, and the thing is, Gertrude's so flaming rich and dreamy it lies empty for most of the year, and David says he's pretty sure she'll let me take it for the summer!'

Clare looked up from stuffing documents into the briefcase. 'Near Rock? But that's brilliant. You know we'll be down again this year, don't you?'

'You will?' I blinked. 'Hang on, I thought you said you'd had it with Cornwall? Said if you saw another sandcastle you'd detonate it.'

'Did I?' She looked vague. 'Must have been pre-menstrual. Oh no, we're *definitely* going. We're taking that cottage again. The one we took with the Mitchells last year. It's so tiny you can't swing a cat in it, but dirt cheap and – oh! So you'll be up the road! In a huge empty house.' She straightened up from her packing and her eyes began to shine.

'Er, yes. But the thing is ... Well, the idea is I finish my book there. In ... you know, peace and quiet.'

'Oh, but that won't take long, will it? Golly, what luck! Has it got a garden?'

'Er, yes. Huge garden, I think, with steps going down to the beach. But, Clare—'

'Steps down to the beach!' she squeaked. 'Terrific! God, Luke and Becky will *love* it – maybe we could get a boat? Giles is mad about sailing. We could, couldn't we? You know, hire one down there between us?'

'Um, yes, maybe.' I scratched my neck uncomfortably. 'But I will of course be working.'

'Oh yes, and we won't invade your privacy too much, but, Annie, a house with effectively its own beach! Gosh, what a find. And just what we all need right now, a *proper* holiday, not just getting by in some tiddly seaside cottage.' She snatched up some earrings from an ashtray and popped them in excitedly. I opened my mouth to protest, then shut it again. She turned suddenly. Frowned. 'Anyway, I thought you'd done most of your book. Didn't you say you'd finished it?'

'No!' I flushed, alarmed. 'God, did I tell you that?'

'Yes, you said someone had rung from the publishers and you'd said—'

'Oh yes, I *said* I'd finished, but I've only actually done three chapters!'

'So why did you tell them you'd finished?'

'Because when this chap Sebastian rang,' I blustered, 'and said he liked the first bit and could he see the rest, I couldn't exactly say I hadn't written it, could I?'

'Why not?'

'Well, because he assumed I had! And I didn't want to put him off, did I? Didn't want him to go off the boil.'

'So what did you say?'

'I said – well, I said it was all in the bag, but

needed a bit of tidying up. A bit of polishing. And it might take a few weeks. But the thing is, I've got to write the whole bloody thing! And incidentally' – I dropped my voice, terrified – 'David doesn't know that.'

'Doesn't know what?'

'That I've told this chap I've finished but haven't really.'

She frowned. 'But ... Hang on, David knows, doesn't he?'

'Oh yes, *he* knows. It's just I don't want him to know I've lied to the publishers.'

'Why not?'

'Because I don't want him to think I'm that sort of person!' I yelped. 'I'm marrying him, for God's sake, Clare!'

'Well, you clearly are that sort of person, so he may as well know now.'

'Thanks! You're being really supportive here and all I'm saying is I need a bit of space to do some work, like you work all bloody hours of the day!'

'Right.' She looked really miffed. 'Well, of course. We'll keep ourselves to ourselves, then. Keep *right* out of your hair.' She threw her purse in her bag with some force.

'Oh no, I didn't mean that either,' I groaned. 'It's just ...' I hesitated. 'I can't do open house. Can't say all round to my place and stay as long as you like. Have to slightly get my head down, because ... well, this is my big chance, Clare! It's my dream to be published one day, and this is the first time I've ever offered up a manuscript which anyone's ever been remotely interested in. And you know how many times I've tried.'

She nodded. 'I know.' She was silent for a moment. At length she sighed. 'OK, so what about Flora? Is she to keep out of your way, too?'

I hesitated. 'I thought I might get a nanny for Flora.'

'Oh, don't be ridiculous. She's twelve! Anyway, she's got all her cousins down the road. We'll have her.'

'Oh no, I couldn't, Clare,' I said, horrified. 'You've got four of your own and this is your only break of the year. No, no, I'll sort something out.'

'Don't be silly,' she said staunchly. 'One more doesn't make any difference. I'll cope. And we're very open house,' she added piously, positively reeking of burning martyr now. 'Very easy-going.'

'Well.' I bit my thumbnail nervously. 'We'll see.' Oh God, I didn't want to be indebted to her. Not now I'd effectively banned her from my grade II listed mansion.

'And what about David?'

'He'll be down at weekends, if he can get away. But it's a hectic time of year for him.'

'Of course it is. And you've got the wedding to organise too, you know,' she warned, busily buttoning up her jacket. 'You can't just leave it all to David, he's a busy man. And it takes longer than you think, there's masses to do. I don't think you've even considered flowers and headdresses yet, have you?'

'No. No, I'll get on to it,' I agreed, biting my nail practically down to the quick. She always made me feel about the same age as Flora.

'And don't forget Mum wants a church.'

'I haven't forgotten,' I snapped.

She raised her eyebrows and I instantly hung my head. Dear Mum, who'd been so upset when I'd barefooted it on the beach with Adam, and who, when I'd taken David down to Devon to meet her, had sat in the Windsor chair by the range in the kitchen, clenched her bony hands in her lap, blinked back tears, and said that all she and Dad had ever wanted was to see us girls happy and settled, but that they'd always hoped we'd get married in church. Would it be possible this time? A blessing, perhaps? Even though Dad was in heaven?'

And I'd been so ashamed, not realising how much I'd hurt her the first time, and how much she'd never said. She'd been pale with shock and worry when I'd returned to the farm from Hawaii, but there hadn't been a word of reproach.

My phone rang in my jacket pocket and I absently answered. It was David.

'I've just rung Gertrude, Annie, and she said she'd be thrilled.'

'Oh!' I perked up a bit. 'She doesn't mind?'

'Not in the slightest. I told you, she's delighted to have it occupied, but I said you might pop round and see her this morning if that's all right. Is that OK? You know, to chat it through?'

'Of course,' I beamed. 'What time?'

'About ten, I said. Any good?'

I glanced at my watch. 'Perfect.'

I rang off and turned round to Clare, who'd disappeared down the hall with Henry to collect the post which had just spluttered through the letter-box.

'I've got to go,' she murmured distractedly from the doormat, flicking through the envelopes.

'Me too.' I got up and flashed her a conciliatory smile. 'And I'm going to get the bus, so I'll walk with you to the station. D'you need this?' I picked up her briefcase.

'Please. Oh good.'

'What?' I carried it down to her.

'Letter from Giles.' She ripped it open eagerly.

Giles, her eldest, was away at school, and Clare missed him dreadfully. Her eyes scanned the page, then suddenly she snorted.

'Listen to this.' She raised her voice.

'Dear Mummy,

We lost again yesterday, twenty-two–nil. I was in goal. We've just had lunch which was lasagne but tasted like toenail, and next we've got PSHE with Matron, which is all about brushing your teeth and sex. Matron just CANNOT draw testicles.

Love, Giles'

I giggled. 'Poor Matron.'

'Quite,' she agreed. 'Can you imagine, a room full of pre-pubescent boys sniggering behind your back as you attempt a cock and balls on the blackboard? And we think we've got problems.' She pocketed the letter and opened the front door.

'Donna!' she yelled up the stairs. 'I'm away!'

'Coming!' came back the cry and, sure enough, moments later, a pair of wide denim flares tripped lightly down the stairs, followed by a pretty freckled face and long blonde hair. Henry's face lit up as he toddled away from Clare to meet her.

'Do-nnaa!'

'Hey, my prince!' She scooped him up in her long brown arms and kissed his nose. Henry chortled and clutched her hair, and Clare had the grace to smile.

'At least he likes her,' I said quietly in the garden after the door had shut behind us.

She looked at me, surprised. 'Oh, he loves her. And actually I'm not jealous at all. I love my kids too much to be small-minded about that. No, no, I'm delighted.'

'And you don't ever think ... I'd rather be her? When you leave him?' I asked tentatively as I followed her down the path.

'Oh, sure I do, of course. Every morning.' She swung round incredulously. 'God, Annie, I wouldn't be human if I didn't think that! But it's not that simple, is it?' She smiled patronisingly at me as she shut the gate behind us with an efficient little click.

I blinked in the bright morning sunshine. 'Isn't it?' Still puzzling, I fell dutifully in step beside her.

chapter three

'So,' said Clare, setting off at a cracking pace, a smile spreading over her face, 'it'll be your turn soon, and I'll be the one doing the consoling.'

I frowned. 'What?'

'Babies!' she said. 'Surely you and David want some?'

'Oh. Oh yes. Well, definitely. He'd love some, in fact. Actually, we're already trying.'

'*Are* you?' She stopped in her tracks. Put a hand on my arm. 'God, I wondered if you were. How long?'

'Just this month. And only because we're not exactly spring chickens, either of us, and David's keen to get a move on, so we thought we'd start now.'

'And the wedding's only a couple of months away,' she reasoned, 'so no one would really notice even if you were pregnant.'

'Exactly. Or care, d'you think? In our circumstances?' I asked anxiously.

She shook her head. 'No. Not even Mum. She'd be

delighted. And anyway, it's only going to be a small family do, isn't it?'

'Exactly, plus a few friends. Just a sit-down lunch in a hotel, I think,' I said vaguely. Then I grinned. 'So yes, you never know, as sister of the bride you could be buttoning me into an extremely tight ivory dress on the day.'

'Ooh, I hope so,' she said, almost rubbing her hands with glee. 'I know I shouldn't admit to it, but I'd have more than a touch of the Schadenfreudes if you were housebound with twins and Henry was safely away at nursery school.'

I smiled down at the pavement. One of the refreshing things about Clare was that she openly admitted to any unpleasant feelings she might be harbouring, which had the effect of diluting them somewhat. She'd even admitted that, having genuinely worried herself senseless about my disastrous situation with Adam and been thrilled to bits about me marrying David, she'd still been just the tiniest bit peeved that he wasn't a mediocre accountant, say, or a mobile chiropodist, instead of a Belgravia doctor with a burgeoning private practice. I knew that she was also secretly alarmed that when the funds from David's flat and my place were amalgamated, it might even buy us a bigger house than hers. She wanted me to be happy, but not to the extent that my happiness eclipsed hers, and not so rich that my wealth exceeded her and Michael's joint income. I was still, after all, her little sister, and had always been slightly less bright and less attractive, and should therefore know my place.

I, after all, had turned down a place at the local college to read sociology, whilst she'd got a first in law at Cambridge. She'd modelled for *Vogue* in her gap year, whilst I'd worked in a Mars Bar factory. True, I'd married first – my one stab at taking the lead – but it had been to Adam: a charming loser, whose career involved more resting than acting. She, on the other hand, had married Michael, another Cambridge first, and now a financial whiz-kid whose hand on the money markets was generally regarded by those in the know to be exceedingly steady.

And I had never questioned the implacable order. I knew, for example, that she'd like me to have more children, but not as many as she had. I knew that she'd like me to work again, but never in the City, and probably writing short stories rather than novels. Nothing that would rival her success. As I walked along the pavement beside her, watching her black stilettoes strut purposefully along, I cleared my throat, unable to resist.

'So the Mitchells are coming to Cornwall again with you, are they?' I asked innocently.

'You know damn well they're not,' she snapped. 'Serena Mitchell proved to be a complete pain in the tubes last year. All that sucking up to me and doing all the shopping in Wadebridge while I sat on the beach, and: "Oh, I in*sist* on cooking lobster for everyone tonight, Clare, *do* let me", all because she wanted

Michael to give her wally husband a job. As soon as Schroders offered him something she dropped us like a cup of cold sick. We haven't heard from them since, *and* she had her fortieth last month without inviting us. Oh no, the Mitchells are definitely *persona non grata* this year.'

She looked downcast and I wished I hadn't teased her. Clare was my favourite person, but you had to know her jolly well to accept her abrasiveness. Sisters are bound irrevocably by blood, and I'd lost count of the times I'd forgiven her myself or been her apologist when others had been wounded by her sharp tongue. She found it harder to make friends than I did, and I knew she envied me my big circle of mates – something neither ambition, brains nor beauty could ever buy.

'So who are you going with then?' I asked. 'You're surely not taking that house on your own, are you? Don't you need some moral support as you're buttering yet more ham rolls for the children to fill with sand on the beach?'

'Oh no, we're not going on our own. We've asked the Howards.'

'The Howards!' I stopped short in the street. Stared at her incredulously. Two familiar spots of colour were rising in her cheeks as she looked straight ahead. Rosie Howard was my best friend, and had been ever since our hips had welded together in the dormitory of St Mary's Convent, Dorset, at the age of twelve.

'Golly.' I moved on slowly, stunned. 'What did they say?'

'They said they'd love to. They're not doing anything this summer. Said they hadn't got any plans.'

'Because they haven't got a bean,' I said shortly. 'Oh yes,' I went on tartly, 'I'm sure they'd love to come and share some all-expenses-paid accommodation. When did you ask her?' And why on earth hadn't I heard, I wondered?

'Only yesterday,' she said hurriedly. 'So she probably hasn't got round to ringing you yet.'

Suddenly my anger dissipated. I felt embarrassed for Clare. God, it couldn't have been easy to go through her address book and end up asking my best mate. And why should I be annoyed with Rosie? With an unemployed husband and no prospect of a holiday this year, who on earth wouldn't leap at the chance of giving their kids a run on the beach at my sister's seaside house?

'Great.' I smiled, nodding. 'That's brilliant.'

'Oh Annie, I'm so pleased.' She looked hugely relieved. 'I was a bit worried you might think . . . you know. Muscling in and all that.'

'Not a bit of it. I'm delighted.'

'And we can all muck in,' she said eagerly. 'You know, meet on the beach every day, share picnics.'

'Yes, except I'm supposed to be . . .' I tailed off. Sighed. No wonder Clare had got so far in life, she was like a ruddy bulldozer. I gritted my teeth and persevered doggedly. 'This isn't a holiday for me, Clare. David and I are having our break later on, in Mauritius. This is for me to work, remember?'

'Oh yes, I know, but not every day, surely? And in the evenings you'll want a bit of company.'

'Well, we'll see. Gertrude's house isn't actually *in* Rock, anyway. It's up a creek around the headland.'

'So you'll be well away from the action,' she placated. 'Perfect. The Todds are going too, you know.'

'Doesn't surprise me,' I said grimly. 'That man thinks he owns the place. He walks into Rick Stein's and pauses at the door as if everyone should drop to their knees and genuflect.'

'Well, he's very successful. And very attractive too, I think.'

'If you like the over-fifties in tight jeans and pink shirts with a paunch and arrogance to match. No thanks.'

'He kissed me last year, you know.'

I stopped dead. 'What? CLARE!'

She narrowed her eyes and looked the other way.

'Where!' I gasped.

'Walking back from Polzeath after the Elliotts' drinks party.'

'No! What – a snog?'

'Not a snog exactly, but when he said goodbye he deliberately planted one full on the mouth. Wiggled his tongue a bit.'

'Oh, yuck!'

'Oh no, quite nice actually. I'm definitely on for more this year.'

I held her arm. 'You're *not*!'

'Not the full works, no. But something thrilling, definitely. Something dangerous and exciting on Daymer Bay perhaps, after the usual barbecue. Maybe I'll let him stroke my tits behind a rock.'

'Clare!' I was genuinely shocked.

'And maybe I'll let Michael find out, too. Maybe he can watch.'

'Ah, right.' I dropped her arm and walked on. 'So that's what this is all about.'

She fell in beside me. 'I can't help it, Annie. I wish I could find it within me to forgive him, but I just want to slap his face every time he touches me.' She squared her shoulders as we reached the entrance to the tube. 'Thought this might help.'

I gave a wry smile and kissed her goodbye. 'I doubt it. But I don't suppose you'll take any notice of me.'

'Doubt it,' she said cheerfully. 'Never have before, have I?'

I couldn't help laughing as she stalked off down the steps to the District Line, her back ramrod straight in her nipped-in grey jacket, handbag swinging jauntily. I watched her go; so outwardly prickly, so defiant sometimes, yet inside, so desperately wanting to be loved.

And Dad had been hard on her, I thought, as I turned to cross the road to the bus stop. Dad had expected so much from the girl who should have been a boy. The boy they'd lost before her, who'd been still-born. She'd been pushed and chivvied out of that farmhouse whether she'd liked it or not. When Dad got up at six to milk the cows, so did his daughter, cramming in yet more homework at the scrubbed kitchen table, and all to please him. All to live up to his expectations and not be a farmer's wife like Mum and his mother before her.

Dad was a feminist, and a first-time buyer at private schools, and if he was going to kill himself on the farm so his daughters could go on to the convent, he was damn well going to get results. And Clare got results, in spades. But still he wanted more. He wouldn't really have been happy unless she'd won a Nobel prize, let alone a form prize. I remembered his face at speech day as she'd mounted the rostrum yet again to receive another cup. He was delighted, of course, and clapping hard in his shiny suit, but his eyes were on that ruddy great shield at the back. Who was getting that then, eh? Not that Barker girl again? Pull yer finger out, our Clare! Modified rapture then, for all her achievements. Yet I, four years behind, had been allowed to be the girl. Allowed to wallow in the slipstream; be Mummy's concern, not Daddy's. Allowed to sit on the back step and feed the chickens, whilst Clare learned her tables in the kitchen behind me with Dad standing over her, thumping his fist on the table in his shirt sleeves and braces, yelling, 'Nine eights are seventy-two and you won't forget that one!' his face reddened by the wind and exasperation.

Yes, I'd been pampered more, indulged; allowed to ride old Meggy bareback around the fields, to watch Dad skin a dead lamb and slip its fleece on an orphaned lamb's back, hoping the mother of the dead lamb would suckle it, and, if not, permitted to take it back to the house to bottle-feed it myself. I'd led a happy, charmed childhood, whilst Clare, growing up in the same house, hadn't.

Later, I'd read voraciously, helping myself to what I felt like in the local library – romantic novels, sagas, not the classics Clare was force-fed – and then later, as a teenager, I developed a passion for the poetry of Emily Dickinson. I'd sit for hours and read it on the same back step where I'd fed the chickens. No one took much notice though. Expectations were lower, you see.

So had Dad enhanced Clare's life, I wondered now as I stepped on to the bus? Would he be proud of her now? Or, with the hindsight I was sure heaven afforded, would he be looking down and wondering if he hadn't 'bin a bit hard on the lass'? Wondered if he could perhaps have loosened the rein? Wished she were at home now, with Henry, playing with building bricks on the floor, cuddling him on her lap as they watched *Teletubbies* together and munched their way through a packet of biscuits, or would he still be up there thinking: That's my girl. Off to show those boys a thing or two in the money markets. Off to kick some ass.

I sighed as I got off the bus at my stop and walked along the High Street. Who knows. Certainly Mum had quietly questioned Clare's life since Dad had gone, wondered if she wasn't pushing herself and her family too hard, but everything Mum suggested was hesitant. Timid. Clare, like her late husband, knew best. On the other hand, Dad's death had made Mum dare to champion me. Whilst he'd scoffed at the romantic stories I wrote, calling them tosh and bunkum, Mum had always quietly lapped them up; she read me in every woman's magazine I featured in and loved every minute as I rehashed the same doctors and nurses, bringing them out in different guises.

When Dad died, it was she who urged me to write a novel. I didn't tell her that what I really wanted to do was write a biography about a certain poet I admired, but didn't feel I was educated enough – or even the right nationality – to do Emily justice. I was pretty sure I ought to be a Harvard WASP. No, some dreams I couldn't admit to, even to Mum, although, to be fair, had she known, I'm sure she would have encouraged me.

I turned the corner into Gertrude's road. Tall, elegant cream houses reared up at me out of a sailor-blue sky. Yes, encouragement, I mused. That's what I could have done with when Dad was alive. Yet when Mum had suggested I try for university, he'd said, 'Leave her be, Mum. She's not the same calibre as our Clare,' rhyming calibre with saliva.

I smiled to myself as I approached Gertrude's house: huge, stuccoed and double-fronted. And maybe he'd been right. Maybe he'd known I couldn't cut the mustard. After all, three attempts later and I still wasn't published, even though ... well, even though this time there really was a glimmer of hope. I clenched my hands in my cardigan pockets in excitement. This time, amazingly, a large publishing house had responded to my last oeuvre, not with the usual polite rejection slip, but with a personal letter from a senior editor. I knew it by heart.

Dear Mrs O'Harran,

Thank you for sending me the first three chapters of your manuscript. I think you show great promise and have considerable talent. I do hope the novel continues in the same vein. I have to tell you, however, that the reading public nowadays demands a great deal more sexual explicitness from romantic fiction. So far, your characters seem reluctant to move in this direction. Perhaps Lucinda could get her kit off in chapter four?

Yours sincerely,

Sebastian Cooper

Senior editor

Now, admittedly that last line had startled me. Shocked me, in fact. But then again, I reasoned, I wasn't used to the right-on ways of hip and trendy publishing houses. Wasn't used to the lingo. I was merely a housewife from Fulham penning my love stories and, actually, straightforward advice was just what I needed right now. And if sex sold, then surely I could steel myself to write it? My toes had curled in my trainers as I'd tried, and recently I'd been having a whopping great gin before sitting down at my laptop to see if that helped the erotic flow. It had, a bit, and I was pretty sure that the combination of Gertrude's house by the sea providing a conducive environment and buckets more gin would do the trick. And hadn't Mr Cooper also said I showed 'great promise' and 'considerable talent'? Of course he had.

I raised my chin defiantly and mounted the steps to Gertrude's gleaming black front door, remembering how awestruck I'd been by these exclusive South Kensington surroundings a year or so ago. David had brought me here to Onslow Gardens to meet his only living relative, with the vague proviso that she was a bit dippy and rather bohemian. Expecting a sweet old thing in a chaotic flat full of cats, I'd dressed accordingly. Stripy socks, baggy canvas trousers and a patchwork jumper had been the order of the day, and I'd bounced up these same steps to find a very grand old lady in grey flannel trousers and a Katharine Hepburn black polo neck, opening the door to the largest London house I'd ever seen. One hand held the doorknob, whilst the other rested on a rifle, nestling in the umbrella stand. As she'd towered over me, regarding me with icy hauteur, I'd nearly fallen over with shock. David explained later that the air rifle had belonged to his late uncle and that she always opened the door with her hand on it to discourage intruders. Believe me, she didn't need to. Despite a rapidly fading memory, she still, at eighty-odd, had the power to scare the pants off anyone.

I had to keep telling myself that she must be kind at heart to have taken on her eight-year-old nephew when her sister and husband had been tragically killed in a boating accident, and Flora assured me that she was. Despite, or perhaps because of the generation gap, she and Gertrude got on famously and, at Flora's insistence, we often popped in to see her after school. I had to steel myself even for these little encounters, but it helped enormously having Flora there. She'd breeze into the house in a way I was totally incapable of doing, give Gertrude a smacking kiss, then make straight for the tallboy in the drawing room where the photograph albums were kept. Plonking herself down on the carpet and with Gertrude perched at her elbow, she'd pore over them, wanting to know exactly who everyone was, and prompting Gertrude if she forgot.

'That's cousin Harold,' Gertrude would say imperiously, pointing a bony, jewelled finger.

'No, Gertrude, it can't be. Cousin Harold was blond. Look.' And she'd flip back a page to prove it.

Gertrude peered again. Sat up straight. 'My dear,

you're quite right. Very blond. He was a faggot, too, if you're interested.'

Flora was.

I smiled as the door opened and Gertrude peered down at me: tall and commanding in an ankle-length purple waistcoat, corduroy trousers and ropes of beads around her neck. Cascades of dark, onyx balls shone from her ears, and her steel-grey hair was cut in a sharp, uncompromising bob. Her pale blue eyes were cloudy though, over her hawk-like nose.

'Annabel! My dear, how delightfully unexpected.'

She presented me with her floury cheek, indicating it should be kissed.

'Unexpected, Gertrude?' I flinched, anxiously. 'Didn't David say I was coming?'

She stared down at me, blue eyes more penetrating now. After a moment, they cleared. 'D'you know, you're quite right. I believe he did. Rang not half an hour ago.' She clapped a hand to her forehead. 'Stupid of me! Come in, come in!'

Her voice echoed flutily down the hall as she strode off into the depths of the house, then paused at the entrance to the lofty drawing room, bowing her head low to indicate I should shuffle through first.

The room was high, with an elaborately moulded ceiling, and painted a delicate shade of duck-egg blue. At the tall sash windows, drapes of deep plum damask hung in heavy folds, and all around the room were dotted Gertrude's potted palms and elegant but delicate antiques. I made firmly for the sofa, remembering how, on my first visit here, I'd heard an ominous creak coming from the dear little eighteenth-century love seat I'd plonked myself on.

'Coffee?' She swooped, then gave a dangerous twinkle. 'Good and strong and black?'

It was a private joke between us, except the joke was firmly on me. The only way I can take my coffee is white and very milky, but on that first disastrous visit, I'd been offered it good-and-strong-and-black. Desperate to ingratiate myself, I'd accepted with alacrity.

'Mmm, please!'

'There's no milk you know,' she'd barked accusingly at me. 'I don't drink it. Makes me heave.'

I remember giving a little cry of pleasure, and assuring her that it had precisely the same effect on me. In fact, I was so nervous, I pretty much led her to believe that had the milkman come jingling round the corner on his jolly old milk crate right now, I'd have lunged for Uncle Hugh's air rifle and slotted him between the eyes. I remember sitting there, in that ominously creaky love seat, one ankle resting on my other knee in a curious attempt to look relaxed, constantly using my stripy sock as an absorber for my sweaty palm, and watching as she poured the filthy treacle from a percolator. I'd stared at it for twenty minutes, raising it to my lips occasionally but unable to get a drop down. Later, when she and David briefly left the room to attend to a broken window lock in the kitchen, I threw it, in desperation, into the nearest pot plant. The next time I visited, it had mysteriously died. Latterly, of course, I'd come clean and she'd deigned to add a drop of milk, but it was still very strong and quite filthy, and I was still too timid to refuse.

'I'd love one, Gertrude,' I said, cranking up a vivacious smile. 'Although' – I licked my lips bravely – 'I've been reading more and more about how bad coffee is for you. I'm thinking of switching to tea.'

'Stuff and nonsense.' She glared. 'It's all rubbish, that propaganda about caffeine.' She fumbled with cups and saucers on a tray. 'I've been drinking five cups a day for the last sixty years and I've never felt fitter. Never felt remotely "high" as they say one should.'

Could account for the violent hand tremor though, I thought as the cup and saucer rattled its way precariously towards me.

'Oh, absolutely,' I agreed spongily, rescuing it from her liver-spotted hand. 'They'll print anything in the papers these days.'

'Well, quite.'

Gertrude sat down opposite me on the club fender and raised her cup to her lips. Then she straightened her long, thin back and fixed me with a stare of stern disapproval.

'Now. I gather you're after the house.'

I flushed. Oh God, that sounded awful! Like

some terrible, grasping arriviste, intent on my future husband's chattels.

'Well, n-no,' I flustered. 'It's just that David said it was empty and . . . But if it's not convenient . . .'

'It's more than convenient, my dear, I'm delighted to have it used. You've seen it, I take it?'

'Er, I know where it is, vaguely, but—'

'But I've shown you the picture?' she persisted.

'Picture? No, never. Perhaps Flora's seen it. In an album, but I don't recall—'

'No no, my dear, not a photograph. We did have one or two of those but something happened to them. Some idiot threw them away for some blasted reason. No, the painting in the dining room. Didn't I show you last week? Showed someone.' She pursed her lips and narrowed her eyes accusingly.

'No, Gertrude,' I said firmly. 'Not me. Must have been someone else. Cecily, perhaps?'

Cecily was a niece on Hugh's side who popped in occasionally to visit and quake, like me. We swapped horror stories.

She kept her eyes trained suspiciously on me for a few long moments, convinced that I was trying to trick her. I tried not to flinch. Abruptly her face cleared. 'You're quite right,' she said quietly, lowering her eyes and brushing some imaginary crumbs from her lap. 'It was Cecily. Came in to fill in some forms for me. Eyes aren't quite what they used to be. I remember now. We did it in the dining room, that was it. So.' She put aside her cup and rose to her feet. 'Come.'

She towered above me, calling me to attention. Hurriedly I put down my cup and followed as she strode towards the double doors which connected the two huge rooms. She opened them with a flourish and swept through into the dining room. Her violet waistcoat fanned out behind her like a cloak as she skirted the vast Regency table and came to a halt by the Adam fireplace. She gazed up at a picture above it.

'There.' She raised her chin imperiously. 'What do you think?'

I followed her eyes. 'Oh,' I breathed. 'It's gorgeous!'

I'd only been in this room once before, and never noticed the painting. It was a large watercolour of a low, long, Elizabethan house, timbered and covered in wisteria, and with a sweeping lawn in front. Flanked by rhododendron bushes, it stood proudly on a cliff top overlooking the sea.

'Just look at that view!'

'But will it suit?' she demanded sharply.

'Suit? Golly, Gertrude, it's fantastic. I mean – to be literally right on the sea like that . . .'

'Yes,' she agreed, head on one side, considering it. 'It *is* a lovely spot. Just at the end of the creek. And the beach is pretty much private. We own the land at the top. So Joe Public can only get to it by boat, or else scramble across the rocks and get marooned, which they do *de temps en temps*. Silly arses. We've had the odd drowning incident, you know. Always a bit tricky.'

For whom, I wondered nervously. Her, or Joe Public?

'And we had a whale of a time there as children, of course,' she mused, fiddling with her beads. 'Pammy and I. With Mummy and Daddy. Picnics and bathing and whatnot. Such larks.'

Her blue eyes clouded for a moment and I thought how awful it must have been to lose her sister like that, suddenly, at only thirty-two.

'And with David too,' she went on. 'When Pammy and Angus died and Hugh and I took him on, we took him down there for the summer. Well, of course we did. No point selling it. Can't think why he doesn't use it more now, but then perhaps . . .' She tailed off, puckering her floury old brow. Miles away. 'Anyway.' She came to. 'Now there's you and Flora to use it, so that's marvellous. And maybe more children in time?' She eyed me craftily.

I smiled. 'We hope so, Gertrude. David would love children, I know.'

'Splendid! So the house will be full again. Of course I still go for a spell in September, but July is so desperately crowded, although admittedly not in our little creek. Take it, my dear. I really couldn't be more pleased. Have it with pleasure. Here, I'll give you a key.'

She crossed to a little inlaid writing table in the corner and pulled out a drawer.

'Somewhere . . . in here . . . ah.' She took out a ring with half a dozen identical keys on it. 'Always keep a few' – she fumbled around and I resisted the urge to help her – 'because I lose them. Hopeless. You'll probably find one or two down there, but . . . here, my dear.' She pulled one off finally and handed it to me. 'Now. David can tell you how to get there—'

'Oh, he already has,' I broke in eagerly. 'And actually, I know the spot quite well, because when I was young we always used to go to that part of the world for our holidays. We took our caravan and parked it in the campsite close by, and I always used to peer down that long drive and wonder who lived there. Tried to imagine what the family was like.' I flushed. God, did that sound awful? Like some frightful below-stairs peeper, or something? 'I grew up in Devon, you see,' I went on hurriedly, 'and Rock's only an hour or so away—'

'Of course, you're a West Country girl. Well then, you'll be quite au fait with the beating of the waves and the seagulls screeching endlessly overhead. And of course they do say the place is haunted by a pirate chief, but that's all baloney.'

'Quite. Show me an old Cornish house that isn't haunted. The estate agents down there know that vendors would be very disappointed if they didn't get the ubiquitous ghost.'

'Exactly, all part of the charm. And you never know, you might get some inspiration for that book of yours. Might do some writing?'

'Well, that is rather the idea,' I said, confused. 'Didn't David say?' I added anxiously. 'That's the whole point. I wanted somewhere quiet to – you know – write in peace.'

Golly, did she think I was deserting her nephew to top up my tan on her terrace? Knock back some solitary cocktails? Go clubbing with the locals?

She frowned down at me. Blinked. 'D'you know,' she said slowly, 'I believe he did mention that. Tell me.' She seized my arm urgently and brought her face down to mine. 'Is it saucy?'

'Heavens no!' I said, terrified.

'Oh.' She looked disappointed.

'B-but I haven't written it all yet, Gertrude,' I said, desperately feeling my way. 'And I *have* been asked to spice it up a bit, but I'm not sure—'

'Oh, I should!' she urged. 'Tell me, am I in it?'

I gulped. What – as the love interest in the Twilight Home, perhaps? A geriatric temptress, corridor-creeping towards the Major's bedroom after lights out? Sniffing for trouser in an angora bedjacket? Would she like that, I wondered? Another dilemma.

'Um . . . not yet . . .' I said guardedly, gauging her response. She frowned. 'But – you will be soon!'

'Excellent!' She clasped her hands excitedly. Then eyed me suspiciously. 'But as the matriarchal old bag, no doubt.'

'N-no.' My hands felt a bit sweaty. 'As the – the distinguished' – her face fell – 'b-but terribly attractive older woman.'

She smiled and patted her hair. 'Ah yes,' she purred. 'A marvellous literary archetype. Frightfully well preserved, but with a hint of come-hither in her eye, eh?'

'Oh, more than a hint,' I said warmly. 'Positively awash with it!'

'Steady,' she admonished, but gave a skittish little toss of her head and I could tell she was thrilled to bits.

I breathed again, exhausted. Clearly an Ealing comedy along the lines of *Carry on, Lady Bracknell* was called for here and I wasn't sure I was up to executing it. Although actually, I reflected, pocketing the key, writing Gertrude in as a raunchy cameo role was a small price to pay for a house on a cliff with its own private beach. And speaking of payment . . .

'Um, Gertrude, are you sure I can't give you any rent for the house? I mean, we are going for quite a long time, so—'

'Heavens no, I wouldn't hear of it,' she said firmly, taking my arm and propelling me back through the drawing room and down the hall to the front door. 'You're family now, Annabel. No no, just go and enjoy, and send me a PC letting me know all is well.' She stopped suddenly in the passage, short of the door. 'Oh Lord. I am a poor hostess, I haven't offered you a thing! Won't you have a coffee with me before you go?'

'You've . . . just given me one, Gertrude.'

She frowned, and I knew she thought I was tricking her again. I made a helpless gesture to the drawing room. She popped her head suspiciously round the door and spied the tray.

'Good heavens, so I did!' She clapped her hand to her head. 'I am an absent-minded old ninny. Well, you can't have another or you'll be flying. Plays havoc with your nervous system, you know. You young girls drink far too much!' She opened the door with a flourish. 'So. Love to David then, and Flora too, and tell the dear girl to pop in before you go, hmm? I love our little chats.'

'I will,' I promised, smiling. Dear old thing. She really was losing it a bit. I made a mental note to tell David. 'She loves seeing you too, Gertrude. We'll pop by soon. And thanks so much for the house.' I turned to kiss her on the step.

'Toodle-oo!' she trilled.

'Toodle-oo!' I agreed, waving as I went down the street.

She watched me go, fluttering her hand from the top step. Once around the corner though, and out of sight, I took to my heels and beetled guiltily towards the bus.

chapter four

When I got back home I found Rosie on my doorstep. Her short red hair looked wild and mussed as if she'd forgotten to brush it, and she was wearing one of her husband's jumpers. She had Phoebe, her four-year-old, on her hip and looked about to leave when she saw me come around the corner.

'Oh! I was about to go!' she yelled.

'Sorry, I was round at Gertrude's. Did you say you were coming?'

'No, just popped round on the off-chance. Have you spoken to Clare?' She looked anxious as I walked up the path towards her.

I smiled down at the ground as I rooted in my pocket for my key. 'I have.'

'Oh Annie, I'm sorry. I meant to ring you last night and tell you. D'you mind?'

'What, that you're going on holiday with my sister? Of course not.' I let her in.

'You're just saying that,' she said nervously as she hastened after me down the long passage to the kitchen. 'I can tell by your tone you're not amused, but when she rang . . . God, I was at such a low ebb, Annie – just contemplating the meths, actually, since I'd run out of gin – and I thought: Bugger it. A couple of weeks by the sea is just what we need right now, Dan and I, but more particularly the kids. I mean, Christ, we haven't had a holiday for nearly two years now and . . . Oh, I don't know. I know she's your sister and not really my friend . . .' She tailed off miserably and sank down in a heap at my chaotic kitchen table with Phoebe on her lap.

'She asked you to be godmother to Henry,' I reminded her, chucking the house keys in the fruit bowl.

'Only because she'd run out of friends, we all know that.' She clutched her head in horror. 'I'm such a bitch! Here I am accepting her hospitality and – oh hell.'

'Listen, Clare's under no illusions,' I said as I whisked around behind her clearing the table, slinging cereal packets in cupboards and slamming the fridge door on the milk. 'She knows the score. She knows you're my friend, but she likes you and desperately wants . . . well, sounds sad, but more mates. Particularly to go on holiday with.'

'And I like her too,' Rosie said quickly, twisting round to look at me. 'Really like her, and would like to spend more time with her, get to know her better. It's just she can be a bit . . .' She hesitated, pulled a piece of loo paper off the handily placed roll on the table and held it to Phoebe's streaming nose. 'Blow, darling.'

'Scratchy? High-handed? Bossy?' I squirted some Fairy Liquid in the sink and turned the taps on hard. 'God, you don't have to tell me, Rosie, I grew up with her. Had to pay twenty pence to get into her room and thirty to borrow one of her conkers, but don't worry, my friend, you won't be alone. I'll be there for you. Round the corner, up the creek, as it were.'

'What creek?'

I plunged my hands into the soap suds and gazed dreamily out of the window. 'The one that snakes sleepily off the estuary under an umbrella of leaves into a thicket of green, far, far from the madding crowd.' I smiled as I took a gleaming plate out of the water. 'Gertrude's lent me her house,' I informed her. 'The one I told you about.'

Rosie swung around again, bog roll clamped to Phoebe's nose. 'She *hasn't*! Annie, that's fantastic! God, so you'll be down there too. Brilliant. Christ, I'm so relieved, I can't tell you.' She flopped back dramatically in her chair, arms and legs out like a starfish as Phoebe wobbled precariously on her lap. Suddenly she sat bolt upright again. 'So why don't I come and stay with you?'

'Because for one thing I'm supposed to be working, and for another, you've just said yes to my sister. The one you want to spend so much time with? No-mates Clare?' I eyed her beadily.

'Oh. Oh yes. No, you're right,' she said quickly. She nodded guiltily, then plunged her hand nervously into her old suede bag to pull out a tin of Old Virginia and a packet of Rizlas – her latest economy drive.

'But golly,' she murmured, 'if *you're* there it'll make all the difference. No, Phoebe, let Mummy do it.' She retrieved a paper from her daughter's hand which Phoebe surrendered with unusual complicity. 'If you become adept at roll-ups, people will think you're on drugs. Not a nice party trick.' Phoebe leaned resignedly against her mother's chest and sucked her thumb.

'Why isn't she at school then?' I asked, scraping dried Weetabix off a bowl and eyeing the little girl's white face.

'The school's got a staff training day, but she wouldn't be there anyway, she's got a bit of a temperature. Nothing serious though, is it, poppet? Hm?' Rosie stroked Phoebe's forehead as the child's eyes began to shut. 'Actually, I love my children when they're like this,' she confided in a hoarse whisper over her daughter's head. 'A bit, you know, below par. Lovely.'

I giggled. 'Rosie, you're appalling.'

'Just takes the edge off them though, doesn't it? I mean, we've just done a huge Tesco's shop and she actually sat *in* the trolley, *in* the seat. Usually she hangs off the side like some belligerent bus conductor, yelling: "Frosties! Lollies!" Or, more embarrassingly, as we cruise the feminine hygiene aisle, "Heavy or light flow, Mummy?" Today, she just sat there quietly with her head on my puffa jacket. Lovely.'

'Why didn't you leave her with Dan?'

She shifted Phoebe on her lap. 'Dan's got an interview.'

'Oh?' I turned from the sink.

'Don't get excited. He's had interviews before. Thirty-eight of them, to be precise.'

'Yes, but you never know.'

'How true. You never know. This could be the one. The one to raise us from the depths of shitty despair and take us sailing into the ranks of the gainfully employed. To take us back into mainstream society full of solvent optimism, with our bank balance flashing miraculously from red to black, and our children back at private schools in nice shiny shoes. I could even tell our vulturine estate agent to piss off back to Barnard Marcus and stop telling me my fixtures and fittings are a bit on the shabby side and my paintwork's looking tired.'

I turned to look at her from the sink. She was lighting an appalling rolled cigarette which drooped down at one end. It was shaking a bit.

'You're selling?'

'We're having it valued,' she muttered. 'That's all. But with a view to selling, yes, and maybe renting and then buying again when the market finally crashes. Dan says it makes sense.'

'Of course,' I said quietly.

Rosie had the prettiest pink Fulham house which

had originally been bed-sits and which they'd bought for a song in the days when one could. Painstakingly, over the years, she and Dan, without builders, had slowly transformed the interior into the elegant house it was today, with two airy rooms on each of the four floors, and all painted in soft, muted National Trust shades. Together, amidst much laughter and swearing, they'd laid a reclaimed slate floor in the kitchen, punched out a bay window in the sitting room, opened up every fireplace, quarry tiled the bathrooms, and agonized in salvage yards over Victorian light-switches and doorknobs. It had been a labour of love.

I turned back to avoid her eye and rinsed a cup under the tap. 'Well, you never know. He might get the job this morning.'

'He might. And then we could relocate to mouth-watering Birmingham. Super.'

'Birmingham!'

'Oh, don't worry, he won't get it,' she said drily. 'He's too old. All these finance houses are looking for nice, cheap graduates. Anyway, I've told him if he does get it he'll have to weekly commute. Either that or I'll divorce him. He's quite keen on option two, actually.' She grinned and looked around for an ashtray. Not finding one, she flicked her ash into a pot of half-dead azaleas.

'Thanks.' I shoved a saucer under her nose.

'Makes great compost,' she advised, taking a bit of tobacco out of her mouth. 'No, what we were actually thinking, last night, as we shared a bubble bath together having celebrated our free holiday with some lukewarm sex, was that maybe Michael could give Dan a job. You know, at Schroders?'

The telephone rang.

'Oh!' I whipped round in horror. 'God, that's what the Mitchells did last year and Clare twigged and went totally insane! Please tell me you won't do that,' I implored her, one hand hovering on the receiver. 'Clare will top herself if she thinks that's why you're coming down!'

'All right, all right, keep your wig on,' she muttered as I lifted the phone. I was still gazing anxiously at her as I said hello.

'Ah. Bad moment?'

It was David.

'Um, no, not at all. Just got Rosie here.'

'Oh, right. So if I were to pop back for lunch and a bit of Midweek Sports Special, would that be inconvenient?'

I giggled. Turned my back on Rosie. 'Not at all, I'll get rid of her. She's only popped round to apologise for using my sister. I'll see you later.' I put the phone down.

Rosie eyed me suspiciously as I turned back. 'Who was that? You've gone all pink.'

'David. He's coming back for lunch, and then we're going to make babies, so you'll have to shift your ass.'

She boggled. 'He comes home for lunchtime sex?'

'Only because it's that time of the month, and David being David knows precisely where I am in my menstrual cycle – which is more than I do, I might add. He knows when I'm ovulating, and when, to the second, would be the best time for sperm-boy to ride that egg. He took my temperature this morning and decided I'd be peaking at precisely twelve-thirty-two. I'll have you know you're looking at a supremely ripe woman, my friend. My apple is fit to bust.'

'Blimey, he is keen,' she said, hastily gathering up her Rizlas and stuffing them in her bag. 'How many does he want?'

'Children? Oh, three or four, I think.' I bit my thumbnail.

'Three or four!' she shrieked, dropping her bag.

'Er, no. Three. Or two,' I said hastily. 'He was an only child, you see, Rosie. He'd love a big family.'

'Right,' she said shortly. 'And would you? You're happy to be still doing this baby lark when you're forty, are you? Because that's what you'll be doing, you know, if he's going for a baker's dozen. It's all right for him, he's younger than you.'

'Only four years,' I said tetchily. 'And of course I am, otherwise I wouldn't be doing it, would I? And it won't be a baker's dozen. You know what these men are like, they think they want loads, but David's never been a father. Speak to him after he's been up at dawn with a filthy nappy that's erupted into the feet of the snuggle-suit and up the back of the vest, and which he's had to change against the clock because his horribly hormonal wife is shrieking that her milk-bar's about to explode. Speak to him after he's been denied rumpy-pumpy for weeks on end for fear of rupturing stitches. I think you'll find he'll be quite content with one.'

'Quite. Dan wanted to put one of ours back. And actually,' she sighed, 'I applaud David's boyish enthusiasm. I haven't the energy to open the cat food at lunchtime, let alone have sex.'

'Well, I must say,' I admitted, '*Bargain Hunt* would otherwise be commanding my attention. But don't tell Clare,' I added hastily. I reached for a carton of soup and poured it into a pan.

'What, that you watch daytime telly or have day-time sex?'

'Either,' I said nervously.

She grinned. 'Don't worry. Your secret's safe with me.' She stood up and hoisted her daughter on to her hip. 'Right, come on, young Phoebe, I'm not sure I want you to be party to this. You're too young to witness the monstrously priapic Dr Finlay bursting through that door, tongue hanging out, hips thrusting, ready to start his dynasty. It's back to the cat food for us.'

At that moment the milk bottles rattled on the step outside and a key went in the door. Rosie and I stared at one another, astonished.

'Bloody hell, that was quick!' Rosie boggled. She laid a hand on my arm. 'No, don't tell me,' she whispered. 'He was in a phone box, he twirled around a few times, and now he's standing outside with his pants over his tights. I always thought he looked like Clark Kent.'

'Either that or he was en route with his mobile when — Oh!'

The door opened and we both turned to see that it wasn't David at all. Sauntering into my house, whistling distractedly and gazing down at the post on my mat, was my ex-husband, Adam.

He stooped to pick up the envelopes and flicked through them nonchalantly, oblivious of Rosie and me watching. He dropped most of them but retained a free magazine which he opened and read, still quietly whistling as he came towards us. Tall, dark and disreputably handsome, he was wearing a grey T-shirt over another long-sleeved white T-shirt, cargo pants and trainers. On his head, in the manner of a gauche fourteen-year-old, a baseball cap was turned back to front. Adam is nearly thirty-eight.

He glanced up from the magazine. Saw us for the first time. Looked surprised.

'Oh. Shit. Didn't see you in here.'

Rosie couldn't speak.

'Adam.' I leaned back against the sink and gripped the rim hard.

'Hi, sweetie.' He planted a kiss on my cheek, then cast a nod in Rosie's general direction. 'Rosie.'

Rosie still couldn't utter.

'Sorry to bust in like this but I had a break in

rehearsals and I wanted to check the diary.' He sauntered round the room and stopped at the cork notice-board, peering at the postcards and invitations. 'Thought you'd be out shopping actually, but still chained to the sink, I see?' He grinned and I loosened my grip on it. 'That's what I like about you, Annie, it's either the kitchen or the bedroom and you know what to do in both. Know the quickest way to a man's heart, as Jerry Hall once famously said.'

'Although, as Ruby Wax once famously said, the quickest way to a man's heart is actually through his chest,' I quipped back, trying to breathe.

He gave a bark of laughter. 'Ah, by Jove, you have to get up pretty early in the morning to get one past you, eh, Annie? That's what I like to see, still coming out fighting. What's this then?' He moved across to the stove and peered in the pan. Stuck a finger in and tasted it. 'Vichyssoise? Oh no, parsnip. Nice. Enough for three?' He glanced around enquiringly.

'Rosie's not staying,' I said quickly. 'It's just – well. For me. And David.'

'David's popping home for lunch?' His eyes widened. 'Really. And then, no doubt, availing himself of your other area of expertise in the bedroom? Oops, spot on,' he muttered as, maddeningly, I flushed. 'Well, I'd better make myself scarce in that case, once I've checked a few dates with you. All right if I help myself to one of lover boy's Stellas? I've got a hell of a thirst on.'

'Help yourself,' I muttered, as he did just that, opening the fridge and offering one to Rosie.

'Rosie? Annie won't, of course, it's her puritanical upbringing, but I know you're a woman of the world.' He glanced down at the ashtray. 'See you're even rolling your own these days. Now there's proletarianism for you. Good on yer, girl. How's Dan the Man? Still drinking at the Feathers? I must pop in for a pint with him one of these days.' He threw back his head and sucked hard on his beer.

Rosie finally found her tongue. 'He just walks in here,' she exploded, her face pink with outrage, 'without a by your leave, *with* a key, helps himself to your fridge – why the hell don't you change the locks, Annie!'

'Ah, but that wouldn't be fair,' said Adam, wagging a warning finger in her direction. He crossed to the larder door where my calendar hung and began coolly to flick through it. 'Annie gave me this here key back in the days when I visited regular, like. Every day, to be precise, and nights too sometimes, eh, Annie?' He grinned over his shoulder at me. I flushed and stared at my feet.

'Oh yes, up until a year or so ago I still had a foot firmly in this door, and a place in her heart, too. Until the flying doctor came winging by and usurped me. Bastard.' He grinned. 'And anyway, apart from anything else, my child lives here,' he reminded her, letting the pages of the calendar fall back. 'So it wouldn't be entirely friendly to lock me out, would it?' He glanced back at the calendar. 'This when her school holidays start then, Annie?' He prodded a date I'd circled in red.

'Yes. That's it,' I muttered.

'Great. I'll have her that weekend then, shall I? That's what I came to say, that I may need to juggle my dates a bit. This new play's taking up more time than I thought.' He pulled a diary from his pocket and flicked through it. 'At the moment I think I've got her every other weekend until then, but we're going to Cornwall soon so I need to change all that.'

'Cornwall?' My heart stopped. 'Why?'

He looked up in surprise. 'For a holiday. Why not?'

I nodded, my throat inexplicably dry. 'Right. Whereabouts?'

'Oh, usual place,' he said airily. 'North coast, some-where. Near Polzeath, I think. Where we went last year, remember? Cozzy's parents have a bungalow down there.'

So Cozzy had lasted a whole year. Unlike Francine. Or Sandra, who'd fallen at the final flourish of the Tour de France flag, the stale stench of urine no doubt too much for Adam as he took her in his arms for a celebratory hug. And I did remember him motoring off from this very house not much more than a year ago, after an illicit night with me, in the days when, to my shame, I still let him into my bed even though he didn't live here. Yes, off he'd gone to frolic in the surf with Cozzy, as I shut my eyes tight and tried not to cry into my pillow.

'Right.' I swallowed. 'It's just – well, we're going to Cornwall too. For six weeks.'

His beer froze at his lips. 'Six *weeks*? Stroll on down.' He blinked his bright blue eyes and took his cap off. Ran a hand through his dark curls. 'Without consulting me? A whole summer, without me seeing my daughter?'

'Well, I would have consulted you, naturally, Adam,' I said hastily. 'But it's only just been decided. And since you're going to be down there too, it's actually quite convenient. I could drive her over to you.'

'Yeah,' he agreed as he weighed it up, considering. 'Or I could come and get her.' He struck a nonchalant pose. 'We were going to go for the whole summer too, actually,' he said blithely. 'But we changed our plans.'

'So you wouldn't have seen her anyway then, would you?' put in Rosie acidly.

'Where are you staying?' he went on, deliberately ignoring her.

'David's aunt's got a place on the Camel estuary.'

'Cool. Big pad?' Adam thought it took years off him to talk like a hippie.

'Um, I'm – not sure.'

'Oh, huge,' said Rosie, reading his mind. 'With a pool, and a billiard table, and a tennis court. You'll have to come over, Adam, use the facilities. Raid the fridge.'

'Might take you up on that.' He winked at her, unruffled. 'Unless you're there already, Rosie, which I have a shrewd suspicion you might be, in which case there may be a conflict of interest. Dan and I could hang out quite happily together by the pool – sink a few tinnies, tell a few jokes – but I suspect you'd get on my tits after a while. How is dear old Redundant Man, anyway?'

'He flourishes, thank you, and is probably more active than you are, Adam,' she snapped. 'At least he actually tries to get work and doesn't just pose about in back-to-front baseball caps pretending he's a teenager.'

'All right, you two,' I said wearily. 'Can we get back to the real reason you're here, Adam? Obviously you want to see Flora over the summer and since we're both in Cornwall it makes things logistically easier, if not . . .'

'Emotionally easier?' he pounced, delighted. 'Surely you weren't thinking what a blessed relief it would have been *not* to see Adam for six weeks? To get over him properly, this time? To get out of the mind-set of lusting after a wayward, impoverished actor and into the mind-set of marrying handsome, successful, *sensible* Dr Kildare? Surely you weren't thinking *that*, Annie? Oops, hush my mouth, you were!' His eyes danced with hilarity as Rosie rose furiously from the table.

'Get out, Adam,' she seethed. 'Go on, piss off. If she won't tell you, I will. Don't flatter yourself that you even impinge on her consciousness any more. You're an amoeba, pond-life, you're not even the lovable rogue you think you are – poor romantic devil, led by his heart, can't help himself – no! You're just a sad old fart who can't say no to his testosterone surges!'

'Nicely said, Mrs Howard' – Adam inclined his head graciously – 'and with lots of righteous indignation on behalf of your friend, but you've overlooked one technicality. You've overlooked the fact that I can't, indeed, help myself, and that despite everything I may still feel very strongly, and very deeply, for Annie here. I might even be prepared to admit that I was a bounder and a cad and all the other unspeakable things you accuse me of and, given a second chance and a fair wind, be ready to mend my ways for the sake of my marriage and my child.' His mouth was twitching merrily, but there was something oddly fixed about his eyes. It brought us both up short.

'Bullshit,' said Rosie at length. 'You're half the man David is and you know it. You're just scared witless she's going to end up with someone loyal and honest and devoted.'

'All of which are excellent canine attributes, I grant you, but are they entirely the spice of life? Entirely what sets the world on fire? Does loyalty make the party go with a zing, say, or does — Ah! The man himself. Or hound dog, should I say. Let him speak for himself. David, welcome!'

David appeared in a shaft of light down the hall as the front door opened. He closed it behind him and advanced warily down the passageway in his pin-stripe suit, carrying his briefcase.

'Welcome to this small kitchen party,' went on Adam, beaming and spreading his arms wide. 'Rosemary I believe you know, and of course my ex-wife, Annabel, and I am merely a wallflower. Here to secure visitation rights on my beloved only child, soon to be your step-daughter. How cosy is that. Stella?' He reached in the fridge. 'Or would you prefer something stronger?'

'No thanks, Adam, and whilst Flora may be your daughter, those are my beers. I don't necessarily begrudge you one, but I'll thank you not to help yourself to another, because on the one hand I've got things to do here and on the other, there's a disgruntled-looking blonde outside in an ancient MG that I seem to recall belongs to you. She's picking her nail varnish and looking mutinous. I wouldn't leave her kicking her stilettoes while you're quaffing in here, or she may shift into gear and leave you stranded.'

'Shit! Cozzy!' Adam clapped a hand to his fore-head. 'Forgot she was out there. I was going to tip her the wink at some point and bring her in and introduce her to you, Annie, but I suspect now is not the moment?' He took in my flushed face and the two icy ones flanking me. 'Ah. No. Thought not. Oh well, at some stage it might be a good idea to get to know each other. Flora thinks she's terrific, and now you've got yourself a man, there'll be less angst all round, eh? No more hard feelings. Less hell hath no fury. Yes. Well.' Even Adam seemed to sense the atmosphere was against him. 'I'll be on my way. Rosie, David.' He nodded at them. 'Thanks for the beer, mate, and, Annie, we'll swap holiday addresses and phone numbers soon, eh? Might even all get together for a barbie on the beach!'

Grinning at David's horrified face, he slid out of the kitchen and slunk down to the front door, whistling merrily again.

Rosie, gathering up her by now sleeping child, her old suede bag and her other belongings, was, after a swift goodbye, gone pretty much in his wake. Muttering darkly about my erstwhile disastrous taste in men she followed Adam out, but made a point of turning pointedly in the opposite direction once she'd reached the pavement.

When the door had shut behind them, David turned to me, appalled.

'He's coming to Cornwall?'

'Er, yes.' I bit my lip. 'Always does, I'm afraid. Well, since last year. Once is often, twice is always in Adam's book. Cozzy's got a place down there, you see.' I avoided his eye.

'I didn't know that,' he said despairingly, scratching his head. 'You didn't mention it, Annie.'

'I forgot,' I said simply. 'And anyway' – I went

across and put my arms around him. Hugged him hard – 'he won't spoil our fun.' I reached up and kissed him softly on the mouth. 'No one can spoil our fun, can they?'

Later, an hour or so later, when our heads were on the same pillow but our legs pointing in opposite directions – mine, absurdly, going straight up the wall to ensure the sperm had the best chance of meeting the egg and not falling out of my cervix – David took my hand. It was tricky, but he took it.

'Does he still upset you?' he asked, looking straight up my nose.

I smiled and looked up his. 'Not in the least.'

'Because I would understand. I mean, personally I think the man's a complete dick, but I do appreciate that you were once married to him and might still harbour certain eccentric allegiances.'

I turned my head sideways and kissed him. 'David, I don't give Adam a moment's thought.'

He smiled. 'Good.' He stroked my hand for a moment. 'And when the houses are sold . . .?'

'When the houses are sold and we buy one together he'll need to send a calling card and book weeks in advance if he so much as wants to set foot in my doorway.'

He smiled. 'Splendid.'

I sighed. 'David, how long have I got to stay like this?'

He glanced at his watch. 'Oh, only about half an hour.'

'Half an hour!'

'You'll be fine, relax.'

'Relax!'

'I'll get you a book if you like.'

'And a cup of tea?'

'Done.'

He flung aside the duvet and got up. I watched as he crossed the room naked and went to reach for his dressing gown on the back of the door. He paused. Turned. 'What are you smiling at?'

I grinned. 'Nothing.'

He padded back to the bed, leaned over and kissed me. 'Call that nothing? Any more cheek and I'll cancel my Miss Monroe appointment at two-fifteen and book you in for a rematch.'

'Miss Monroe?'

'My new patient. She has unsightly hives in unlikely places.'

'Ah. Attractive?'

'The hives most certainly are not, and Miss Monroe might have been once, but is now a desiccated seventy-nine.'

'I see.'

'And no, Annie, I do not get my rocks off when female patients strip for me, which I know is your next question.'

'It was not!' I snorted as he pulled on his dressing gown.

He gave me an arch look. Then he disappeared downstairs to get the tea, leaving me contemplating the wallpaper between my feet, and smiling like the cat who's got the cream.

'But I don't believe you!' I yelled.

chapter five

'Come on, Flora!'

I crammed the suitcase into the boot and slammed it shut, glancing back through the open front door to where she stood in the hall talking to David, his fair head bent over her dark one. I paused for a moment, watching, as David, clean and pressed in his attire of Oxford cotton shirt, pale khaki trousers and a cashmere sweater slung artfully around his neck, got some batteries from his briefcase and gave them to her. Fumbling a bit, she slotted them into her personal stereo.

I smiled. It was typical of the man that he should check her batteries before a long journey, but then get her to fit the new ones herself. Just as he helped her with her homework, but only when asked, and came to watch her in lacrosse matches only when invited – something Adam never quite managed, invited or not. He was supportive, but not too step-fatherly. Not too over the top. He was alive to the delicacy of the situation, just as Flora was alive to it too, but in a different way. She knew he was good for me.

A year ago, when Adam had first heard about David, when he'd returned from his Cornish holiday with Cozzy and the grapevine had filtered down to him, he'd rung us, distraught. Flora had answered.

'It's Dad,' she whispered. 'He's heard you've met someone. He wants to come back. For good.'

My heart, and I know it shouldn't have, leaped. But her dark eyes had filled with tears. She shook her head. 'No, Mum,' she whispered.

I'd stared at her for a long moment. Then I swallowed hard and took the mouthpiece from her.

'Sorry, Adam, we don't want you back. No. No dice.'

And that was that. But the awful thing was, if it hadn't been for my eleven-year-old daughter saving me from myself, I'm not sure I would have got off the roundabout. Not sure I wouldn't still be spinning around now, sharing a niche with his harem of women, scanning the cast list when Adam brought it home, looking to see who his leading lady was, wondering if she was his type or if he'd slept with her before – in which case it was an odds-on certainty he'd sleep with her again. But Flora, who loved her daddy more than anyone, knew better. She knew that even though he made us laugh like no one else did, took life by the scruff of the neck and made every day a holiday, he wasn't good for me. And actually, when David came along I realised that there was more to life than clutching one's sides. That life wasn't necessarily one long party. He'd been so good for us, David, so completely what we needed.

'And take some spares,' he was saying as he popped a couple in her denim shoulder bag, 'in case you want to listen to it on the beach.'

'Ready, love?' I walked up the path, smiling at them. At my two.

'Ready. But, David, *please* don't forget my fish. They hate slimy water and it only takes a second, I promise.'

'It takes precisely twelve minutes because I did it for you last weekend, and no, I won't forget them. Or your plants,' he added to me. 'Although someone should really tell your mother, Flora, that those spider things with trailing babies went out with hostess trolleys and Arctic Rolls. I've half a mind to replace them with winter-flowering jasmine while you're away.'

'Don't you dare,' I warned. 'Those spiders have been with me through thick and thin, and I know precisely how many offspring they've got, so don't go getting scissor happy either. Now, Flora, map?'

'Got it.' She tapped her bag. 'Come on, Mum, let's go. Bye, David.' She reached up and gave him a kiss.

'Bye, hon. Take care and look after your mum.' He took me in his arms and kissed my nose. 'I'll be down in a couple of weeks to check up on the pair of you.'

'A couple of weeks?' I stepped back from him. 'Can't

you come sooner? Can't you come this weekend?'

'I'll do my best,' he said, walking us to the car, 'but I'm up to here with paperwork at the moment and it is a hell of a long way, Annie. I mean for the weekend.'

My heart lurched. 'I know, but you said you didn't mind. We went through this,' I said anxiously.

'I don't.' He opened the car door for me. 'And I'll do my best, I promise. Now, for God's sake drive carefully, and stop for lunch, and *don't* drive if you're tired. Go for a walk or something. It's always the last bit of the journey when people plough on because they're nearly there that something disastrous happens.'

'I will,' I promised, glowing slightly under his protection. When had Adam ever exhorted me to drive carefully?

He kissed me again and we both saw Flora, despite her protestations, turn her head away. We parted quickly.

He waved us off and, as my ancient Fiat pulled out into the sunny Fulham street, the dusty plane trees spreading their mottled shade over the baked tarmac, I gave a hoot and a backward wave to him, standing watching on the pavement.

'Lovely man,' I said, admittedly a trifle smugly, as I eyed him in the rear-view mirror. 'Can't quite believe he's marrying me.'

'Neither can anyone else,' murmured Flora distractedly, fiddling with her CD player. 'Damn. This thing's really crappy. I knew I should have borrowed Rachel's.'

'What d'you mean?' I said sharply. ' "Neither can anyone else"?'

'Only joking,' she grinned, snapping the case shut. 'No, I just meant he is quite cool. I mean, for us,' she added, generously offering herself into the equation. 'Let's face it, we are a bit scruffy, Mum.'

I negotiated the sunny streets out towards the A4 and regarded my daughter beside me in her cropped jeans, immaculate white T-shirt and freshly washed hair caught back in a pony-tail. She looked, as ever, with her beautiful heart-shaped face, like a Ralph Lauren advert.

'Well you're not,' I said shortly. 'So you must mean me.'

'Well, you must admit,' she said, regarding my filthy old espadrilles and faded man's shirt which was hanging over the top of my trousers because the zip had gone at the side, 'you're not exactly Coco Chanel.'

'David doesn't mind about that,' I retorted, hastily adjusting my shirt over the gaping zip. 'He's not marrying me for my sartorial style.'

'Just as well, with your wardrobe. But honestly, Mum, you might try. I saw your pants in the bathroom the other day, and they're outrageous. Full of holes, and all that crumbling grey elastic – anyone would think you were trying to put him off.'

'I just haven't made it to M & S recently,' I said heatedly. 'And anyway, I have got some nice ones. I only use those in an emergency.'

'You should throw them away. It's embarrassing.'

I looked at her. The colour was high in her cheeks.

'Right,' I said shortly. 'I will. Anything else destined for the rubbish bin?'

'Well those trousers you're wearing now, and those horrid stained espadrilles and your nasty grey jumper with the moth holes, and your *dress*ing gown. With that huge great coffee stain on the back that looks like you've pooed or something, and that you wander around in from nine o'clock onwards every evening. Honestly, Mum, it puts men off.'

'Men? You mean David?'

'Well—'

'What? And Daddy?'

'I don't know, do I? I'm not a man. All I'm saying is . . . don't let yourself go.'

She stared out of the window fixedly, her face and neck pink. I got the impression she'd been meaning to tell me this for some time. Clearly she felt it might be my fault her father had strayed, had wandered from the pack. This was news to me.

'Right.' I gripped the steering wheel hard. 'Any other areas I should clean up on? I mean that's easy, the superficial stuff: wash hair, buy new pants, or even a cropped leather jacket worn with the collar turned up like your father's,' I added sarcastically. 'God, we can all do that,' I scoffed.

'Why don't you then?' She turned in her seat to look at me. 'And actually, I thought Daddy looked great last week. I like him in cool clothes, and Cozzy's got some great stuff too. So what if they don't want to look old yet?'

I gaped at the injustice. 'Oh, and I do?'

'No, I'm just saying you don't care, Mum, and you could look terrific. I just don't want . . .'

'What?' I turned sharply. This fun trip to Cornwall was turning sour on the A4. *'What?'* I repeated. 'For it to happen again? You think that's why your father and I divorced? Nothing to do with his tatty morals but everything to do with my tatty underwear?'

'You know I don't mean that,' she muttered.

And I knew she didn't, but it was too late now. She'd backed me into a corner and I was going to come out fighting. I was going to have it out. She slumped defeated in her seat, knowing the tables had turned.

'So what else?' I insisted furiously.

'Oh, I don't know,' she muttered. And then rather bravely: 'Well, OK, the house.' She sat up. 'You never bother to tidy up, just wait for Yvonne to come in once a week, and all the washing up in the sink builds up, all day long—'

'But I do it, eventually. It does get done.'

'I know, but in between, it's such a mess. And David's so immaculate, and . . . well, I mean look around you. Look at this car, Mum.'

I looked. Sweet wrappers and old magazines rolled luxuriantly on the floor; an empty McDonald's carton basked in the sunshine on the back seat; a shrivelled apple core festered on the dashboard. All my detritus. Nothing I could blame Flora for, who was scrupulously conscientious about throwing litter away. Caught and shamed, I retorted angrily.

'Oh, don't be so prissy, Flora!' I roared. 'D'you want a gleaming four-wheel-drive that's never seen a spot of mud? Is that what you want? One of those, hm?' I jerked my head angrily as an immaculate Jeep whizzed past driven by a coiffed, middle-aged blonde. 'D'you want to be as genteel and scrubbed as that?'

'No, but you deliberately go the other way,' she persisted. 'As if it's two fingers to people like Adam, and Clare, who take such pride in their cars.'

I swept a despairing hand through my hair. Couldn't believe we were having this conversation. Couldn't believe I was being unfavourably compared to my sister, my totally anal, control freak of a sister who shined her bath with a duster and whom Flora and I joked about constantly, and my ex-husband, whose desperate attempts to recapture his youth I openly ridiculed. Although I had noticed recently Flora didn't always join in. Declined to comment when I railed against him. Had she really begun to wonder if it was all my fault?'

'Right!' I said, fury mounting. 'Well, I'm glad you spoke up, darling.' I swung into a BP garage and joined the queue for petrol, fuming. 'Clearly I've got some thinking to do if I want to keep a man. Clearly I've got some drawers to tidy, some cushions to plump, some freezer bags to label and date.'

'Mum . . .' she muttered miserably, picking at the seam of her jeans.

'Oh no, I'm obviously totally out of touch with my feminine side. Instead of trying to write a novel in the attic, I should be languishing between designer sheets painting my nails! I should be buying pot-pourri in John Lewis and arranging it in chi-chi little bowls in the sitting room. I should be wiggling my pert little backside as I vacuum the car with a Dustbuster! Well, let's start now, shall we?' Furiously, I leaned across her, grabbed a grotty plastic bag from the floor by her feet, and began madly stuffing it with rubbish.

'Mother, chill.'

'In fact' – I raised my head from the floor as I threw in an old sock, glanced about wildly and spotted it – 'let's get this whole flaming shooting match sorted out now, shall we? Look, there's a car wash!'

I shunted triumphantly into reverse gear, lurched backwards, and then roared towards it. I jerked to a halt in front of it.

'Mum, no.'

'No? NO?' I turned to her with mock incredulity. 'Why not? Golly, perish the thought we should drive to Cornwall in a dirty car! Come on, money in!'

I pulled a tenner from my bag, leaned out of the window and tried to stuff it in the slot.

'Mum, you need a ticket. And you've never been in one of these things before so why start—'

'Heavens, darling, that's not the attitude! There's always a first time for a bit of spit and polish.' I jumped out and dashed to the kiosk. Happily there was no queue so I quickly secured my ticket and raced back.

'Right, in it goes!' I panted, flopping back in the driver's seat and shoving the ticket in.

The little light on the control box flashed to green and I sped grimly up on to the ramp. Over the ramp. Was that right? Or had I gone too far? I reversed up a bit, revving madly.

'You're supposed to put the aerial down,' muttered Flora. 'Most cars have a button to retract it, but since ours is practically pre-war, it'll get snapped off.'

'So be it!' I barked, all reason gone now. God, even my *car* was too old.

She shook her head in wonder, folding her arms. 'Right. Fine. Leave it. A five-hour drive to Cornwall with no radio. Perfect. I've got my CD player, of course, so I'm all right. Your lookout, Mum.'

I glanced at her. Her arms were folded, eyebrows raised. A triumphant little smile played on her lips. She knew she'd won. Well, bugger that. I jumped out of the car.

'It's too late, Mum, you've put the ticket in!'

Bugger that, too. Quickly I nipped around the bonnet, reached up and deftly pushed the aerial down. The concrete was wet and slippery underfoot though, and as I started back I lost my footing and fell to my knees with an agonising crack. A white light of pain shot through me and I swore furiously, just as jets of water shot at me from every direction in great horizontal sheets. While I shielded my face from the onslaught and tried to breathe, huge rolls of blue polyester fabric lunged towards me, fringed and whirring, advancing and converging on me, knocking me flat to the ground. More and more water was fired at me as I struggled to my knees, gasping, grabbing at the front bumper and trying to breathe through the deluge.

The blue rolls retreated for an instant, and I saw Flora's horrified face, mouth open, eyes huge, gazing at me through the windscreen. Struggling to my feet I clutched the streaming bonnet, my fingers desperate for some purchase, ridiculously imagining I could struggle round to a door, get back in, but no sooner was I up than the buffeting rolls returned – from behind, this time – whipping me with their sodden fringes and biffing me over again like a skittle.

As I clawed my way back on to the bonnet and clung there, spread-eagled like a sacrifice, I wondered if I was going to be killed. Was that possible? In a BP service station in West London? Had a precedent been set, or would I be the first? And what would the papers say? Housewife drowned en route to beach?

As I eyeballed the streaming bonnet, struggling for air, the machinery miraculously halted for a moment. Gasping, I lurched upright, turned and staggered, arms outstretched blindly, towards the drier concrete of the forecourt. I made it by a whisker, just as the mechanical rolls whirred up again, helpfully smacking me on the back of the knees for luck. I faltered, but boy did I stay upright.

On the forecourt, all business had come to a standstill. On this swelteringly hot, busy day in West London, people stood transfixed as a woman, pouring with water, staggered out of the car wash. Some had been lucky enough to witness the whole episode, and were standing by their cars having unloaded the entire family to watch, open-mouthed, nozzles limp in petrol tanks. The water was gushing from me in rivulets; as I glanced back, I saw Flora shrinking down in her seat and pulling her hair over her face.

A young Indian attendant in a turban came running out of the kiosk.

'What happen!' he shouted, gaping at me. 'You no supposed to get out!'

'I thought I had time!' I gasped, shoulders heaving, legs planted wide apart for balance.

'Time? You have no time! Once you put ticket in, you had it! Bingo! Curtains! Kaput!'

'Clearly.'

I turned back to the car just in time to see it being deposited by the ramp, gleaming, on to the forecourt. I lurched towards it, swinging my wet legs wide like John Wayne, the water squelching out of my shoes. I went to the boot and opened it. Found my case. Flora shot out of the passenger seat and ran around to me.

'Are you all right?' she shrieked.

'I'm fine,' I muttered grimly.

She gaped at me, speechless, as I rooted for a towel and some dry clothes. Then: 'What are you going to do?' Her voice was very shrill.

Aware that I still had a large captive audience, I cleared my throat and regarded her squarely.

'Do?' I said loudly. 'Why, Flora, I'm going to strip naked. Then I'm going to dry myself with my towel, and change into some other clothes.'

'Here?' she squeaked.

'Of course.'

Her face paled. A palpable frisson rippled around the forecourt. This woman was mad. Clearly certifiably bonkers. And it's not often one meets one of those, is it? Collectively they held their breath and settled in for some street theatre. I seized some clothes, rolled them efficiently into a towel, and slammed the boot.

'Please, Mum,' Flora whimpered.

'Relax,' I growled at her out of the corner of my mouth. 'I'm going to the loo.'

'Oh.' She gulped with relief. Then, with a quick, terrified glance around, shot back into the car.

With my togs rolled up under my arm, for all the world as if I'd had a pleasant dip in a public pool and was off to get changed, I made sodden progress, head high and with as much dignity as I could muster, towards the kiosk. As I passed by the car, I paused at Flora's window. She buzzed it down.

'Don't ever, *ever*, tell David,' I hissed.

chapter six

I cried aloud at my first view of Taplow House.
Although to be fair, of course, it wasn't my first view.
I'd spied it, as I'd told Gertrude, years ago, when I
was about twelve, on a family holiday, and on other
holidays since.

The first time was in a little boat that Dad had
hired to take us up the estuary. I was leaning over the
edge, trailing my fingers in the water and Clare and
Mum were chatting in the bows with Dad at the
stern. As we floated past the mouth of the creek, I
caught a glimpse of an old stone house covered in
creeper with a slate roof, up a secret, green alley.

'Look!' I'd pointed.

'Mmm. Lovely spot,' Dad had murmured, his eyes
gleaming with envy, hand on the tiller, puffing his
pipe as he guided us past.

Later in the week I persuaded Clare to go for a
bicycle ride with me, not telling her where we were
going. I was longing to see the house again, but not
for the reason I'd seen in Dad's eyes. We'd cycled

down the narrow country lanes, the high banks and hedges rearing over us, a riot of cow parsley, red campion and wild honeysuckle as we freewheeled past, and I'd stopped at the end of the long drive. 'Taplow House', said the sign.

'Why have we stopped?' panted Clare, planting her feet wide apart.

'I don't know, I just thought . . .'

'We can't go down there, it's private.'

'I know.'

I got off my bike though and climbed the five-bar gate, craning my neck. Yes, just. I could just see the edge of the creeper-covered façade, a gravel sweep, and a lawn with croquet hoops on it.

'Come on!' Clare was already on her saddle, wobbling on. Reluctantly I followed and we pedalled on, heading back to the campsite in Trebetherick, where Dad towed the caravan for a week every year.

Later, much later, I remembered my astonishment when David described the house his aunt owned.

'She *owns* it! What, Taplow House? The one up the little creek, the one all on its own – are you sure? Sure it's the same one?'

'Quite sure.'

'But, David, that was the house I dreamed about! As a child! I made up stories about it, fantasised about the people who lived there, the family who owned it. I imagined all these brothers and sisters, you see, and a beautiful mother who was an artist's muse, constantly draped over chaises longues in little bits of chiffon, and a domineering father who ran the house with a rod of iron and was terribly jealous of the French artist who painted his wife. And I made friends with one of the sisters – Tabitha, she was called, with long red hair – and went to the house and played croquet on the lawn with them. Oh, and there was this tall, frightfully attractive brother who wrote poetry and—'

I'd stopped at his astonished face. Yes. Steady on, Annie. You've only just met the man. And a lurid imagination, coupled with what could wrongly be construed as a covetous nature stemming from an upbringing diametrically opposed to his South Kensington one, were not necessarily the first traits one should be exhibiting.

Now, though, as I got out to swing open the five-bar gate at the end of the drive, my heart was pounding just as fast as it had twenty years ago. We purred down the gravel drive, Flora and I, around a bend and, as the rhododendron bushes parted, it appeared out of a sweep of gravel. A long, low, stone house, its crumbling grey façade almost entirely covered by wisteria, its bay windows so low they almost touched the ground, whilst the upstairs windows, under deep eaves, glinted in the sun like sharp eyes under brows. I stopped the car and my eyes feasted. I gazed at the overgrown garden: a tangle of weeds which gave way to a lush lawn, almost field-like it was so strewn with daisies and buttercups and cowslips, which swooped down in turn to thick undergrowth and trees, and then gave a glimpse of the sea beyond. Hidden among primeval green, here was a beautiful, forgotten time-warp. For a moment I couldn't move.

'Pretty,' commented Flora, scratching her leg.

'Pretty!' I squealed, reaching for the door handle and flinging it wide. 'Flora, it's heaven!'

'Bit neglected though. That lawn could do with a mow. I'm surprised Gertrude hasn't got someone down here to do it. Great setting though.' She peered around. 'Did you know it was going to be like this?'

'I had an idea, but I was willing myself not to be disappointed. I'd only ever seen a glimpse.' I shielded my eyes with both hands against the sun, taking in the peeling green shutters at the windows, the little wooden porch with its seat where I imagined I'd sit in the morning sun, cup of coffee and book in hand. Greedily I drank in every detail.

'So how do we get to the sea?'

'Down there, through those woods, I imagine.' I pointed. 'Come on, let's see.'

We walked quickly across the mossy gravel and the overgrown lawn. I was practically running, and actually, Flora was too; both tacitly agreeing to deal with the cases and interior later; hurrying to explore, each wanting to be the first to exclaim.

'Oh, I can see where, because look, there are steps!' She ran ahead of me, and I revelled in her excitement. On the cusp of her teens, but happily still such a child. Still longing to kick off her shoes and run down the steps, to show me first.

Sure enough, the thick undergrowth at the bottom of the garden yielded to granite steps, and then a track leading downwards, twisting and turning sharply through the woods. As I hurried to follow her, plunging into sudden shade, steadying myself occasionally by hanging on to tree trunks to stop myself falling headlong, she cried out.

'Except it's not the sea, it's a river! Mum, look. Our own river, and a beach!'

I hastened to join her, loving the excitement in her voice. As I reached the shore, I caught my breath. It was indeed a very private little beach on a slip of a creek which snaked in from the main estuary. The late afternoon sun away in the west cast ribbons across the water, which, full and limpid with the tide, lapped against the sand, accompanied by all the scents and sounds of midsummer. Gulls whirled and cried overhead in the sailor-blue sky and, higher up the creek, a heron stood motionless, only to rise as we approached, gliding away over the trees with his great soundless wings.

I gripped Flora's shoulders from behind. 'Like it?'

'Totally love it,' she murmured back. Then: 'So quiet!'

'I know.'

'And so private.'

'Isn't it,' I agreed, glancing about. No one, literally no one in sight, not a house, not even a boat. 'Almost indecently so. When you think of Daymer

Bay, heaving around the corner.'

Flora considered this. Bit her lip.

'Perhaps we could ferry people across? Take a boat round and get them to pay to come here for the day?'

I laughed. 'A philanthropic gesture with a touch of commercial zeal thrown in for good measure? Admirable, but no. No, I have no problem being selfish about this place. This solitude is what I came for. I can see myself sitting on that rock with my notebook, sunhat on, words flowing copiously, inspired by the glorious seascape – oh, I can't wait.'

'While I, meanwhile?' She raised her eyebrows.

'You, meanwhile, will . . . you know. Skim stones, paddle, make castles—'

'Castles! I'm not six.'

'Well, I don't know . . .'

'Cycle round the lanes? Pop into Polzeath and hang out at the beach café like you and Clare used to?'

I hesitated. I had heard tales of the Rock youth, streaming down from Robbie's campsite, patronising the Oyster Catcher, leaving spliffs – and worse – on the beach. 'Flora, there were two of us, remember.'

'So?'

'And times were slightly different then. Safer.'

'Rubbish,' she scoffed. 'You told me you slipped away from Grandpa and had a whale of a time with local boys on the beach. Smoking and partying and—'

'Well, we'll see,' I said curtly, wishing I hadn't been

quite so sisterly with her in what had clearly been a rash, confidential moment. 'Come on, let's see the house.'

Linking her arm with mine, I walked her back up the shore to the path through the woods, not wanting to lose the mood of a moment ago and have her sulking on me.

We crossed the garden and went round to the front door, ducking under the little wooden porch as I dug in my pocket for the key. It was stiff in the lock, and for an awful moment I thought it wasn't going to turn, but it did, and we went into the dark, flagged hall, gazing around, blinking in the gloom. If the interior was distinctly subfusc and cool, it was, in a way, rather comforting after the intense glare of the sun and sea without. Dark beams loomed low over bulging, cream walls, and bits of ancient Persian carpet made a poor fist at covering the plain oak boards. In the sitting room there was a scuffed old leather sofa, two upholstered chairs with exploding arms, and an oak bookcase which ran the length of one side of the room, groaning with books. We wandered on.

The kitchen, with its chipped blue lino floor, yellow Formica work surfaces, glass cupboards on the walls and ancient Rayburn, was straight out of the 1950s. All I needed was a pinny and some rollers, I decided. There was also, we discovered, pushing open a heavy oak door, a rather austere dining room housing a long table with barley twist legs, and matching throne-like chairs. Off the hall was a small, surprisingly light study – which I made a mental note to make use of in bad weather – with a vast leather-topped desk, and a captain's chair. Dotted all around the walls of the house, where beams permitted, were tatty prints, badly framed and almost exclusively of seagulls.

One could, I thought, as I made my way back to the dark-panelled hall and watched Flora clatter up the uncarpeted wooden stairs in her flip-flops, have a decorating field day here, but actually, it could so easily be spoiled. The overwhelming sense of nostalgia, of bygone days, of holidays past, was this place's charm. It reminded one of a gentler age, when cakes were made every week; when children pressed their noses to window panes on rainy days; when parents, in the evenings, listened to the gramophone with a book; when the pace of life was slower, less frenetic.

Upstairs, Flora had discovered three bedrooms and a bathroom on the first floor, and then right in the attic, where I followed her up to now, two more tiny ones with faded rose wallpaper, and another bathroom.

'Perfect,' I said, throwing up the sash window in the larger of the two bedrooms and sticking my head out. I looked straight across the creek to the other side, where cows grazed in a patchwork of lush fields, and where, in splendid isolation, a little grey church nestled in the fold of a hill. To the right, the creek flowed down into the estuary. A lone wind-surfer swept past. Rather nice to know someone was alive, I thought. He tacked to port and swept across the creek to the church. Perhaps it was the vicar, I thought idly, about to slip out of his wetsuit and don his cassock. I grinned. Shut my eyes, and breathed deeply.

'Mmm . . . lovely. Smell that view.'

'I'll be up here then,' said Flora decisively, flopping down on the bed behind me.

'And I'll be on the floor below,' I said, turning. 'In the main bedroom, overlooking the garden.'

She sat up quickly. 'Not the one right at the end of the corridor?'

'No,' I said patiently, 'just below you. Literally just down the stairs.'

'Oh. Good.'

I sensed the relief in her voice and tactfully avoided her eye. She wanted to appear independent, but still wanted me close by. She'd never quite grown out of that. At nearly thirteen, a lot of her friends were going to boarding school – had done, some of them, at eleven – but there was no question of Flora following suit. The subject hadn't even been broached, which had meant a new London day school, and because she was bright, an academic one. A hot house, where the only two girls she knew she loathed for the lipstick in their pockets and their smart-alec ways. I glanced at the eczema on her legs, which hopefully would abate in the summer sun. But then back to London, to start a new term . . . She saw me looking and scratched it.

'What?'

'Nothing. Come on, let's go downstairs.'

We spent the rest of the afternoon unpacking and making beds, and then I scrambled some eggs for supper. No garden furniture apparently, so we ate side by side on the warm stone steps which led down from the kitchen to the garden. As we sat, dreamily admiring our bucolic idyll and gazing into the last rays of the sun as the mayflies gathered, Flora scraped her plate thoughtfully.

'Anyway, the others will be down soon, so I can cycle round to see them, can't I?'

'You can,' I affirmed graciously. 'I don't mind that at all. Just no wandering about on your own.'

'And if I'm over at Clare's, you'll have David. I mean, at the weekends.'

I smiled at her attempt to give me some space. Let me have time with him on my own.

'I will, my darling.'

A silence ensued.

'Will you miss him?' she ventured, at length.

'During the week? Yes, I'm sure, but you know I'll be terribly busy.'

Privately I couldn't help thinking: Golly, what heaven. No man to cook for, no house to clean. We'd live outside mostly, I decided, and anyway, it was so dark inside no one would notice if I didn't dust. Didn't hoover. But then – suddenly I brought myself up sharp – that wasn't the attitude, was it? The new attitude ... I narrowed my eyes over the treetops to the glimmer of bright water on the horizon. A plan was beginning to form.

'Flora,' I said eventually, 'would you mind very much if I nipped into Rock? Would you be all right here on your own?'

'What, now?'

'Yes, just for an hour or so. The shops will still be open. I thought I'd look around. Will you be OK?' I challenged her briefly with my eyes.

'Of course,' she said, rising to it. 'I'll raid the bookcase. I notice there's no telly, but there are masses of books. Why? What d'you need?'

'Oh, this and that.' I smiled and took the plates inside.

I left her humming to herself in the sunshine and nipped upstairs. Pulling open all the drawers I'd just filled, I threw the contents on to the bed. Ten minutes later I'd left the house, armed with a bulging black bin liner which I dumped in the dustbin in the garage. Hopping in the car and tooting cheerily to let her know I was away, I purred off down the long drive.

And an hour or so later, I was back. The wind had got up a bit now and it was getting squally outside, heralding a storm, perhaps. As I blew in with a gust of wind, the front door slammed shut behind me.

'Phew! Quite a storm brewing out there!'

Flora didn't look up. She was spread-eagled face down on the old leather sofa, her head firmly between the pages of *Jamaica Inn*.

She grunted.

I cleared my throat and struck a nonchalant pose. 'Whadya think?' I drawled. Still no response.

'Flora, what d'you think?' I resorted to finally, and slowly she turned. She gaped. Dropped her book.

'Mum!'

'Pretty hot, huh?' I twirled.

She got off the sofa, incredulous.

'I'm not sure "hot" is the word. Preppy, or Sloaney perhaps but – God, you look like Clare. Clare on holiday!'

I beamed down at the navy blue polo shirt tucked neatly into crisp cream trousers with a smart leather belt. Flexed the squeaky new deck shoes on my feet and swung my bulging carrier bags.

'I've got a whole wardrobe in here. Shirts, trousers, shorts, pleated skirts, all brand spanking new with lots of lovely logos on, and all my old summer clothes are in the bin.'

She blinked. 'All of them?'

'Pretty much. Except the underwear. Crew Clothing didn't quite run to that, but I'm sure somewhere in Wadebridge will oblige tomorrow. Oh, and I bought a tennis racket too.' I took it out of a bag and swung it jauntily.

'Mum, could you take that cap off? And untuck your shirt?' she said, circling me nervously. 'And take your hair out of that band. You really do look like Clare like that.'

'Really?' I beamed. 'So why take it out?'

'Please.'

'Oh well.' I shook my curly dark mane back over my shoulders. 'Might get it all cut off tomorrow.'

'No! Don't,' she said, alarmed. 'I mean – not until you see what David thinks. He may not like it. Any of it.'

'Nonsense, he'll love it. And anyway, it was your idea.'

'I know, it's just you don't look like you.'

'Of course it's me,' I scoffed, marching past her and heading for the stairs with my bags. 'The new me. The new, improved, organised, dynamic me. We'll get the Hoover out tomorrow, Flora,' I warned as I bounced upstairs. 'Just because we're on holiday there's no reason to let standards drop. That hall carpet's a disgrace.'

That night we fell gratefully into our soft, plumped-up little beds, tired after the long journey. The wind had whipped up into quite a storm, and the rain was beating a fast tattoo on the black windows. I lay there and listened for a while, loving that feeling of being snug within whilst it raged without. After a while though, I realised it would be quieter with the shutters closed, so I nipped out and shut them, sliding the wooden bar across.

Up above me I heard Flora get into bed, and then, predictably, get out again. I listened as she rearranged the curtain – there had to be a carrot shape of light at the top – turned around twice, touched the floor, muttered a Hail Mary, turned around again in the opposite direction, and then got back into bed. A little ritual – amongst others – that had to be performed every night of her life, or who knew what horrors would befall her or her loved ones.

Yes, I thought, turning on to my side, this was just what Flora needed: a break from the stresses and strains of London life. A break from keeping up, fitting in, getting on, being cool; a licence to be young and free, with world enough and time to enjoy it. In my mind's eye I had her rambling the cliffs, finding gulls' nests in the wind-tossed grass, picking wild flowers and exclaiming merrily at rare orchids, until my eyes closed and Morpheus led me tactfully away down the dark corridors of sleep before I spotted the cigarette butt by the orchid.

It was some time later that I heard footsteps in the passage. I opened my eyes, unsure why I'd woken, and then . . . yes. There they were again. I turned my head and peered at the illuminated hands on my clock. Two-thirty. Still the footsteps continued, slowly padding around the galleried landing. It was a deliberately careful tread, but in an old house like this, the floorboards creaked ominously. They were getting closer now, coming towards my door. I sat up in bed, my heart hammering. In the dark, I reached down and my hand closed over my new tennis racket. Slowly, the door handle turned. I held my breath. The door opened and, in a long white night-dress, her eyes huge and staring, Flora wafted towards me, looking exactly like a ghost.

'Shit!' I dropped the racket with a clatter. 'Flora, you frightened the life out of me! What the hell are you doing creeping around like that?'

'There's someone downstairs!' she gasped. 'Mum, I'm sure there's someone moving around down there!'

'Oh, don't be ridiculous, you stupid girl!' I spluttered, terror instantly turning to anger. 'I nearly brained you, for God's sake!'

'No but, Mum, there's creaking and bumping and all sorts!'

'Well, of course there is! There's a ruddy storm raging outside and this house is three hundred years old. It feels it in its bones, just as I do, the poor old relic. Now go back to bed.'

'No, Mum, I can't,' she whimpered, climbing in. 'I'm too frightened up there. Can I sleep with you?'

'Oh, *Flora*!'

But it was a foregone conclusion and I knew it. I moved across as she fastened herself tightly on to me, like a flea on a frowsty old labrador.

'When will you grow up?' I fumed, furiously.

As ever, with Flora, I lurched between supreme patience and out-and-out frustration. I clamped an arm around her shoulders and glared at the ceiling. God, when would she grow out of this? She was nearly a teenager, for heaven's sake. She'd be dating boys soon; would they be in bed with me too? Would she, at nineteen, be dragging some loose-limbed Lothario into my room, getting his hair gel all over the pillow, because something had gone bump in the night? Would I wake up with David on one side and Flora and Trev on the other? I sighed and turned over. And the worst thing was, I knew it was my fault. Mine and Adam's. Knew that she was fall-out: a timorous casualty of our terminal marriage.

'Sorry, Mummy,' she muttered.

'It's fine,' I muttered back. 'Not your fault.' I squeezed her shoulder tight. We were silent.

'There it goes again.'

'It's the wind, you wretched child.'

A pause.

'Well, what's that then?' She raised her head sharply from the pillow.

I have to say that, even to my cynical ears, it sounded very much like a chair scraping back from a table. I sat up. Listened. 'Probably Gertrude's ghost.'

'What!'

'No, nothing. Probably just an old beam creaking. Go back to sleep.'

'No, Mum, please! There's definitely someone down there!'

'Oh *God*!' I threw back the bedclothes. 'Right. Let's go down and see them, shall we?' I snapped on my bedside light but nothing happened.

'There's no power.'

'Why not?' Flora yelped.

'Clearly there's been a power cut, darling. These things happen in old houses in a storm. We're in the country now.'

'So how are we going to see?' she whimpered. 'How are we—'

'Come on, we'll manage.'

I got up, irritated beyond belief, and groped for the door.

It was pitch black in the passage outside, blacker even than in the bedroom. Together, we slithered along the landing wall towards the head of the stairs. Then with Flora behind me, gripping on to my T-shirt with both hands, we shuffled, like a panto-mime horse, across the landing – me with arms outstretched and hoping to goodness I wouldn't fall down the stairs – towards the banisters.

I grasped them firmly. 'Got them.'

With Flora still clinging to me, I groped my way down slowly, slowly, step by step. Didn't want to break my bloody neck. All the curtains were closed in the hall and, apart from a chink of light coming through a leaded pane in the front door, all was blackness. I kept my eyes firmly on that chink.

'See, Flora?' I said in a loud voice as we reached the bottom step. 'There's no one here. No one at all. Come out, come out, whoever you are!' I sang jovi-ally, as I'd done when she was small, rattling broom handles under her bed at imaginary monsters, stark naked on my haunches usually – and, come to think of it, when she was not so small either.

'And there's a torch in the car,' I went on as we shuffled as one towards the door. 'If I get that, at least you'll have a light in your room.'

'Your room,' she corrected.

'All right, my room, just for tonight.' I patted the door, searching for the doorknob. 'But, Flora, you really must get a grip, you can't keep creeping into my— AAAAAGGH!'

I let out a shriek of terror as a hand closed firmly over mine on the doorknob.

'Not so fast,' breathed a man's voice softly in my left ear. 'Hold it right there.'

119

chapter seven

The scream I emitted was worthy of a B-movie actress in a Hammer House of Horror. I snatched my hand away and leaped backwards into Flora, who was also squealing like a banshee and ducking down behind me as if under fire. In the dark, I could just make out a man's shape, vast and looming, with a huge hunched back, black and mutinous by the door. I shrieked again, backing furiously and pushing Flora back with me.

'Get out! Get out of my bloody house, or I'll call the police!'

'Your bloody house?' drawled an American accent. 'Some mistake, surely?'

A yellow flame snapped up in the gloom. In the light of a Zippo lighter, I found myself looking into a pair of bright blue eyes in a brown, weathered face.

'Where the hell are the lights in this place? Don't they run to electricity in this part of the world?'

'There's been a power cut,' I breathed, trying not to

scream again. 'Who the hell are you? What are you doing in my house?'

I was still bloody scared, but not totally terrified. He didn't have the face of an axe murderer: more of a Red Indian actually, with those slanty cheekbones; and the hunch turned out to be a backpack.

'*Your* house again. Jesus. Well, what I'm trying to do is occupy the accommodation I took for my summer vacation. Listen, are you sure the lights have gone? Haven't you got any candles or anything? And can't we discuss this so we can see some faces and not just follow the dialogue? Seems to me that might be a little more civilised than standing around in the dark.'

'There's some in the drawer,' said Flora. She fumbled over to the hall table. 'I saw them while I was looking for some matches.'

It occurred to me to wonder what she'd wanted matches for, but I had other things on my mind.

'How did you get in?' I demanded.

'With a key, of course. How did you?'

'With – a key,' I faltered, as Flora produced a bunch of candles.

I stood, bewildered and open-mouthed, as he expertly lit four or five, holding them in a bunch in his hand. He glanced about, then, seeing nowhere to put them, strode into the sitting room and set them carefully in line on the mantelpiece. A soft-focus glow developed as the room began to resemble a Renaissance still life. I scuttled in after him.

'But where did you get the key?' I yelped.

'From Mrs Fetherston-Hall. She mailed it to me. Here.' He whipped it from a pocket and dangled it on a piece of string in front of me. 'Together with confirmation of the dates I booked, and handy hints on how to cajole the washing machine into life, and the location of the butcher, the baker, the candlestick maker and other local amenities. I'm sorry, ladies, but it seems to me you're in the wrong place. I took this house for a summer vacation and that's just what I intend to have. I've also just got off a flight from Boston and driven five hours down your so-called freeways at some godforsaken hour because my plane was delayed, and what I didn't expect to find when I got here was two shrieking females in white winceyette playing Lady Macbeth in stereo. Not only occupying my house, but giving me the third degree about what goddamn right I've got to be here. Now, before you shift your asses down to the nearest motel, perhaps you'd be good enough to show me where the fuse box is so I can get this place illuminated.'

'Ooh!' I bristled when I'd finally found my tongue. 'Mrs Fetherston-Hall – how impertinent! *Mrs* Fetherston-Hall just happens to be my fiancé's aunt, and she has kindly lent me this house, not just for a vacation, but for the entire summer! Clearly there's been some mix-up with your dates, but I think you'll find that if there's anyone's "ass" that needs shifting, it's yours!'

He frowned. 'She's your aunt? Mrs Fetherston-Hall?'

'My fiancé's aunt,' I hissed.

'And you've paid good money?'

'Well, no,' I faltered. 'Obviously I haven't paid money—'

'Because I have to tell you' – he whipped a letter from another pocket and waved it rather rudely in my face – 'that a financial transaction has taken place here. It's here in black and white. Clear and binding.' His blue eyes challenged mine.

'Clear and . . . Oooh!' I seethed, and snatched the letter. I began to read it: 'Dear Mr Malone . . .' Then I glanced up warily. 'That's you? Mr Malone?'

'My passport is only moments away in the car, lady,' he said testily.

'My name is Mrs O'Harran,' I snapped back, wishing I had a dressing gown over this stupid short nightie. I tugged it down and read on.

Further to your letter of the 4th, I'm writing to confirm your stay in Taplow House. The key is enclosed. Do have a marvellous time. The place is a little haphazard, as you'll discover, but charming, and I think you'll enjoy it. I've enclosed a list of reliable local shops, and an inventory. If you have any problems, please don't hesitate to telephone.

Yours sincerely,
Gertrude Fetherston-Hall

123

I sat down slowly on the arm of a chair and shot a despairing hand through my hair. Oh God. I recognised her spidery hand and the thick, headed, Onslow Gardens writing paper. Oh *God*. I licked my lips. Took a moment. Then I glanced up.

'She's made a mistake,' I said defiantly. 'She's getting old and rather doddery, and clearly she forgot she'd promised the house to me. I'm sorry, but I think you'll find that when we iron this out in the morning and speak to Mrs Fetherston-Hall, you'll appreciate the situation. I'm sure she'll refund you in full, Mr Malone. Meanwhile, I suggest you drive back down the road and follow it into town. There's a very pleasant hotel called the Priory Bay on the corner; I'm confident they'll accommodate you tonight, and perhaps for the rest of your stay. We'll speak again when I've contacted her tomorrow. Good morning.'

His blue eyes, in the candlelight, looked dumbfounded. Then they hardened.

'I'm not driving anywhere, Mrs O'Harridan, or whatever the hell your name is. I told you, I've just driven five goddamn hours from London. It's two-forty-five in the morning, for Chrissake. I'm not going to some Priory Bay, I'm staying right here, in this house, that my family and I rented for two weeks!'

'Don't be ridiculous,' I retorted, 'of course you can't stay! *We're* here, my daughter and I. This is *our* house. We've unpacked, made up beds—'

'Mum, we can't just turn him out in the middle of the night,' muttered Flora at my elbow. 'He's got a letter. From Gertrude. Something's obviously gone wrong.'

I glanced down at her, astonished.

'Finally, the voice of reason,' he snapped. 'Something *has* gone wrong, very wrong, the bottom of which we will get to in the morning, be sure of that, Mrs O'Have-a-go. Meantime, since you ladies are presumably occupying the first-floor accommodation, I will unroll my sleeping bag on this couch. That is unless you want some strange man prowling around the upstairs corridors.'

'Certainly we don't!' I bristled. 'I don't know you!'

'Neither you do, but unless you get your butts back to your beds and let me get some sleep down here, you're gonna know me a whole lot better, because I tell you' – he unhooked a sleeping bag from his backpack and threw it on the leather sofa – 'I haven't put my head down in thirty-six hours and I sure as hell could use some sleep.'

'But I can't have a perfect stranger down here while my twelve-year-old daughter sleeps upstairs!' I spluttered. 'You can't just—'

'Watch me.' He unbuckled his belt and dropped his trousers.

'Oh!' I yelped and hurriedly turned Flora around. She giggled and glanced back. He winked.

'Now. Bathroom?'

'*Mr* Malone,' I seethed, 'there is a downstairs

125

lavatory which I suggest you use. As you so rightly pointed out, I do not want you prowling around upstairs while my daughter and I are asleep. Kindly do not take one step in the direction of my quarters.'

'Mrs O'Harrods,' he said, looking me up and down, 'I swear to God your quarters are the last thing on my mind.'

'Oh!' I clenched my fists impotently. Glared at him. He grinned back.

Seething, I snatched up a couple of candles, handed one to Flora and pushed her ahead of me, towards the hall and up the stairs. 'Go on, Flora,' I hissed. 'Up, up!'

God, the *nerve* of the man. Barging in here, sending us back to our beds – *oooh*. If the china were mine I'd throw it at him. I strode – as defiantly as I dared in a T-shirt that just about covered my bottom, horribly aware that he was watching me – on up the stairs. And Jesus, what the hell was Gertrude up to? Had she really got her wires so comprehensively crossed? No, of course she hadn't, I decided as I hustled Flora ahead of me along the gallery. It was unthinkable. And she'd get rid of him, too, or David would. Golly, yes, it was practically David's house, I thought with a start, since it was Gertrude's, which made it . . . yes, as David's prospective wife, almost mine really! *My* house. I stopped. I had a good mind to shoot back downstairs and order him out, but actually – I glanced over the balcony and caught a glimpse of a brown chest in the candlelight as he whipped his sweater over his head. I hurriedly looked away. Actually, the thought of those steely blue eyes and those bulky shoulders made me think better of it.

'Where are you going?' I hissed as Flora went on, up the next flight to the attic.

'Back to bed.'

'But I thought you wanted to sleep with me?'

She turned on the stair to look back at me. 'Oh, that was when I thought there was a crazy mass murderer lurking downstairs. I'm fine now.'

'But, Flora—!'

'Mum, don't fuss.' She grinned. 'Looks a bit like George Clooney, don't you think?'

I stared at her, horrified. 'Nothing *like* George Clooney!'

But she'd gone on, up to her room.

Except perhaps in that TV horror movie I'd seen him in, way before *ER*, I thought suddenly. The one where he'd played the neighbourhood nutter. That sinister smile. That axe coming through the front door. Horrified, I raced up after her and hurtled into her room as she was getting into bed.

'Flora, lock your door!' I panted.

'What? But, Mum—'

'Lock it!' I slammed it shut, leaving her within. 'Lock it!' I instructed again, putting my ear to it and waiting. Finally I heard her pad across the room, a deep sigh, and then a click.

'Satisfied?' she muttered.

I nodded grimly and hurried down to my room again. Red-hot candle wax dripped over my hand in my haste, and, swearing with pain, I got into bed. I lay still for a moment, picking the wax off my hand, listening for sounds downstairs, listening for – God forbid – his tread on the stairs. But at length, in the silence, I blew out the candle. I shivered and turned over, pulling the covers right up to my chin. The rain was still beating hard on the windows. Bloody man, I seethed. Bloody, *bloody* man. That was all we needed, some Yank wandering in from the storm, but Flora did have a point. I couldn't exactly turf him out, seeing as how he had a letter. I'd better speak to Gertrude in the morning. Send him packing then.

Hours later, I awoke to find the sun streaming through my window. One of the shutters had blown open in the wind, and a great shaft of light was beaming through, illuminating the opposite wall and filling the room with a golden glow. I sat up and opened the other shutter, gazing out at a sparkling lawn, and then the sea: blue, limpid and calm beyond the trees. It was a fabulous day. The storm had indeed abated and, for a glorious moment, I completely forgot about Mr Malone downstairs. And then I saw him. Emerging from the back door below me with a plate piled high with bacon, eggs, fried potatoes, baked beans and tomatoes. In his other hand he held a sloshing mug of coffee, and behind him was Flora, dressed, and carefully carrying a similarly laden plate and a mug. They made their way, the two of them, clutching knives and forks, to a table and chairs I'd never seen before set out on the lawn. My jaw dropped.

'Christ!'

Hurriedly I lunged for my clothes. I threw them on, splashed water on my face, and then – catching sight of my reflection as I spun out of the room – hastened back to drag a comb through my hair. I ran downstairs, my feet echoing loudly on the wooden stairs. Through the kitchen I sped, and out of the back door, where, in a sylvan scene straight out of *The Darling Buds of May*, ankle deep in cowslips and dandelions, the pair of them sat, mouths full and chewing hard, making serious inroads into their groaning platefuls.

'What the *hell* d'you think you're doing!' I panted, legs planted wide for support, hands on hips.

He looked up surprised. His dark hair was tousled and unkempt, and he had an old blue fishing jersey on.

'Having breakfast. Have some.' He waved a fork idly towards the kitchen. 'We left some fries in the pan for you. You just need to slap another egg on the griddle.'

'I will not "slap another egg on the griddle",' I gasped. 'One of *my* eggs no doubt. I told you, I want you out of here! Not enjoying *my* sunkissed garden with *my* daughter, eating *my* bloody breakfast!'

'Ah.' He nodded. 'Yep.' He wiped his mouth with the back of his hand. Stifled a burp. 'I rang the Priory

129

Bay, incidentally. They've got a couple of rooms vacant.'

'Excellent,' I snapped.

'They don't come cheap though,' he warned, waving that fork again. 'It's high season now, and the smaller ones have all gone. I reckon you'll be paying upwards of a hundred and fifty pounds a night, but the guy on reception said they were pretty sumptuous.'

I opened my mouth to speak. Finally made it. '*I'll* be paying? I'm sorry, Mr Malone, *you'll* be paying!'

He regarded me for a full moment above a forkful of egg. 'No, I don't think so, Mrs O'Haggard.'

'O'HARRAN! And we'll soon see about *that*!'

I went inside and made for the phone. The kitchen, as I stalked through it, was a profusion of greasy pots and pans, half-empty bean tins, egg shells, crusts and dirty mugs. The sitting room was equally chaotic: clothes were strewn all about; a half-unpacked suitcase spewed out on to the floor; a sleeping bag lay in a heap; and piles of papers from a case had been knocked over on to the carpet. It looked as if we'd been burgled.

'Bloody *hell*!' I seethed as I picked my way precariously through the debris to the phone by the sofa. I perched on the edge, then, remembering he'd slept on it, moved smartly on to a chair. I flicked furiously through my address book looking for Gertrude's number – except I suddenly realised I didn't have to. Mr Malone had thoughtfully propped his letter up, quite ostentatiously, by the telephone. Gertrude's number, under her address, was underlined purposefully in red. I stared, taken aback. Then rallied. Right. *Fine!* I dialled.

Gertrude answered almost immediately, her distinctive, cut-glass tones echoing musically down the line.

'Helleau?'

'Hello, Gertrude? Oh, thank goodness you're in.'

'Annabel! My dear, how lovely. How are you?' she bellowed. She always bellowed on the telephone. Didn't trust the equipment. 'Enjoying the weather? Glorious here, and hopefully with you, too?'

'It is, Gertrude, it's lovely, but listen. We have a slight problem.'

'Oh?'

I briefed her elaborately, explaining at length, exclaiming, protesting – but hopefully not too vehemently because it was, after all, a pickle of her making – and then paused, breathless and triumphant, waiting for her indignation to match mine. There was a pause.

'Oh. Oh dear . . .' she faltered eventually.

'Gertrude?'

'Yes, yes, I do see. Oh dear, what a dilemma.'

'Well, no, not really. No dilemma really, Gertrude, I'll just tell him to go, shall I?'

'Well, you see, my dear, it's all rather awkward. As a matter of fact I *do* remember meeting him now, him and his family, a couple of years ago, in Cornwall.

131

They were staying further along the coast from Taplow House, with the Masterses. Tom Masters was a old pupil of Hugh's and a great friend. If I remember rightly, Mr Malone was a cousin of theirs, American fellow, I believe. Anyway, you're quite right, I did offer him the house this year – he contacted me recently about it . . .'

'Well, offer, yes,' I spluttered. 'But, Gertrude—'

'But, my dear, he's paid me, you see,' she said anxiously. 'Quite a lot of money, as I recall. Sent a cheque, and all gone, of course, on the blasted roof. So hideously expensive, builders, these days. Oh my dear, how ghastly. I'm most dreadfully sorry. Perhaps the Priory Bay? Up the hill? For a week or so, maybe? It is frighteningly expensive, though.'

'You mean . . .' I swallowed. 'For me?'

'Well, and Flora, obviously. It's just, well, now that you're down there, it does seem awfully silly to come all that way back again, doesn't it? Oh dear, how perfectly stupid of me, I've ruined your holiday. I do apologise. What a forgetful old fool I am! Honestly, sometimes I forget my own name. Do forgive me!'

She was genuinely distressed now. I gazed out through the bay window at the other end of the room. In the garden I could see Flora and Mr Malone scraping their plates in the sunshine. Flora laughed, albeit a trifle nervously, at something he said. I gulped. All my dreams . . . my hopes for a long, restful, productive summer in this glorious house by the creek: writing, fishing with Flora, teaching her to sail, all turning to dust and ashes.

'Never mind, Gertrude,' I said quietly. 'It's not your fault.'

'But, my dear, I feel wretched.'

'No. Don't. Really, it's fine.'

We said goodbye and I put the receiver down. Then, almost immediately, I picked it up and rang David. He'd see. He'd tell her she was wrong. That it was, after all, her house, and that we could . . . well, pay Mr Malone back, David and I. And David could speak to him. Be, you know, authoritative. Firm. Tell him his aunt had made a mistake.

'I'm with a patient,' he murmured, *sotto voce*, when I'd finally bullied his receptionist into putting me through.

'I know, Laura said, but, David, this is important,' I insisted. I set off at speed and gave him a swift résumé of the last eight hours. He was silent for a long moment.

'David? David, shall I give him a cheque? Would that be the best way to handle it?'

'Well, you can try, but I doubt he'll take it. And why should he? He's flown all the way from America expecting vacant possession. God, what a balls-up.'

'I know, I know!' I wailed, wringing my hands on the other end.

'I'm so sorry, my darling, because I know how much this means to you, but I'm afraid you're going to have to go up the road until we sort this out. Perhaps that letting agent, John Bray, will have a bungalow left. You never know.'

A bungalow. This glorious, glorious house. A *bungalow*!

'Annie? Annie, darling, I'm in the middle of a consultation. I must go. I'm so sorry. My blasted aunt . . . honestly, sometimes I think she's got Alzheimer's.' Now he felt wretched.

I nodded miserably. 'No no, it's OK, David. It's fine. Don't worry.'

Slowly I replaced the receiver. I gazed up at a print of a seagull, soaring high into the sky on the wall above the fireplace. Blinked hard, willing back the tears. By the phone, a small local guide book lay, interspersed with adverts. I flicked through it bleakly. Slowly, I picked up the phone again. Made a few more calls. Finally, I replaced the receiver and walked back to the garden.

Mr Malone was leaning back in his chair, which he'd clearly found in an outhouse I hadn't discovered, stretching languidly and letting out a deep sigh of contentment after his heavy artillery breakfast. There were holes in the underarms of his jumper, I noticed as he locked his fingers behind his head.

'Well?' He grinned as I approached. That maddening, blow-torch grin.

'Well.' I swallowed. 'Yes. It seems you're quite right, Mr Malone. You do, indeed, have a contract. A right to this place, because a financial transaction has taken place. And I don't.'

'Great.' He grinned some more. 'So you'll be off then.'

'Yes.' I averted my eyes to the grass. 'So we'll be off then.'

I felt Flora's huge brown eyes upon me. 'You mean . . . we have to go?'

'I'm afraid so, my darling.' I raised my chin and gave a brave smile. 'It seems Gertrude forgot she'd already rented the house out to this gentleman when she offered it to us. You know how forgetful she is.'

'Oh!' Her face fell. 'So . . . where will we go? Priory Bay?'

I gave a bleak little laugh. 'What, at two hundred pounds a night? No, I'm sorry, darling, it's way out of our league. They've only got suites left, and all the bed and breakfasts are full – I've tried. High season, you see. John Bray says he might have something in a couple of weeks, a bungalow, but he can't be sure. He's waiting on a possible cancellation. But no, my love, I'm afraid it's home time for us. Back to London.'

There was a silence. Flora got up from the table.

'But, Mum—'

'Come on, my darling, chop-chop. You go and pack, and I'll do this.'

I bustled over to the table to clear the plates, to avoid her eye. Avoid saying sorry. I knew my voice would crack, and anyway, I could do that in the car. Say sorry I'd mucked things up for her, as usual. Mucked up her holiday, just as I'd mucked up her short life. Say sorry, I couldn't even get that right. I fumbled miserably with the plates and cups and saucers, loaded them into a pile, and turned for the kitchen.

Mr Malone cleared his throat. 'Er, listen. When did that estate agent guy say a house would be free?'

I paused, plates in hand. Didn't turn round though. 'A couple of weeks. He couldn't be sure, though.'

'Well, hey,' he said gruffly. 'This place is huge. I'm not expecting company for a while, why don't you stay on 'til you get someplace else?'

I turned. Gave a tight little smile. 'Mr Malone, that's extremely kind, but we couldn't possibly accept.'

'Why not?' said Flora.

'Because . . .' I turned to my daughter. 'Well, darling, we just can't! We don't know this man and—'

'Oh, not that old baloney again. Whadya want, a formal introduction? My full résumé?' He got to his feet and stuck out his hand – then, realising my hands were full, thrust it in his pocket. 'Matt Malone, OK? So quit with the Mr Malone routine. I head up the psychiatric department at Boston University Hospital – and you can check that out with the boys in the white coats back home if you wish. I'm here to get some peace and quiet – not to cut up bodies and put them in bin liners as you clearly assumed, although I know a man could – and to do some work. By day I'll be working on a thesis I should

136

have had finished months ago as it's getting published in the fall – I might, incidentally, commandeer that study I spotted earlier – and when I need a break, I might get a bit of fishing in. Unless you're the house guests from hell, I can't see our interests are going to conflict that much, since I guess you'll want to be either out on the beach or on the ocean. Am I right?'

'Yes! Yes, you are right. We will be out for most of the day, won't we, Mum?' Flora turned to me eagerly.

'Yes, but—'

'And since the house is on three floors, I suggest I take the top one – which I see has a tub but no shower in the quaint old English style – and leave you the first floor, which also has a bathroom. Would that suit?'

I stared at him speechless.

'Midday meals could be taken on the beach for you, and on the hoof for me – unless we happen to coincide in the kitchen, in which case it might be friendly to open a can of beans together like Flora and I did this morning, without you flying into a rage and waving a rolling pin like something out of welfare. Am I going too fast for you?'

'N-no, but . . .' I put my fingertips to my temples and shut my eyes. 'Hang on, what about your family? Gertrude said she'd met you with your wife. Surely she'll be coming out? Surely she won't want—'

'Not for some time,' he interrupted, shortly. 'She's working.'

'Oh. Right. What as?'

He paused. Raised his eyebrows. I blushed at my nosiness.

'As a consultant radiologist, since you ask.'

'Oh, right,' I mumbled, taken aback.

'I, on the other hand, being semi-academic, get a much longer semester break, which is why I took this place on in the first place.'

'You're . . . a psychiatrist?' I ventured. 'A shrink?'

He gave a glimmer of a smile. 'With elegant consulting rooms in midtown Manhattan? Where movie stars come to lay their coiffed heads and share their innermost thoughts with me for hundreds of bucks an hour, is that what you're thinking?'

'Well . . .'

'I'm a clinical practitioner specialising in drug research. I treat psychotically ill patients in a high-security hospital.'

'Oh!' I stepped back in alarm. Nearly dropped the bloody plates.

'Wow.' Flora blinked in awe. 'Real psychos.'

He smiled. 'Not necessarily.'

I straightened up. 'My fiancé's a doctor too,' I said importantly. 'A general practitioner. In London. Belgravia, actually.'

'Excellent news,' he said quickly, 'I'm delighted for him. So we can all be medics together. And now I must go commandeer that study. Do I take it you accept, Mrs O'Harran?'

I licked my lips. 'Annie.'

'Annie.'

'I'd – obviously have to pay you?'

'Why? This place belongs to your relative. You expected to have it free. I didn't.'

'No, but . . . well. Perhaps we could share it. Share the rent.' I wasn't entirely sure I wanted to be beholden to him. Didn't want a landlord–tenant situation going on here. 'I'd feel happier,' I said decisively, standing up straight. 'What did you pay?'

He mentioned a sum of money so colossal I nearly fell over.

'Gertrude asked you for that!'

'Listen, I'm not asking for anything.'

'No, but I . . .' I gripped the plates hard for support. 'I insist.'

He shrugged. 'OK. Now all I ask is for some peace and quiet and to be left alone.'

I bristled. 'Certainly I'll leave you alone! You may have a thesis to deliver, but I'll have you know I have a book to write. A novel to finish. A certain well-known London publisher is clamouring for my next chapter, and if anyone needs peace and quiet, it's me!'

'Fine, whatever,' he said brusquely. 'Do we have a deal?'

'Golly.' I swallowed hard. 'I suppose we do. But I don't know what David will say . . .' I dithered for a moment. 'Maybe I should . . .'

'Well, go ask his permission, for God's sake,' he said, exasperated.

I stiffened. 'I don't have to do that!' I snapped, raising my chin. 'Yes, Mr Mal— Matt. You have a deal.' I turned to stalk inside, then thought better of it. Paused. Turned my head. 'And, um . . . thank you,' I said doubtfully. 'Very much.'

'My pleasure.' He nodded curtly before stalking inside himself.

chapter eight

It was only later that evening, as I went to ring David, that I realised the enormity of what I'd done. My hand rested hesitantly on the receiver. Golly, what would he say? How favourably would he react to the news that I was sharing a house with a complete stranger? David was an easy-going man, but he did marvel at my impulsiveness sometimes. Lunacy, he'd been moved to call it on occasion. Would this be just such an occasion, I wondered? It was.

'You've done what?' I held the receiver a couple of inches from my ear. 'Annie, are you mad?'

'No no, listen,' I insisted, 'it's fine, really. You haven't seen this house for years, David, I know, but if you recall, it is jolly big. Deceptively big, and on three floors with . . . ooh, six or seven bedrooms, and he's right at the top with his own bathroom. I promise you, we hardly see him. We've spent a whole day together, and I swear you wouldn't even know he was here!'

This much was true. Matt had indeed holed up in the study as promised with a pile of books and files, emerging only occasionally to make himself cups of strong black coffee which he overfilled and then slopped, in a slovenly manner, all the way back to the study. Slightly unnerved by his presence and not being able to get straight down to work as smartly as he had, I'd hovered, on the pretext that I was dusting or hoovering the sitting room, but actually wanting to be around in case – well, you know. In case he made improper remarks to Flora or something. Not that Flora was around to hear them. Having discovered the bookcase from heaven, she'd taken a pile and decamped down to the creek with her boogy-pack, her Ambre Solaire and a large bottle of Evian.

I crept down mid-morning and found her, supine at the water's edge, lying on a towel in a bikini, foot tapping, engrossed in Daphne du Maurier and totally at peace with the world. She looked up when she saw me.

'YEAH?' she yelled loudly, above her music.

'Everything all right, darling?' I called.

'WHA'?' she bellowed, squinting in annoyance at me.

'Shh.' I held a finger to my lips. 'I just wondered if you were OK? Not bored? Or lonely?'

She took her earphones off and regarded me witheringly. 'No, Mother. I thought you were going to work in the summer house?'

This we'd discovered at the bottom of the garden,

a little green wooden slatted affair, on the crest of the hill just before the woods, with a perfect view of the sea. And since Matt had commandeered the study, it seemed the perfect place for me and my laptop.

'I was. I mean – I am.'

She nodded, snapped her earpiece back on smartly, and went back to her book.

I crept back up the hill through the leafy glade, following the twisting, sandy path. She was right, I should get my head down, get on with some work, but hell, it was nearly lunchtime. Flora would be hungry soon. I'd better make her some sandwiches. Oops, no butter in the fridge. Better nip to the shops.

I knocked tentatively on the study door.

'Yep!' he barked. I jumped. Popped my head around.

'Just going to the shops,' I said brightly, eyes roving quickly round the room, taking in the chaotic mess he'd made of the place already. I glanced back at him. He was staring at me incredulously.

'And your point is?'

'Well, you know,' I said quickly. 'I've left Flora on the beach. Thought she might wonder where I was.'

'She's thirteen, isn't she? Can't she handle being alone for five minutes?'

I bristled. 'She's *nearly* thirteen, and rather immature, actually. I also thought we should discuss shopping.' I sidled inside. 'If you like I could buy a load of groceries and we could halve the bill. Only it seems rather silly for us both to buy food when—'

'Whatever,' he interrupted brusquely. 'Whatever domestic arrangements you'd like to implement will be just fine. Shop till you drop and hand me a bill, only please . . .' He jerked his head eloquently towards the door.

'Well!' I shut the door soundly and stood, fuming, on the other side. Was he the rudest man? Still, I reasoned, at least we didn't see him.

'I promise you, David,' I echoed down the phone, 'we don't see him at all. He's writing some paper, totally wrapped up in it.'

'But you don't know him, Annie. He could be anyone!'

'But he's not anyone, Gertrude's met him, and he's the head of the psychotic – or whatever – department at Boston Hospital. He's a medic, just like you!'

'He's a bloody shrink, you mean,' he retorted.

'Well, yes,' I said nervously. 'Sort of.' I'd forgotten David's rather low opinion of that branch of the profession. 'But on the academic side. Research and all that. You can look him up.'

'Thanks. I will. I can't quite believe you've done this, Annie. Why didn't you go to a hotel?'

'Because all the cheap ones were booked up and . . . Oh, David, the thing is, it's so heavenly here: the house and the creek and the beach, and Flora's loving it and . . . well, we'd unpacked and everything, you see. Spent a whole night here. Thought it was ours. We'd got used to the idea of it being ours, I suppose,' I said lamely. Like a child, not wanting to give back a toy.

He sighed. I was moderately encouraged. A sigh was better than a bark.

'Oh well, what's done is done, I suppose. But – how does it work? I mean, what's happening this evening, for instance?'

'Oh, that's easy,' I said eagerly. 'He worked for most of the day, but this afternoon he went out fishing and caught loads of mackerel. He's cooking them now on a barbecue for our supper.'

'Is he. How cosy.'

'Oh no, not at all. Not cosy. I mean . . . he's not like that at all, David. He's much older than me – well, about ten years, I suppose – and sort of going grey at the sides.'

'Excellent news.'

'And quite sort of . . . thick set. Not my type at all.'

'Now there's a relief.'

'And terribly grumpy, too. I mean really really bad-tempered. Only comes out of his study to grunt and bark about something. Deeply unpleasant actually and— Oh!'

I broke off to find Matt standing behind me in the hall. I blushed hotly. He held out his hand.

'I'm on the phone!' I said, horrified. Bloody man. What was he up to? And how long had he been there?

'You're also doodling with my pen. My fountain pen. May I?'

'No I'm—' I glanced down. 'Oh.' I handed him the pen. He turned and went back to the kitchen.

'See?' I hissed down the phone to David. 'That's what he's like. All the time! Just emerges from his cave to spit at us. That's what we have to live with!'

'Right,' he said wearily. 'I don't think there's any "have to" about it, Annie, but as long as you're happy.'

'Oh I am, I am, but I'd be so much happier to see you. When are you coming, David?' I asked eagerly.

'Not for a bit, I'm afraid. I've got one or two tricky . . . Well. Things are a bit difficult at work at the moment.'

'Oh? Why?'

It suddenly occurred to me that his voice was strained. And it wasn't just to do with me sharing a house with a total stranger. I frowned.

'What is it, David?'

'Um, nothing really. But . . . remember I told you about Mr O'Connell? The jeweller? The one who drank a lot?'

'God, yes. The one who was convinced he had every medical condition under the sun. Didn't he think he was having a heart attack the last time he came to see you?'

'Yes. Well, he did,' David said shortly. 'He died.'

'What!' I gaped.

'He came to see me again this morning – still reeking of the night before – and complained of a pain in his arm. The man could hardly stand up, he

146

was so drunk. I sent him home to sober up, and he collapsed on the stairs outside as he was leaving.'

'Oh my God. You mean he died there?'

'Almost. Laura heard him cry out and shrieked for me to come. I ran downstairs and tried to resuscitate him, tried everything. We called an ambulance, but he died on the way to hospital.' His voice wavered slightly at this. I'd never heard it do that before. I sat down heavily on the hard oak pew.

'That's not your fault, David.'

'Isn't it? I'm a doctor, aren't I? He comes to see me for the second time, suspecting a heart attack, and this time with a pain in his upper arm. And I send him packing.'

'Yes, but he was drunk, and – and he's been coming to you for years like that. Plastered, imagining things . . .'

'Not really years. Months. And his wife says he drank out of fear. Says he knew he was dying.'

'His wife?'

'She rang me. An hour or so ago. She was almost incandescent with rage and emotion.'

'Well, upset, obviously—'

'Telling me I was a fraud. A quack. Saying I'd effectively killed her husband. Saying . . .' he struggled.

I was appalled. How *dare* she! David, my sweet, kind . . . I licked my lips. 'David. David, listen to me. This is ridiculous. Outrageous! God, how on earth can it be your fault? Even if you'd sent him off in an ambulance, he'd have died anyway!'

'Not necessarily. They could have resuscitated him in the ambulance and treated him in hospital.'

'Yes, but how many doctors would have done that with an outrageously pissed patient? You did what anyone else would have done, you sent him home to sober up! Relax, darling, it'll be fine. It'll all blow over.'

'That's not really the point though, is it, Annie? Yes, professionally, and in the eyes of the BMA, I'm sure it will be fine. But a man's dead. It's how I feel about it that's important.'

I swallowed, humbled. Anything I said now would be wrong.

'Anyway,' he rallied slightly, 'the point is I don't think I should just swan off on holiday at the moment. It wouldn't look right. Wouldn't *be* right.'

'Oh. Well, no, I can see that. But maybe at the weekend? Not this one, but next weekend?'

'Maybe. I'll ring you, darling. Sorry to sound so gloomy. Doesn't help that I miss you so much too.'

'Oh, and I miss you!' I said enthusiastically. '*So* much. Think of the wedding, David, the honeymoon in Mauritius. Think how happy and relaxed you'll be then!'

'Yup.' He sounded unconvinced. 'Anyway, have fun. I've got some paperwork to do now. Bye, my darling. I love you.'

'I love you too. Bye.'

I hung up. Stared dismally out of the mullioned window into the front garden, at the wind-tossed, overgrown lawn. Poor David. How awful. And how unfair. He was such a dedicated man; he worked so hard. Too hard, I often thought, putting in too many long hours. And he was always so careful. Always sought a second opinion if necessary, and sent patients straight round to Harley Street specialists if he wasn't sure. His uncle, Hugh, had impressed upon him the importance of doing that, when he took David on as a partner; when he'd worked alongside David for a few years before he died.

And I knew David missed him. Personally, obviously, but professionally too. Missed having a sounding board, a buffer; someone to nip next door and thrash out a problem with, discuss a diagnosis, say: Take a look at this rash, Hugh, or this lump, what d'you think? I'd tried to persuade him to take on a partner, to have another doctor in the practice, and not be quite so solitary, but he'd said he wasn't busy enough to warrant it, and if he couldn't work with Hugh, who'd been such a brilliant man, he'd prefer to work alone. So he did. And he was so conscientious. So meticulous. To have this sort of accusation levelled against him was outrageous!

Pensive and maudlin now, I let myself out through the front door, and wandered slowly round the side of the house to the back garden. On the terrace, Matt, who made such a colossal mess inside, was making an equally spectacular one outside. Bags of charcoal had tipped out on to the York stone, and a white wine marinade and piles of slimy fish were slopping

149

from a dish over on to a table he'd set up beside a brick barbecue. All of this was just about visible behind clouds of billowing black smoke. I sat down at the table and chairs, slightly apart from the action, and bit my thumbnail anxiously.

Surely this was the nature of what David did? People got sick. People died. It was like any job – like being a mechanic. Cars went wrong; you fixed them; they went wrong again. Sometimes terminally. It was an occupational hazard.

Matt looked up as he took a fish out of the marinade. Saw my face.

'Problems?'

I hesitated. It would be nice to share it, to talk it through with someone who knew the territory, but . . . no. No, I wouldn't tell him. God, I didn't even know him, and it would be the last thing David would want. My boyfriend the doctor, who thinks he's responsible for someone's death. David would loathe it. And I'd feel disloyal. I straightened up.

'No. No, it's nothing.' I smiled. 'Wedding plans, actually. So much to do, and so difficult to know where to start!'

'Ah.' He went back to his fish.

'You know, flowers for the church, a restaurant to organise for the lunch afterwards – not a big do of course, because I've been married before – but still, it all needs doing.'

I felt myself flushing. Why was I blurting all this out? About being married before? I reached instinctively to pour a glass of wine from the bottle on the table, then realised I hadn't bought it.

'Oh. Sorry, I—'

'No, go ahead.' He waved the barbecue tongs. 'I noticed you'd missed it off the groceries, so I bought a few bottles on the way back from fishing.'

'Thanks.' I took a large gulp. A silence ensued.

'So,' I said brightly, keen to deflect the conversation his way. 'When will your wife be joining us exactly? I mean' – God, that sounded awful – 'joining you.'

'When she can,' he said shortly. 'Head off, or on?'

I flinched. 'Sorry?'

'Your fish. You want me to take the head off?'

'Oh. Please. Yes.'

Another silence. Was it because I'd been too nosy about his wife, I wondered? Or prattling too girlishly about my wedding in an annoyingly frivolous manner? In an effort to appear serious, I adopted a creative slouch in the chair. Threw a leg over the arm.

'And of course my book is such a worry, too,' I confided. 'As I said, my publisher is desperate for it, but you know, I can only work at my own pace.' I wearily rubbed the side of my face with the palm of my hand, as if already exhausted by the demands of a literary public, greedy for the fruit of my intellect. I smiled a trifle morosely. 'And naturally, it all depends on whether or not the muse is with me.'

He nodded. 'Naturally. How many books have you had published?'

'Oh. Um, none. I mean, one. Hopefully. This is the first one.'

'And how far have you got?' He expertly turned the fish on the rack.

'Er, well. Three chapters so far. In my head. One, actually on paper.'

He smiled. 'I see. Maybe if you did a little less vacuuming the muse would come back to you?'

It was said pleasantly enough, but I bristled at the audacity.

'I'm sorry?' I said, with measured quietness.

'Well, I couldn't help noticing you spent a lot of time keeping house this morning.'

I stared. 'Yes, because this house is so dreadfully dusty. And yes, I did hoover, but only—' I broke off. Shook my head in wonderment. 'Good grief. I certainly don't have to explain my movements to you.'

'No, ma'am. You don't.' He turned the rest of the fish over. I stared at him. Licked my lips. 'And it doesn't just happen, you know,' I said testily. 'This writing lark. There's a lot of . . . thinking involved. Ruminating over plot lines, characterisation, that sort of thing.' I sniffed importantly and shifted in my seat. A regrouping gesture.

He smiled down at his fish. 'Ah.'

Ah. Now what the hell did that mean? And what was that supercilious little smile all about?

'Anyway.' I glanced at my watch, determined not to rise. 'Suppertime. I'll get the plates, shall I? Where's Flora?'

I glanced around anxiously, suddenly aware that I hadn't seen her for hours.

'She's making a salad in the kitchen. I asked her to.'

'Oh!' I got up hurriedly. 'She doesn't have to do that. I'll do it.'

'Sure, take over. I guess she's too young to make a salad.'

I'd risen from my chair and started back to the house, but now I stopped. Turned.

'Right,' I said quietly. 'I see. You're making some mighty big assumptions about me, aren't you, Mr Malone?'

Despite my irritation, I couldn't help noticing I'd slipped into American. Mighty? When had I ever said that?

'I am?'

'You're suggesting, for the second time today, that I mollycoddle my daughter.'

He shrugged. 'I'm just saying she's not a baby.'

'And you're also suggesting that when I'm not fussing over my offspring, I'm cleaning the house and making excuses for not working. Is that it?'

He smiled. 'Let's just say I know the type.'

'Type?' I bridled. 'What type?'

He paused in his cooking and looked straight at me, his blue eyes bright and slightly mocking. 'Well, you know, you've got a growing child, about to be growing out of you, out of your jurisdiction, but you're still hanging on to her. Hanging on in there.

Half of you knows you shouldn't, 'cos she needs to spread her wings, so you're desperately looking around for something else to do besides nurturing her. You hit upon writing' – he shrugged – 'but it could be anything. It could be painting, or pottery, or mosaics or any other dilettante occupation – but it's an occupation, not a job. Not actual employment. It's to fill a gap in your life.' He paused to push the fish around on the barbecue rack.

'So, OK, you give it a go,' he went on. 'This writing lark. But actually, your heart's not in it, because all you've ever done up 'til now is keep house. Either that or go shopping at the mall in your squeaky clean car' – he nodded over to my gleaming Fiat – 'in your neat preppy clothes' – he gestured at my outfit – 'or maybe play tennis with the pro. So work, in whatever guise it takes, and the application of it, comes as something of a shock. Am I right?' He grinned.

I gaped at him, horrified. Appalled. Finally, I found my voice. 'No, you are not right. You are so wrong. And – and – so *rude*, Mr Malone, and no I will not call you Matt. *So* rude, and so . . . Flora! FLORA!' I bellowed, fists clenched.

She appeared at the double at the kitchen door, clutching a bowl of salad. Nearly dropped it.

'What?' she called

I couldn't speak. She took in my furious face, hurriedly set aside the salad, and hastened across the terrace to us. 'What is it? What's happened?'

'Flora,' I said, breathing hard, 'please tell this – this

know-it-all shrink the state of our house.'

She blanched. 'Our house?'

'Yes, our house at home. Do I keep it tidy? Do I – Keep House?'

'Well . . .'

'IT'S A BLOODY TIP, ISN'T IT, FLORA!' I roared.

'Er, yes.' She blinked. 'A bit.'

'And the car?' I breathed. 'Tell him about the car before I put it through its exotic make-over on the A4.'

'Oh, yeah, the car's really dirty, usually,' she said cheerfully. She jerked her head to where it sat in the drive. 'Doesn't always look like that. It's usually gross, but Mum washed it on the way down. Oh God, it was so funny, she got out in the car wash to put the aerial down and—'

'NEVER MIND! And my clothes? Prior to yesterday?'

'Your clothes? Mum . . .' She looked confused. 'I thought the whole idea was to turn over a new leaf. Impress people, not—'

'My *clothes*, Flora!'

She shrugged. 'OK. Really tatty. Holes in the sleeves – bit like you actually.' She glanced at him. 'Old trainers, odd socks, a mess.'

'I've a good mind to show you my underwear, Mr Malone,' I seethed. 'A good mind to show you my old grey pants, right now!'

He backed away alarmed as I went for my belt. 'Hey,' he murmured, palms raised. 'No need.'

'You think you're so clever,' I spat. 'You think you can meet someone for five minutes and, because you spend your life psychoanalysing people, do a quick thumbnail sketch of the little English memsahib – just like that!' I snapped my fingers under his nose. 'But you're way off, *way* off, because actually, you've been dealing in appearances, and that's not very clever. You think I spend hours constantly tarting up myself or my house because I have no other interests, but I'll have you know I've worked hard all my adult life.'

'Hey, Annie, I didn't mean to—'

'You think that this – this occupation of mine, this "writing lark", is a little bland diversion, but it's actually the result of years of hard graft. Years of selling stories to magazines to pay the mortgage, to keep the bank manager from snapping at our heels and turfing us out, because I wasn't just supplementing my ex-husband's income, Mr Malone, I was the bloody breadwinner! This doesn't keep me amused while my daughter's at school, this is what keeps her *in* school. This is what puts the food in our fridge and the shoes on our feet! I've kept our heads above water for twelve years with this "dilettante" occupation, and all by writing about a life I didn't have. A romantic life, full of hearts and flowers and happy endings, a life that didn't exist for me.' I was horrified to find my voice breaking.

'Mum!' Flora stepped forward in alarm.

'Hey, look, I—'

'And sometimes,' I went on tremulously, 'it would have been a pleasure to have had the smart lunch-and-shopping existence you describe, Mr Malone, but it was never an option. But now it is.' I raised my chin. Took a deep breath. 'Now, I have a lovely, respectable doctor boyfriend who wants to indulge me and make my life a bit more comfortable, and d'you know what? I'm going to let him. I'm going to wear nice clothes for him and spruce myself up, and I'm going to let him take me to Provence in the summer and skiing in the winter, because I've worked hard and I deserve it! Oh, you've got it so wrong,' I said, shaking with resentment now. 'I haven't had the sybaritic life of leisure you describe and am now looking for a little hobby, I've had a bloody tough time and now I'm looking to put my feet up! So the next time you think you – Know The Type, and want to get pat and analytical with someone you've known all of five minutes – PICK ON SOMEONE ELSE!'

And with that, I inexplicably burst into tears and raced back into the house.

chapter nine

The following morning, he knocked on my door. Happily I was up and dressed. I opened it an inch. He cleared his throat.

'I, um, came to apologise. Clearly I upset you last night, and I'm sorry.'

He regarded me steadily. Clear blue eyes in a tough, lined face. I nodded. Twelve hours later, I felt faintly stupid.

'It's fine,' I muttered. 'Forget it. I probably over-reacted.'

He shrugged. 'Maybe, maybe not. Leastways, I had no idea I'd hit such a sore spot. In fact' – he scratched the back of his head – 'I don't remember hitting a few of those spots at all. All that stuff about letting your boyfriend take you skiing, Jesus. I don't even recall *men*tioning him.'

I took a deep breath. 'No. No, you're absolutely right. I brought him up. It's just . . . well, he seemed part of what you were accusing me of, somehow. Funding my leisurely lifestyle. Something like that.'

He shook his head. 'Hey. I've never met the guy, and like you said last night, I've only known you five minutes. It was crass of me to overgeneralise, and also to knock your writing like that. I'm sorry.'

I recognise a genuine apology when I hear it. I glanced down at my feet. Nodded curtly.

'Forget it.'

There was an awkward silence. He made as if to go, then turned back. 'There's, uh, some bacon on the stove, if you like. Only you didn't get to eat last night. Have some.'

'Thanks. I'll do that.'

He withdrew and, a few moments later, I heard the study door shut downstairs behind him.

It was true, I hadn't come down for supper last night, because once I'd bolted to my bedroom and punched a few walls, it was slightly difficult to save face and extract myself. I'd foolishly backed myself into a corner, and could either skulk down looking dark and mutinous, or swan back breezily as if nothing had happened and compliment him on his marinade. Since I could see that the former was counter-productive but didn't have the grace to do the latter, I chose another option, which, I told myself as I eyeballed my wet pillow, was equally necessary. To stay in my room and work out exactly why I was so angry.

Clearly, Mr Malone had unwittingly voiced something that had got me spitting; something that perhaps I'd been aware of but had subconsciously tucked away in a drawer. Now though, there it was, out in the open, and there I was, too, up in arms. Flailing them actually; protesting, justifying, but why? Surely my shiny new lifestyle was only what I deserved after all those lean years with Adam? My cushy ménage with my doctor husband in my soon-to-be purchased Hurlingham pad only what was due to me after all those years of struggle? But did I secretly feel uncomfortable about it? Question any motives? And had a stranger I'd known for precisely two days inadvertently lit the blue touch paper, failed to stand well back, and taken a bit of heat?

I'd flipped miserably over on to my back on the bed and concentrated hard on the ceiling. And did I miss my work, I wondered? My proper work? My articles, my stories, meeting deadlines, dealing with magazine editors. Was I just playing at being a novelist? Was a crack appearing in my life like the one I was staring at now that ran the entire length of the ceiling? No, not a bit of it, I'd decided firmly, averting my eyes to the window and the sylvan scene surrounding the little grey church on the opposite side of the creek. And I'd show him. Show him in the morning. Show him what hard work and application was all about. Show him how it was done. Full of resolve, but also exhausted by my tears and tantrum, I slipped under the covers and promptly fell asleep.

Now, this morning, as I emerged from the bath-room, I bumped into Flora coming out of her new bedroom, having shifted down a floor to accommodate Matt.

'Oh, hi, Mum.' She tottered sleepily in the long khaki T-shirt she always slept in. 'We were worried about you last night. I didn't like to come up, though, 'cos you were so stressed. Are you OK, or have you still got a bastard on?'

'Don't use that expression, darling, you sound like your father. No, I'm fine. Sorry, Flora. Something . . . set me off.'

'Phew, just a bit. Scary. You didn't have any supper either. We couldn't believe you didn't come down. Aren't you starving?'

'I am, and I'm going to have some of that yummy sausage and bacon I can smell down there. What are you going to do today, sweetheart?' I linked arms with her chummily as we went downstairs, wanting to dispel all memories of the mad, unhinged mother, spilling out her life story in front of total strangers and generally making a spectacle of herself.

'Well, isn't it today that the others are coming? I'm going to cycle round to Rock and see them.'

'D'you know, I think you're right,' I said slowly. 'It is today, isn't it? You do that, darling. I'm going to be working in the summer house.'

'OK.'

We went arm in arm to the kitchen, where she plucked a couple of pieces of bacon from the pan with her fingertips and sandwiched them together with two slices of Mother's Pride. She took a huge

161

bite. 'First though,' she mumbled through her mouthful, 'I'm going back to bed with this and *Northanger Abbey*. See you.'

As she shuffled past me, book in one hand, sandwich in the other, dripping crumbs everywhere, I opened my mouth to say, Take a plate, then shut it again. God, there'd be crumbs in that bed however she ate it and she had to sleep in it. When had I started to worry about things like that? And the fact – I gazed despairingly about – that yet again, this kitchen was awaiting a good fairy to deal with all the greasy pots and pans? On an impulse I piled them high in the sink and turned the taps on hard. Right. Well I wasn't going to pussy-foot around cleaning up like I had yesterday, I'd foster a little war of attrition. Leave this lot to soak and see what happened. Get off down to the summer house.

Armed with a cup of coffee, a bacon sandwich and my laptop, I set off purposefully – and a trifle ostentatiously – across the garden, past Matt's study window and down to the little hut that Flora and I had discovered yesterday.

I pushed open the creaky green door. Inside, it smelled of musty deckchairs and wooden framed tennis rackets and old summer holidays. The past. There were three Lloyd Loom chairs with faded, chintzy cushions, and in the window, a small, rather rickety bamboo table. I pulled up a chair and sat down delightedly. Through a gap in the trees, the sea could just be glimpsed, and it struck me, as I arranged my laptop and switched on, that someone had deliberately cleared that gap in order to see the view better. In order to sit perhaps, like me, and paint, or write, or even just think. Perfect, I beamed. A perfect place for the creative juices to flow.

I turned on my screen and read my first chapter. My only chapter. In which Lucinda De Villiers, my elegant, highly strung heroine, had just discovered – courtesy of a hotel bill found in husband Henry's suit pocket – that whilst Henry was closing a multimillion-pound deal for Chase Manhattan in New York last week, he might also have treated his attractive female assistant, Tanya Fox, to more than just a celebratory plate of sushi at the Waldorf Hotel. Pacing her Holland Park mansion now, waiting for him to come home from work, Lucinda was unsure how to handle the situation.

I tapped my fingers on the bamboo table and gazed out at the view. I was unsure how I was going to handle it, either. I mean, sure, on the one hand, the man was a complete bastard. His behaviour was treacherous, the situation untenable and therefore she should turf him out *tout de suite*. But on the other, there were her three gorgeous children asleep upstairs. There was this huge London house, another one in Tuscany, a Caribbean holiday booked with the Frowbishers next month, their vast network of friends and ... OK. I raised my hands. Tapped.

Lucinda paused for a moment by the Adam fireplace in her eau-de-Nil drawing room. She glanced up and regarded her reflection in the antique overmantel mirror. Her face was pale, and her grey eyes huge with fear in her heart-shaped face. She glanced down at her Cartier watch again. Ten-fifteen. Where was he? With her, Tanya? In a hotel bedroom in the West End, somewhere? Suddenly, she heard a key in the door.

I broke off exhausted and pushed back my chair. Phew. Golly. Eight lines. This creative malarkey was jolly hard work. Perhaps I needed a coffee. Or some chocolate. I scraped back my chair and got up. I was uncomfortably aware, too, that I wasn't quite sticking to the brief as outlined by my new editor, Sebastian Cooper. After his fulsome letter of praise and acceptance some time ago, I'd rung to introduce myself properly, and he'd been equally complimentary on the phone. Couldn't have been nicer, actually. He'd praised my style, my dialogue, my – something else – but he'd also volunteered a hope that we might see the story from Henry's point of view. Maybe even see him in action with Tanya.

'You mean . . . you want sex?'

'Sorry?' he'd said startled.

'No no,' I'd said hurriedly. 'In the book.'

'Oh. Oh, in the book! Yeah, definitely,' he'd agreed. 'Lots of it, yeah. Sells really well, you know, that sort of thing. Why don't you, like, chuck it in all the way through? A bit in each chapter?'

'Er, well . . .' I'd faltered. 'I'll . . . do my best.'

'Great. T'rific. Just let it – you know – flow. Go with the flow.'

He'd sounded awfully young, I'd thought in surprise as I'd put down the phone. I'd had an idea a senior editor would be about forty, but perhaps not, these days.

It was important to keep him happy though, I decided as I took my mug and went out of the summer house. Perhaps we ought to see him in his boxer shorts? Henry, I mean. Maybe he could have a bit of a raunchy tussle in chapter three, wrestle with Tanya on the dealing-room floor after lights out or something? But I wasn't convinced I could keep it up for twenty chapters. Wasn't convinced Henry could, either, so to speak.

In the kitchen, Matt was pouring boiling water into his own mug.

I smiled, cheerily. 'Phew. See you've taken a break too! Hard work, isn't it?'

He looked at me blankly, grunted something noncommittal, and made to move past me back to his study, when the phone rang.

'I'll get that. It might be David.'

'It'll be for me,' he said curtly, heading me off at the pass and disappearing into his room to pick it up.

The door slammed behind him. Well. Not necessarily, I thought, irritated. Rude man. I mean, I lived here too, it could just as easily be for me, couldn't it? And he had a habit of doing that, didn't he? I ostentatiously slammed all the cupboard doors he'd slovenly left open. Being perfectly pleasant one minute, and then ruining it by being perfectly foul the next.

As I stirred my coffee, I heard his voice rising angrily behind the door. Unable to resist, I tiptoed across.

'Listen, I'm not gonna put up with it, OK? I've told Madeleine before,' he snapped, and then his voice dropped again. Golly. I inched away. Glad I wasn't on the receiving end of *that*. Some minion, no doubt, back in his Boston hospital getting it in the neck. Not doing things the way the Führer liked them done.

I cradled my coffee and sauntered out of the back door, down the stone steps, and into the sunshine streaming across the daisy-strewn lawn. God, it was a beautiful day. Not a cloud in the sky. Such a waste to be shut up in the summer house like that. Maybe I'd just sit out here for a bit, take a break in the clover, and recharge the old batteries. Give Lucinda some thought. I went to the far edge of the lawn where it met the long grass, lay back with my hands locked behind my head, and contemplated my heroine. The sun was in my eyes though, so I put my head right back, and shut them. Fatal, really. The next thing I knew I was waking up to sounds of shouting and whooping coming from people messing around on a boat, below in the creek. I sat up with a start. Felt hot and sweaty. My face felt burnt, too. I touched it tentatively. God, how awful. Had I really fallen asleep? Mid-morning? I looked at my watch. Damn, I had. Been asleep for about twenty minutes.

I swung around to make sure no one had seen, and realised I'd chosen to kip, albeit at a distance, but pretty much in a beeline from Matt's study. Behind the bay window his head was bent studiously to his task, but he'd have to raise it occasionally to breathe, wouldn't he – if indeed he did breathe. He'd have been unable to miss me, spread-eagled on the grass, legs splayed, mouth open, snoring loudly.

I got up quickly and brushed myself down. Damn. *Damn.* And damn the fact that I couldn't just do that. Couldn't have a kip on my holiday on my own sunny back lawn if I felt like it. Irritated now beyond belief, I stalked back to the summer house, where Lucinda De Villiers was still flicking back her long blonde hair and blinking nervously in the mirror.

Oh, don't be so wet, Lucinda, I seethed, viciously snapping on my laptop. Chuck Henry out and get your own back, for heaven's sake. Go have some rumpy-pumpy with one of the zillions of blue-collar workers you must have crawling around your mansion, watering your begonias and changing your lightbulbs. Go unzip your Armani jeans, girl, and get on with it!

I settled down to empower Lucinda and incapacitate Henry, forming a vicious plot to give Tanya a nasty bout of piles – or even crabs – in chapter two. But just as I was getting into my stride, I realised that those raised voices I'd heard down on the creek not a few moments ago were awfully familiar. They were getting closer now too, and louder, and through the gap in the trees, I could just see the top of Flora's head as she came up the steep slope through the woods, pushing her bike. I stood up and craned my neck. Down below at the water's edge, I could also see Michael, trousers rolled up to his knees, steadying a boat on the shore in which Rosie and Clare wobbled precariously, shrieking with laughter, as they tried to climb out.

God, already? It hadn't taken Clare long to offer to bring Flora back in the boat and take a quick shufti at our house, had it, I thought drily. I switched off my machine and went out to meet them. They'd left Michael in charge of the boat, and the pair of them came puffing up the hill towards me through the woods, Flora arriving just ahead of them.

'Mum, look who I found!'

I forced a grin. 'So I see.'

She disappeared towards the house as I went across to kiss my sister, then Rosie, who was panting hard. She stopped, clutching her knees.

'God, what a hill!'

'Steep, isn't it? Sorts the men from the boys, we find.' I shot Clare a look. 'Lesser pilgrims never even make it to our little abode; they fall at the first hurdle, at the first hint of an incline, but then they lack your determination. Come to spy on me already?'

'There's no already about it,' snorted Clare, gasping.

'We got here yesterday morning, actually, came a day early because the weather was so glorious, and left it a whole day before coming to see you. Is that OK?'

'Absolutely fine,' I soothed with a placatory smile. 'Where are the others?'

'We left Dan in charge of the children. There wasn't room in the boat with Flora's bike.' Clare was still holding her sides, panting. 'Blimey, is this it?' She squinted up into the sun at the house. 'Shit, it's all right, isn't it?'

Clare, who rarely swore, having far too much self-control, was evidently impressed.

'Pretty,' agreed Rosie, shading her eyes with both hands. 'And so out of the way, too. The rest of the north coast is heaving, let me tell you, but you wouldn't know it here. God, it's no good, I've got to sit down.' She flopped dramatically on her back in the long grass.

'I know, and so few people come down to this creek,' I enthused, kneeling down beside her. 'I don't think they even know it's here. It's incredibly private.' I was keen to show off.

'Well' – Clare made a face – 'except that it's not now, is it? Flora says you've got some man living here with you. Honestly, Annie, you are extraordinary, I can't quite believe it!' Her eyes were incredulous.

Ah. So she'd told them. 'Yes, well, that's all fine too, actually,' I said quickly. 'It was a misunderstanding. All Gertrude's fault, but not a problem in the least. He just keeps himself to himself.'

'Yes, but he's living here!' insisted Clare. 'With you and Flora! I mean, does David know?'

'Yes, he does, and shush, would you?' I glanced nervously back to the house. 'He'll hear you. He's working in the study. And he's married.'

'So where are you working then?'

'In the summer house.'

'That grotty old thing? That's a bit rough, isn't it?' Did I detect a hint of glee in her voice?

'No, it's fine.'

'So what's he like, then?' asked Rosie, sitting up to cup her hands around a match and light a cigarette.

I hesitated. 'Nice,' I said, finally. 'I mean . . . fine.'

'Really?' She glanced across, catching my tone.

'You'll meet him later,' I said quickly. 'Anyway, how are you lot all getting on? How's life down at Penmayne Terrace? Children thrilled to be here?'

'Delighted,' said Rosie, resting her head back in the dandelions again and taking a deep drag of her cigarette. She exhaled slowly. 'We've been down on the beach from the moment we got here, and we haven't been off since, have we, Clare? Splendid. We are having,' she enunciated carefully, 'the time of our lives.' There was an edge to her voice which didn't escape me. I had to look away quickly before I laughed.

'And so this is, what – how many bedrooms?' Clare was still on her feet, arms folded and surveying the house pseudo-casually, head on one side, like a prospective buyer.

'Four. No, five, I think. Have a wander, if you like.'

'I might just do that,' she mused. 'Yes, I could do with a pee. Back in a mo.' She sauntered nonchalantly up the lawn, but there was nothing nonchalant about her eyes. She was looking around greedily, taking it all in: the sweeping but unkempt acres, the old fish pond encrusted with moss and lichen, the tennis net, the large crumbling terrace with barbecue; clearly impressed, but not wanting to show it. Not wanting to race up the garden shouting, 'Oh, you lucky thing, Annie, it's fantastic! Quick, show me around – it's divine!' As I'd have done.

'She is driving me mad,' muttered Rosie in measured tones, head back in the grass, eyes shut.

'I gathered,' I muttered back. 'But, Rosie, come on. You've only been here a day. Give it a chance.'

'She won't let me smoke,' she exclaimed, sitting up abruptly. 'I mean, even on the terrace! "Couldn't you do that down on the beach, Rosie," she says in that imperious voice of hers, *and* she told me off for drinking too much last night. "This isn't the Munich beer festival, dear," she said lightly, but believe me, that "dear" went through me like a poisoned arrow.'

'Well, she doesn't drink, you see.'

'Clearly. And then this morning she woke us all up at eight o'clock – *eight o'clock!* – to send Dan off to get the papers, and me to the bakery. "Come on, Rosie," she said, shaking me – *shaking me* – as I dozed. "Got to get in that bread queue, or it'll all be gone." For a moment I thought I was in Poland, with a coup on or something. Thought I'd be shuffling out with a black shawl wrapped round my head. Anyway, ten minutes later – no cup of tea, mind, no breakfast, haven't even washed my bloody face – there I was, standing in this queue of women who, spookily, *all look just like Clare*! It was like something out of *The Stepford Wives*. I promise you, there they all were in their immaculate sailing shorts and sporty little polo tops – the sort of gear one imagines comes straight out of a drawer marked "Cornish Holiday". Not dissimilar to yours, actually.' She eyed me with dismay.

'It's a long story,' I muttered, hurriedly untucking my shirt.

'And they've all got these pristine deck shoes on and recently waxed white legs which are looking a bit embarrassed to be out on display, and there am I in Dan's old shirt and ripped jeans with sleep in my eyes and a bloody shopping list in my hand!'

'Ah yes, the bread queue.' I nodded solemnly. 'That's all part of the ritual, I'm afraid. Part of the initiation ceremony.'

'And then it was back to the kitchen to join a production line of bap-buttering whilst Clare filled them with one hand, washed fruit with the other, and simultaneously, it seemed, poured coffee into a Thermos with her toes, whilst the men sat in the sunshine with the papers and did bugger all!'

'Hm. She has rather got that fifties mentality. Very like my mother. Very much the bap-maker.'

'And then off we all trooped to the beach – at

nine-thirty, mind, sharp, to bag the best spot – where, apparently, the intention was to stay all day, with no alcohol whatsoever, and no prospect of nipping to the pub at lunchtime. Just a sandy ham roll, a force-eight gale, and a hard rock to sit on, followed by a game of rounders with the children, French cricket, more rounders, more French cricket, rounders, cricket, rounders – *all bloody day*! Dan and I were pretty frightened and confused, I can tell you. At one point I abandoned first base and made a break for it. I toddled down to the freezing cold water feeling like John Stonehouse, where I was accosted by an ex-colleague of Dan's, whom I last saw in a pin-stripe suit at the Fulham ABC, and was so frightened by his huge naked paunch hanging over his jokey Boden swimwear I hurried back up the beach again. It was only when Flora arrived and we had the bright idea of coming up to see you that the nightmare ended. Please tell me it's not going to go on like this?' she begged. 'Not day after day? I'm coming out in a rash.'

I giggled. 'But this is a Cornish holiday, Rosie. Surely you know the rules? *We* did it as children, and have glorious, rose-tinted memories, and now we have to ensure that *our* little darlings have them too. Bugger the fact that the world has moved on and it's not just the rich and pampered who are renting villas in Portugal, but Tracy and Wayne too. Oh no, the show must go on. And of course the children really *do* love it, so much so that Clare can smugly say: Oh, they'd much rather go to Cornwall than to Italy.'

'Well, I think she's mad,' Rosie said shortly. 'I bloody wouldn't, and neither would Dan. What – she'd rather butter bread rolls and sit on a windy beach than sip an aperitif in a sunny piazza, stroll to the harbour arm in arm with Michael, and then back to the villa for a *siesta complet*?'

'Oh, I think the *complet* bit would be right out of the question,' I said drily. 'Clare's off games. At least as far as Michael's concerned.'

'So we noticed. He's grovelling around for some attention like a dog hoping to be tossed a bone, and all she's throwing him is a cold pasty. And meanwhile, she's been very ostentatiously putting lipstick on on the beach, in case a certain Todd family appear.'

'Ah yes. The Todds.'

'Which as yet, they hadn't, but good old Clare looks up expectantly from the sandy rug that we call home every time another familiar family droops past, weighed down with windbreaks and chairs and dogs and buggies and kites and God knows what else, poor bastards, all greeting us like long-lost buddies – which of course they are, incidentally, since the whole of south-west London is here. And then finally the Todds *did* drip past with Mr – who I assume is the object of Clare's desire – so engrossed in chat with the French au pair that he didn't even see her. There she was, Clare, lying back, elbows in the sand, bosoms pointing skywards like heat-seeking missiles, lips glossed – and he walked straight past! She nearly spat her ham roll in the sand, she was so livid. What's that all about, then?'

'Oh. Yes.' I shifted uncomfortably. 'Well, Clare had a bit of a flirt with Theo Todd last year. Nothing serious, but she's trying to get at Michael, you see.'

'Ah. After his fumble with the fund manager at the Christmas party.'

'Who told you that!'

'You did.'

'Did I?' I was horrified. 'God, I'm so indiscreet. And the thing is, Rosie, I just don't think she's terribly happy. All this jolly holiday lark – what she really needs is two weeks on a tropical island with no children and just Michael, to remember who she is and who she's married to. But she has to do this frantic earth mother bit every year, because she works so hard in the City and feels guilty about it. She's a bag of nerves, actually. It's all a big cover-up. And Michael's terrified of her, of course.'

'Aren't we all,' she muttered. 'God, I'm petrified. I tell you, I'm going to set my alarm for seven-thirty tomorrow, and I'm going to be in that queue with my white legs on parade and my handbag swinging and— Oops, look out, here she comes. Look busy.' She hurriedly stubbed her cigarette out. 'Just tell me quickly though, what's he really like, this lodger chappie?'

'Frightful,' I muttered back. 'Really bolshy and chippy and opinionated, and frankly downright rude. He makes a terrible mess, too.'

'Well, so do you, don't you?'

'That's not the point. The only good thing is that he doesn't actually appear very often.'

'Ah.' She smiled. 'So you're selling your soul for the sake of a luxury holiday?'

I raised my eyebrows back. 'And you're not?'

Clare, looking much more buoyant than usual, and slightly less tight around the eyes and mouth, was striding confidently back down the lawn towards us.

'Lovely house,' she conceded as she approached. 'Charming.'

'Thanks.' I smiled. If she could flatter, I mustn't crow too much. 'It is, isn't it?'

'And he's sweet.'

I sat up. 'Sorry?'

'Matt. In the study.' She sat down beside us, curling her legs efficiently under her.

'Oh Clare, you didn't go in, did you?'

'Certainly I did.'

'But he's working!'

'Yes, on some paper or other. Golly, Annie, do grow up. You haven't got the American president locked up in there, ironing out the Middle East peace treaty or something. Anyway, I wanted to find out more about him. Can't have my little sister living with just anyone, can I?'

'So what did you say?' I breathed. 'You . . . knocked first?'

'Yes,' she said wearily, 'I knocked first, *and* stuck out my hand politely and said: "Hi, I'm Clare

Faraday, Annie's sister." So he stood up and introduced himself and was perfectly pleasant. And you're right, he is married, but separated. His wife is living here in England, in Cambridge, with their son.'

'Oh!' My jaw went slack. 'But . . . hang on, he said his wife was coming. He said—'

'Well, perhaps she is, perhaps she's delivering the son or something, perhaps she'll stay the night. Golly, I don't know, Annie, I don't know how friendly they are, didn't get that far. I'm not that nosy.' She smartly swatted a fly on her leg. 'Gotcha. Anyway, I asked him to come to our barbecue tomorrow night, and he said he couldn't. Got too much to do, apparently.'

'Blimey, Clare!' I snorted. 'You might have asked me first!'

She blinked. 'Well I rather assume *you're* coming.'

'No! I mean, if you could ask him!'

'Why?'

'Well . . . I don't know,' I blustered. 'I just . . . anyway, he's not coming. That's a relief.'

'Why? I thought you liked him?'

'I do, I just – well I don't want to get too matey, Clare. We're lodgers, for crying out loud!'

'Lodgers?' Clare raised her eyebrows. 'Right. I'll remember that. Remind him of his place, next time I meet him.'

'Oh, for God's sake! Anyway, who's coming to this barbecue you've organised within two minutes of getting here?'

'The world,' murmured Rosie *sotto voce*, blowing dreamily at a dandelion clock.

'Well, all the friends we met on the beach today, obviously. The Elliotts, the Fields, the Todds—'

'Ah, the Todds.' I couldn't resist it. She ignored me and swept on.

'The Frasers, hopefully, you and David—'

'Oh no, David can't come down this weekend.'

'Oh? Why not?'

'He's working.' I said shortly. Later, I'd tell Rosie. Definitely. But not Clare. No, not Clare. Oh, she'd be terribly supportive, say how ghastly it all was and that of *course* it wasn't poor David's fault, but secretly, might she not feel a little frisson of delight that all was not going so well? Or was that just me being a cow?

I gave myself a little inward shake, confused. 'Um, no, he's too busy. But he'll be down the weekend after, for sure, and that suits both of us, actually. I've got so much to do.'

'Ah yes, the famous book,' she drawled. 'How's it coming along?'

'Lucinda got her rocks off yet?' asked Rosie sleepily from the grass.

'Lucinda? Who's Lucinda?' demanded Clare, irritated that Rosie knew more than she did.

Rosie turned her head in the grass. 'The manicured wife of Henry the investment banker, who's been caught in flagrante with some tart from the office. Isn't that it, Annie?'

'Investment banker? Tart from the...' Clare stared. 'Right,' she said softly. She licked her lips. 'So it's about me, is it?'

I stared back, horrified. 'No, of course not!'

'Really? But he's a City boy, is he?'

'Well, yes, but—'

'And she goes to work in Armani suits, I take it?'

'Well, she *wears* Armani, but no, for God's sake, of *course* it's not about you!' I was appalled.

'Three or four children? Large house in London?'

'Yes, but—'

'Shops in Harvey Nichols?'

'Well—'

'Great,' she fumed. 'Really, really great, Annie. Terrific. Positively sisterly of you. Loyal.' She stood up. She was trembling, she was so angry. 'And this is the one they're so enamoured with at the publishing house, is it? This is the one they're awaiting with bated breath, holding the Booker prize for, jacking up film deals?'

'Clare...'

'Well, good on you, Annie. Well done. Nice to know at least someone's going to benefit from this family's misfortunes!'

And with that she turned on her heel and strode back down the hill to the boat.

chapter ten

'Bloody hell,' muttered Rosie.

'Bloody, *bloody* hell,' I agreed.

We watched in shocked silence as Clare crashed through the wood, brushing branches roughly aside, pulling innocent saplings up with her teeth no doubt, muttering angrily as she lost a shoe. 'Sod it. Sod it!'

'But you didn't, did you, Annie?' Rosie swung round to me bewildered when she was out of earshot. 'I mean—'

'No, of course I flaming well didn't!' I said hotly. 'Not deliberately, anyway. Would I do that?'

'No, but . . . subconsciously?'

'Who knows?' I ran my hands despairingly through my hair. 'Who knows what goes on up there amongst the grey matter and the dust and the pigeons?' I put my hands over my eyes. 'Ooh God, I'm *sure* I didn't, though,' I moaned as, just at that moment, Michael appeared at the top of the hill through a gap in the trees. He looked shocked and flummoxed.

'Well, bugger me.'

'Michael!'

'I've just met Clare flouncing down that hill,' he said, wide-eyed, 'and all I said was I was just popping up to say hello to you, Annie, and then perhaps we'd better think about getting back to the children, and she told me to fuck off!'

'Ah, yes. She would have done.' I nodded solemnly. 'Sorry about that, Michael. My fault, I fear. How are you, anyway?' I got up to kiss my poor beleaguered brother-in-law.

'Thoroughly pissed off and insulted, since you ask.' He rubbed the back of his head bleakly, where it was thinning slightly. 'What's that all about then?' He turned again to stare down the hill at his departing wife's back. I told him.

'Shit, Annie.' He looked appalled. 'You can't write about us!'

'I'm not!' I wailed. 'At least, not intentionally, it's just the way Clare's taken it. But, Michael, what am I going to do? I can't change it now, they love it at the publishers, they're clamouring for more!'

'Easy,' said Rosie suddenly. 'You just change the characters a bit. Instead of Lucinda being a successful businesswoman in a Holland Park mansion, she's a – I don't know – a Colour Me Beautiful rep. In Leighton Buzzard. Chigwell, even.'

I blinked. 'Colour me what?'

'Beautiful. You know, they pick out the colour that suits you, tell you what to wear; that sort of thing.

Waft different coloured scarves in front of your face, then boss you into lilac because of your insipid complexion. Just the sort of thing Clare would have done, actually, had she not been a banker. And the husband,' she went on, warming to her theme, 'doesn't have to be a City chappie like Michael, does he? He could be . . . I don't know . . .'

'A Burger King chappie?' Michael put in caustically. 'With a Big Whopper?'

'Yes!' she agreed. 'Why not?'

'As long as he's the manager,' Michael murmured, narrowing his eyes thoughtfully at the horizon. He squared his shoulders. 'I'm not having him doling out the cheeseburgers.'

'It's not you, Michael, remember?' I snapped.

'Oh, er, no. Quite right.' He looked momentarily disappointed. 'Shop floor then.' He nodded.

'You think that has the same cachet?' I asked, biting my thumbnail nervously as I sat down beside Rosie. 'I mean, d'you think my editor will go for that?'

'Well, it's not cachet you're after, is it?' Rosie insisted. 'It's raw human emotion. Pulsating passion played out in sensual suburbia with real people doing real jobs – catching buses, picking their toenails, that type of thing. Oh no, this is much more gritty and realistic, Annie. Much better than sex among the smart set. And the guy that the betrayed wife gets the hots for,' she went on, eagerly, ''cos presumably you need that little revenge motif before it all ends happily, he needn't be a theatrical type like Theo Whassisname.' She caught my horrified eye and hastened on: 'He could be – I don't know – different. From Kosovo, or something. A refugee!'

'Who's wondering if he's wearing too much lilac?' I ventured, drily. 'Is that how they meet?'

'What?' Michael was looking totally bewildered now. 'Hang on, why has this Lucinda woman got the hots for anyone in the first place? And what's Theo Todd got to do with it?' he asked suspiciously.

'Absolutely nothing,' I said quickly, glaring at Rosie. 'It's just Rosie getting carried away.'

'I mean,' he struggled, 'surely Lucinda's husband has apologised, hasn't he? For whatever he's – you know – done? So surely it's all over and done with?' He sat down beside us and lit a cigarette, nervously. 'Surely that particular raw nerve was smoothed over months ago, and now she's forgotten it and forgiven him, hm? Particularly since the poor chap was as pissed as a fart when it happened and can't remember a bloody thing about it,' he added miserably.

'Absolutely,' I soothed. 'You're quite right.'

Rosie laid a hand on his arm. 'You smoke,' she said in awe, her eyes huge.

'Only in secret,' he admitted. He turned equally huge eyes on her. 'Don't tell her,' he said quickly.

'I won't,' she promised. She gazed at him in silent respect and they exchanged a conspiratorial look like a couple of Resistance fighters hiding an airman in the attic.

183

'Anyway, this won't do,' Michael said abruptly, taking another quick drag. 'She'll be alone down there, pacing the beach, wishing she had the children to take it out on and panting to be taken back. There'll be steam coming out of every orifice. Come on, Rosie, let's go.' He stubbed the cigarette out quickly on the grass. 'We've still got the shopping for the barbecue to do yet, remember,' he warned. 'We were told to do that this afternoon.'

'Oh God, so we were,' said Rosie nervously, getting quickly to her feet. I'd never seen her move so fast. 'But will I see you before then?' She gave me a pleading look.

'I'll try,' I promised. 'But obviously now that I've got to rewrite my entire novel, time is not exactly on my side.'

'Sorry,' she muttered and, looking severely chastened, tottered after Michael in her inappropriate wedged shoes. She followed him down the hill through the trees.

'But make sure you come to the barbecue!' she yelled back at me. 'I'm not bloody doing *that* without you!'

I watched them go. After a while, I heard subdued voices coming from the creek, and the sound of a motor starting. Hopefully Clare had calmed down a bit and wasn't actually killing anyone yet. Probably waiting until they were out at sea and she could tip Michael smartly over the side, dusting her hands off efficiently afterwards.

I wandered back to the summer house, shut the blistered green door behind me, sat down at my little bamboo table, and stared at the screen. Could Lucinda become Lorraine, I wondered? Not pacing her Persian carpets, but nervously touching up her roots in Chigwell? And could Henry really look dashing in a polyester shirt complete with Burger King logo and a jaunty little red and white paper hat? And would Tanya still want hot sex with him if he reeked of Tom Ketch? I wasn't convinced.

On the bright side though, I thought, chewing a pencil, at least the blue-collar worker Lucinda was poised to have a ding-dong with – who naturally couldn't be an asylum seeker or whatever ludicrous idea Rosie had come up with – could now become a sizzling ski-tanned executive with pads in Mayfair and Miami. But then there wouldn't really be a critical plot dilemma, would there? Surely Lucinda would just stick two fingers up to Henry and his quarter-pounder, and swan joyously into the sunset with her square-jawed smoothy. And where would that leave the dénouement? Or the kids for that matter? (For Lucinda's offspring would now surely be kids, not children.) Wherein lay the feel-good factor, as Lucinda packed her Braun hair-styler and ran down the path to her boyfriend's Ferrari, leaving Henry, tearing his paper hat to pieces, with three bairns to feed – bairns now, mind – and all on a minimum wage from a fast-food outlet?

No, I decided firmly. Clare could think what she

bloody well liked. I was keeping my Holland Park ménage – who, to my mind, had never remotely resembled my rather boring sister and brother-in-law – and she could lump it. This was my story, and I was sticking to it.

I tapped away furiously – and eloquently, actually, now I'd got up a head of steam – with purple passages flowing. I'd just got to the bit where Henry, having finally fallen out of a taxi outside his house at two in the morning, is mounting the stairs looking pissed and post-coital, while Lucinda awaits him in the marital bedroom looking wide-eyed and vulnerable between the toile de Jouy sheets, quivering in her Rigby & Peller nightie, when someone rapped loudly on the door.

'What!' I barked, swinging round in annoyance in my chair.

'Sorry, Mummy.' Flora turned to go.

'Oh! No, darling. Sorry. I was miles away. What is it?' God. *Constant* interruption. How on earth had Jane Austen managed it, I wondered? Had sister Cassandra barged repeatedly into her sanctum? Twirling her parasol and imploring her to take a turn in the garden?

'I was just wondering if you wanted to come for a swim. The tide's right up now, Mum, and it's amazing out there. Really deep, like our very own swimming pool, and you can swim straight out from the bank!'

I took a deep breath. Squared my shoulders and

forced a smile. 'Lead on, MacDuff. Nothing I'd rather do.' I glanced longingly at my screen as I turned it off. 'I'll just nip up to the house and get my things, and then I'll see you down there.'

'Got them!' She smiled smugly, holding a towel and swimsuit aloft – albeit an ancient one I'd brought as a spare. 'And we can change in here, can't we?' She hopped inside, glanced around, and in seconds was peeling off her leggings.

We could, and we did, and then, taking our clothes with us, picked our way gingerly in bare feet down the granite steps and the twisting sandy path, to the water's edge. As we emerged through the trees, I was startled by the transformation. As Flora had said, the sand and mud flats had completely disappeared and the creek had become a winding river. Deep and limpid and overhung by rustling trees which crowded darkly to the water's edge, it snaked invitingly before us, glinting in the sunlight.

'Oh!' I breathed. 'Isn't this beautiful?'

But Flora had already raced ahead of me, running a little way along the bank to a rock. Moments later, she'd climbed up and dived off into the water. I, meanwhile, shrieking my way in gingerly from the bank, held my arms up high as the water crept up my swimsuit.

'It's freezing!' I gasped, turning blue with cold.

'Not once you're in. Come on!' She did a splashy crawl across to me, grabbed both my hands and pulled. I shrieked again as we both went under, but she was right, and after the initial shock, we were both swimming delightedly in beautifully clear water.

I lay on my back and floated dreamily out to the middle of the creek, savouring all its drowsy, mid-summer beauty, my face turned, salamander-style, to the sun. On the opposite bank, the land was lush and open: pastures dotted with Friesian cows, or golden stubble fields bare and shorn, their bounty already tied up in neat bundles for the harvest; our side though seemed more secret, more primeval, as the woods reared up to the house, its old slate roof just peeping above the tops of the trees. I trod water and gazed about. I could see now that as the creek narrowed inland and the trees crowded ever more thickly to its banks, it dwindled finally to a stream, which twisted mysteriously into the woods. I turned the other way, where the mouth gaped wide open to the broad waters of the estuary, and where, on the hazy blue horizon, windsurfers and boats dodged and weaved about, but didn't trouble our little creek.

'Isn't this heaven?' I shouted to Flora, bobbing beside me.

'Total!' she yelled back, and I could tell she meant it. 'You were so clever to get this place, Mum.'

Despite the freezing water, I glowed with pleasure. We ducked down and swam to the sandy bed below, trying to do handstands and pick up shells, then soaring up and breaking through the surface to the cloudless sky. When we were beginning to feel the Cornish water penetrate our very bones, we clambered out, laughing and gasping, on to the bank again.

'That was brilliant,' I panted. 'And presumably we can do that every day, at high tide.'

'Exactly, and then lie on the bank to get dry!' She flopped down. 'Ouch. Quite prickly, though.'

'This isn't the Mediterranean, Flora,' I said, trying to dry myself on the ineffectual scrap of towelling she'd brought down and watching her shake with cold. 'Where's your towel?'

She shivered. 'Only brought one.'

'Oh Flora!' I threw it at her. 'Come on.' I picked up my clothes. 'Back to the house to get dry, and then you can come back down later.'

She got up, not unwillingly, shuddering with cold now, and, clutching our clothes, we picked our way through the tangled wood, along the little path.

'That towel's hopeless, Flora,' I scolded, watching her white shoulders shaking in front of me. 'Just a bit of rag. Why didn't you bring our beach towels?'

'Couldn't find them,' she said, teeth chattering.

'Didn't look, you mean. They're in my bottom drawer, along with my new swimming costume. This one's ancient.'

'Sorry. Well, we can go back to the house and get them. I'll race you, OK?'

I grinned. 'OK.'

She stopped and got on her marks. 'Ready, steady— Oh, *cheat*!'

But I was off. Knowing my daughter at nearly thirteen believed that she could beat me, I sprinted ahead of her. Flora, shrieking with indignation behind me and yelling that she hadn't said go and wasn't ready, was nevertheless gaining on me. I heard her pounding up behind me. She'd never beaten me yet though, I thought, hysteria mounting. We raced past the summer house and up the back lawn, screeching with laughter and shoving each other aside, neck and neck, up to the house, and were just hurtling around the corner, yelling at the tops of our voices and heading for the back door – when suddenly we skidded to a halt in our tracks. Flora cannoned into me, nearly knocking me over, and we held on to each other, gulping and wheezing, steadying ourselves, as we gaped, horrified. For there, in the sunshine, on the crumbling, mossy terrace, around a wrought-iron table and sharing a jug of Pimm's, sat Matt, Adam, and a girl of quite astonishing beauty. My jaw dropped.

'Well, hey,' drawled Adam, looking me up and down. 'Look at this. What have you come as, Annie? Lady Godiva?'

I glanced down at my white swimsuit, which, being old and thin, had become completely transparent in the wet, so that with a dark patch between my legs and pink nipples poking through I looked totally naked. Horrified, I snatched the scrap of towel from Flora and dangled it ineffectually in front of me.

'Adam!'

'Daring, Annie, at your age, don't you think?' he mused. 'But actually, I'd say you pretty much pulled it off, wouldn't you, Matt? Oh, this is Cozzy, by the way, who's totally intrigued by the cool little ménage à trois thing you and David have got going here. She's dying to find out more. Hi, Flora, darlin', how ya doin'?' He broke off to kiss his daughter who'd draped wet arms delightedly around his neck.

'Daddy!' She kissed his cheek, tipping his baseball cap off. 'Didn't know you were coming!'

'I'm going up to change,' I muttered as I sidled past them. Matt, I noticed, tactfully averted his eyes. I darted through the back door and scurried through the house to the hall and on up the stairs, appalled.

When I got to my room, I recoiled in horror as I gazed at the apparition in the mirror.

'Shit!' I squeaked, instinctively covering my bits with my hands.

I ripped the wretched costume off and threw it angrily on the floor, grabbing a towel. Damn. *Damn*. How could I have stood there like that in front of Adam? And what the hell was he *doing* here, for Christ's sake, without even ringing me, sitting on my back step with Matt, sipping a glass of Pimm's? Matt, for crying out loud, who wouldn't even stop for a cup of *coff*ee with me. And – and her, Cocksy or whatever the hell her name was: God, she was gorgeous. She wasn't what I'd expected at all, so – so tactlessly young, and unlined and slim and ... Steady, Annie, steady. I gripped the rim of my chest of drawers for support and breathed hard. Shut my eyes tight.

When I opened them again, I regarded my reflection in the mirror. My dark eyes looked wide and scared in my pale face. My heart was racing. Hardly surprising, I thought grimly. I'd never actually trod this territory before, had I? Never actually been here. Because in all my years of anguish with Adam, all my years of broken hearts and dreams and promises, although I'd known about the other women, I'd never actually seen him with one. Never seen him sitting beside one, in the flesh, as a couple, like they were down there. I swallowed hard, knowing the palms of my hands were sweaty as they clutched the furniture, knowing still what he could do to me.

Steady, Annie, I muttered to myself again. Just take it easy. Get dressed, and go down. Slowly.

A few moments later I was walking back out, nonchalantly drying my hair with my towel, dressed in a linen shirt and silk trousers, going for sophistication in the face of her youth. God, how young *was* she, I thought as she smiled up at me. Nineteen? Twenty? She didn't look much older than Flora, with her long blond hair and those endless legs coming out of tiny frayed denim shorts. She looked like one long, slim erogenous zone sitting there, rendering my own little zones – the ones I'd so brazenly displayed to the assembled company less than two minutes ago – risible in comparison. I breathed deeply as Matt pulled out a chair for me.

'Thanks.'

I smiled and turned to my ex-husband with what I hoped was breezy confidence. 'Adam, you should have warned me. I didn't know you were coming. I would have stocked up the fridge. Got in some alcopops or whatever it is you youngsters drink.'

He grinned good-naturedly. 'Didn't know your number. I only had your address, and your mobile was turned off, so Cozzy and I thought we'd head on over. I had no idea your place was so close. We're literally only about half an hour away, aren't we, honey?'

He turned to honey, slumped as he was in his chair in his baggy cargo pants and white T-shirt, and stretched out a tanned hand to take her tiny one. He looked gorgeous, as ever. *They* looked gorgeous. Made a gorgeous couple.

'Thanks,' I muttered as Matt poured me a drink from the jug of Pimm's.

'And when I looked it up on the map, I thought, well, hey, that's so close. I know, we'll pick Flora up and have her here for the night. Take her out for a curry or something. Would you like that, sweetheart?' He turned to look at her.

'Oh Mum, can I?' Flora, curled on the grass between Adam and Cozzy's feet, glanced up. I noticed she was fiddling with the fringe on Cozzy's suede bag.

'Of course.' I smiled. 'But don't forget there's Clare's barbecue tomorrow night. You might like to be back for that. See all your cousins.'

'Oh, I'll drop her back, don't worry,' Adam said. He grinned. 'And you'll be going to that with Matt here, will you?' He jerked his head and winked. 'Matt very kindly showed me to your drinks cupboard earlier and explained your domestic arrangements. Exotic, I must say.' He waggled his eyebrows.

'I think you'll find your husband's setting you up,' said Matt, easily. 'I certainly explained the circumstances, but I don't recall mentioning anything exotic.'

'Oh, don't worry,' I said, hopefully equally easily. 'Adam delights in setting me up. It's his speciality. And he's my ex-husband, incidentally.'

'Only according to a bit of paper,' said Adam quickly.

'A legal and binding bit of paper,' I retorted. Then I remembered Flora. No fights. 'So,' I went on brightly, 'you're close by. That's nice.'

'Not as nice as this,' he said, looking around in grudging admiration. 'Really landed on your feet here, Annie. I can see why you didn't want to give it up, although I'm surprised the good doctor condones this arrangement. Cozzy was pretty staggered by that, weren't you, sweetheart?'

He turned to her, and she flicked back her hair in preparation for speech. She'd yet to utter a word.

'Well, I jus' thought it was everso funny, that's all. I thought it was reelly reelly strange, like, all three of you sharin' together!' She giggled, and I nearly went down on my knees with joy. Oh thank you, God, thank you. A truly terrible voice. *Terrible!* A high-pitched, Liverpudlian whine that would make even Cilla wince.

'Your mother rents a place down here, I gather?' I said, pointedly ignoring her last remark, but wanting to hear more of that spectacular accent. She set off obligingly, fulsomely even, regaling us with the pros and cons of renting a house in the West Country, and all in a high-pitched monologue.

'. . . yeah, an' on the one hand it's reelly luverly to be in a familiar 'ouse by the sea, like, but it is a bit of a tie 'cos you never get to go abroad like yer mates do – you know, Soty Grandy and Ibifa an' that – 'cos then you lose yer slot. But what's *reelly* lucky is we're a reelly big family – I've gorra lorra brothers an' sisters, see – so there's always someone to fill the slot.'

Adam chuckled smuttily. 'I'd always fill your slot, darling.'

'So that's reelly nice, like, and you know, if the weather's orright, well, why go abroad? You only get a lorra dodgy food an' the runs an' that – our Gary got terrible trots in Gozo, everso poorly 'e was – so you might as well be 'ere 'avin' a pasty and . . .'

Excellent. *Ex*cellent. I sat back, lapping it all up, and hoping every tortured decibel was destroying her sexual allure, although I have to say neither Matt nor Adam seemed put off by it; they were hanging on to every word that fell from her bee-stung lips.

Finally though, after another weighty chapter entitled 'How all me brothers an' sisters' kiddies love fishin' in the rock poowels and how I still like doing it wiv them', she ground to a halt.

I cleared my throat. 'Well, Flora.' I turned to my daughter. 'If Daddy's taking you off for the night, perhaps you'd better go and pack a bag?'

'OK. Oh, Cozzy, d'you want to see my room? It's got a really cool view of the sea.'

'Oh yeah, I'd reelly love to. Thanks, Flora!'

And up she bounced from her chair in her tiny denim shorts and followed Flora inside. They looked for all the world, the pair of them, like a couple of schoolgirls. Adam even reached out and patted her pert little behind possessively, grinning proudly as the pair of them disappeared.

It hurt me though, to see how well they got on, Flora and Cozzy. I could see how Flora might adore having this big girl around, as younger girls did, and that Adam had been telling the truth when he'd said Flora thought she was terrific. And no doubt she was. No doubt she was sweet and kind to Flora, and I was just being a snobby cow because she was with Adam. I breathed hard. I mean, how much worse would it be, I told myself sternly, if she was a matron of my age and Flora was fond of her? Wanted to show her her room? Wouldn't I be even more devastated?

'Annie?'

I came to, and realised Adam was talking to me. I

also realised I was gripping the arms of the wrought-iron chair and that my hands hurt.

'I said, where's the good doctor? Isn't he gracing us with his presence this afternoon?'

'Oh no, not for a while actually. He's got a problem at work,' I said, without thinking.

'Oh? Not another misdiagnosis, I hope?' He laughed and turned to Matt. 'David had an unfortunate episode last year when he told a mate of mine he had herpes, when in fact he had impetigo. Quite a lot of steroid cream was rubbed into delicate parts for no good reason and my mate, understandably, was not exactly chuffed to the bollocks. Didn't do much for his marriage either. His wife never quite believed he hadn't got the clap.' He grinned. 'These days though I think David tends to cover himself. Sends all the "don't knows" round to Harley Street for a second opinion, isn't that right, Annie?'

I stared, horrified. 'Certainly not!' I blustered finally. I felt myself turning scarlet. 'Impetigo and herpes are actually incredibly similar, and the fact is he's simply got too much work on at the moment to be swanning off on holiday. Too many patients!'

God, I could have kicked myself. Adam was always looking for a soft spot, waiting to pounce. How stupid of me!

'Ah, popular man,' he said with a mocking smile. 'Must be that devastating bedside manner. I must send Cozzy along to see him. She's got an interesting little mole she wants removed' – he lifted his arm and pointed – 'right here. Just underneath her left breast. Think he could handle it?'

'He'd handle it with pleasure,' I purred, thinking hopefully his knife would slip and a mastectomy would be performed instead.

At that moment, Cozzy reappeared on the terrace with Flora, their arms linked, giggling, although Flora hastily withdrew hers when she saw me. I glanced away, wishing she hadn't. Children are incapable of subtlety and Adam and Matt had both noticed.

'So,' I said crisply, getting to my feet. 'Packed a bag, Flora?'

'Yep.' She grinned and held up a floral rucksack. 'And yes, before you ask, I've got my toothbrush, and everything else.'

She eyed me, letting me know that yes she'd got her STs and her eczema cream and the three teddies she had to sleep with, *and* the scrap of old blanket to wind around her finger and her birthstone necklace. My heart lurched for her though, as she jauntily swung the bag on her back. Despite her show of bravado it wasn't that easy. She could just about manage her father's for the night – nowhere else – but even then, only with a huge dollop of nerve.

And this was a strange house, I suddenly thought anxiously as I walked her to Adam's car. Not his usual London flat. Where would she sleep? Would her room be miles away from his in the night?

Behind Flora's back, I exchanged a quick glance

with Adam. It said it all. No, it's OK, I'll put her next door, and no, of course I won't go to bed until she's asleep. Relax. He knew. Of course he knew. He was her daddy. I thanked him with my eyes as we walked around to the front drive.

'Bye, Mum!' She hugged me breezily, and ran across the gravel to the black convertible Jeep.

'Cool. New car, Dad?'

'Well, hired actually. Just for the holiday.'

But as Adam and Cozzy got in the front, she suddenly darted back. 'Say it,' she muttered quickly as I hugged her goodbye again. 'Say goodnight, quickly.'

'Love you loads, love you thousands, love you millions,' I muttered.

'Love you up to the sky,' she gasped.

'And to the bottom of the sea,' I gabbled back. I squeezed her, then, after squeezing me hard back, she turned and fled.

I folded my arms, holding myself tight. Adam and Cozzy got in, and Adam started the car. He gave it an inordinate amount of revving, and as I waved them off with a bright, fixed smile, a spray of gravel shot up over me.

I stood there for a moment, in the empty drive, blinking in the cloud of dust he'd left in his wake, then turned to go back to the house. I felt cold, suddenly.

As I walked around the side to the terrace, I was surprised to see Matt still sitting there. He hadn't, as

I'd expected him to, bolted back to his study and locked the door. As he glanced across, he gave the first approximation of a friendly smile I'd seen since I'd met him, and let the Pimm's jug hover over my glass. He cocked an eyebrow enquiringly.

'Drink?'

chapter eleven

I hesitated. What I really wanted to do was to go to my room, throw myself on the bed and howl, but actually, I could do with a drink too. I sat down.

'Thanks.'

He poured out the Pimm's and we were silent for a moment. The heat had gone out of the day now, and the sun was low in the sky across the bay and behind the woods. So low, I could put sunglasses on without him thinking it peculiar.

'Won't be a mo'.'

I nipped through the French windows and into the sitting room, digging them out of my bag with a shaky hand. Then I came back and smiled breezily. I had a feeling he was going to ask me about Adam.

'So, how's the thesis coming along?' I said quickly as I sat down.

He smiled. 'It's more of a book, actually. It began as a thesis, but has grown rather.'

'Oh, a book! Right. So that makes two of us. Have you got a publisher? An agent?'

'A publisher, yes, but not an agent because it's not that sort of a book. It's an academic work. It'll be published by the university press in Boston.'

'Ah. Called?' I enquired brightly even though I couldn't care less. My hand was still shaking, I noticed as I picked up my glass. Just keep up the breezy chit-chat, Annie, get the booze down your neck, then go for a lie-down.

'It's called *Molly goes Mental*.'

I glanced up.

He smiled. 'Only kidding. No, no catchy title. It's essentially a collection of papers on the extensions of clinical psychosis in the paranoic mind.'

'Oh. Heavens.' I sank humbly into my Pimm's.

He smiled. 'And yours?'

'Oh, er, *Love All Over*, at the moment. But it's um, a working title.' I nodded. 'Might change it.'

'Ah. A romantic work.'

I eyed him sharply. Was he laughing at me? 'Well, amongst other things,' I said haughtily, straightening up. 'There's – you know – mystery and intrigue in there as well, a bit of pathos and, um, black comedy, that kind of thing.' I cast about wildly. 'Not an entirely intellectual work, like yours, of course, but hopefully not too, well . . .'

'Trashy?'

'God. Hope not. Probably will be though.'

'I doubt it.'

I squinted up at him through the sun's rays, think-ing he was being uncommonly nice to me all of a sudden. It also occurred to me that actually, he wasn't unattractive, in a last of the Navaho Indians sort of way, if only his hair weren't so long and wild-looking and he brushed it occasionally. Oh, and changed out of that horrid old fishing jumper. His eyes were as blue as the sea.

'And is it autobiographical?'

'Hm? Oh heavens no, I make it up.' I gave a hollow laugh. 'Golly, if I wrote something autobiographical it would be about me and Adam, and that would run into volumes. Be longer than *War and Peace*, with the emphasis firmly on the former. I'd probably end up slitting my wrists.' I took a big slug of my drink. Stared balefully into the bottom of my glass. A silence ensued.

'And is that the first time you've seen him with anyone? I mean' – he jerked his head eloquently – 'with that floozie?'

I wondered if this wasn't rather rude? Then quickly decided it wasn't. I grinned, grateful for his support.

'Yes, it is as a matter of fact.' I sat up a bit and flicked back my hair. 'But ... it's fine. It's good.' I nodded firmly. 'I've done it now, and it feels OK. Another hurdle over.'

'And for him, too. I mean, he's seen you with David now, presumably?'

'Oh yes, a few times, but that's not the same.'

'Really? But you are getting married?'

I laughed. 'Yes, but I assure you that wouldn't

impinge on Adam's consciousness one iota. He couldn't care less if I stripped naked and fornicated in front of him.' I swirled the ice around in my drink. 'Probably join in.'

'That's not what I observed.'

I glanced up sharply. 'What d'you mean?'

He shifted his weight on to his other thigh and crossed his legs. 'Annie, in my experience, middle-aged men only flaunt their extremely young girl-friends in front of their ex-wives for a reason. He didn't have to bring her along today, did he? Could have picked Flora up alone?'

'Yes, I suppose, but—'

'And all his derogatory remarks about your fiancé: he wouldn't bother to denigrate him unless he was jealous or unhappy, believe me. He should be relieved you've found someone, relieved to have you off his conscience and have his guilt assuaged, but he doesn't look like a blissfully happy man to me.'

I stared at him intently. Suddenly I laughed. 'Non-sense. Adam doesn't give a fish's tit about me. Not in any real sense. Oh, he likes the idea of the nuclear family and would prefer to live with his wife and child and he's sad about the break-up of all that, but that's the only reason he'd want me back. He fell out of love with me years ago.'

Matt shook his had. 'People don't bother to hurt each other unless they care.'

I regarded him, slumped casually in his chair, narrowing his eyes thoughtfully over my shoulder into the sunset, cradling his glass in his hand.

'In your experience.'

He nodded. 'Sure.'

'As a psychiatrist.'

'Well, no, not just that. My experience of life too.'

'Ah yes, life too.' I took off my glasses, the better to see him. 'Which, according to my sister, has not been so smooth. Not that dissimilar to mine. A few casualties along the way, I gather. A wife and child?'

He smiled. 'Ah yes, your sister. Very different to you, if I may say so. A very . . . direct lady. Forthright. In control.'

Well he was spot on there, but – what, and I wasn't?

'And they're over here, I gather?' I went on doggedly. Yes, quite forthrightly and in control, actually. 'Your family?' I was determined to pursue my line of chat rather than his. Show him I wasn't that easily deflected.

'They are.' He conceded. 'In Cambridge.'

'Ah, so—'

'My wife and I are separated,' he interrupted shortly. 'As I'm sure Clare told you.' He regarded me steadily over the rim of his glass. 'And Tod, my son, lives with her. And with her boyfriend, an English psychiatrist by the name of Walter Freedman. He's a doctor at the University Hospital there.' With that he threw back his drink, draining the glass.

I watched him. Right. So that hurt.

'She . . . left you?' Awful, but I wanted to know.

He looked down at the ice left in the glass. Swirled it around. Then glanced up. He seemed about to say something, but didn't.

I shook my head. 'I'm sorry, I shouldn't have—'

'Walter Freedman and I had an exchange professorship going on, d'you know what I mean by that?'

'I think so.'

'The idea was that I'd go to Cambridge for six months and work alongside him, see how his department ticked and how he ran it, which I duly did, and then he'd come to Harvard to work alongside me, which he duly did too. Except that – and this is where he deviated wildly from the script – when he went home, he took my wife with him.' He smiled wryly. 'That wasn't part of the deal. And no, before you ask, I wasn't tempted to take his wife, neat though that would have been. Her penchant for small yappy dogs and her ample backside were not to my liking.'

'Oh, how awful!'

'Her ass?'

'No! Your wife.'

'Ah.'

'And she took your son with her?'

He glanced down. I realised he couldn't speak for a second. 'Yup. Took Tod too.' I saw his eyes penetrate his glass to the grass below. He recovered. 'He's not far off the age of your Flora, as a matter of fact – who's a great kid, incidentally.'

'Flora?' I beamed. Knew he wanted to change the

subject, but he'd chosen a good one. 'Yes, she's getting there. Gradually. She's had some tough times though. You know: me and Adam . . . the split. You can't always shield them . . .'

'Oh sure,' he nodded. 'And neither should you. Not entirely.'

'But she's coming through. And David's helped enormously. It's just . . . she's so anxious.'

'Sure she is; I've watched her. She has some compulsive obsessive tendencies, but it's understandable.'

'What?' I looked at him sharply. 'Compulsive what?'

'Obsessive. But hey, so mildly. Nothing major. And most kids have it in some small way; they grow out of it. You know, the way you see lots of kids who won't step on the lines of the sidewalk, or have to eat their food in strict rotation: peas, carrots, chicken. Well, Flora won't pick up something she's dropped unless she counts to ten first. And she has to tap her spoon three times on her bowl before she starts her cereal. I've seen her.'

I stared. 'Yes, you're quite right. Both those things. And more.' God, he'd noticed all that, already.

He grinned at my anxious face. 'It's fine, relax. Trust me, she'll grow out of it.'

'Will she?' I panicked. 'Not necessarily. I mean – God, look at me. I can't sit down for a meal without reciting my Latin grace from boarding school under my breath, and I still can't get into a strange bed at night unless it's pushed right up into the corner of the room with walls on two sides. It used to drive Adam mad, and now Flora's exactly the same, spinning like a top before she gets into bed and muttering Hail Marys. We're freaks, both of us, Flora and me,' I concluded miserably.

'Quirky,' he said. 'Not freaks. Believe me, I've seen a lot of those, and that, lady, you ain't.'

'And horribly impulsive, too,' I went on, knocking back the Pimm's and sinking deeper and deeper into my gloom, 'which David just can't understand. He's so organised. So steady. And I just get carried away on the back of – I don't know – a strange impulse. I *do* things, like—'

'Throw all your clothes away?'

I was startled. 'Yes. Exactly! Things like that, or that stupid car wash, or—'

'Your clothes are in the closet, incidentally.'

I blinked in astonishment. 'Which closet?'

'The one in the spare room. I found them in the garbage can on your floor and took them out. Figured you might regret it later.'

'Oh!' I stared. 'Oh, well, thank you. I looked, actually, but assumed the dustmen had been and . . . Thank you.' I regarded him for a moment. Glanced down at my navy blue linen and silk ensemble. 'I hate all these new clothes, actually,' I confessed, tugging viciously at my top. 'So conservative. I feel like a prison warder.'

'You look like one.'

I giggled. 'Thanks.'

The atmosphere had indeed lightened perceptibly. Whether it was the drink or just the fact that our jaw muscles were loosening with practice, I don't know, but when he refilled my glass I didn't try to stop him. I thought how much better I felt than I had done an hour or so ago, and how much more pleasant this was than sobbing on my bed. He was rather convivial company once a few barriers had been broken down, and his angular features had softened a bit too in the hazy evening light. Either that or it was my hazy eyesight. There was still something forbidding about him, though, I decided as I played with the mint in my glass. He had a distancing technique which made it hard to get beyond a certain point. I glanced up.

'So when are you going to see your son?' I asked, suddenly brave. 'I mean, is he coming down?'

He took a moment. 'He is,' he said carefully. 'In a couple of days.'

'Oh! Great. That'll be nice. Nice company for Flora. I mean – assuming you don't mind this arrangement,' I added hastily. 'We could still get the bungalow, maybe, or—'

'Forget the bungalow,' he cut in. 'I don't mind at all.'

Something in his tone brought me up short. Scared me, even. 'Good.' I smiled.

Every time I mentioned his son he changed the subject, but the drink and pure nosiness made me persevere. 'So, is his mother bringing him? I mean, how's he getting here?'

'Yes. His mother is bringing him to Bodmin. To his aunt's house.'

'He has an aunt in Bodmin?'

'She's my cousin, actually. Louise is married to an Englishman, a GP. Tom was a friend of your Gertrude's late husband. That's how we met Gertrude, two years back. My family and I were visiting Tom and Louise when we lived in Cambridge.'

'Oh yes, of course. I remember Gertrude saying now.' I waited. No more was forthcoming. 'And . . . he's staying there in Bodmin? Your son? Or here?'

He hesitated. 'That's where Madeleine – his mother – thinks he's staying. For a week. Louise has three boys, you see. But I'm gonna pick him up from there as soon as she's dropped him off.'

I was confused. 'But why? Why doesn't he just come straight here?'

'Because he's not allowed to. I'm not allowed to see him.'

'Why on earth not?'

'Because we had to go to court over Tod. Madeleine got sole custody.'

'*Sole* custody? God, how awful! But presumably you can still see him occasionally? I mean—'

'No. I have no access.'

Suddenly the garden seemed very still. Very quiet. I went cold.

'But why? I mean . . . why won't they let you see him? At all?'

'Because Madeleine has a scar at the base of her throat. Which I allegedly inflicted on her when I attacked her with a piece of glass.'

I felt ill. 'You . . . attacked her?' I said, appalled.

'I said, allegedly. Of course I didn't. It happened the night Madeleine finally told me about her and Walter. We were back home, at our house in Marblehead. It was late, around eleven, and Tod was asleep upstairs. She was sitting opposite me on our deck overlooking the sea. We'd been having a brandy together after dinner, which was quite normal. There was nothing unusual about the evening at all.' He narrowed his eyes into the distance. Went on softly.

'I can see her now, perched on that calico couch, elbows on her knees, hands clasped purposefully, talking to me softly – calmly even – as she sat there in the moonlight, telling me her plans. Breaking my heart. I couldn't believe what I was hearing. That she loved another man, that she was planning to live with him in England. That she was leaving me. When she told me she was planning on taking my son too, I slammed my hand on the table between us and put my fist right through the glass. A great shard flew up and hit Madeleine in the neck. Cut her badly. There was blood everywhere, and she was screaming as it ran down her throat and chest, soaking her white silk shirt. She was covered, and I was trying to help her, when Tod came running downstairs in his pyjamas. Madeleine was crying hysterically, pushing me off and pointing a quivering finger at me.'

'God. And he believed her?' I whispered.

He shrugged. 'His mom was covered in blood. At the time, I think he probably did, because that's what it looked like, but not now. Now he knows. But what Tod believes isn't the point. The courts are behind her, you see.'

'She went straight to court?'

'Oh sure. To get an order. And when she got up there, in the witness box, her neck still bruised and bandaged, her wrist too where more glass had slashed her, this tiny, petite figure with a quavering voice, telling the judge how I'd come at her, attacked her, how she'd put up her hands to protect herself and her wrist was slashed . . . Oh boy, there wasn't a dry eye in the house. She was good. She gave an Oscar-winning performance. And she had to. She had to fight dirty like that, because she knew she'd broken up the happy home, knew she was the adulteress. She was the one leaving, going to England, taking her son out of school, and she also had a full-time job lined up, whereas I, on sabbatical from Harvard and writing this book, could quite easily have looked after Tod. Kept his life on track. The cards were stacked against her and she had to use every trick in the book to get that judge alongside her. And boy, did she.'

'But surely that wasn't enough? I mean . . . OK, you'd had a fight, hurt her, allegedly, but you hadn't hurt Tod. So surely—'

'When Tod was four months old I put him on a

changing mat on a table at our flat in Boston to change his diaper. Madeleine was at work. I left him, stupidly, to grab the wipes from across the room, for – oh – two seconds, and he moved. He fell off on to the kitchen floor. He seemed fine, but I was horrified and took him to hospital just in case. Sure enough, he'd sustained a hairline fracture. All the doctors were really understanding and sympathetic and said it could have happened to anyone, but none the less, you go on their records as a risk.'

'No!'

'Oh yes, for sure. And a good thing too, as a matter of fact. You wouldn't believe the number of "accidents" that occur, and then a baby dies after just one too many. No, it's a good procedure. Anyway, Madeleine told the court I'd dropped him deliberately. Said I'd admitted it to her later.'

I stared at him, horrified. 'That's unbelievable!'

He shrugged. 'I don't know. Yes, on the one hand it sounds it, but at the time . . . I didn't find it so unbelievable. What lengths would you go to to secure your child, Annie? What lengths if it were Flora? If Adam wanted her? Madeleine was desperate. She wouldn't give up her man, and she wouldn't leave her child, either.' He paused. 'But there are limits. And I was the one who stopped short.'

'What d'you mean?'

'She wanted Tod to go in the witness box. She was going to get him to say he'd seen me attack her as he came downstairs.'

'Oh, surely he wouldn't have done that!'

He shrugged. 'Maybe not. But he was living full time with her then, remember. And I guess she'd talked to him about never seeing Mommy again if the courts ruled against her, about how she'd be in England and they'd be so far apart . . . I don't know, Annie. At the time he was only eleven. Scared. Terrified, probably. But I wouldn't let him go in that witness box. Wouldn't let him perjure himself, go through a barrage of questions, trembling, crying. I gave him up at that point. And that was the point at which Madeleine won. I gave in, and the judge took that to be evidence of my guilt.'

'So when did all this happen?'

'Over a year ago.'

'And you haven't seen him since?'

'Haven't seen him since. And let me tell you, Annie, you think you've got it tough sending Flora off with Adam and that bit of skirt every couple of weeks, but Jeez, I look at you guys, shuttling that child between you, exchanging glances to ensure she'll sleep well at night and not be frightened in the dark, and I think: Hey. That's civilised.'

I swallowed. There was a silence.

'So . . . that's why you're here? To see Tod?'

'That's why I'm here. You think I'd come all the way from New England to Cornwall otherwise, pretty though it is? My cousin, Louise, arranged this place for me, after that meeting with Gertrude way back. She mailed me your aunt's address and I wrote to her, reminded her where we'd met, reminded her that she'd mentioned this house. She mailed me back a bill, and a key.'

'So, Madeleine has no idea? That Tod's coming here, to this house?'

'None at all.'

'But Tod does?'

'Oh sure. We email regularly.'

I nodded, getting the picture. 'He wants to see you.'

He looked stunned. 'Sure he wants to see me, we miss each other like—' He stopped. Licked his lips. 'Listen, Annie, he's my son. I'm his father. I haven't seen him in over a year. And I've done nothing wrong. I've done nothing, other than look after him all his life, and his mother. Love them, protect them. I've done nothing that warrants my life being in pieces like this.'

He looked very pale. Suddenly I realised what the tough mask was all about. What a vulnerable core he was protecting by distancing himself. What the habitual darkness in his face, which only occasionally lifted, was hiding. It was pain. A pain that wouldn't go away, and was so deep-rooted it wouldn't abate for a moment, either. A huge hole had been blown in the landscape of his life and, as a result, he was reeling down a far-away precipice of horror I couldn't even begin to contemplate. He'd lost his wife, and then his child, in one fell swoop. He was watching me.

'Tod's coming here on Sunday, Annie. But that's not on general release. No one else knows. Aside from Tom and Louise, of course. It's a secret.' His blue eyes regarded me intently. 'And I need to know that you can keep it that way.'

chapter twelve

That night I went to my room feeling full of sorrow for Matt. How ghastly to lose your wife and son in one nightmarish moment, and what an appalling woman she must be to pull a stunt like that. I knelt up on my bed and shut the wooden shutters tight against the wind which was whipping up from the sea, then lay down and pulled the covers up around my chin. On the other hand, I thought as I lay staring into the blackness, as he'd said, who knows what desperate lengths one would go to to secure a child? What if Adam had tried to get custody of Flora; would I have lied, claimed he'd abused me? And what about mental cruelty? I'd certainly suffered plenty of that in my time as a spectator to his blatant philandering; might I not have exaggerated a bit, said he brought his women into the house, fornicated with them in front of me and Flora? If I had been really desperate? I shivered under the duvet and gazed into the total darkness that the shutters afforded, the windows rattling in their frames behind them.

I turned over and tried to sleep, but my mind's eye repeatedly conjured up the scene on the deck of the beach house. I saw her, Madeleine, cool in her white silk shirt, smooth blonde hair (I imagined) swept back in a band, perched on the calico sofa he'd described, not dissimilar to the ones I'd seen in *Elle Decoration* that graced the decks of prosperous American waterfront houses. Then I saw Matt, opposite, perhaps slightly more groomed in those days when there was a wife around, his dark hair shorter and brushed, in a chambray shirt, shaved and tanned. And I heard her low Boston Bay voice as, with jewelled hands clasped, she quietly gave him the shock of his life. Calmly unfolded the horror story no man wants to hear when they get home from work. That his English friend and colleague, the one who no doubt had shared meals with them at that very house, perhaps a brandy afterwards, just as they were doing now, had stealthily muscled in on his family, betrayed him, stolen them from under his nose, and that they were all leaving for England. How angry would he be? How justified in putting his fist through the table?

I tossed about in bed, trying to find a cool spot on the pillow. But then supposing . . . supposing he'd been so livid that, in a moment of white hot rage, he'd picked up a slice of broken glass from the wooden deck. Clutched it in his hand. Suppose – and here I sat bolt upright in bed – suppose he'd lunged at her, gashed her face, again and again, slashing her hands as she put them up to protect herself, and which he'd told me had been bandaged in court. Who knew what madness had possessed him? And suppose the boy had come down and found them like that, and screamed and screamed, and suppose, if he hadn't – would his father have gone further? I didn't know this man, this scruffy American stranger with the manic grin and the strange hooded eyes. Didn't know his true mental state and whether what he'd just told me was a pack of lies, and yet here I was, sharing a house with him.

I drew up my knees and clasped them tightly, huddled in the darkness. I glanced at my clock. Midnight. Midnight, and yet – I listened – yes, I could still hear him; pacing around down there, on the terrace beneath my window, just as he had every night since we'd been here. Pacing, drink in hand, no doubt, and – what – plotting? Plotting what? My mind whirled. Was he insane? Was I insane? What was I *doing* here? Was I sharing a house with a violent man for the sake of a beach, a sea view and a bucolic idyll? The alcohol stormed wildly in my blood and, for a moment, the room spun. Suddenly I was glad Flora wasn't here; glad he wasn't going to walk past her bedroom on his way up to bed, pause for a moment at her door . . . slowly turn the handle . . . open it softly, gaze at the sleeping child, almost the same age as the child he'd lost and . . . Christ! I gave a strangled yelp and ran to my door, my hands fumbling for a key. No key. Bugger. I flicked on the light and glanced around. That chair, heavy and old, wedged underneath the handle, would do, then at least I'd hear if he tried to come in. I dragged it across, wedged it firmly, then scurried back to bed. I turned off the light and shivered. Tomorrow, I determined, we'd go. Definitely. Spend a small fortune at the Priory Bay if needs be, but oh boy, we'd get out of here. I shut my eyes fearfully. And of course I'd never get to sleep now. Never.

The following morning I was woken by a thump and then a crash as the chair fell over and the door opened an inch.

'Jesus, what have you got against there?' Matt's voice came around the door. 'I tried to rouse you by knocking but I couldn't get any answer. David's on the phone for you downstairs.'

I unstuck my eyelids and peered around, motionless. Morning? Surely not. I'd only just gone to sleep, and – David? So early? I flung back the winding covers and stumbled out of bed like some rough beast, fumbling my way along the gallery, eyes half closed. Clearly the glassman hadn't struck in the night, which was a relief, I thought as I tottered unsteadily downstairs; and actually, in the bright morning sunshine which was flooding through the open front door and illuminating the dark hall like a stage set, causing me to squint it was so bright, I suddenly felt awfully stupid. How could I have been so idiotic? How could I have let the drink and the night demons get to me like that? Why, he was a perfectly harmless man with a very sad past and a story to tell, not a lunatic poised to eviscerate a mother and her young daughter. What planet was I on?

'Hello?' I mumbled as I picked up the receiver.

'Morning, darling. Another beautiful day!'

Golly, he sounded chipper, but then he liked mornings. 'Yes, isn't it.' I yawned, blinking out at the sunny lawn where the buttercups were playing host to bumble bees as they hummed and supped before flitting to the next watering hole. 'Where are you?' I yawned again.

'At work, have been for ages, but I just thought I'd ring and see if you'd got any news.'

I scratched my leg. Frowned. 'News?'

'Yes, you know!'

I concentrated like mad. 'Do I?'

'Well, come on, darling, you're late, aren't you?'

I blinked. Christ. Was I? Where was I supposed to be? 'Late for what?' Heavens, I wasn't even dressed.

'Your period's late, silly! Wasn't it due yesterday?'

'Oh!' Blimey, was it? I hadn't the faintest idea. 'Oh, er, yes. Probably. You may be right.'

'I know I'm right, because yesterday was precisely fourteen days since ovulation, which we carefully pinpointed with a rather hot little baby-making session, if you recall.'

'Oh. Yes. Right.'

'So?'

'Sorry?'

'So you haven't started?'

'Um, no. Not to my knowledge.' I pulled up a chair and sat down, pulling my T-shirt over my thighs.

He laughed. 'Well, darling, you are fairly clueless but I think even you'd know that. How d'you feel?'

'Fine, thanks.' I yawned. Thirsty, actually. Very thirsty. A drink of water or a cup of tea were becoming crucial. I also wondered if a small furry animal had crawled into my mouth and died during the night. Tasted rather like it. My head was throbbing horribly, too. Too much Pimm's.

'How about your breasts?'

'Sorry?' I sat up.

'Are your breasts sore?'

'Um, I don't think so, David.'

'Well, check,' he said impatiently. 'It's always a good sign.'

A good sign. Right. I had a quick feel. 'Er, bit sore, yes.'

'Good. Particularly the nipples?'

I felt again. 'Yes, very.' Cup of tea. Cup of *tea*. Now. And bacon. I could smell it. I turned towards the yummy smell, obediently fiddling with my other nipple, but realising, as I did, that the bright sunlight had blinded me to the fact that Matt's study door was open and he was at his desk, watching me in the mirror above it. My hand flew from my breast in horror.

'Mucus?'

'David, stop it!' I hissed, hurriedly turning my back on Matt. 'I am not giving myself a gynaecological examination at this hour of the morning on the telephone!' God, what must he think? That I was feeling myself up as I chatted to my boyfriend? I went hot with shame. Must think I was desperate for it.

'You women never cease to amaze me,' sighed David. 'You never check your breasts for lumps and you don't even know how your own bodies operate throughout a monthly cycle. Imagine if men had babies; we'd know every sign, every nuance. We'd have it taped. Darling, there are signs of menstruation and signs of impending pregnancy. They are similar, but different, and you should be on the lookout for both.'

'Right. Yes, I'll . . . be very alert,' I flustered. 'From now on. Only please, David, I've just woken up. Dying for a cuppa. What time is it?'

'Nine-thirty. If you've just woken up you've had a jolly good lie-in.'

Lie-in? I called eleven o'clock a lie-in, and what was he so chirpy about?

'How are you, David?' I asked cautiously. 'No more news of Mr O'Connell?'

'Not a word,' he said happily. 'It's all blown over rather satisfactorily, actually, just as I'd hoped it would. Everything appears to be back to normal. I realise now I was worrying unnecessarily. After all, these things do happen, in medicine.'

'Of course they do,' I said warmly. 'Except they don't usually happen to you because you're such a good doctor! That's why it came as such a shock.'

'Well, thank you, my darling, for that vote of confidence, and on that note, I really must get back to my administerings. I've got a patient waiting in reception.'

'OK, but I'll see you next weekend?'

'Definitely at the weekend. I'll drive down on Friday.'

'Good,' I beamed.

'And fingers crossed.'

'Sorry?'

'About . . . you know!'

'Oh! Oh yes, definitely. Fingers crossed.'

I put the receiver down and sat gazing distractedly into the floodlit garden. Then I got up and sauntered into the kitchen. Lovely man. Such a lovely man. So . . . concerned for me always. I mean, how many men would know the finer nuances of their girl-friend's menstrual cycle? Not Adam, that was for sure. He wouldn't know a fact of life if it hit him in the face. I poured a cup of tea from a convenient pot that was still warm, then, as was my wont these mornings, picked a piece of bacon out of a pan that had all the hallmarks of not being washed up from yesterday – and why bother, I thought, it was only reheated bacon grease – sandwiched it between some sliced bread, and wandered idly outside, munching away and dropping crumbs as I went. I pulled my T-shirt down and perched on the worn stone steps in the sunshine.

Narrowing my eyes at the silvery-blue water that glistened through a gap in the trees on the horizon, I thought how stupid I'd been to have my guts wrenched by Adam last night. So idiotic to care, when I had the lovely David. I sipped my tea. And of course I didn't really care, it was just force of habit. And seeing him with another woman . . . I stared intently at the glassy water. Shivered. Suddenly I wished we could hurry this wedding along. Everything would be so much simpler when we were settled, when it was all official, and when we were finally Dr and Mrs Palmer. I smiled. That had a lovely ring about it, didn't it? Yes, Dr and Mrs Palmer, entertaining in their charming London town house, a baby asleep upstairs in the nursery, a pram in the hall – or perhaps not in the hall. I had a feeling David wouldn't want guests barging past baby clutter. I had a feeling I might have quite a few guests too, be doing quite a bit of entertaining. He had a lot of smart London friends who gave proper dinner parties with cocktails and canapés and a choice of puddings – I quaked at the very vocabulary – but no doubt I could get some help. Or learn. Yes, I'd learn. Maybe do a cookery course after we were married.

And actually, it wasn't that far off, now. The wedding. Only six weeks. Only six weeks to go, and we'd be bowling back down the aisle in that dear little church in Cadogan Street, grinning from ear to ear at all our delighted friends in their smart hats, cameras flashing, and then off to – oh. Golly. Where was it? Where were we going? Claridge's, David had suggested, even though I'd favoured something a little less grand. But yes, a table for fourteen at Claridge's – close family and a few friends – and I'd promised to book it. Suddenly I went cold. I'd promised to book it! Because David had joked that I couldn't organise a piss-up in a brewery and I'd said I'd jolly well show him. That was *weeks* ago, and I'd done nothing!

Hastily I got to my feet and hurried back inside, making for the phone in the hall again. I got the number from directory enquiries. A smooth, continental voice answered.

''Ello?'

'Oh, yes, hello,' I flustered. 'Um, look, could I book a table please, for quite a few people actually, about twelve or fourteen, on Saturday September the sixth, for lunch? Would that be OK?'

'One moment, madam.' The line went quiet. I thought he was never coming back. Finally he returned.

'I'm sorry, but for zat day, we are fully booked.'

'No! Damn. Are you sure?'

'Quite sure, madam.'

'Oh God, I'm going to be in such trouble! It's a wedding party, you see. Might you . . . possibly get a cancellation?' Blimey, this wasn't the hairdresser's, Annie.

'Unlikely, madam, but shall I take your name?'

'Yes, it's Mrs O'Harran. Oh, except by then I'll be Mrs Palmer. Dr and Mrs Palmer.'

There was a pause. 'But a Dr Palmer 'as already booked a wedding party for dinner, on zat day.'

'Well, how extraordinary! Two Dr Palmers getting— Oh! Dr David Palmer?'

'Yes, madam.'

'Well, that's him! My boyfriend!'

There was a pause. 'I see,' he said politely.

'God, that's a relief. But dinner – golly, I thought . . . Oh!' I went hot. How stupid. I remembered now, David had told me the church wasn't available until six o'clock so we'd have to have an evening reception. How could I have forgotten? I licked my lips.

'Right. So. Dinner for – what, fourteen?'

'For forty-two, madam. In zee Plantation Room.'

'Forty-two! Heavens. So, what's the form, I mean, has he ordered the – you know, whassisname – menu or whatever—'

'After zee champagne you will be sitting down to chilled vichyssoise, followed by wild salmon wiz seasonal vegetables and *bébé* new potatoes, followed by profiteroles, frash razberries and cheese.'

'Oh! Well, that sounds . . . lovely,' I said, humbled. 'Thank you,' I added cravenly, deeply ashamed.

What must he think? That I was a hopeless future

wife who hadn't even discussed the menu with her fiancé? But he hadn't exactly discussed it with me, had he? I thought as I put the phone down slowly. Not that it mattered, I decided quickly. No, no. At least we had a table, that was the important thing. Well, private room, actually. I bit my thumbnail nervously. And for a moment there, I thought we'd be having a knees-up in the pub! I smiled, gazing abstractedly at the sunny lawn. Quite fun, actually. A knees-up in the Nag's Head. And I knew someone who would have enjoyed that.

On an impulse, my hand strayed back to the receiver and I dialled a familiar number. I was aware, as it rang, that the study door was firmly shut now. Too much frivolous chit-chat going on, no doubt, and I was still in my nightie, damn it. What must he think? But the *mo*ment I'd made this call, the *mo*ment I'd put the phone down, I'd get right down to that summer house and—

'Hello?' A familiar voice echoed far away.

'Mum? It's me!'

'I know that, my love, I was hopin' you'd call. Clare said you were down.'

'Oh, did she?' Suddenly I was ashamed. I hadn't rung since I'd been here, unlike Clare who religiously rang Mum every day. I did it when I thought of her, which was often, but perhaps not often enough.

'How are you, Mum?' I asked anxiously.

'I'm fine, Annie love, an' you? Enjoyin' the sea air? And Flora?'

'Oh Mum, it's so lovely here,' I gushed. 'You'd adore it. Right by the sea and so tranquil and pretty; I wish you could see it. In fact – why don't you? Take a few days away and come and stay with me and Flora? We're only an hour or so from you, you could get the train.'

I glanced nervously at Matt's door wondering how he'd take to this invasion, but my mother chuckled predictably.

'What, no one here to feed the ducks and hens? Don't be daft, love. No, I'll stay put, thank you.'

Mum had sold most of the livestock when Dad had died and she rented the fields out to a neighbouring farmer, but she'd hung on to the poultry. She said it was for the eggs, but Adam had commented with a wry smile that it gave her a convenient excuse never to leave North Devon. Surprisingly, they'd got on well, Mum and Adam, whereas he and Dad hadn't. She'd appreciated his humour. His free spirit. Been sad when it hadn't worked out.

'Well, in that case I'll come and see you,' I said decisively. 'Probably next week, because we're here for ages. But, Mum, I was really ringing about the wedding.'

'Oh yes?'

'I've booked a table at Claridge's,' I said happily. 'And the church is booked in Knightsbridge, so everything's organised!'

'Claridge's, eh? I thought you fancied your local place. That French restaurant at the end of your road, where you know the owner.'

'I know, I did, but David decided this would be better. More – you know – appropriate for a wedding. Oh, and he's organised a florist, too, someone who does big society weddings apparently, to do the church flowers and table decorations, and it's going to be in the evening now, not lunchtime. There'll be forty-two people there, and everyone will change into black tie – you can get a new dress!'

'Black tie. And you're right, I would need a new dress.' She sounded worried. 'Oh, I don't know, love. You young are much more used to all that razzmatazz. And it will be all young, aside from me.'

My heart lurched. 'No! No, and Gertrude. Gertrude will be there, too.'

She chuckled. 'Gertrude, who was born and bred in Knightsbridge. She'll be right at home.'

My mouth dried. 'But what are you saying, Mum? You will come? You will, won't you?'

'Now don't you fuss, my duck, we'll sort som'at out. But it is a long way, London, and you know, with my legs. Wasn't you goin' to do it down here at one stage? In the village, like Clare did?'

'Yes. Yes, I was, but David thought it was a long way for all our friends to travel. All our London mates . . .' I trailed off miserably.

'And so it is. Sensible lad. Now don't you fret, Annie, I'll think on it, all right? Leastways, you'll have a lovely party. Forty-two in black tie at Claridge's, eh? What'd your dad say?' she marvelled.

'I . . . don't know, Mum. What would he say?' I asked anxiously.

She paused. 'He'd have been right proud. Right proud, love.'

'Yes,' I said. 'Yes, he would.'

I said goodbye and, chewing my thumbnail again, moved on upstairs. I reached my room and slowly picked up the chair from my bedroom floor. I began mechanically to wash my face and get changed. It was true, Mum's legs were bad. Her diabetes had gone to her feet now, and she couldn't drive any more, but . . . even so. Even so, there were trains, or – or I could come and get her. But then I was going to Mauritius with David, so how would she get back? Well, there was Clare, she could drive her back, or Mum could stay with her, but somehow, deep in my heart, I knew she wouldn't. I had a feeling she'd find some reason for that not to work either. Not to come. And not because she didn't want to, but because somehow she felt she might let me down. And I thought of her in Claridge's, in her good grey suit that she'd had for ever and her black patent shoes and bag to match. Thought of her sitting at a long table covered in white linen and silver, surrounded by braying young things, gloves tightly clasped in her lap, nervous, uncomfortable and I thought: How stupid of me. *Stupid!*

I trudged gloomily downstairs and down the garden to the summer house. Angrily I kicked open the green door. I sat down and flicked on my computer. Stared at the screen. Damn. She was right. And now it was all arranged. All organised. And I so badly wanted her to come! My eyes burned. I gulped down tears and scanned the screen in a desultory manner. Blinked hard and made myself reread yesterday's offering. Somehow, in my present mood, the prose didn't seem quite so elegant, so sparkling.

Henry had finally slunk home smelling like Harrods' perfumery, and Lucinda, after a sleepless night, had risen to find that the nanny had taken the children to school, Henry had gone to work, and she, with a throbbing head, had one hell of a day ahead of her. A lunch date with her best friend in Harvey Nichols followed by a spot of shopping. *Merde.* As she stepped out of a taxi in Sloane Street, I suddenly had her twisting her ankle badly. Well, get real, Lucinda, I thought savagely, as she hobbled off on her broken heel to the Miu Miu franchise for some new slingbacks. If you're not careful I'll give you food poisoning on the Fifth Floor, too. Christ, you don't know how lucky you are! And for God's sake stop fannying around and get your kit off, we haven't got all day!

Talitha was late as usual. Still ensconced with her personal trainer, no doubt, thought Lucinda as she perched her pert little Versace behind on the banquette seating. Her hand trembled slightly as she picked up the menu. She was tempted to go mad and have a spritzer instead of her usual mineral water, she felt so low.

'Are you ready to order, madam?' said a badly disguised northern voice at her elbow. As she turned, she was surprised to find herself looking into the steady hazel gaze of one of her employees. It was Terence, her dog-walker-cum-window-box-gardener.

'Terence!' She was startled. 'What on earth are you doing here? Why aren't you walking my Patch? Or tending my patch?'

'Mrs De Villiers! Eh oop! Ay, well I've done that already, like. Been oop since dawn, so I'm doin' a bit of moonlightin', like, as a waiter. But now the game's oop and I expect you'd like me to go. Leave yer employ.' He cast his eyes down morosely.

Lucinda looked up at his anxious young face. So appealing and open, and those heavenly long lashes brushing his cheek. Her gaze travelled up his muscular legs to his tight little backside, protruding provocatively, like a Masai warrior's, from the long white apron wrapped around his washboard middle. There was something about a man in an apron. Lucinda's eyes widened.

'Now why would I want you to do that, Terence?' she murmured huskily.

'Well, I thought, you know, you'd be angry, like. Mr De Villiers would be, I know. 'E'd 'ave me sacked!'

'Mr De Villiers isn't here,' she murmured. A girlish blush spread over her face as, impulsively, she reached out her hand and caught his rough brown one. Her rings sparkled in the overhead lights. 'Don't worry, Terence,' she breathed. 'Your secret is safe with me. What you do in your own time is your own affair. Your affair . . . and mine.'

With a deep sigh, I leaned back in my chair whilst my eyes scanned the screen again. At the end, I smiled. Filled my lungs. At last. Perfect. Here we go.

chapter thirteen

That evening, to my surprise, I found myself almost looking forward to Clare's barbecue. It was one of the compulsory rituals of a Rock summer, and whenever I'd rather glibly snatched a few days at my sister's seaside house in the past, sometimes with Adam, sometimes just me and Flora, I'd always felt that, aside from Clare, who ran about beaming madly and organising everyone, there was a distinct air of forced jollity about the whole event. This evening, however, as I made my way across the golf course, following the sandy path as it wound its way through the gorse bushes and down the sand dunes to the beach at the foot of Brea Hill, I decided that a bit of jollity would do nicely thank you, forced or otherwise. I was glad of it. Glad to get out of the house.

I'd felt Matt's presence very keenly that day – perhaps because I'd been alone with him, without Flora – and there was something disconcerting about it. We seemed to be tiptoeing around one another, as if trying to forget our long and fairly intimate conversation in the dusk the night before. I'd wanted to tut loudly in the kitchen at the mess he'd made as he got his lunch, but found myself cleaning up after the wretched man, and when he uncharacteristically murmured an apology for the trails of fried egg, potatoes and beans decorating the work surfaces, I'd assured him it couldn't matter less. I'd be glad when Flora returned, I decided, and I could get back to the ritual sniping and door-slamming I was more comfortable with.

As I'd left the house he'd been ensconced in his study, but years of habit and living with a husband and child had made it difficult for me to leave without saying goodbye. I dithered. Hovered without, then: 'See you in the morning!' I called cheerily through his door. Anticipating the usual grunt, I was surprised when he opened it. In the gloom of the hall, his blue eyes were bright in his dark, Apache-like face.

'You're off then?'

'Yes, to my sister's barbecue, remember? I think she asked you.'

'She did.' He paused, as if perhaps wondering if I was reissuing the invitation. Was I? I wasn't sure. Then he nodded briefly. 'Have a good time.'

I scurried away, dismissed.

Now, though, as I stood at the very top of the dunes with the wind in my hair, my rug under one arm, cooler bag full of mixed salad and garlic bread

under the other – Clare knew better than to task me
with the more exotic components of the menu like
béarnaise sauce or apricot roulade – I was glad to be
alone. I stood, feeling the salt on my cheeks as my
hair was tossed about like the rough grass at my feet,
and gazed down at the scene below. It comforted me
to see that on the stretch of pale sand, the evening
was running true to form. About a dozen or so adults
stood around in little clutches, chatting, laughing,
and holding plastic champagne glasses. Most of
them I knew: the Fields, the Stewart-Coopers, the
Todds, the Elliotts, the Frasers. The men predomi-
nantly wore pale summer trousers, bright but tasteful shirts – often pink – and deck shoes, and the
women, pretty much the same, but with a floral
summer dress adding a spot of colour here and there.
Masses of children frolicked around; the younger
ones making sandcastles and damming moats, whilst
the older ones sloped off to chat in little huddles. The
pre-teens were still vehemently single sex, but the
teens mixed determinedly, walking much further up
the beach than was strictly necessary, and hunkering
down in the dunes where I walked now with illicit
cans of beer and cigarettes stolen from their parents. I
nearly fell over one little clutch, and recognised Theo
Todd's boys from his first marriage, who must be
fourteen or fifteen by now, giggling with two blonde
girls in a bunker, eyes swimming, laughing uproariously, presumably half-cut.

I tactfully averted my gaze and walked on. I

spotted Clare instantly and was surprised. She usually looked like a lifeguard at this event, uncompromising in navy shorts and a white T-shirt, and once even with a whistle around her neck until her embarrassed offspring had forced her to remove it. This evening, however, she was looking extraordinary in a swirling sarong skirt and a low-cut black bikini top. The sun was going down and it was getting quite chilly, added to which she was a heavily breasted woman.

As she tasked a couple of the men off to light a bonfire – always crucial to the ambience – I saw that Theo Todd was one of them: tall and greying in a biscuit linen jacket with a bright blue shirt, very natty and full of himself, but carrying a paunch before him these days, and redder of face – a drinker. His voice boomed out as Clare gave him the matches, waving her arms extravagantly as she explained which way the wind was coming from, and giving him ample opportunity to view her cleavage.

Quite apart from the main group, in a little huddle of dark baggy jumpers, like Albanian refugees, sat Rosie, Dan and Michael, heads down in a pow-wow as they tried to light a cigarette between them. I grinned and raised my arm, and Rosie looked up and waved back. I kicked off my shoes and slowly made my way down the shifting sand of the dunes, knowing of old that momentum could send one flying, but getting increasingly faster as I broke into a run at the bottom. I made my way towards them, the sand cold between my bare toes, and dumped down my bag, breathless.

'God, you'll get shot sitting here, you lot. Don't you know the rules? House guests must pass around drinks and nibbles, and, Michael, I'm surprised at you. Barbecue duty, surely?'

'I know, I know,' he muttered, getting wearily to his feet and brushing sand off his legs. 'And then later, fire maintenance and guitar-strumming I suppose, but I just thought I'd have a quick drink first. She's got eyes in the back of her head though, sadly.'

At that moment Clare turned. 'Michael!'

'*Arrivederci*, my friends,' he murmured. Then: 'Coming, my darling!' as Clare frantically beckoned him over.

I sat down beside Dan who was huddled with his back to the wind, arms around his knees. He looked horrified.

'You do this every year? Whatever the weather?'

'Well, obviously we try to pick a clement evening, Dan, but that's not always possible in this country. How's it going, anyway?' I grinned sideways at him as I handed him a Pils from my bag. 'Having a lovely time, wish you were here and all that?'

'Well, obviously it's going swimmingly,' he said, taking the beer gratefully. 'Simply splendid of your sister to invite us chickens down, and the kids are having a ball, but' – he looked around despairingly – 'Jesus Christ!' He lowered his voice. 'It's this wretched obsession with sand! We've been on this sodding beach all day, battered and windswept, shivering and wet, and even bashed on the head by windbreaks at times of force eight gustings, and lo! Eight o'clock at night, and here we are again. *More* bloody beach, and more bloody beach rounders no doubt, and by the look of that campfire and that poor sod Michael lugging that wretched guitar around, we've got fucking *Kumbaya* to look forward to later. I mean, what's she playing at? This is England, for Christ's sake, not some sun-baked hippy trail in Morocco.'

'The children love it,' I soothed. 'The barbecue, the volley-ball, being up late with their parents, all of that.' I looked around for Flora. Not here yet, but Adam had said he'd bring her, and he'd know where.

'Yes, but I'm not a child!' he said petulantly. 'I'm nearly forty shagging years old. Why aren't I having steak and chips and a bottle of Chablis in a nice warm pub while the children shiver outside with a packet of crisps and a bottle of pop like we used to? It's this bloody Children's Charter, it creeps into everything. It's insidious. These working mothers feel compelled to ensure their little darlings are having a splendid – and stimulating – time, whatever inconvenience it is to the poor adults. It's all born of guilt, of course. And she should lay off those kids a bit, incidentally.' He wagged his finger over at Clare's brood. 'They need some space.'

'I know,' I agreed. 'She knows it too.'

He ran his hand despairingly through his mop of dark, shaggy hair.

'I mean, I'm not complaining or anything, Lordy no. Lovely holiday – and beautiful countryside too, incidentally, and I mean that. I should know. I was born and brought up round these parts. Well, Dartmoor.' He took a slug of beer.

'No! Dan, I didn't know that. I'm a Devonshire girl myself. So you like all this rugged granite cliff and rolling seascape stuff?'

'Can't get enough of it – in small and, as I've qualified, clement doses. No, it's the old Pol Pot regime I object to. Between you and me, that sister of yours needs a good slap. Either that or a good—'

'Thank you, Dan,' purred his wife. 'Your answer to most things.'

'Works a treat, I find.' He grinned. 'Anyway, thanks for smuggling in the beer, Annie. We're only allowed warm pink fizz in Stalag Faraday, you know.' He pulled gratefully on his Pils. 'I put a six-pack in Clare's cooler bag this evening, and she took it straight out again, saying crisply, "It's not really that sort of a party, Dan," and giving me a look which said who the devil was I to make catering suggestions anyway? I am, after all, only Dan, Dan, the Redundant Man, not a financial adviser or a theatrical impresario like that tosser over there.' He nodded across to where Clare was flirting wildly with Theo over the bridge rolls. 'What do my opinions count? I'm practically invisible.'

'Only in her eyes,' said Rosie staunchly.

'Well, no, in many people's eyes, actually,' he corrected her. 'It's rather interesting really.' He cocked his head thoughtfully. 'In fact, I'm thinking of writing a book about redundancy. You'll be interested in this, Annie – Dante would have been too – because it's a sort of limbo state, you see. Neither one thing nor the other. Neither living, nor dead. And rather unnerving for other people, because no one quite knows what to do with me, how to categorise me. At the school gates, for example, when I'm dropping off the kids, I'm regarded with wild-eyed suspicion by the mothers as they hurry past, heads down, not letting me muscle in on their car-park gossip or their coffee mornings – I'm not sure if it's their bodies or their Bourbons they think I'm after – but they certainly find it disconcerting to see a man about, when surely they've just packed one off to serve his purpose in the workplace and have finally got the house to themselves?

'And I'm not one of them now, either.' He nodded across to a group of men, knocking back the booze and braying loudly. 'Because I don't strut off in pin-stripes of a morning and come home at seven, sniffing the air as I open the front door, and crying, "Ah, stir fry. It must be Wednesday!" I'm the one in the pinny *cook*ing the effing stir fry.'

'You've just temporarily lost your balls, that's all,' said Rosie consolingly, patting his arm. 'But it's all right, you'll get them back. Actually, I quite like you emasculated,' she mused. 'Never had you so humble.'

'Make the most of it,' he growled. 'Because one of these days I shall rise up and be counted. Be master of my own universe.' He sank balefully into his beer.

'What is she wearing?' muttered Rosie in my ear, looking at Clare. 'And is it all for him?'

I glanced over as Clare bent forward unnecessarily low to hold a cricket stump as Theo obligingly banged it in.

''Fraid so,' I sighed, as Theo boggled into her cleavage. 'And his wife, of course, couldn't care less. Turns a blind eye. Seen it all before.'

'Which one?'

'Helena. Short blond hair, pink linen shirt.' I nodded over at an elegant but pinched-looking girl, struggling to take jellies off a recalcitrant three-year-old.

'Quite young,' remarked Rosie.

'Second marriage. Fifteen years younger than him, and jaded already. Tired. So complacent is she, in fact, that she seems to have brought along the same staggeringly pretty French au pair that Theo was all over last year. And guess what? He's all over her this year, too.'

Theo drifted away from Clare to help the au pair, who'd been tasked with emptying the car, and was struggling back down the dunes with another full wicker basket.

'Please don't tell me he's doing it with her.'

'Oh no, Helena's not that stupid – or Céline for that matter. No, there's a tacit understanding between those two women, with Helena's eyes saying: Let him think you might, but never do, and Céline's saying: Believe me, I'd rather slit my throat. Although Theo would like you to think he is getting it, and since it keeps him happy, they both maintain the fiction. He is jolly rich after all, and keeps a tight hold on the purse strings. Puts on plays, you know, musicals, in the West End.'

'Yes, I've heard of him. Met him once, briefly,' Rosie said, watching as he took the basket from Céline, making eye contact and letting his hand brush gently over her bare arm. She shivered. 'Doesn't he realise everyone just thinks he's a sad old tart? And that it makes him look older to flirt with a girl young enough to be his daughter? Just accentuates the age difference. I mean, God, he must be fifty if he's a day.'

'You and I would think so, but not necessarily the men.' I glanced at Dan who was looking at Theo with something approaching blatant envy, until he caught his wife's eye and sank nervously back into his beer.

'If he has to bottom pinch, he'd be better off doing it with an elegant, older woman,' snorted Rosie, glaring at Dan. 'At least there's some dignity in that.'

'Clare's sentiments exactly,' I agreed, watching as Clare eyed Theo and Céline with fury, her lips disappearing, they were so compressed. 'Although I'm not convinced it's dignity she's going for tonight.'

'Come on, everyone!' Clare called sharply, cupping her hands round her mouth like a loudhailer, clearly keen to break up the happy couple. 'Let's get things under way! Michael and I have picked teams, so everyone should know which side they're on. Now, we'll bat first, so my team – behind me. Dan, come on, you're on Michael's side, so you're fielding. First base!'

'First fucking base *again*!' Dan fumed, savagely biting his beer can. 'Bossy cow. I swear she hates me. And I love the way Michael doesn't even get to place his own fielders!'

'Come on, darling,' muttered Rosie, nervously. 'Keep the peace. You'll enjoy it.'

'Oh I would, I would, I'd adore it, if only I hadn't been first base five times today already. How many times do we have to play this sodding game. She's obsessed! And you can bet your bottom dollar it'll be sodding Monopoly again tomorrow night, and she'll be the sodding banker.'

Nevertheless, he trudged off, hands thrust deep in pockets, tattered jeans trailing in the sand.

'Doesn't exactly look the part, does he?' said Rosie fondly. 'Amongst all these Boden types. You're looking more relaxed today, incidentally,' she said, eyeing my frayed old Monsoon shirt approvingly. 'You looked terrible yesterday.'

'Thanks,' I grinned. 'That was me trying to smarten up my act. D'you think I can get out of this game by dint of the fact that I arrived late? I don't think I'm on a team, and I've just come on, too. Doesn't that incapacitate me?'

'Course it does. Always used to at school, and anyway, you can be deep square leg with me.' She got up and hauled me to my feet. 'We might stand, though, just to show willing. Over here, Clare!' She grinned and did a mock catch to show she was prepared. Clare nodded approvingly and, when she turned away, Rosie lit a fag.

'Anyway, the children are loving it,' she said, blowing smoke out in a wispy line and gazing fondly at her elder two, leaping up and down in the queue to bat, whilst Phoebe played with a bucket by the shore with some other toddlers. 'Oops, look out,' she murmured. 'It's the ageing Lothario.'

'Might I join you ladies? Out in mid-field?' Theo was suddenly upon us, appearing from nowhere. His hair was greyer than I remembered. Longer too. He kissed my cheek, unnecessarily close to the mouth.

'I must say, Annie, you're looking quite lovely this evening,' he purred. 'And if I'm not very much mistaken this is Rosie Howard, who I distinctly remember trying to chat up at a dinner party at the Osbornes' once, to no avail.' He twinkled lecherously at her. 'And I thought I was being charming and amusing!'

Rosie smiled sweetly back. 'Well, that's a lethal combination, Theo, and pretty hard to pull off. Are you sure you weren't being drunk and outrageous?'

He laughed good-naturedly. 'Well, I do usually get the MP prize.'

'Most pissed?'

246

'Precisely.'

'Ah, then clearly you blew it. You see, I've got one of those at home, so why on earth would I want another— Ooh, I say, good shot Clare!'

We watched in awe, as Clare sent the ball sailing way up to the sky and into the dunes. Roared on by the crowd of excited kids behind her, she set off for first base.

'Drop the bat, drop the bat!' they all yelled, as she tore past Dan, and as, unbeknown to her, one of her pendulous white breasts dropped out of her bikini top.

'I've dropped it!' she yelled, throwing down the bat.

'Hasn't she just,' murmured Theo as she pounded furiously along the sand, head thrown back. She spotted him out of the corner of her eye and, keen no doubt to impress him with her athleticism, gave a huge grin, bare breast bouncing happily.

'Clare! Darling!' Michael's hands went up in horror as he tried vainly at last base to intercept her.

'Oh no you don't!' she cried, shoving him roughly aside. 'I'm going for a second!'

'By golly, she is too,' muttered Theo excitedly in my ear. 'Look, the other one's come out!'

Sure enough Clare was streaking now, bare-chested like a bust on a galleon's prow, as she set off on a lap of honour, tits swinging joyously, impervious to her husband's and children's horrified faces.

'Mum!' screamed Becky, fists clenched, pink faced and appalled.

'Clare!' Rosie and I shouted, frantically clutching our chests.

'Can't stop me!' she chortled, streaming past us.

'Oh God,' I moaned, 'she'll never forgive us. Never. This will go down in the annals of history. Our cards will be marked for ever and it'll be our fault for not stopping her.'

'Why is Auntie Clare running around with no clothes on?' said an awestruck voice in my ear as Michael finally, with a valiant lunge, rugby-tackled his wife to the ground at last base with a mighty 'Ooomph!' I turned to see Flora wide-eyed behind me.

'This isn't one of those embarrassing grown-up parties where you all chuck your car keys in the sand, is it?' she said in disgust.

'Sadly not,' murmured Theo. If he'd had a Terry-Thomas moustache, he'd have twiddled it. 'Although I must say, I'd snap up the ones to your auntie's Volvo any day. Magnificent,' he purred. 'Truly magnificent. That's what a woman should look like, not like those two anorexic washboards over there.' He nodded dismissively at Helena and Céline, who, along with most of the batters, were clutching each other, crying they were laughing so much.

I looked anxiously back at Clare, who, puce in the face with horror, was smartly swatting away

Michael's attempts to restore her modesty and frantically pulling her top up herself.

'Thank you, Michael. I *can* manage.'

'I wonder if I can be of any assistance?' Theo mused quietly. 'Smooth ruffled feathers and all that?'

He reached into the cool box at his feet and pulled out a couple of glasses which he dexterously filled with champagne. 'Excuse me, ladies.'

Rosie giggled as Theo sauntered over with the bottle under his arm, just as Michael was being shooed away like a dirty fly.

'Looks like she's unwittingly played her trump card,' she observed. 'Snared her prey in one fell swoop and – oh God, look!' she said in awe. 'Now she's going to get pissed!'

We watched as Clare took the glass and, uncharacteristically, knocked it back in one. Theo proffered another and, pink with humiliation, but not objecting to the arm he put around her shoulders, she allowed herself to be led away to be commiserated with on the rocks.

The rounders match continued; in a less professional manner without Clare at the helm, perhaps, but with more enjoyment from the kids, who, after all, it was supposed to be in aid of, and who took over with alacrity, employing their own school rules and yelling instructions to their parents. Flora ran off happily to join in with her cousins and other friends she hadn't seen since last summer, and I watched her go, pleased.

Without the gym mistress's beady eye upon us, Rosie and I sank down in the sand again, leaning back on our elbows, legs stretched out before us, happily dissecting the rest of the assembled party, analysing marriages, clothes, highlights – before I stopped suddenly. At first I'd assumed Adam had just dropped Flora and gone, but then I saw him over by the fire, chatting amiably to Dan and snapping open a can of beer. He was alone. Cozzy wasn't with him, and for that I was grateful. Adam and Dan rocked with laughter at something one of them had said, clearly delighted to see each other again.

'I'm afraid Dan's got no sense of propriety,' muttered Rosie uncomfortably. 'He doesn't know he's supposed to knee him in the balls.'

I smiled. 'Men don't. They don't take sides. They're much more relaxed, and actually . . .' I hesitated. '. . . nicer than us in many ways. They accept people's weaknesses and carry on regardless. They don't hunt them down and damn them to hell for ever, as we do.'

'I suppose,' she said doubtfully.

'And I wouldn't expect Dan to take sides, anyway. They were always friends. Why should they stop now?'

Michael approached the pair of them, also patently pleased to see Adam, and pumped his hand enthusiastically. They'd always got on well, too.

'Let's face it,' said Rosie grudgingly. 'For all his faults, he's an amusing guy. Good company. Just a complete dead loss as a husband.'

'Mm,' I murmured softly, knowing she'd like more from me than that. More: 'Dead loss? Complete bastard, you mean!' But I couldn't oblige her. Couldn't give her the affirmation she was looking for.

It was lovely to see him here, actually; greeting other fathers who wandered up, men he'd known for years and whom he hadn't seen for a while, and who, I noticed, all drifted up to say hello. No pointed remarks. No recriminations, whilst the women, who were aware of his presence, stood back, kept their distance, out of loyalty to me, perhaps. And I saw the pleasure on Adam's face, too. Saw the unexpected delight he took in being recognised and accepted by people who, a couple of years back, he might have scornfully written off as predictable middle-class bores who played the money markets, skied in Switzerland at Christmas and went to Cornwall for their holidays. More than anything though, I saw the pleasure on Flora's face. It brought a lump to my throat. Yes, both my parents, her expression seemed to say, as she chatted, glowingly, to a friend she hadn't seen for ages. Mum's over there, and that's my dad. Yes, fine to be in the same place together. They get along fine.

I caught her eye. She flushed and grinned and I nodded back. Yes, it's OK, darling, I don't mind. He can stay. For a bit.

The evening sailed on into a beautiful sunset. The rounders players drifted back to the fold, and the barbecue was loaded up with steaks, chops and sausages. Children were fed first, a few younger ones tired, hugging blankets and sucking thumbs, and being shepherded on to rugs to eat and spill their orange squash. Parents stood around in happy groups, getting more and more intoxicated, the men munching the children's burgers instead of waiting for their steaks. I moved around, reacquainting myself with people I hadn't seen for ages, drinking and laughing, and, suddenly, it felt good. Suddenly I was glad not to be in a Corsican villa, swatting mosquitoes away having been delayed for eight hours at Gatwick, but here, under an English sky, with the gun-metal sea stretching out like a ripple of silk before us, the gulls swooping and calling, amongst friends and family.

Michael, as usual, strummed his party piece by the fire after supper, some Beatles, some old Cat Stevens, but actually, it didn't feel too corny and, helped by the alcohol, we all joined in, including the cooler teenagers. I even noticed Dan singing along to 'Wild World'. It was easy to mock, but there was value in what Clare tried to do here. Whopping great dollops of family value: if only she didn't go at it so doggedly, with such a vengeance, with a metaphorical clipboard under her arm. But someone had to organise it and, in many way, it was a Herculean task. I looked around for her. I couldn't see her, but Michael was getting happily pissed with Adam, so she was probably safely counting cutlery somewhere.

Through my sozzled haze, I was dimly aware that Flora had joined Theo's boys and another couple of older girls for an illicit swig of beer in the dunes. I hoped it wasn't more than that. I swung around anxiously to see, and caught Adam's eye over the fire. In one eloquent exchange I knew that no, he'd checked, and she wasn't far away, and he had his eye on her. Extraordinary, that when it came to Flora, he could be so responsible. I leaned back in the cold sand with a sigh, and gazed up at the dark vault of the heavens above. I listened to the sea, beating its endless rhythm against the shore as it had since time immemorial, and wished that life could always be this simple.

chapter fourteen

The following morning, Flora and I sat side by side on the warm back step which led from the kitchen to the garden, pulling at croissants and sharing a pot of tea. Aside from the house martins and the swallows swooping low over feathery whirls of grass, and a few pale green butterflies flitting about the buddleia, all was still and quiet. In fact, it took me a moment to realise we had the place to ourselves.

'He's not here,' I observed, peering cautiously round into the study window, which protruded to the left of us in a wide bay. 'He's usually in there, tapping away by now.'

'Unless he's still in bed,' commented Flora, dunking her croissant in her tea.

'No, he's always up before us. Must have gone for a walk. It is a lovely morning. Probably down on the beach. Oceanside.' I affected his deep American drawl and Flora giggled.

A silence ensued as we gazed into the hazy horizon: the low sun was just breaking through the morning mist, glancing on the water in the creek and lighting up the fields of corn and barley on the other side, heralding another beautiful day.

'Mum?'

'Hm?'

She drew up her bare knees under the T-shirt she slept in. I knew by her tone it was something heavy.

'I had a chat with Dad last night.'

'Oh yes?' I said lightly.

'Yeah. Well, in fact, he had a chat with me.'

I stayed silent, continuing my contemplation of the view. She glanced at me. 'Don't you want to know what about?'

'Well, you're obviously going to tell me, Flora, whether I want to hear it or not.'

'He'd had a row with Cozzy. That's why she didn't come last night, and when he drove me to the beach, he was just, well, talking about what might have been.'

'And what did he think might have been?' I said with measured quietness, fixing my eyes intently on a seagull perched on a buoy out at sea.

'Well, if he hadn't . . . you know. Messed up.'

'At least he sees it as *his* mess,' I commented.

'Oh he does,' she said eagerly. 'Very much so.'

'Don't say very much so. It's what footballers say when they're being interviewed by Gary Lineker.'

'Sorry. But he does, really. He knows he was at fault and irresponsible, and – and something about a terrible betrayal of trust, but – well, what he did say was that you and him got married awfully young. And that he hadn't exactly played the field.'

Played the field. My daughter's vocabulary as learned at the knee of her philandering father.

'What are you saying, Flora?' I said evenly.

'Well, just that I think he – you know – regrets it. Regrets what a bish he made of it, and really wishes it was different.'

'Really.' My hands were tightly clasped. Hot, through the knees of my pyjamas. 'And what about Cozzy?'

'Oh, I don't think he's ever really been serious about Cozzy. I mean, she's fun and nice and pretty, but, you know, she's very young.'

I nodded. Couldn't speak for a moment. My throat felt tight. Constricted. I cleared it. 'An amusing diversion.'

Flora considered this. 'Yeah. Yeah, you're right.'

'Get to the point, Flora.'

'Well, it's just that . . . I think if you played your cards right, I think Dad would come back for good. He really misses you, Mum. Both of us.'

I turned to look at her for the first time. Her eyes were wide and earnest. 'Flora, we had all this a year ago, remember? Remember he rang? Begged us to have him back, and you shook your head and we both agreed?'

'I know, but it was different then. You were like . . . I don't know, so low. So sad.'

'Pathetic?'

'No, but it wouldn't have been right. He'd have been doing us a favour. And he didn't really know himself, then. Didn't know for sure if he'd be off in a few months with someone else. And you weren't in a position to stop him, Mum, you were all sort of defenceless. But now you're much more, like, up. Together. And it would be much more of an equal partnership. You could, like, call the shots more.'

I marvelled quietly at my adolescent daughter's knowledge of relationship games. From whence did it spring? *EastEnders*, or *Northanger Abbey*?

'Flora,' I boggled, 'one small point. I'm marrying David. Where exactly is this conversation going?'

'Nowhere. I'm just telling you, that's all, before you do!' Her voice was getting shrill now. 'Before you do get married. I mean – better I tell you before than after, surely?'

I struggled. 'But – but you like David, surely?'

'Yes, of course I like David! But I'm not the one marrying him, am I?'

She turned angry, tear-filled eyes on me, and I gazed back, digesting this non-sequitur, as a car tore briskly up the gravel drive beside us. I gulped. Turned to look.

'He's back,' I muttered. 'It's Matt. Must have been shopping.'

Flora frantically blinked back her tears. 'There's someone with him. In the front.'

'Oh,' I breathed, staring. 'I forgot. It's his son. He's been to pick up his son.'

We watched as a small fair-haired boy in glasses got out of the passenger door, pulling a huge back-pack after him.

'His son!' echoed Flora in disbelief, our previous conversation suddenly forgotten.

'Yes, I forgot to tell you,' I said hurriedly. 'His son's staying for a week. He lives over here with his mother. He's about your age, I think.'

'Oh terrific!' she stormed. 'That's all I bloody need. Some arrogant gum-chewing Yank hanging around for my entire summer holiday – thanks, Mum!' And with a strangled sob, no doubt due to a combination of factors, she got up off the step and fled back into the house.

My heart still beating fast, I stood up to greet them. What had Adam been saying? And why was he fostering false hope in her, for something he had no intention of following through? And how badly *had* I been falling apart last year, for her to have had the maturity to know I couldn't handle having him back then? But now, now that I was 'up', apparently I could?

I swallowed hard as they came towards me, trying to forget my inner turmoil and to smile kindly at the boy, whose eyes didn't leave the grass. All I got was the top of his head: a mop of blond curls like a Franciscan angel. He was small for his age, and skinny, wearing old jeans and a plain, pale blue T-shirt.

'Tod, this is Annie,' said Matt, with an arm around

his shoulders. 'And if you're quick, you'll just catch the back of Flora, just pounding up the stairs, there.'

'Tired and bolshie,' I muttered apologetically to him, holding my hand out to Tod. 'Hi, Tod, good to see you.'

'Hi,' he muttered, raising huge and limpid blue eyes for a split second from the grass.

'I'm going to show Tod his room, and then take him around the place. Give him the lie of the land.'

'Good idea,' I agreed, my eyes glued, now that I'd greeted the boy, to Matt. I couldn't get over the change. He was wearing a clean cornflower-blue shirt I'd never seen before, and his hair had been washed and cut. Gone were the dark locks straggling around his brow, and his eyes, as he looked down at Tod, had lost their dark, haunted look. The effect was staggering.

'You've had your hair cut!' I said, unable to stop myself.

He grinned. 'I do, periodically, otherwise it'd be down by my knees. Tod, you want some breakfast?'

The boy shrugged. 'Sure,' he said listlessly, scuffing his toe. Head down, he followed his father indoors.

I watched them go and, knowing better than to prise Flora out of her room and persuade her to be friendly and welcoming, wandered down to the summer house to work. I was still in my pyjamas, but these were decent ones, bought down here, and hell, I was supposed to be on holiday. I bit my

259

thumbnail miserably and tried not to think about Adam. What the hell was he up to? Winding poor Flora up like that, weeks before I was due to get married – and me, too. What was his game? Because a game it surely was. God, it was outrageous. David would be furious. Not that I'd tell him, I thought nervously, sitting down at my table and switching on my screen. I didn't want to set that particular cat screeching amongst the pigeons.

At my feet was my ancient cassette recorder and, as was my wont when I was writing, I reached down, selected a tape, and snapped it in, as my laptop simultaneously lurched into gear. Both machines were as old as the hills and took a while to respond, but when they did, Mahler's Fifth Symphony somehow seemed more arresting than my last paragraph. I leaned back, shut my eyes and listened.

Ten minutes later I was aghast to find tears of regret running down my face as memories flooded back. Horrified, I snapped to. I sat up smartly, nervously wiping my face, and, glancing around to check no one had been peering through the window, switched off Mahler and shoved in a jolly Chopin concerto, before turning my attention to Lucinda De Villiers instead.

Actually, her needs were quite pressing. Having spent an hour in here last night after the barbecue – knowing for various reasons that I wouldn't sleep immediately – I'd manoeuvred Lucinda into a tantalising position in her garden shed. Terence was expected at any moment, to prick out the dahlias, and she was draped seductively against the potting bench, wearing only the skimpiest of Joseph shirt dresses. For a moment I couldn't quite remember what she was doing there, then . . . ah yes, on the verge of an adulterous afternoon bonk. Now, last night, with the champagne storming in my blood and the moonlight flitting across my screen, this had seemed like a good idea, but this morning, with Flora's cracked little voice ringing in my ears and the makings of a monumental hangover, it didn't, necessarily.

I rested my chin in my hands, chewed my little fingers and gazed out of the window. When Flora went past a few minutes later, en route to the beach, I raised my hand, but she stalked haughtily on, fully dressed – patently emphasising the fact that she was unable to wear a bikini now she had an audience – with an armful of books and her headphones clamped to her head. I sighed. Then, raising my hands for all the world like a weary concert pianist forced to embark on yet another ground-breaking symphony, tapped away.

Lucinda paced the tiny shed, wishing she'd thought to install a bigger, more sumptuous one, with a sofabed perhaps. Why were these structures so rudimentary? She'd have to lure Terence into the comfort of the house – thank God it was Consuela's day off – but her bedroom was so overlooked. That sinister artist chappie, Justin Reynolds, who lived at the back, was bound to be painting in his studio again. It would have to be the spare room at the front. She tapped her foot impatiently. If only Terence would hurry up! Her new thong was killing her. More like dental floss than lingerie.

Suddenly she heard his masculine tread echoing across the York stones. The door handle turned.

'Mrs De Villiers! By 'eck, what are you doin' 'ere!'

His young face looked startled in the gloom, and Lucinda wondered nervously just how young he was? Could he remember the Bee Gees, she wondered?

'I was ... looking for a reference book, for plants,' she murmured, letting her manicured nails linger over a pile of Suttons Seeds catalogues. 'Thought we might have some of that topiaried box in pots on the terrace.'

'Oh aye. Golden balls?'

Lucinda blinked. Golly. Quite forward. Still, nothing wrong with that.

'Why not?' she purred. 'And maybe some pointy dwarf conifers as well?' She edged closer, letting her Poison waft towards him.

He took off his cap and scratched his head. 'Could do, but the common dwarf's only semi-erect. You might want summat more upright.'

Lucinda caught her breath. 'Yes!' she breathed. 'Yes, definitely. Don't want anything – semi – about it.'

'Aye, well you'll be looking at summat more vigorous then. I've got one in mind that shoots up a treat. It's a big 'un.'

'Splendid,' she gasped wantonly.

'Eh oop, lass, yer shirt button's coom undone!'

Lucinda glanced down at the pearl button on her dress, deliberately left provocatively open.

'Oh!' She clutched at her bosom, which was small but heaving. 'So it has. In fact' – she pulled hard – 'it's come off!'

'By 'eck, that's torn it. You'll never see in this light. 'Ere, let me look.'

He got down on his hands and knees, thus affording Lucinda another glimpse of his tantalising backside. Heroically she resisted scrambling about with him, but feeling rather faint now, wondered how on earth she was going to lure him housewards, away from these dirty, uncomfortable surroundings . . .

I glanced up, thoughtfully. Perhaps I should have made more of the dog-walking side of Terence's job? That could have placed this particular tête-à-tête in the nice warm kitchen, where Patch and Woo-Woo had their cushions. Wouldn't that have made more sense? Then, as Terence was brushing her little Woo-Woo, Lucinda could toy playfully with the terrier's fringe, thus demonstrating how sensual she could be, when lingering in Terence's own, secret thickets?

I gazed out of the window to the seascape beyond. Beside me, next to the comfort cassettes, was a pile of poetry books, and, on top, my favourite, Emily Dickinson's. I reread a classic for the thousandth time, wishing, as ever, I could write like that, when something made me glance up. Tod was passing by my window, hands deep in his pockets, his thin shoulders hunched, making for the beach.

I read a bit more, choosing her later poems, which usually inspired me to mediocre things, but, after a while, could resist it no longer. I put the book down, turned off my computer, and crept out, shutting the door softly behind me. I tiptoed to the edge of the lawn where the rough grass marked the edge of the wood. The tide was out, and if I stood on tiptoes and craned my neck, I could just see a flash of sand through the trees. But no more. I hesitated for a moment, then carefully picked my way through the leafy glade, down the steep winding path, until I came to a clearing.

I crouched down, shaded my eyes, and peered. There was Flora, standing on a rock at the water's edge, with – yes, Tod beside her. I sat down quietly, careful not to snap any twigs. They were plunging their hands into rock pools searching for smooth stones, then skimming them across the estuary. I watched as one jumped three – four times. There didn't appear to be much chat going on, but quite a lot of shrugging and toe-scuffing, the adolescent equivalent of communication. Good. That was a start. Mindful of being seen I carefully stretched out my legs and leaned back in the soft emerald ground cover. I watched a while longer, then held my face up to the sky. I shut my eyes, savouring the dappled sun on my face, when suddenly I heard a rustle behind me. I swung round, just as Matt, silent as a cat, crouched beside me.

'Oh! You startled me!'

'Shh . . .' He put a finger to his lips. 'Seems we had the same idea. Indulging in a spot of spying?'

I flushed. 'Well, I wasn't spying exactly, but I just thought I'd see . . . you know . . .' I gestured vaguely beachwards.

'Whether or not left to their own devices and without us poking our noses in, they could perform the human equivalent of canine bottom-sniffing?'

I smiled. 'Something like that.'

He peered through the trees. 'They appear to have achieved it. Gratifying to know they've acquired a few social skills along the way, albeit Neanderthal. Not at each other's throats yet then.'

'Not yet, but early days.'

'Oh, sure.' Matt settled back on his elbows beside me. 'Tod's a bit' – he squinted into the sun – 'on the shy side, I suppose. With girls.'

I considered this. 'Funnily enough, Flora isn't. She's better with boys, more relaxed. She finds girls scarier. Admittedly, most of them at her school are pretty fast. And I suppose certain boys would intimidate her, but not a boy like Tod.'

'I'm sure my son will be delighted to know he has such a devastating effect on women.'

I smiled. 'I didn't mean it like that. I just meant . . . Well, I don't think he's entirely what Flora was expecting.'

'Oh? So what was she expecting?' He turned to look at me. 'An all-American jock, already six feet tall with a bull neck and visible testosterone surges, chucking a ball in the air and chewing gum as he ran a practised eye over her in her nightie?'

I smiled. 'Something like that.'

We watched as, tiring of their stone-skimming, they squatted down together on a rock. They appeared to be intent on drawing some sort of hieroglyphics on it, with sharp stones.

'Odd age,' I reflected. 'This stage. Neither a child, nor an adult.'

'True,' he muttered back. 'Old enough to know what you want, but not old enough to make any choices.'

I glanced across at his moody profile; his eyes fixed on the beach and his mouth set, and wondered what he meant by that? He caught me looking.

'Just the one?' he murmured.

'Sorry?'

'I can't help noticing Flora hasn't got any siblings.'

'Oh. Oh no. Well, I had her very young, when I was only twenty-three. And it was such a struggle, we didn't have any money, so we thought we'd wait a bit. Have a couple later on, when we were more solvent. Of course we never *were* solvent, but when we tried again later, I lost them. Lost three, actually.' I swallowed.

'Miscarriages?'

'Yep. And the last one' – I sat up and hugged my knees hard – 'well, it was at twenty-two weeks. Almost a proper baby. Was a proper baby. We ... named him. And I had to deliver him. Then bury him.' I breathed hard, remembering. Adam and I, in a heap, sobbing on the bed in the ward with the curtain closed around us. Then later in the hospital chapel, holding each other so close.

'I couldn't face going through it all again after that. Neither could Adam.' I shook my head.

'But ... I thought you were going to try again? Didn't you say—'

'Oh yes, with David.' I turned to him. Smiled. 'But that's different. David says medical science, and in particular obstetrics, has come on leaps and bounds since then, and there's all sorts of things we can do to ensure I hang on to them. A snip here, a tuck there – I don't know.' I laughed gaily. 'And certain drugs, too, that I can take. He's very clued-up of course, being a doctor. Knows all the right people.'

'Of course.'

'And then straight into hospital for bed rest the moment there's even a hint that all's not well. He says he knows one woman who spent seven months in bed, but had a perfectly healthy baby, which is, after all, all that matters. Emotionally he's very different from Adam. Adam and I both went to pieces. Like a couple of kids. We couldn't even help each other.'

'Well . . . naturally.'

'Yes, but David's much more of a rock. So much more stable. Which is what I badly need. And he's much more pragmatic too. He says if it doesn't work, we don't collapse in a heap, we just try again.'

'You try again.'

I glanced at him. 'Hm?'

'Nothing.'

He pulled a beech leaf from a low branch on a sapling beside us and began shredding off the green with his thumb and fingernails, revealing a skeleton. I laughed.

'I used to do that.'

'So do it.'

I expertly skinned one and put it next to his. We regarded our two skeletons, laid bare together.

'He seems like a nice guy,' he said, at length.

I frowned. 'You haven't met him, have you?'

'No, I meant Adam. Just from the drink I had with him on the terrace the other day.'

I gave a hollow laugh. 'Oh, Adam. Yes, men always like him. He's one of the lads. Always at the bar buying a round, hail fellow well met and all that.' I shifted my bottom on the hard ground, realising I was still in my pyjamas. He didn't appear to have noticed. And I didn't want to talk about Adam. Didn't want to think about him, after what Flora had said.

'And you?' I said quickly. 'Only one, yourself?' I shaded my eyes with my hand, regarding his granite-like profile. Don't come the personal questions with me, mister, without getting one winging straight back in return.

'Yes,' he agreed, 'just the one. Madeleine . . . well, she found Tod quite a handful. And he was a tricky baby, up at night for years, that kind of thing. We did try later, but she'd developed something called endometriosis.'

I nodded. 'I know. Sticky tubes.'

'Exactly.'

He spread his hands. 'And, of course, as things have turned out . . .'

'Quite,' I agreed softly. 'Hurting one child is bad enough, why bring more into the equation?'

We gazed down at the beach below, where Tod and Flora had rolled up their jeans and were wading in the shallows, trying to catch crabs with their bare hands. Tod dropped a rock into the water causing a huge splash and making Flora shriek as the water sloshed up at her, whereupon an even louder shriek went up behind us.

Matt and I swung around, then looked down at the water again to check it hadn't echoed up from there, but the children had heard it too, and had turned, shading their eyes and gazing up at us.

'Annie!'

I stood up and turned around.

'ANNIE!'

This time, as my name rang out, I saw Clare, plunging through the trees into deep shade, looking wildly about for me, then spotting me. Ignoring the winding path, she came crashing straight from the top, through the brambles and branches, towards me. Her face was scratched and her hair all over the place. She was covered in mud, but still in the ridiculous clothes she'd been wearing the night before.

'Clare!' My hand shot to my mouth, appalled.

'Oh Annie, thank God! Thank heavens I've found you, something terrible's happened.' She clutched my wrist, trembling, her voice cracking.

My heart stopped and I went cold. Thought of Mum.

'What!'

Her eyes were huge in her grubby face, and they gazed out at me, anguished. She swallowed hard.

'I think I've slept with Theo Todd!' she gasped.

chapter fifteen

I stared at her, horrified. 'Think? What d'you mean, *think*?'

She collapsed on my arm. 'Oh Annie, it's awful,' she sobbed, tears streaming down her cheeks. 'I got so horribly drunk, and you know me, I've never been drunk, never!'

It was true, she hadn't. Hardly touched a drop.

'And – and Theo, well, he led me away, up the dunes, and I was so excited. It was so exactly what I'd wanted, what I'd fantasised about for ages, and he kept pouring me drinks – he had a bottle of vodka and some orange juice – and the thing was, we could see you all, sitting by the fire, happy and singing, and the children were fine and no one seemed to have missed us, so we crept even further away, giggling and holding hands like a couple of teenagers, right up on to the golf course. And it was so dark and thrilling and – oh I felt such a rush, Annie! I felt so brave, so young, and, oh God, I was *so pissed*! And Theo kept pouring more and more liquor down

271

me, and then we found this bunker—'

'A bunker!'

'Yes, and we lay down in it – collapsed into it – and then he was all over me. His hands were everywhere, and—'

'Er, Clare?' I jerked my head, alarmed, at Matt, but she was unstoppable.

'And I remember him taking off my bra top – I still had this ghastly bikini on – and I kept giggling and thinking it was terribly thrilling and romantic, and he had his face buried in my bosoms going "brrrm-mmmm" ' – she vibrated her lips – 'like that, and sort of batting them from side to side, calling them my fun-bags and jelly buns, and I was joining in and—'

'I'm out of here,' muttered Matt, holding up his hands and turning away.

'Clare, for God's sake!' I hissed. I shook her arm. God, her *breath*! I took a step back. 'What on earth were you *think*ing of!'

'And there we were lying in this bunker,' she gasped, 'and rolling around and kissing and, oh God, I don't remember if he took his trousers off, and I don't know what happened to my sarong but it's all torn and – I just don't know!' she wailed, wringing her hands.

'Clare, what are you saying?' I said, aghast. I held her shoulders and shook her. 'Of course you'd know! You'd remember if you *slept* with a man, for crying out loud, and your clothes were all over the place, so – presumably you did!'

'Presumably I did,' she sobbed, raking her hands desperately through her hair, 'but the next thing I knew, I was being shaken awake by Michael, in the back garden!'

'Michael found you in the garden?'

'Yes, at four o'clock this morning! Oh God, Annie, and *everyone* knows, literally everyone. What am I going to do?'

I turned away, dumbstruck for a moment. Then I swung back to her.

'And you can't remember how you got there?'

'Well, I vaguely remember Theo and me staggering back there from the golf course – I mean, it's only down the lane – staggering and burping and holding on to each other, but other than that, no, not a thing.' She dropped her voice very low suddenly. 'And Michael's so furious. *So* furious.'

'Well, I'm not bloody surprised!'

She put her hands up to cover her face, then sank down on her knees to the ground. 'He's thrown me out!' she sobbed through her fingers. 'Told me to go. Sent me home, says he doesn't want me here, says he'll tell the children Mummy's been called back for an urgent meeting in London.' She took her hands from her wet face and wiped her cheeks with the inside of her wrists. 'He says it happens all the time anyway,' she said bitterly. 'Says it's the story of our family life, so they won't question it.'

I crouched down beside her. 'Yes, well, of course he has to say that, Clare. He has to save face, but

273

don't worry, he doesn't mean it.'

'He does though, he does!' She turned her grubby, tear-stained face towards me. 'He means it this time. What am I going to do!'

She started pulling up clumps of grass in a tortured fashion, just as, through the bracken, Flora and Tod suddenly materialised, having climbed up the path from the beach.

'What's wrong?' asked Flora in astonishment, stopping short in front of her aunt, who appeared to be enacting a dying swan in the fens.

'Never mind,' I muttered briskly, getting to my feet and ushering the pair of them quickly on past her. 'Now listen, Flora. Clare's had a bit of a shock and I need to talk to her in private. Why don't you take Tod up to the house and play table tennis in the garage or—'

'Tod's brought his surfboard. I'm going to get mine and we're going to go round to Polzeath to surf. Can I have some money for a burger?'

'In my purse on the hall chair,' I muttered. 'Take a tenner, and be careful. Take your mobile, too. How are you going to get there?'

'We'll walk across the cliffs,' she yelled back at me, as they raced as one up the path towards the house, taking advantage of my abstraction to surf alone and have money.

'Come on,' I said firmly, squatting down beside my sister again and taking her arm. 'I'm going to get you into a nice hot bath and then we'll decide what to do.'

I hauled her to her feet. She was heavy and dumbly quiescent now. I put my arm around her and helped her through the rest of the wood like an invalid. We made our way up the overgrown lawn and, as we got to the house, I glanced nervously in at the study window. Matt, happily, had his head down, deep in the paranoia, and had the tact not to look up as I led her past and in through the kitchen door.

Once upstairs I started running a bath for her. She was quiet now, shivering a bit as she stood in the bathroom, a pathetic figure in her dirty bikini top and torn sarong, her white shoulders hunched and miserable. She started to pull off her bra strap with shaky hands. I took her in my arms. Hugged her hard.

'It'll be fine,' I assured her fiercely. 'Honestly, Clare. It'll all be fine, don't worry.'

She nodded miserably into my shoulder, hiccuping wordlessly.

When she'd taken off her clothes and got in the bath, I flew next door into my bedroom, shut the door, and rang Rosie.

'What the hell happened last night?' I demanded.

'Ooh, Annie, it's awful,' she breathed excitedly. I could tell she was horribly gripped. 'Clare's had a ding-dong with Theo Todd!'

'Yes, I know that,' I said through gritted teeth, going to the far end of the room, away from the bathroom. 'She's here! But what the hell happened?'

'Well, after you and Flora went, we all started packing up, you see, putting the barbecue stuff away and everything, and then we suddenly realised Clare and Theo were missing. It was all a bit embarrassing actually. Michael was wandering round the dunes looking for them rather hopelessly, sort of half-heartedly calling "Clare!", and everyone was standing around looking awkward, heads down as they packed their cooler bags, trying not to notice but exchanging knowing looks, and you know everyone was there, Annie, the Stewart-Coopers, the Fields, the Elliotts, all that London crowd, all the people Michael and Clare have regular dinner parties with—'

'Yes, I *know* who was there, Rosie!'

'And all the time Michael was trying to pretend to the children that it was quite normal for Mummy to go for a walk with Mr Todd.'

'Oh God,' I groaned. 'Giles and Becky and Luke!'

'Well, Giles guessed immediately, of course, and went very pale and started whacking the sand with a cricket stump and swearing softly, and then Becky started to cry because she was frightened and didn't know where Mummy was. And of course Michael knew. And we all knew that he knew, that was the worst thing, and then suddenly he stopped searching and went absolutely still and quiet. He just stood there, staring out to sea, and everyone was hovering around looking embarrassed and trying to pretend they were still packing their picnics, and then someone muttered something stupid about calling the police.'

'Oh, for God's sake.'

'At which point Helena gave a strange, hollow laugh, like a bark almost, and said that if she did that every time her husband disappeared she'd be on intimate terms with the police by now, and that she for one was going home and he could bloody well find his own way back. And she stalked off to her car with her children and her nanny, at which point Michael said quietly, "Right. Let's go too."

'So we all trooped back up the dunes and across the golf course, and piled into his people carrier, about ten of us, in complete silence. Even my children were quiet, which is a first, but they'd sensed something pretty dreadful had happened. So anyway, we drove back, and Dan and I put all the children to bed – Becky and Phoebe were really upset, I can tell you – and Michael went out looking for her again.'

'And that's when he found her? In the garden?'

'Much, much later, at about four in the morning, having been searching all night. He said he knew she was with Theo, but he was worried in case they'd gone for a swim or something. And knowing she was pissed—'

'Rosie, she's *still* pissed,' I insisted. 'Honestly, she stinks, and you know Clare, she doesn't even *drink*, for heaven's sake. And she says she can't even remember if she slept with him!'

'Course she bloody did,' retorted Rosie caustically.

'Convenient amnesia. Christ, she was with him all night! Anyway, Michael's livid. I mean really fire-breathing livid. Didn't think he had it in him, to tell you the truth, in fact— Oh. Gosh, sorry Michael. I didn't . . . No no, it's Annie. I was just . . .'

There was a muffled exchange. A pause, then: 'Annie? Is she with you?'

I hardly recognised his voice. It was harsh and rough.

'Yes but, Michael, listen,' I said quickly. 'I know you're furious and I don't blame you, but honestly, she was so out of it. She doesn't remember—'

'Oh she's out of it, all right. She's out of it full stop,' he said tersely. 'I've had it with her, Annie, after this. Completely had it. For precisely seven months she's broken my balls over one inadequate fumble with a girl at a Christmas party which I stupidly admitted to. She's made my life a total misery, to the point where I'm scared to open my mouth for fear of her flying at me, wondering if she'll bite my head off, or the children's heads off, all of us treading on eggshells and pandering to her every whim, and then she bloody well fucks Theo Todd at a family beach party. With all our children present, and our friends, and in a completely tarted-up, tits-out, premeditated way. Well, I'm thrilled actually, Annie. Thrilled to bloody bits, and you can tell her that from me. I didn't know I was looking for an excuse to get away from her, just thought my miser-able life would go on ad nauseam, but now I've got one, I'm clinging to it with both hands, I can tell you. I'm not going to pussyfoot around the queen bee any more, pander to her sour, bullying ways; I'm not going to wonder if every sentence I utter is going to be pounced on and sneered at, or stay late at the office, dreading going home, and longing for Monday mornings so I can escape the house. Oh no, she can sod off. Tell her to go back to London and pack up, and make sure she's out of our house in two weeks when I get back with the children. I'll speak to her through my solicitor then. I'll sue her for adultery. We'll have a nice, old-fashioned, no-holds-barred divorce.'

'Michael, you don't mean that,' I breathed. 'You're just upset.'

'I bloody do mean it, Annie. I can't tell you the sense of relief I felt when I realised what this meant about an hour ago. At first I thought: What the hell am I going to do? Then I thought: Well, I'm going to bloody leave her, that's what. Halle-bleeding-lujah. I think I've been subconsciously looking for a chance to leave this mess of a marriage for years, and now she's provided me with one. You can thank her for that, from me.'

'Michael—'

'Tell her goodbye, Annie. And tell her I'll see her in court. You can't imagine how relieved I am not to be seeing her sour, accusing face glaring at me over the breakfast table tomorrow morning.'

I breathed in sharply as the line went dead. Stared

at the receiver. There was a sound behind me. I turned to see Clare, hair wet, eyes wide, wrapped in a bath towel, in the doorway.

'Michael?' she breathed.

I nodded. Licked my lips.

'And?'

'And . . . he's a bit cross.'

'How cross?'

'Well,' I struggled, 'he wants you to go home.'

'I know,' she nodded. 'Back to London. And then?'

I swallowed. 'He wants you out of the house. But he doesn't mean it,' I said quickly, seeing her face collapse. 'It's just because he's upset now. He's angry, that's all. He'll come round; he'll get over it.'

She shook her head dumbly. Came slowly into the room and sat down, ashen-faced, on the side of my bed.

'No,' she whispered. 'He won't. I know Michael. Once he's decided something, set his mind to it . . . he's much stronger than you think, you know.' She looked up at me. 'Not really a timid little man at all.' She stared beyond me, through the window to the sea. 'But you wouldn't know that, because I've knocked all the gumption out of him. I've pushed him, you see, Annie,' she said flatly as I sat down beside her. 'Been needling him for years. This isn't just about last night. But now I've pushed him too far.' She shot her fingers up through her hair and held on to her head tightly. Gripped it as if it might explode. 'Oh God,' she whispered. 'I've pushed him over the edge!'

'But . . . why, Clare? Why have you been so hard on him?'

She let her hands drop and shrugged hopelessly, tears streaming unheeded down her face now. Clare never cried. 'I don't know,' she whispered. 'I just couldn't help it. I just kept nagging and digging at him – I always have done, in a way. But after his thing with Patty—'

'It wasn't a thing, Clare,' I said sharply. 'Just a snog, for God's sake. At an office party!'

'I know, I know,' she whispered, 'but I used it. Pretended it was more! *Wanted* it to be more, to fuel my cause, to gather ammunition against him, so he had no defences. Used it to make his life a misery!'

'But why, Clare? Why?' I asked again, mystified.

'Because . . .' She tilted her face to the ceiling. Gazed up, eyes swimming, searching, racking her brains for the truth. 'Because . . . because *my* life is such a misery!'

Her face dropped and she buried it in her hands and wept. I put both arms around her heaving shoulders and held her close.

'It's always been such a misery,' she sobbed, 'for as long as I can remember, and I've always had to pretend it was so bloody perfect! Right from way back, when I swotted for exams and was hassled by Dad, and got into a better university, and got a better job, and a richer, more successful husband than anyone else, and had more children and a brilliant

281

full-time career and up and up the sodding ladder of life I went, climbing at quite an astonishing rate, like a bleeding mountain goat I was so flaming agile. And then this exhausting holiday every year, self-catering and relentless bucket and spading.' She paused for a moment, wiped her nose with the back of her hand, sniffing loudly. She gave a cracked laugh. 'No cushy Mark Warner hotel for us with three meals a day and crèche facilities thrown in, oh no. Not for the Faraday family; that would be cheating. God, Annie, I'm so tired. So utterly exhausted, and actually, not ever even remotely happy.'

Her face was empty, naked almost in her despair.

'And Michael was, you see,' she went on sadly. 'Before I squashed it out of him. He was often happy. Larking with the children, enjoying them, wrestling in the garden with them, playing the fool with them, and I hated that. Resented it.' She looked bleakly into space. 'All rather unattractive and undernourished, isn't it?' She gave a wry smile. 'But it's the truth. And I resented you, too.'

'Me?'

'Yes, you. In your scruffy clothes and your terrible car with your one child and your little house and your failed marriage—'

'Oh, thanks!' I blinked.

'Because even though you've been through some ghastly times,' she ploughed on regardless, getting it all out, 'you've had some really riotous, throw-back-your-head-and-roar times too. With Adam, in the old days, when you two used to come to our dinner parties and laugh so much about things I didn't understand you nearly fell off your chairs; and then taking off, the two of you, in that dreadful old van to France, to camp by rivers with Flora in a pouch; no money, no cares, just lots of laughter and sex and having – well, *fun*. With Flora too. I've seen the two of you clutch each other you're laughing so much, and hopefully with David, and – and I've never had that! Do you know, last night, in those dunes with that ghastly, groping, geriatric pisshead, Theo, it was the first time in years – ever, even – that I've felt . . . free. Liberated. Happy. Just being pissed and taking my clothes off and laughing and . . . Oh I don't know,' she trailed off miserably.

'But . . . why don't you do that with Michael?'

'Because Michael has to suffer!' she screeched, fists balled. 'Michael has to suffer because I have to suffer, because my life is so shitty. Don't you see?'

She regarded me slightly manically now, her eyes wide and green, full of tears and anguish.

I blinked. 'I . . . think so, Clare. A bit. But . . .' I wrestled with something. 'This huge ambition—'

'To be the best,' she said fiercely. 'The first. To succeed at all costs, always. Crucial.' She nodded. 'Yes, crucial. You were so lucky, Annie. You got away. You were the one that got away.'

She stared down sadly at the carpet. I followed her eyes to a tiny beech leaf, blown in through the open window probably, being wafted about on the tatty pink carpet in the breeze. This way and that, whichever way life took it. How she saw me, I supposed.

'And he does mean it,' she said flatly. 'He's had enough of me. No man could take the assault I've sustained on Michael and not crack at some point. It's just ironic that I dealt the final hammer blow myself. Smashed it for him. Smashed our marriage,' she said sadly.

We were quiet for a moment, huddled on the edge of the bed, my arm around her. Silent. It took me back to a day at the farm, long ago, when we were about ten and fourteen. Her very first boyfriend had ditched her, and she'd allowed me to console her. I'd felt hugely grand and proud, my arm round my big sister's shoulders in the room we shared together, overlooking the rolling, sheep-dotted hills. I remember being disarmed and touched by this rare and human collapse, but suddenly she'd snapped to. 'He was too much,' she'd hissed abruptly, shaking me off. 'Too good-looking. That was it.'

After that her men had tended to be less attractive, and if there was any ditching to be done, she did it. Always had the upper hand. As she had done with Michael.

'What will you do?' I murmured. 'I mean, now. Will you go home?'

She licked her lips. 'I'll have to ring Donna first. She's at her mother's. Ask her to come down here. Cut short her break, and come and help Michael.'

She started to get off the bed. 'He'll never cope, never. Four children—'

'He'll cope,' I interrupted softly, pulling her back by her towel. 'Don't. Don't ring Donna. Let go, Clare.'

She turned back. Stared at me. 'Yes,' she said flatly. 'You're right. He will cope. That's the awful thing. They'll be fine. It'll be me who won't be.' Her voice was very small. 'But I can't just leave!' Her face crumpled. She turned to me appealingly. 'Can't I stay here?'

'Yes, of course, but . . .' I hesitated. She needed to get away. Michael needed her to get away. 'Why don't you go to Mum's?'

She gave a hollow laugh. 'What, alone? Home to Mum without my husband and kids? Hi, Mum, Michael's kicked me out?'

I shrugged. 'She's never judged. Always just been there. Should you ever need her.'

'For you, maybe.'

'And you. It's just you've always been too proud to ask.'

She ran her hands through her hair again, despairingly. 'Such an admission of defeat . . .'

'Dad's not there, Clare,' I reminded her softly.

She looked up and met my eyes. Nodded. 'No. Dad's not there. Just his ghost.' She shivered. Then sat up straight. 'Right. Well, maybe. Maybe tomorrow. That way, I'm not alone in London, am I? Still close by. But – tonight?'

'Of course. Of *course* stay,' I assured her, hugging her hard. My eyes filled as she rested her damp head on my shoulder. My big sister. So much more crushed in defeat for her seeming invincibility normally. So much more humbled through her colossal, misplaced pride.

After a moment, she took her head off my shoulder and held it in her hands like cracked china. 'Tired. Just so tired,' she muttered. 'And my children, Annie . . . My children. Can't bear to think about it.' I could sense a wave of terror approaching.

'Don't,' I said firmly, as more tears threatened. 'Here.' I reached up and pulled back the bed covers. 'Come on,' I urged gently, helping her in. 'Sleep. You're exhausted.'

'Don't think I will,' she muttered dully, but she let me fold her legs up anyway, her face pleated with fatigue. 'So much to think about. So much I've wrecked.'

'Try,' I insisted, lightly crossing the room and closing the shutters, instantly plunging the room into darkness. 'You've been up all night, and we'll talk later, when you wake up. Things will seem so much better then, they always do. You'll see.'

Leaving her murmuring bleakly to herself, I tiptoed from the room, shutting the door softly behind me. Even if she didn't sleep, I thought, she needed to be alone. Alone, for once, with her thoughts, and her conscience. Alone to examine her soul.

I went downstairs with a heavy heart, desperately

sad for her. Sad that she'd ever felt the need to trample so resolutely on her own dreams.

The sun had gone behind the clouds now, and I shivered, reaching for a cardigan on the hall table as I went on through to the kitchen. I poured myself a large glass of wine, then padded back to the sitting room. Climbing up into the bay window seat that overlooked the garden and the creek beyond, I gazed across to the little church buried in the tawny landscape, the fields browning off now in the summer sun. I curled my legs under me and pulled the cardigan around me for warmth.

Clare was right, I never had felt the same pressure. Quite the reverse, in fact. From a very young age I'd always assumed I was expected to fail, so anything more was a bonus. Any painting I brought home from school was admired and exclaimed joyfully over, any piano grade I scraped – just the one – was regarded as a major triumph, whilst Clare, who played three instruments, all to distinction level, gained grades with little drama from my parents. Just a gruff, 'Good girl,' from my father as he beadily inspected her certificate, before going out to his cow sheds. And so, in a way, my life had been a series of small celebrations. It could only go up, whilst Clare's could only go down. Be a series of disappointments. And not through anything crueller than love. My father had only ever loved her, but in the wrong way. Children can't take too much scrutiny. They need to go unwatched in order to develop their inner lives.

My father didn't just watch Clare, he inhaled her. She was made to feel constantly significant.

I wondered too if my refusal to make something of my own life over the years – not to study too hard, not to go to university – had hardened into a stubborn statement. A reaction to my sister's all-consuming passion to make a record of her life. To not give a damn as Clare went down in the annals of working-mother history.

I hugged my knees and shivered as I looked out to sea. The wind was whipping up the trees to a frenzy, swirling their tops as they danced amongst the gathering clouds, and beyond, the surface of the water was shaking, making white horses farther out in the mouth of the estuary. Suddenly, I went cold. The house was so quiet. So still. I leaped off the window seat and reached for the phone on the bookcase, my heart pounding. It rang for ages, twenty rings or more. I held on though, pacing the sitting room, worry stealing over me like a shadow. Then her answer machine: 'Hi, this is Flora, please leave a message—' Panicking, I ran through the hall to Matt's door and knocked.

'Matt?' No answer.

I rattled the handle. Locked. The bloody man had locked himself in.

'Matt! Are you there?' God, what was he doing? Asleep at his desk, or – no. Just not there.

I dashed back in a panic to the sitting-room window, clutching the tops of my arms tight as I gazed out at the surf, breaking out there in the distance, and even in our little creek now. Hurriedly snatching up my shoes, I ran to the kitchen and through the back door, not bothering to shut it behind me.

As I fled down the garden towards the woods, I peeled off at a tangent to the right, following the path that ran, not down to the creek, but along the edge of the undergrowth, and then up the hills to the cliff path beyond. My heart was pounding high up in my throat as I belted through the rough, scrubby grass, the wind streaming into my open mouth as I climbed, panting, up and up around the headland. Then suddenly, as I rounded a bend high up on the cliff top, I stopped. Swayed almost, in the wind. Because there, coming around the top of the cliff, in a row – in formation almost – were the three of them, striding towards me.

Flora and Tod were in wetsuits, laughing and soaked, caked in salt and sand; Matt was between them. His hair was wet, and he was wearing old shorts and a T-shirt, his arms and legs tanned. He was laughing at something one of them had said, head thrown back, his eyes as bright and blue as the sky he lifted them to. As he raised his face and roared out loud to the heavens, it seemed to me his face was alive with happiness.

chapter sixteen

'Hi, Mum!' Flora ran ahead to greet me as I stood there, holding my sides and panting with the uphill exertion.

'Hi.' I smiled, hugging her, but my smile was for Matt. A beam, actually. 'You went with them.'

He shrugged. 'Well, I figure the creek is fine, but surfing . . . You know, bashed heads, all that stuff. The current—'

'I know,' I said quickly, 'and I would have gone. I always go with her, only Clare was so upset and—'

'Mum, chill. Matt came, OK? Stop fussing,' interrupted Flora, embarrassed, barging into me playfully with her elbow. 'And you should see Matt surf, he's ace. No wetsuit or anything!'

'Well, where I come from wetsuits are for pansies, but I gotta tell you, in these Cornish waters I can almost see the point.'

'Freeze your knackers, eh, Dad?' grinned Tod.

He winced. 'More than that.'

I fell in beside them as we walked down the cliff

path towards the garden, sneaking a sideways look at Matt as we went. He looked absurdly young suddenly, his hair wet, joking with his son. But then, children did that to you, didn't they, I mused as I stood up straight, deliberately walking jauntily now that relief had flooded through me. In many ways they made one feel a hundred, but they also had the capacity to make one feel nineteen.

'Hose off those wetsuits,' Matt instructed as they began peeling them off as soon as we reached the terrace. 'And then later on we might go see if we can get anything for supper.'

Tod turned, half out of his suit. 'What, fishing?'

'Well, I'm not going hunting. I've seen the size of the rabbits round here and you couldn't make a sausage out of them. Come on, get the salt off those suits. Properly, Flora.' He took the hose from her and showed her. 'Otherwise the salt dries real hard.'

'And could Mum come too?' Flora asked, taking the hose back, keen to do it properly herself. 'We've never been fishing, have we, Mum?'

'Sure. If she wants?' He half turned, enquiringly.

Unaccountably, I found myself flushing. 'Well. Yes. I'd love to. Why not? I've done enough work today, and Clare should be sleeping, so . . . lovely.'

'Good,' he said shortly, turning back to help Flora. 'The wind's dropping now, so I reckon in a couple of hours we should be fine.'

In a couple of hours we were fine. Dandy, in fact,

in his parlance. There we were, right out near the mouth of the estuary on the left bank, the trees with their arching green limbs like a shady umbrella over us, in a little blue boat called *Pandora* which Matt had hired from the pontoon. An anchor had been tossed over the side and the boat rocked gently in the swell. Matt and I were in the bows, Tod and Flora on the centre thwart, and each of us was equipped with a vast orange lifejacket and a fishing rod, which he'd also managed to hire from somewhere. The wind had indeed dropped, and the water was calm; just a gentle ripple on the surface. Every so often, a fallen leaf or twig came down the ebbing tide, but other than that, all was still. Quiet. Around the corner we could see a slim slip of a beach with people on it, but their voices didn't carry.

Tod's face was intent on the water and, as I rested back in the prow, I took a moment to study him. He was a beautiful boy, his eyes huge and blue and brimming behind his cumbersome glasses, his features thin and refined in his pale face. He sat pensively, passively, whilst Flora, I noticed, shifted about, impatiently tugging her line up every now and then to examine the hook. The worm remained untouched, but for a dark ribbon of seaweed.

'You're letting it touch the bottom,' Matt murmured from under his hat which was pulled down over his eyes. 'Here.'

He reached across and pulled it in a length or two, then he continued with his own fishing, quietly content. At length, I found my own line slipping. I let it slide and, out of the corner of my eye, considered the line of his jaw, the set of his shoulders, the shape of his hands. Strong, capable hands, my mother would have called them; his back, too. I couldn't quite see his nose on account of the hat, but it's fair to say I wasn't exactly fishing in earnest, which was why it came as a shock when something tugged.

'Oh!' I stood up in excitement. 'I've got one!'

'Steady,' he said as the boat rocked madly from side to side. He put his arms out to steady it.

'But I can feel him there!' I began to reel frantically, laughing at Matt over my shoulder. 'I'm not kidding, he's there, on the end of my line!'

'Brilliant, Mum!' squealed Flora.

'Not so quickly,' Matt said quietly. 'You might lose him. Slowly, bring him in gently.'

But I wasn't listening and, still standing, I jerked harder than ever, and caught the flash of a silver fish streaming to the surface, head first. I felt a tug, saw its underbelly gleam as it streaked sideways, and then away into the depths.

'Oh! I've lost him!' I turned to Matt, absurdly disappointed. 'He's gone.'

Matt looked up at me, laughing, pushing his hat up out of his eyes. 'You got over excited!'

'Damn. And it was such an amazing feeling when it tugged. Now I want to catch another.'

But I didn't, of course. The children did though; they got two apiece; Flora pink with pleasure as she hauled hers in. Matt bashed its head on the side of the boat, which made her squeal, then showed her how to take the hook out, which, to her credit, she did. She eagerly tossed the line out again, and then I saw Matt reeling his in, too.

'Have you got one?' I leaned forward excitedly, my shoulder touching his.

'Yep. D'you want to pull it in?'

'Of course,' I said, longingly. 'But I won't. It's your fish.'

Laughing, he gave me the rod and, accompanied by great cheers from the children, I brought the frantically flapping fish slowly over the side and landed it gingerly in the bottom of the boat. I knelt down to examine it as Matt unravelled it from the twisted line, gripping it in his hands.

'It's not nearly as big as the one I lost,' I observed.

He smiled. 'Funny that. They never are.'

We fished a bit more, and when Tod had caught another, Matt deemed it enough for supper.

'How are you going to cook them?' asked Flora. 'On a campfire down on the beach?' she teased.

'Sure, why not?'

Flora looked taken aback.

'Dad and I often do that back home,' explained Tod. 'I mean in Connecticut.'

'Golly,' I boggled. 'Very Huckleberry Finn.'

Matt sat back in the stern and pulled the string hard out of the outboard motor. It spluttered into action. 'Hardly. I tend to use a cutting-edge non-stick pan, a firelighter and lashings of olive oil, but other than that it's authentic.'

I watched as he guided us around some rocks and back along the more populated side of the estuary. He gazed about, looking at the beaches and the little boats we passed with interest. I had other things on my mind, though. I wanted to ask him about his life now, since the split; since the days when he caught fish with his son and cooked them on the beach. He steered us expertly along the shoreline towards the creek, one hand on the tiller, his eyes, far beyond me, searching the distance.

'Can I do that?' I asked suddenly.

He looked at me, surprised. 'Sure.'

He shifted across, and I got up unsteadily, wobbling down the centre of the boat past the children, to sit beside him in the stern. His hand was on mine as I took the tiller, then he got up and went swiftly to the bows, to distribute the weight.

'Done it before?' he called.

'Sure.' God, stop saying sure, Annie. In an American accent.

Flora looked at me in surprise, but loyally didn't utter a word as I steered us gently along. Piece of cake.

'Little bit faster?' I called, confidently.

'Yeah, OK, but — Hey, steady!'

Suddenly we shot off, the bows rearing right up out of the water. I hadn't appreciated quite how sensitive the throttle was and, frozen with shock, was suddenly gripped by the sheer speed of the thing. We hurtled along at a million miles an hour, heading for the beach. Not our beach, you understand, but one in the main estuary, accessible by both foot and car, and certainly with quite a few families on it this afternoon.

'Other way!' yelled Matt, holding on to the sides and attempting to stand up, but I was beyond all rational instruction. Rigid with fear, I stared wildly as the shore loomed, dotted with people, their faces getting more distinct as we raced full pelt towards it. THWACK! We hit it with a mighty smack, just short of a family enjoying a late tea at the water's edge. The force catapulted me and the children forwards, and we landed in a tangle of orange lifejackets on top of Matt in the bows.

The family, sandwiches frozen en route to mouths, watched wide-eyed as we struggled to collect ourselves, inches from their picnic rug and their bare toes.

'Hi!' said Matt, leaping out and sticking out his hand. 'Lieutenant Matt Malone, US Marines.'

The father, red-faced and corpulent, struggled for speech. 'You could have killed us!' he spluttered, spitting crumbs.

'Oh sure,' agreed Matt, 'and ourselves too, but my friend here is training for the élite female boat squad, and that's the way we teach these cadets. Just hit that beach full throttle. Pretty gutsy, huh? Nice work, corporal.' He threw me an approving look and, without waiting for a response from the family, turned and pushed the boat athletically out to sea at a run.

'Come on, you guys, move it!' he bawled. 'I wanna see you MOVIN', let's get OUT there again!'

As we clambered back to our seats, shocked and wordless, Matt waded to his waist then jumped in, cocking a smart salute to the astonished throng. 'Sorry to have troubled you people,' he yelled, and we shot off.

'Nice one, Annie,' he muttered as we roared out to sea again. 'Nearly had us all up for manslaughter.'

'It got away with me!' I gasped, when I'd finally found my voice. 'Just – got away with me!'

'Jeez, you were freaky!' said Tod, in awe. 'Your face was like – like this mask!'

'She does that,' affirmed Flora, nodding, her eyes huge in her white face. 'She just freaks. But, oh God, Tod, your dad was awesome!'

He was awesome, but I was still horrified. Horrified by the carnage that might have been: bodies floating bleeding in the sea, legs severed like *Jaws*, white heads floating like *Titanic* – so many seafaring disaster movies to draw on – and could only lie back, shocked and supine, in the prow. The children were giggling wildly now, thrilled to bits with their adventure, re-enacting it as they lunged forward, then shrieking with laughter as they mimicked the shocked faces of the family, mid-HobNob. Matt looked through them and found me. He grinned ruefully. Shook his head.

'Jeez, I had half a mind you knew what you were doing back there. Thought you were about to do the cutest little cut to starboard, just at the last minute, before we smacked that shore.'

'I'm sorry,' I whispered. 'I'm so, so sorry.'

'Thought you were gonna tell me you were flotilla captain back at high school.'

'I'm so ashamed,' I gulped. '*So* ashamed!'

Later, however, I permitted myself to see the funny side, and it was a very giggly supper we prepared in the kitchen at Taplow House that evening. Clare had presented herself as we were all gathered there around the kitchen table, Matt instructing the children in cleaning and gutting the fish with plenty of squealing from Flora as she pulled out bloody entrails, whilst I whisked up olive oil and balsamic vinegar to make a dressing for the salad. She'd appeared in the doorway, politely refusing our invitation to join us for supper, and affording a very different picture from the one she had earlier. Clean, and wearing some old blue trousers of mine and a T-shirt, her face devoid of make-up, hair swept back in a band off her face, she looked more like her usual self; but there was a sheepishness about her, a new humility, an embarrassment, as she stood, hovering, without her usual poise, at the door.

'No. Thank you though. You're very kind, but I'm not particularly hungry. I'm going to go for a long walk, actually. Around the headland.'

Matt tactfully resumed his fish-gutting as I

regarded her anxiously. 'On your own? Why don't I come with you?'

She shook her head bravely, eyes brimming. 'No thanks. I just need some time to myself at the moment.'

'Did you sleep much this afternoon?'

'No, but I will tonight, I'm sure. If I walk enough I'll be exhausted. I want to, you know. Exhaust myself.'

I nodded. Exorcise the pain, the memory of last night and everything that went with it. Get that bracing sea wind in her face; force some uphill exertion until her legs ached. I remembered doing that in the face of Adam's affairs; pounding up and down the Embankment from Hammersmith to Victoria and back again, with Flora in a pushchair, legs aching, arms and back stiff, but clinging resolutely to exertion; wanting to wipe my mind to a blank sheet with physical pain, strengthening my body whilst my heart curled up and died elsewhere. And not always succeeding, either. Sometimes having to bolt home to cry, or be sick. I glanced up from my salad.

'Well, we'll be down on the beach, if you need us.'

'OK.' She turned to go. 'Oh, and I've rung Mum. I'm going to the farm tomorrow.'

I crossed the kitchen quickly and gave her a swift hug. 'Well done. It's what you need. Some time at home with her.'

She smiled ruefully. 'Home. You still call it that. You always have done, Annie.'

Supper on the beach was a raucous affair. Tod and Flora had been allowed a lager apiece and, after their pre-dinner cocktail, were now chucking the canapés in the air, attempting to catch peanuts in their mouths and falling in a heap in the sand. Tod's glasses went flying, perilously close to the fire, and Matt yelled for calm as he expertly cooked the fish. He'd built a wall for his fire with stones to protect it from the wind, and put a barbecue rack on top to balance the pan. He turned the fish carefully, then slid them on to plates. Sprinkled with herbs and lemon, and with a salad, olive bread and new potatoes to go with it, it turned out to be a splendid feast, and I told him so later, when we were all sitting around the fire, plates balanced on our knees, carefully picking flesh from the bones.

'So this is what you did in Connecticut? On the beach?'

'At weekends, sure. Tod and I made it a regular Saturday night fixture, didn't we?'

'Yeah, it was wicked. The house was right on the ocean.' Tod turned to Flora. 'You could literally step right off the steps down from the deck, and be on the beach in seconds.'

'Cool,' she agreed. 'Have you still got the house?'

'Yeah, but we don't live there.' Tod looked out to sea.

'I still own it,' Matt explained, 'but it's rented out. I live in Boston these days. In an apartment.'

'Did your mum like the beach house?' persisted

Flora with the tactlessness of youth, but Tod didn't seem fazed.

'No, it wasn't really Mom's thing. She preferred the city. I like the city,' he added loyally, 'but not all the time.'

'Madeleine finds the country dull. She calls herself a people person,' offered Matt, without rancour.

It was the first time he'd volunteered information about his wife. I wiped my plate with some bread and waited until the children had finished their meal; until they'd moved further down the beach to talk, to drink Coke, and cover their legs in sand.

'Do you miss her?' I ventured bravely.

He pushed his fish skeleton to the side of his plate. Considered this. 'Miss is perhaps the wrong word. If she'd just walked out and left me, sure, I'd miss her. But she took Tod too, so any feelings I had for her were overwhelmed by such anger and longing for him.'

'But you did have feelings for her?'

'For the girl I'd married, yes. For the sweet, smiling, serene girl I'd once known, but I have to force that image from my mind and remember the bad-tempered, faithless woman she turned into.'

I nodded. 'I have to do that too. Force myself not to remember Adam as he was, but look at what he became.'

'Exactly. And that's not easy, because you don't just stop loving someone. But their changing into people you don't recognise helps. It hardens the

301

heart. What you're left with is a longing for how things were long ago, not for the more recent past.'

'Does . . . your work help you do that?'

He gave a short shout of mirth. 'What, my work as a psychiatrist? You think it gives me inner vision?'

I felt stupid. 'Well, you're used to delving into other people's minds, so I thought—'

'No, Annie,' he said kindly, 'it doesn't. It simply highlights the fact that I'm not doing so well. I do cling to my hate because it helps, and it gives me strength to get through the next bit of my life, but of course I shouldn't, I know that. And not just because I'm a psychiatrist. It stands to reason. Hate leads to bitterness about everything. It colours your whole life, from buying your morning paper, to meeting a friend for lunch, to working with colleagues. You feel dead inside. But you carry on going through the rickety old motions, only with a more contemptuous feeling towards your fellow man, and that's not nice. You feel quarrelsome, hostile, guarded, intolerant. It turns you into a deeply unattractive human being.' He smiled. 'Ring any bells?'

'Oh, absolutely. Only I never had the guts to harden myself as comprehensively as you did. I just crumpled every time I bought that paper, or had lunch with that friend. I was pathetic. And I went to pieces every time Adam called for Flora, in the beginning.'

'Yeah, I guess that's one blessing in disguise. Madeleine took off so comprehensively – emigrated,

302

in effect – that I don't have to see her.'

He stoked the fire with a stick and I thought about what he'd said. About his toughness, his shell, which I'd originally thought was the real man when I'd first met him: gruff, belligerent, angry, barking at me and locking himself away in his room; and yet there'd been moments even then when his sudden, blow-torch smile would explode across his face and I'd think: No. That's not him. There's someone else in there, hiding. I remembered his kindness to Flora that first morning as he cooked her breakfast, and to me too, when Adam had appeared unexpectedly, and today . . . well, today a positive prankster had emerged. I looked up. He was watching me.

'What?'

'I was just thinking how you really blew it today. The tough, intolerant, hostile image. Your mask slipped on the beach there, lieutenant.'

He grinned. 'Don't know why I didn't go for admiral.'

'Oh, I think you pulled rank quite enough.'

'Yeah, well,' he said softly after a moment, poking the fire around a bit more. 'Today was a blast. First day I've enjoyed for a long while, actually.'

He carried on stirring the embers, and somehow, I knew it was very important that we both stared hard into that fire and didn't look up. We steadily contemplated the gleaming twigs simmering in the white hot ash. A log shifted suddenly in the fire, breaking the moment, and I looked across to the shore, where the children had lain down in the sand and were staring up at the stars. Their eyes were shutting and they were murmuring only occasionally to each other under the inky sky. I glanced at my watch. God. Half-ten.

'Yeah, come on, kids,' called Matt, stirring himself and reading my mind. 'Bedtime.'

Uncomplaining and clearly whacked, they dragged themselves to their feet and trudged towards us, huge denim flares dripping in the sand.

'How come?' whined Tod, but it was a token gesture without any real conviction.

'Because you're bushed, that's how come. Now go on.' His father reached out and patted his leg affectionately. Tod leaned down to kiss him. Flora bent likewise to say goodnight.

'Will you come up?' she murmured anxiously in my ear.

'Course I will. In about ten minutes. Clare's probably asleep next door to you anyway, so you're not up there alone.'

'Oh. OK.'

I watched as she followed Tod, climbing up through the dark wood behind him, with only the light from the fire and the moon to guide them, something she'd surely never do on her own. I gave it a few minutes, then turned back to the house again. Lights had gone on in the upstairs windows, which we could just see through the tops of the trees. Clare's window was dark, though. Presumably back from her walk and asleep, I thought. I hugged my knees and gazed out to sea, to the still black water, where the moon on the horizon was sending a shimmering ribbon of light towards us. As we sat, either side of the fire in the cool sand, I felt the warm night air envelop us.

'Your sister's in a mess, I gather,' observed Matt at length, reaching for the wine bottle and refuelling our glasses. I was grateful to him for deflecting the conversation away from us.

'Yes,' I sighed. 'Michael's chucked her out. And quite right too, in a way. She did behave stupendously badly.' Without being too disloyal I gave him a quick thumbnail sketch of last night's events. 'And actually,' I went on, leaning back on my elbows in the sand, 'she needed this kick up the backside. But the problem is, it might not just be a kick. It might be permanent.'

'Once he realises what a relief it is not to have her around, you mean.'

I glanced across, startled. 'Well, yes. But how did you—'

'Because that's another emotional target I hit with a bull's-eye after Madeleine left. Having a secretive affair had made her tense, snappy, nagging at me and Tod, and that part of her I sure as hell didn't miss. Felt something like the surge of relief Michael might be feeling now, as he throws his clothes on the floor, picks his teeth and watches the ball game all day on TV if he feels like it. Buried amongst the bitterness and anger, there's a sense of release too. Like someone's pulled the ring pull back on the beer can and let the bubbles out.' He lay back in the sand beside me, propped up on his elbows.

'Yes, that's what bothers me,' I said nervously. 'That he'll think: Yippee. Toss his bonnet, as my mum would say. Anyway, it's a good thing she's going there. To Mum's. If anyone can talk some sense into her it'll be . . . God, what's that!'

I swung around. There was a crashing and rustling coming from the woods behind us: the sound of snapping branches and heavy breathing, saplings being bent and trampled underfoot. Matt and I got to our feet as one. It was as if an animal was moving directly through the wood towards us, crushing everything in its path, except that an unsteady, wavering light – which I suddenly realised was a torch – told me it was human. The beam emerged, brighter than before, at the bottom of the wood, and shone straight in our faces. It was coming towards us fast, blinding me. I put my arm up as a reflex, and as I blocked out the white glare, saw the face behind it.

'David!'

chapter seventeen

'God, David! You gave me a fright. What are you doing here?'

He switched the torch off.

'Well, I've come to see you, obviously. Came a few days early, that's all.'

He came towards us. The embers of the dying fire flickered softly over his face, but it was too dark to read his expression.

A few? Heavens, he wasn't due until Friday.

'But – I thought you were on call today . . .' I felt flustered, ridiculous, standing here on the beach with Matt, around a campfire. What must he think? But David, consummately polite as ever, was functioning normally.

'I was, until six, then I got a locum to take over. I've just got here. Took me a while to find the place.'

'But why didn't you phone?'

'I tried all day, but you were out. And your mobile's off.' He turned to Matt with a smile. 'David Palmer.'

'Matt Malone,' Matt immediately responded, shaking his hand. 'And, uh, I'd offer you some supper 'cos I guess you could use some after your drive, but I'm afraid we're all cleaned out here.' He gestured hopelessly to the empty pan and plates. 'Those kids have appetites.'

'Kids?'

'Um, Matt's son is here as well,' I faltered. 'He's come to stay.'

'Ah. That explains the boy asleep in the upstairs room. I must say I was quite surprised to arrive at a darkened house and find three sleeping bodies, but not the one I expected. Seems you have a pretty full house party here, Annie.'

For the first time I detected a hint of rancour in his voice.

'Oh, well, Clare's here too, yes. She's, um, had a bit of an argument with Michael. Nothing serious, but she's off to Mum's for a bit tomorrow. Just 'cos – you know – she hasn't seen her for a while.'

'I see,' said David, although he clearly didn't. 'Well, obviously much has gone on here in a short space of time, but I think I'll catch up on the minutiae of it in the morning, if you don't mind. I'm ready for bed. Are you . . . staying down here, or . . .' He gestured casually to the fire.

'No no,' I said quickly. 'We were – I mean I was just on my way up.'

I knew I was flushing to my roots now, but hopefully he couldn't see in the dark.

'You go on up,' said Matt quickly. 'I'll just put the fire out and gather these plates together.' He bent down to chuck stones on the fire.

'Right,' I said gratefully. 'I could take the salad bowl, or—'

'I'll manage,' he said, taking the bowl from me firmly, head bent, not looking up.

'Come on, Annie, I'm exhausted.' David put his arm around my shoulders and led me away.

I glanced fleetingly back at Matt, but his head was still lowered to the business of clearing up. David and I went on up the beach together and then, out of necessity, walked single file through the woods, up the sandy path in silence. David went ahead, shining the torch, even though I knew the way backwards now.

'Very cosy,' he murmured when we got to the top.

'Oh, not really,' I said uneasily. 'It's just it makes sense for us all to eat together. You know, rather than separate meals.'

'Yes, I can see that,' he conceded as we went up the garden.

'And since we caught some fish today,' I rushed on nervously, 'we thought we'd cook them on the beach.'

'Right. Ging Gang Gooly.'

'Sorry?'

'Nothing.'

He held the back door open for me and I went through, still flustered.

'I must say, I was surprised to find it all unlocked,' David remarked. 'You don't lock up, if you're down there at night?'

'Well, I'm not normally down there at night, David. I told you, it was just tonight, and Flora and Tod had only just gone to bed. We were about to come up.'

'Ah.'

We climbed the stairs, wordlessly.

'Strange house,' he commented, when we reached the landing. 'Rather small windows. Gloomy, I'd imagine, during the day. All that wood panelling.'

'It is quite dark,' I admitted, 'but lovely when the sun streams through. You need to see it in daylight, David,' I said eagerly.

'Oh, but I have. Many times, when I was young. I'd just forgotten about the panelling.' He ran his hand along it pensively as we went down the corridor. 'Haven't been here since I was about ten.'

'Oh. Yes of course. I forgot, you must have come here a lot. And of course houses feel so much bigger when you're small. It must seem a bit poky now.'

'Indeed.'

He was being studiously polite, and I felt unaccountably nervous as we reached my room. Wished I could break the tension.

'It's lovely to see you,' I said, putting my arms around his neck when the door was shut behind us. 'I'm so pleased you came early.'

He held me tight. Very tight. 'It's lovely to see you,

too,' he murmured into my hair.

'And – I'm sorry about being on the beach with Matt.'

'No, not at all.'

'But it must have looked . . .' I trailed off miserably.

He pulled me down to sit on the bed beside him. 'You're here now, with me. That's all that matters.'

He kissed me warmly, and I responded, perhaps over-enthusiastically, still feeling horribly guilty.

'But, David, why did you decide to set off so late?' I asked, when our lips had parted. I stood up and started peeling off my clothes to get into bed. 'It's a long journey to contemplate at that time of night, isn't it?'

'Oh, I don't know,' he said wearily. He began to massage his face with the flat of his hand. 'Stupid, really,' he reflected, picking a bit of sleep out of the corner of his eye. He put his head in his hands, clearly exhausted.

I went to the little sink in the corner to brush my teeth. When I'd finished, I wiped my mouth and looked back at him in the mirror. He was still sitting on the edge of the bed, staring down at the carpet, head in hands.

'David?' I turned off the tap and came back, frowning. Sat down beside him. 'What's wrong?'

He looked up. Gave a thin smile. 'Nothing, really. I've just had a hell of a week, that's all.' He reached out and squeezed my hand. 'One hell of a week. And I don't particularly want to go into it, because the whole point of coming here was to get away from the stresses and strains of London and forget the bloody surgery.'

'I know, but if something's bothering you—'

'Hey.' He stopped my mouth with a kiss. 'Shush. Come on, let's go to bed.'

He took off his clothes, brushed his teeth, and slipped into bed beside me. He held me close. Slipped a hand up the back of my T-shirt.

'Mmm . . .' he murmured sleepily, nuzzling into my hair. 'If I hadn't just driven two hundred miles and wasn't completely knackered, I'd make love to you.'

I was appalled to feel a surge of relief flood through me. 'Plenty of time for that,' I whispered back, hugging him hard.

'Exactly. Anyway, I always wonder if it's such a good idea. When it's so tiny.'

'You're not tiny, David,' I murmured sleepily. 'In fact, from my limited experience I'd go so far as to call you Big Boy.'

He laughed. 'No, I mean, when the egg's so tiny. Right at the beginning. Just a speck of life.'

I froze in his arms.

'Oh.' I drew back. 'Oh David, I forgot to tell you. It's not. I mean – I started.'

He went very still beside me. Very quiet. Finally, his voice came out of the darkness.

'You're not pregnant?'

'No. No, I'm not. Such a shame,' I hastened on

quickly, 'and I would have told you, only—'

'Bugger.' He sat up suddenly in the dark. 'Bugger!'

I sat up beside him, dismayed. 'I – I know. It's very disappointing. But, David, we've got so much time.'

'Yes, but it *is* disappointing, none the less.' He turned to face me, to look at me. I could see his eyes burning in the dark. 'Only you don't seem to think so.'

'David, I do!'

'God, you didn't even ring me and tell me. Didn't even mention it!'

'No, well, of course I would have done, but you've only just got here!'

'Don't you want a baby, Annie?'

'Of course I want a baby! Of course!'

We stared at one another in the darkened room, our words ringing out, keeping us still.

'Rather puts the kibosh on any imminent nookie, too, doesn't it?' he said bitterly.

'Yes. I suppose it does. I wasn't thinking.'

'Wasn't thinking. As usual.'

'David!' I was shocked.

Suddenly he drew his knees up, put his head on them, and cradled it in his arms.

'Sorry,' he said in muffled tones into the bed-clothes. 'I didn't mean that. I just feel everything's going wrong at the moment. You telling me that was the last straw, really.'

I instantly swooped and hugged him hard. I'd never seen him so upset. Felt bewildered by it.

313

'Everything's not going wrong,' I soothed, stroking the back of his neck, 'it's all fine! We're getting married soon, and – and then we'll have a baby. Which is, after all, the right way round. You're just tired, darling.'

He raised his head. I saw him swallow. Compose himself. 'Yes, you're probably right,' he nodded. 'I am very tired. I must find a way to reduce my workload.' He sighed, pinching between his eyes with thumb and fingertip. 'Been working much too hard. Sorry, darling. Let's go to sleep.'

We lay down and held each other close. We stayed in each other's arms for a while that night, facing the same way – David behind me, nestling into my back – like two spoons, fitting perfectly together. We hadn't done that since we first met. In those days, it was me who needed the reassurance. Tonight, I felt it was him. Before I dropped off, I heard Matt climbing the stairs up to the top floor. Heard the taps running in the little bathroom up there, then his door softly close. David was asleep, and I gently disentangled myself and moved across to the other side of the bed. For a long while my eyes were wide open as I lay on my back, staring into the darkness. Eventually, I fell into an uneasy sleep.

The following morning, David seemed much chirpier. The three of us, David, Flora and I, had breakfast in the garden together, sitting at the table on the terrace and looking out over the clover and the buttercups. The morning, unlike the last few, wasn't yet sunny, but if anything it threatened even higher temperatures with an already muggy feel to the air and an insistent pale haze over the horizon. David had got up early and been out to buy croissants and fresh bread which we sat down to now. Flora reported that she'd seen Matt and Tod go off fishing together early, and Clare too, it seemed, had risen and left for Mum's before I was awake. Rather tactful of everyone, I thought nervously as I sank into my cappuccino. Not crowding David out on his first day.

Mmm . . . proper coffee. Well, naturally, I smiled, now that David was here. And a table laid with a cloth, complete with marmalade, jam, cups and saucers.

'You're a little wonder.' I twinkled at him over my cup. 'Normally we sit in a slovenly fashion on the back step in our jim-jams, eating greasy bacon and beans.'

He winced as he buttered his croissant. 'Not convinced my digestive system could cope with that. Silts up my arteries just thinking about it, actually.'

I grinned and regarded him over his propped-up *Telegraph*, leaning back in his cane chair. He looked different. But then I'd never seen him in holiday gear. Never seen him in shorts. They were pressed, and khaki, and his legs were very white. His deck shoes were pristine, as was his pale pink polo shirt, still with two fold creases down the front, and likewise his hair, parted immaculately. I giggled.

'Presumably you didn't feel out of place in the bread queue this morning?'

He glanced up, smiled. 'Sorry?'

'I was just remarking on your sartorial splendour. Very North Cornwall.'

'Hm. I don't know about that.' He went back to his paper. Winked at me over the top of it. 'Unlike you, you mean.'

I glanced down at the faded orange T-shirt of Flora's I seemed to be wearing with inexpertly cut-off jeans. It had occurred to me that one leg might be longer than the other.

'Working gear,' I retorted.

'Quite right,' he grinned, still reading. 'And will you be working this morning?'

'Oh no. Since you're only here for a couple of days, I'll give it a miss.' I wiped my mouth with the napkin he'd thoughtfully provided. 'I can start again when you've gone.'

'Won't lose the thread?' he murmured.

Thread? What thread? 'Er, no. Don't think so.' Didn't sound terribly professional, did it? 'Anyway,' I hurried on, 'what would you like to do today, David?' I put my cup down eagerly. 'We can show you the creek, or any number of beaches—'

'Oh yes, Polzeath!' said Flora, looking up from her book. 'You'd love it, David, the waves are huge!'

'Well, I know it sounds dreary' – he scratched his head bleakly – 'but I've actually got to work this morning. I've got a load of calls to catch up on.'

'Oh, David!'

'I know, love, but patients don't take kindly to holidays. I've got to enquire about hospital beds, operation lists, that sort of thing, but it won't take long. Why don't you work for an hour or two, Annie, and then I thought we could all go to Tintagel? It's only forty minutes away, and there's a terrific ruined castle there reeking of Arthurian legend. Flora would love it, and I haven't seen it since I was a boy.'

'Fine,' I said in surprise. 'But it's going to be boiling hot today, are you sure you wouldn't rather flop on a beach?'

He cast his eyes about. Narrowed them warily out to sea over the treetops. 'Not much of a beach man, to be honest,' he reflected. 'The sea doesn't do that much for me, either.'

'You sound like Dan,' I laughed. 'Doesn't do much for him. They're down here, you know. We might see them later, have supper with them or something. You'd like that, wouldn't you?'

'Of course,' he said evenly. 'But it's you I've come to see, Annie.'

He got up and ruffled my hair as he went past. 'I'll be on my mobile in the dining room. I can spread my papers out in there. That is, since Matt seems to have commandeered the study.' It was said lightly, but I glanced nervously after him as he went in.

'Mum, do we have to go to that castle thing?' hissed Flora, the moment he was out of earshot. 'Tod and Matt are going to Polzeath later, the surf's meant to be wicked today.'

'Well, yes, I think we do, darling. If that's what David's got planned.'

'Oh Mu-um!'

'Although . . .' I hesitated. 'Maybe he'd like some time alone with me.'

'Exactly!' she said eagerly. 'He would, of course he would. I'll go with Tod and Matt.'

I looked at her expectant face. 'Hang on.'

I got up quickly and nipped inside, through the kitchen to the dining room, hoping to catch him before he started his calls. The door was shut. I knocked and went in. David swung around quickly, mobile to ear.

'Oh, sorry, darling.' I turned to go.

'Hang on, Hugo,' he said into the mouthpiece. Smiled at me encouragingly. 'It's OK.'

'It's just . . .' I hovered in the doorway. 'Well, Flora quite wanted to go surfing with Matt and Tod today, and I wondered if you'd mind. Thought we could have some time alone together.'

He frowned. 'I think not, Annie. We're a family, after all. No, I think Flora comes with us.' He turned and went back to his phone call. 'Sorry, Hugo . . .'

I gazed at his back for a moment, feeling like a fourth-former in the headmaster's study. Dismissed. Right. Well, no, quite right, actually, I decided. I shut the door quietly, and went back to Flora in the garden, biting my thumbnail.

'Um, he thinks not, sweetheart. After all, we are a family now.'

'But, Mum, you said!'

'I said I'd ask him, darling. But actually, I think he's right. We are a family, and—'

'And a boiling hot car all the way to some crummy castle is just what we need to bring us together, is that it? To bond us? Terrific!'

She grabbed her book and ran off into the house.

I sighed as I watched her departing back. Heard her thump-thump-thump upstairs. Waited for the door to slam. There. Hormones, I decided wearily, picking up a tray from the grass and clearing the table, had an awful lot to answer for.

In the event, of course, she was right. We didn't set off until nearly midday, when the sun was at its hottest, since David's phone calls took longer than expected. Flora had stayed in her room all the while, with a book, and I'd got so bored with hanging about I'd taken to the summer house, even though I didn't feel remotely in the mood for work. Well, I can just sit here, can't I, I thought petulantly, slouched in my chair in an immature fashion. Pretend to work. I bit my thumbnail. Who's fooling who? my dad would have said. Or – and I could hear his voice now – 'Don't do *me* any favours.' I sighed, snapped on my screen, and tried hard to concentrate; not look too wistfully out to sea.

Trouble was, Lucinda De Villiers seemed like such an old tart this morning. Trying to seduce her gardener in the potting shed, I ask you. Didn't she know there was more to life than a quick bonk? Yesterday that had seemed exactly what she needed, but today ... Oh, today, as I gazed out of the window, over the treetops to the beckoning water beyond, knowing it was lapping at the shore, shimmering out there in the sunshine, full of sparkle and promise, today she needed more than that. She needed romance in her soul, passion. Love, even ...

Hastily I had her retrieve her button from the floor of the shed, along with a few shreds of dignity, and enquire as to whether Terence would like a latte on the terrace. Yes, that's it, I thought, tapping away confidently. Get to know him first, Lucinda.

'Well, I dunno, like,' stammered Terence, twisting his hat nervously in his hands. 'I've never 'ad one.'

'Surely they serve them at Harvey Nichols?' said Lucinda, a trifle irritably. 'It's just a milky coffee. Come.' She called him crisply to heel and he fell in meekly as they adjourned to the terrace.

Without Consuela to help, though, Lucinda couldn't work the wretched machine, so they ended up with lemon barley water, which Terence gulped down in one go, making a rather common 'Ahh ...' noise as he drained the glass, wiping his mouth with the back of his hand. Golly, a very rough hand, thought Lucinda nervously. Didn't he use an emollient?

'You were thirsty, Terence,' she purred. She was sitting alongside him in a steamer chair.

'Terry,' he grinned, stifling a burp. 'Only me mam calls me Terence.'

'Is that right, Terence?' Lucinda said distractedly, her eyes narrowing into the distance, her mind suddenly on other things. Justin Reynolds, for instance; the neighbouring artist, who even now was up in his studio again, looking down at her from the top-floor window. She shivered. But something stirred deep within her. Writhed, almost. Was it her fallopian tubes? What exactly were her fallopian tubes?

Terence was easing back in his chair a mite too casually now, Lucinda thought. Any minute now he'd swing a leg over the arm and scratch his armpit like an ape. She felt rather relieved she hadn't let his tongue loose in her throat, or his hands on her silk undies. The dear boy was beginning to get on her nerves. She turned on him a dazzling smile.

'My husband called, Terence, from New York. Asked how his water feature was coming along. Any progress?'

'Oh aye.' Terence got stammering to his feet. ''E asked me to plant it out for 'im. Only, I don't rightly know if 'e means with bog plants, or aquatic.'

'Whatever,' she purred, eyes back on the studio window. But it was empty. Justin had gone.

She felt an odd little pang of disappointment, again somewhere rather agricultural.

'Aquatic? You think?' Terence asked anxiously, hovering over her.

'Perfect,' she said dismissively.

Heavens. She sat up. Was that her garden gate opening? Down there, in the wall? Her heart pounding, she watched as Justin Reynolds emerged, framed in the gateway. Tall and chiselled, his arty chestnut curls blew in the breeze. He paused for effect, before making his way up the garden towards them.

'See, I'm not an aquatic lover, meself,' Terence was saying. 'It's the devil's own job to keep the mildew off 'em, whereas bog plants—'

'Fine, bog it is. Go now, Terence,' she breathed as Justin approached.

'—are more flexible, like. You know where you are wiv bog—'

'Yes, bog. *Bog!*' hissed Lucinda, gripping the chair arms and going pink in the face.

Justin stopped short, embarrassed. 'Have I . . . called at an inconvenient moment? Do you need to avail yourself . . . of facilities?'

Lucinda stared at him, horrified. 'No. No, of course not!'

She got up, and turned smartly to her gardener: 'Terence, just piss off, will you?' she hissed, then back to Justin, patting her hair and trying to collect herself.

'I'm sorry to barge in like this,' he murmured, looking deep into her eyes, 'but I'm having an exhibition at the Le Touche Gallery on Friday, and I wondered if you and your husband—'

'We'd love to,' she broke in happily. 'At least, I would. My husband's away. All week, in fact.'

'Is he indeed!' said Justin huskily, his dark eyes smouldering. Lucinda basked in his warm gaze, feeling the heat penetrate her very bones.

'I've got a stiffy for you,' he murmured.

'A – what!' she gasped, as he pushed a stiff, formal invitation into her hands. 'Oh! Oh, a – a – gosh. How lovely, yes!'

'Blimey, who's Justin? I thought she was getting her rocks off with Terence?'

I swung around to find David peering over my shoulder.

'David!' I stood up quickly, knocking my chair over in my haste. 'You startled me.' I scrambled to pick it up.

'Could have sworn you told me it was Terence the gardener she was after.' He grinned. 'Now that she's sussed her husband's such a rat.'

'Yes, yes, it was,' I flustered, fumbling for the switch to turn off the screen. 'Is, I mean.'

'But now she's got her eyes on someone else?'

In my haste I pulled out the socket. Damn, it might not save now. Probably just as well. I turned, pink-faced.

'Um, no. No, not really. Are you – you know – ready?'

'All present and correct.' David smiled, straightening up and clicking his heels together, which he did occasionally. It slightly drove me mad, but then he had been in the Blues and Royals. 'And ready to drive the O'Harran contingent to Tintagel Castle.' He offered me his arm and grinned. 'Shall we?'

I beamed back, took it and, with my heart pounding mightily, sailed out of the summer house beside him, and up the lawn to the house.

chapter eighteen

Flora's words were worse than prophetic. Horribly accurate, in fact. We finally crawled through the castle walls – having sat in a two-mile queue in order to gain entry – and emerged from our metal box in the car park, gasping with suffocation and dripping with sweat, at half past one. Flora crowed but got short shrift from David and me, because, by now, we'd both decided that this trip was going to be a success if it bloody killed us. Paying no heed, therefore, to her gasps of protest and her entreaty to 'lie down in the shade just for ten minutes, *please,*' we mopped our brows, paused only to glug down some warm Evian water from the boot of the car, and set off on our sightseeing tour.

As we paid for our tickets at the little kiosk at the bottom of the hill on which the castle sat, I gazed around, marvelling at the spectacular coastline, the gulls circling and cawing in the bright blue sky, the waves crashing against the rocks below. It was all rather majestic and suddenly I felt a bit more jaunty and optimistic.

I grinned at Flora. 'This isn't so bad, is it?'

She scowled wordlessly back.

'All right, my party?' called David, who'd gone ahead to another booth to secure the guide books.

'Fine!' I smiled, marshalling Flora onward.

The jaunty optimistic feeling was short lived, however, as it soon became glaringly apparent that if this castle was to be viewed properly, it could only be done so by mounting the five hundred granite steps that led to the ruin itself.

As we embarked on the first hundred, falling in behind David who had a camera slung around his neck and was looking about, smiling appreciatively and bounding up the steps like a gazelle, Flora muttered in my ear, 'I've seen it before. I remember now.'

I stopped in my tracks, peering ahead into the sun. 'D'you know, I think you're right. Looks awfully familiar. I think we came with Mum, when you were little.'

'We did, on a cooler day,' agreed my daughter bitterly.

David turned back, a few steps ahead. 'Come on you two, what are you belly-aching about now?'

'We've been here before,' called Flora, before I could stop her.

'Have you? You didn't say?' David regarded me with surprise.

'Um, no. I didn't realise till we got here. Forgot the name of the place.'

He laughed. 'Oh really, darling. There aren't that many ruined Norman castles in North Cornwall, surely?'

'Er, no. I suppose not.'

'Well, I wish you'd said,' he added a trifle petulantly. 'We needn't have bothered.'

'No, but you haven't seen it, so come on.' I walked quickly past him, gazing brightly at the piles of rubble and stone where the walls must once have been. 'Looks terrific.'

And so it would have been in Arthurian days, perched as it was right up on the highest cliff top, looking out imperiously across the sapphire sea, lord of all it surveyed, daring anyone to come close, let alone threaten to invade. Now, its proud fundaments had crumbled and only its shell remained, but it was still possible to cast one's mind back a few hundred years and imagine the terrified French foot soldiers scrambling up this steep slope, heads down, roared on by their commanders from the boats, and simultaneously being felled by arrows that came winging over the battlements from the fearless Brits, and collapsing in a heap – rather as Flora was doing now – as they struggled but failed to reach the first set of ramparts.

'Drink!' moaned my daughter in a very fearful, unBritish fashion. 'Now!' But David was soldiering on ahead of us and I lugged her bodily back to her feet.

'No, darling, come on, we've only just started,' I insisted. 'Make an effort.'

She grumbled hotly but complied, albeit hanging on to my arm, and we toiled onwards and upwards under the boiling sun, me practically carrying her. And neither were we alone, I couldn't help noticing. The place was crawling with other pilgrims who, unaccountably, had also deemed this the perfect day, at thirty degrees in the shade, to climb a one in four gradient, and all, it seemed, much happier about it – and ergo much fitter – than we were.

Half an hour later, when we'd got another hundred-odd steps under our belts and reached the second set of ramparts – where, happily, the castle shop was conveniently placed – I buckled pathetically beside Flora on the grass.

'Not sure I can go much further, David,' I gasped, as Flora emitted a death rattle beside me. 'Why don't you go on and we'll wait for you down here?' I looked up at him pleadingly, flat on my back in the daisies.

His face was bright red against the blue sky, and he was panting with exertion and mopping his brow. The next stage was another three hundred steps away and a coronary looked imminent, but I could tell he didn't want to be beaten.

'I might just have a little look at the turrets,' he panted, clutching his sides and narrowing his eyes up the hill. 'Seems crazy not to, while we're here.'

'Crazy,' I gasped.

'But you wait here. Catch your breath.'

We did just that, arms and legs splayed out like

starfish on the grass, whilst David trudged on. I knew I should ask Flora to put more sun cream on her face, but I couldn't be bothered to sit up and fiddle around in my handbag getting it for her.

'Two more minutes,' I groaned, 'then I'll get us some water from the shop. I promise.'

'Now,' she moaned. 'Please, Mum, I'm dying.'

My temples were beginning to throb rather ominously, and I had a nasty suspicion I might be on the brink of a thumping headache. I shut my eyes tentatively. Ah yes, something up there was definitely beginning to bite; a paracetamol was crucial. I sat up slowly, scraping myself gingerly off the grass, knowing any sudden movement was fatal. Pausing only to bully Flora into the shade, I tottered off into the shop.

Naturally it was heaving, and naturally there was no air conditioning, but I forced my way singlemindedly through the throng. As I was paying for the water and simultaneously popping down a handful of paracetamol from my bag, I spotted Theo's wife, Helena, just to the left of me by the till. She was fingering National Trust tea towels in a rather desultory fashion, and had a small child in tow, tugging at the hem of her skirt and whinging. I wasn't in the mood for idle chit-chat and wondered if I could possibly get away without her seeing me, but our eyes collided at the same time.

'Hi,' I beamed, overcompensating in case she'd seen me hesitate. Taking a second to register, she smiled rather bleakly back.

329

'Oh, hi, Annie.'

I pocketed my change and moved across. 'Not here doing sightseeing duty alone, surely?'

'Oh no, Theo's around somewhere; he's got Rollo with him. But I wish he'd hurry up, I'm dying to go home. It's far too hot for this one.' She glanced down at her toddler, then around for Theo, despairingly.

'I know, I've got Flora complaining like mad outside.'

'Well, at least you got her to come along. I couldn't persuade the older ones. Not that they ever do much that I ask them, anyway,' she added bitterly.

I glanced at her, noticing the fretted lines on her pale forehead and around her mouth. It couldn't be easy taking on a fractured family and having older step-sons to contend with as well as young children of one's own, I thought, all with very different demands. She looked worn out with effort.

'I suppose they are rather beyond the sightseeing stage,' I said consolingly.

'They're beyond anything, except nicking cigarettes from my bag and helping themselves to beer from the fridge,' she snapped.

I followed her eyes pretending to help her look and remembered how pretty she'd been, four or five summers ago when I'd first met her. I recalled Theo, his arm protectively around her shoulders, proudly showing off his new wife with her mane of blond hair at the Commodore's drinks party at the sailing club, the older model having been traded in. But the older model was no has-been, and had graced the pages of *Vogue* in her time; she was a rather lovely arty lady called Tilda, who painted beautiful water-colours, and whom I'd got on well with on the odd occasions we'd met. I wondered what had happened to her and made a mental note to ask Clare.

I glanced back at wife number two. Petulance had spoiled her face, and I wondered if either, or both, of them regretted it? Regretted getting married. Wished they'd let their affair go by as a quick, lustful bit of nonsense, with Theo going back to his wife and Helena marrying someone younger. Theo could be sitting on his boat now, with Tilda beside him, sipping Pimm's in the sunshine, whilst their teenage boys, back from boarding school and requiring no parental supervision, windsurfed and water-skied around them, instead of which he was pushing a buggy around a hot castle, and explaining archery skills to a bored and squirming three-year-old.

'Bloody man, where is he? It's like an oven in here!'

I couldn't help remembering how madly, blindly in love with him she'd been that first time I'd met her, when she was still his production assistant; how she'd gazed raptly into the theatrical impresario's eyes, hanging on to his every word. Now he was a 'bloody man'.

'At least we're off to Corsica tomorrow,' she said with a sigh. 'No doubt it'll be baking, but at least we'll have a pool.'

331

'You're off tomorrow?' I turned to her. 'I thought you usually did three weeks here?'

'We do normally, but this year I put my foot down. I wanted a hot holiday as well, because as you know, it usually rains here. Little did I know we were in for a sodding heat wave.'

Suddenly I felt a bit alarmed. God, if they were off tomorrow . . .

'There he is,' I said suddenly, spotting Theo's greying head right over the other side of the shop by the postcards, a changing bag over one shoulder, buggy with sleeping child in the other hand. An idea occurred to me.

'Tell you what, Helena, if you take this bottle of water out to Flora and find some shade, I'll push across and tell him you're waiting for him.'

'Oh, would you, Annie? Thanks. I'm folding up in here, and I don't particularly want to shove through this throng with Millie.'

She took my water bottle and, picking up her daughter, moved gratefully away towards the door. I put my head down and squirmed through the multitude, all avidly poring over clotted cream, tablecloths, mugs, key rings and assorted pixie memorabilia, and finally made it to Theo, who was flicking wearily through the postcards.

'Hi, Theo.'

He looked up. 'Oh, hello, Annie.' He glanced around warily for his wife, not wanting to be caught talking to another woman. 'You've been press-ganged into this wretched trip too, have you?'

'Well, it was David's idea, but we've rather enjoyed it,' I lied loyally.

'Ah, the good doctor. Yes, well, it's all highly educational, according to Helena. She's been shoving flash-cards under the poor little buggers' noses as we hustle them around in the heat. Seem to remember we let the last brood grow up rather more casually. Just let them get on with it,' he said wistfully. 'Prior to packing them off to boarding school, of course. And apparently I'm not going to get away with that, either. I've got the little darlings at home until they're at least eighteen,' he finished gloomily.

'You'll love it,' I assured him. 'They'll brighten up your old age.'

He grinned. 'Cheeky. But actually I do like them as teenagers, they're good fun. It's this wretched toddler stage that's such a grind, and anyone who says otherwise is lying.'

'At least you still get your older boys to come on holiday with you,' I tried to console him.

'Only because I bloody pay,' he said bitterly.

'So they're both coming with you to Corsica? Helena said you were off tomorrow.'

'Oh no, they'd much rather be here, sailing, as I would, but apparently that's all over for me this year. No, I've got to sit around some poncy hotel pool in Corsica and teach Rollo to swim while the boys stay on another week here with the Fields and sail the Laser. My bloody boat,' he growled. 'They'll probably trash it. Anyway, I must go and pay for these. No doubt you came over to tell me The Power And The Glory is tapping her foot outside, waiting for me?' He made to move on.

'Yes, she is, but the thing is, Theo, I wanted to talk to you about the other night.'

'The other night? Oh, you mean with Clare.' His already ruddy face coloured up quickly. He scratched the back of his neck, looking awkward. 'Yes, that was badly done. Got it in the neck for ages afterwards, as you can imagine.'

'Yes, but the thing is, Theo, Clare can't remember—'

'Oh, you're *here*!' Flora barged in between us. 'I thought you were just getting water, didn't realise you were buying up half the shop. David's ready to go.'

'Yes, all right, darling. Here, get these for me, would you?' I snatched a handful of cards and shoved them at her.

'Oh, Mum, the queue!'

'Go on.' I gave her a shove. She went off huffily. 'You see,' I went on quickly when she was out of earshot, 'she can't remember whether or not any-thing . . . you know . . .'

He frowned. 'What?'

'Well – whether or not you did it,' I said desperately.

He blinked. Looked shocked. 'Well, bugger me. That memorable, am I?'

'So you did? Oh God, Theo, I'd rather hoped—'

'Ah. Chattering. I told you, Helena, if you get Annie to drag anyone away, you're sunk.'

David stuck his head between us, grinning. Helena, beside him, looked mutinous.

'You've been so long, Millie wants the potty again,' she seethed.

'Oh, sorry, love,' said Theo, contrite. 'Shall I—'

'No, I'll do it, just give me the sodding wipes.' She snatched the changing bag from his shoulder and made for the Ladies. 'Meet me at the car, OK?'

'OK, OK,' he muttered meekly.

'Perhaps we should get some postcards,' mused David, fingering the rack. 'Send one to Gertrude?'

'Yes, good idea.' I blithely grabbed another handful and thrust them at him as Theo attempted to push the buggy out through the scrum to the door. 'You line up.' I pushed David towards the queue. 'I just want to show Theo something.'

'Theo!' I lunged after him and grabbed his arm. 'Theo, look at this.' I swung him round and seized the first thing that came to hand.

He frowned. 'Must I? A willie-warmer with a Cornish pixie on it? To wear with my incontinence pants perhaps?'

I dropped it hastily. 'But, Theo, did you really?' I hissed. 'Clare was so pissed she can't remember!'

'And so was I, if you must know,' he said huffily. 'Otherwise I'd never have let that lardy old she-devil—' He stopped. Cleared his throat. 'Sorry,' he mumbled. 'No, we didn't as a matter of fact. We had a bit of a fumble, and then she tried to undo my flies and threw up all over my trousers.'

'Oh!'

'Not the most seductive come-on I've ever had, and funnily enough I resisted the temptation to take it any further. I frogmarched her home across the dunes and dumped her in her back garden. Didn't particularly want to bang on the door and face Michael.'

'Which is where she passed out.'

'Lucky her. I went home to Helena, who'd put the babies to bed but not the sniggering teenagers, who rolled about clutching their sides, having a great laugh at Dad being so pissed he'd been sick down his strides.'

'Ah.'

'Well, I could hardly say it was Clare's puke, could I? What would she have been doing in such close proximity to my groin? I then spent an attractive ten minutes scraping it off in the garden and washing the trousers at the sink because the bloody washing machine's on the blink, with Helena standing over me, enjoying every minute of it. So no, I didn't get my leg over, Annie. And neither would I have tried, actually. She was slaughtered.'

'She doesn't drink,' I sighed.

'Well, now we know why,' he snapped. 'Now, if you'll excuse me, I've got an irate wife pacing the car park, and, as you can see, I'm in enough poo this holiday as it is.' He stomped off.

Well, that was something, I reflected, biting my thumbnail as I pushed my way out of the shop. Clare would be hugely relieved.

Outside, David was waiting, hands in pockets jingling change, clearly determined not to appear irritated.

'What was so urgent you had to drag Theo away like that?'

'Oh, um, nothing really,' I muttered. 'He wanted . . . some advice. About schools. For his little boy.'

'Ah. And you, as the mother of a twelve-year-old girl, are the perfect person to ask, eh? Come on then. Flora, all set?'

Flora, looking less than set, moodily clutched her water bottle to her chest and trailed behind us as we trooped back down the steps to the car park. We drove home in silence.

The house was empty when we got back, although not locked of course, because Matt never bothered. This infuriated David as we walked straight in.

'I mean, anyone could wander in,' he said incredulously, standing in the middle of the sitting room and holding his arms out in wonder. 'Anyone!'

'Hardly likely though, is it?' I said wearily, sinking down exhausted into an armchair in the corner of the cool, darkened room. That was what I loved about this house: the cool mustiness within, contrasting with the glaring brightness without. It would be cosy, too, I imagined, in the winter, with a fire blazing in that huge old inglenook. 'I mean, let's face it, it's pretty remote,' I went on, 'and this is the country, for heaven's sake. Not thieving Notting Hill.' I leaned my head back and shut my eyes.

'Fine. No need to snap.'

I opened my eyes, surprised. 'I wasn't. I was just saying it's not exactly very accessible.'

'No, and not ideal either, is it, Annie? Not for six weeks, or however long you plan to be here.'

'What d'you mean?'

'Well, with that . . .' He waved his hand. '. . . character. Matt. I mean, it's all very well for a few days while you get yourself sorted out, but any longer is absurd. Particularly when this place is stuffed full of pubs and hotels you could go to. I rang the Complete Angler this morning, and they've had a cancellation. Got a couple of very reasonable rooms. I booked them for you.'

'What!' I sat up.

'Only on the phone, no deposit or anything, but honestly, Annie, what does this arrangement look like? To Matt; to everyone? You staying here?'

'Oh, David, you're being ridiculous! Completely overreacting. And I can't believe you booked rooms without telling me. Why shouldn't I stay here? I like it, and Flora likes it, and the house is huge, for heaven's sake!'

'And creepy.' He shivered.

'It's not creepy! I don't know why you keep saying that. What have you got against this place, David?'

'Oh, never mind.' He sank gloomily into the armchair opposite me. Rubbed his forehead wearily. A silence ensued.

'Fine break this is turning out to be,' he muttered.

I stared at him. Don't say anything, Annie. Just . . . don't speak. At length he leaned forward and picked up a piece of paper by the phone on the low table between us.

'David, ring Hugo,' he read aloud. He glanced up quickly. 'Did you take this?'

'No,' I muttered, still cross. 'Must have been Matt. Who's Hugo, anyway? Wasn't that who you were speaking to this morning?'

I looked up suddenly. David had got very quickly to his feet. He looked rather pale and drained.

'Darling? Who is this Hugo?'

'Oh, he's . . . an old friend,' he murmured. 'I'll just go and ring him back.'

Ignoring the phone in front of us and digging his mobile out of his pocket, he disappeared into the dining room, shutting the door firmly behind him.

I sighed again and slumped back in my chair, leaning my head against the old leather. I shut my eyes. Well, my headache had abated, that was a relief, but everything else felt – so wrong. So tense, somehow. Not how I'd planned this bit of the holiday at all. I stayed like that for a few minutes, then, after a while, my eyes flitted to the telephone. I should ring Clare, of course. Give her the good news. Let her know she wasn't the mother of Theo's unborn child. I dialled her number but her mobile was turned off, and I didn't like to ring the farm in case she picked up in the kitchen and Mum was there too. I couldn't very well go into the no-shagging-but-lots-of-puke details with Mum sitting across the scrubbed pine table, pouring from the old brown teapot and eyeing her eldest beadily over a home-made scone. No, I'd ring later, I thought, putting it down. After the ten o'clock news, when I knew Mum went to bed.

Instead, I phoned Rosie. I suddenly had an urge to see her and Dan tonight, make a party of it. Have a jolly barbecue here in the garden with all the kids, whatever David had implied about wanting me to himself. I had an idea he'd perk up with a bit of company and a few drinks; we both would. Yes, and I could see Michael, too. Gauge whether he'd calmed down a bit, and hopefully report back positively to Clare when I rang her later.

'God, I'd love to, Annie,' Rosie said, 'but the thing is, we've said we'd go to Rick Stein's with the Hamiltons.'

'Lucky you. Who are the Hamiltons?'

'Friends of Michael's; they live down here. He's an estate agent, sweet, actually, and she's nice too. The five of us are going out. Michael's treat.'

'Golly,' I boggled. 'That's big of him. It's pricey.'

'I know, but he's in such a good mood.' She lowered her voice. 'Honestly, Annie, I've never seem him so chipper, and I can't tell you what a nice day we've had today.' She giggled guiltily. 'We all had a lie-in while the children watched telly, then we read the papers in the garden, declared an early drinks at eleven-thirty and went off to the pub. You know, that really pretty one at Port Gaverne. Then on the way back, we got fish and chips from the shop and ate it from the newspaper with *no napkins*! And, on top of that, we haven't been to the beach all day. In fact, that's not quite true, Dan and Michael have just taken the older ones down to Polzeath for a surf, but honestly, it's been so relaxing. I now get this place, whereas a couple of days ago, I didn't get it at all.'

'Because Clare insists on doing it so flat out,' I said ruefully. 'It is lovely, if you let it all drift over you. Don't let it become a mission.' I felt sad for her. For Clare. She could do it like that, if she tried. I hesitated. No, all right. Not without napkins.

'Well, maybe tomorrow night, Rosie. Why don't you all come over at about seven? Bring some booze and I'll get some sausages and chicken legs and we'll — Oh! Darling? What's wrong?'

I broke off to stare at David who'd emerged from the dining room. He looked as white as the walls behind him. His fists, at his sides, were clenched.

'They're going to do it,' he said incredulously, oblivious of the fact that I was on the telephone. His lips were thin and bloodless and his eyes slid past me, over my shoulder. 'They're actually going through with it.'

341

'What? Going through with what?' I said, bewildered.

'They're going to sue me for professional misconduct. And not only that . . .' He struggled for composure. His eyes found mine. 'They're suing me for manslaughter, too. Manslaughter, Annie!'

I stared at him aghast, as to my horror he put his hands over his face, sank down into a chair, and wept.

chapter nineteen

'I'll ring you back,' I muttered to Rosie.

'Manslaughter!' she gasped, agog. 'But who — Why—'

Brutally I cut her off, dropping the phone and flying over to David's side. I knelt beside him, cradling his head in my arms, horrified. 'David, don't! What's happened, why—'

'They're suing me, Annie.' He jerked up suddenly, his face wet. 'The wife, the family of the man I told you about. The one who died on my surgery steps.'

'Yes but . . .' I licked my lips, my mind whirring frantically. 'I thought that had all blown over. I thought—'

'Obviously not!'

'But, David, it wasn't your fault! And – and so what if they sue? So what? It was just a misdiagnosis.'

'Which is medical negligence.' He got to his feet abruptly, wiping his face savagely with the back of his hand, pacing around the room. 'And it's quite possible I'll never be able to practise again, and just remotely possible I might go to prison.'

I stared at him, horrorstruck. My jaw dropped as I knelt there on the floor.

'Oh, don't be ridiculous,' I spluttered finally. 'That's absurd! You're overreacting, David. They don't send doctors to prison for making a mistake, for missing something. And you said yourself this chap was always crying wolf, always in your surgery complaining about something or other—'

He swung around, eyes burning. 'Yes, and then he fucking died!'

I swallowed. 'Well, I know. I know, but – but with his track record, being a hypochondriac and all that, how were you to know which particular pain was real? He had a history of—'

'*I* have a history,' he interrupted, stabbing his chest viciously with his forefinger. He was over by the window now, staring at me with huge full eyes I didn't recognise. 'I am the one with the fucking history, Annie.'

I'd only ever heard him swear before once.

'What?'

'I have a history of misdiagnosis,' he said with a terrible crack in his voice. 'Remember last year, that woman with a lump on her neck, and I told her it was a harmless ganglion and it turned out to be malignant?'

'Yes, but you said anyone could have made that mistake. They look so similar!'

'But I should have had it looked at. Should have

had a biopsy done. And then last winter, the boy who got septicaemia – and recovered, thank God, but only after a month in hospital – and all because I hadn't got to his wound in time, hadn't checked if he'd had a tetanus injection. And then back in January, the old lady in Battersea who died of pneumonia, who'd refused to come and see me, said she was fine even though when she'd been in previously I'd detected something on her chest—'

'But she wouldn't come in! You said you asked her, and she wouldn't—'

'Yes, but I should have gone to her, shouldn't I? Paid her a house call, which was what she wanted, but I said I was too busy. She was eighty-two, for Christ's sake, and with a psychiatric history too. I should have known she was ill and shielding it. Shouldn't just have taken her word for it, I'm the bloody doctor! And her daughter . . .' He shuddered as he remembered. Shook his head. 'Oh God, her daughter, at the hospital, shaking with emotion—' He broke off.

My throat felt dry and constricted. 'That wasn't your fault,' I repeated. 'She said she felt better. None of those cases were your fault!'

'Hugo only just managed to keep me out of court that time,' he said, turning his back on me and raking a despairing hand through his hair. He gazed out to sea. 'Says he won't be able to do that for me this time.'

'Who's Hugo?' I whispered.

'My solicitor. And an old friend.' He was silent a moment, his back to me. Then he turned. 'I'm not up to it, Annie. Never have been.'

I stared, horrified. His face was pale but composed. There was a terrible clenched calmness about him. I got up from the floor and went to him; I shook his arm.

'That's nonsense, David. You know it is. You're a wonderful doctor, everyone says so!'

He gave a tight smile. 'You say so. I say so, occasionally. But no. Not everyone says so. In fact an awful lot of people say it's not so. Ask Gertrude.'

'Gertrude?' I was stunned.

He turned away from me. Looked out to the horizon again. 'I was so desperate to be a doctor, Annie,' he said softly. 'So desperate. Like my father, a great surgeon. Well, it was clear early on I could never be that, didn't have the brain power, but – well, OK, like my uncle then. Gertrude's husband, Hugh. An excellent general practitioner. So I trained. And failed my exams. And trained again and failed, but eventually . . . eventually I got there. Got my bits of paper. Got those precious letters before my name, changed the boring Mr for something more sonorous. Something with a bit more gravitas.' He put a hand to his brow. Stretched it across and rubbed his temples wearily. 'But you know, Annie, the awful thing was, I always knew. Knew I was a fraud.'

'No!'

'No, OK, not a fraud,' he said quietly, 'but I knew I couldn't cut the mustard. Knew I'd be terrified when it came to actually doing it.'

'But – but Hugh took you on. You were fine! And he must have trusted you to work with you.'

'Well, he'd brought me up from the age of eight,' he said bitterly. 'He was like a father to me. Who wouldn't do that for their nephew? Let them into the family business in Sloane Street? What an opportunity. Also . . .' He wrestled with something. 'I always felt that he liked that arrangement. Him looking over me. It meant he could watch me, you see. Keep me safe. Keep an eye on me. But when I'd been with him a year or two, I saw the worry in his eyes.' He swallowed. Fixed his gaze on a small red boat out at sea. 'Before he died, when he was really quite ill – and knew it – he called me into his room next door. Asked me if I was sure I was in the right profession. If I wouldn't prefer research or something. And then when he died, I had to persuade Gertrude to let me take over the practice.'

'She didn't want you to?' I breathed.

'She did, but she was worried too. Hugh had told her about his misgivings. But when she saw I was so utterly determined to carry on, she urged me to find a senior partner to work with. Someone like Hugh. And I knew she meant a sounding board, someone I could nip next door to, discuss a tricky diagnosis with, but I didn't. I was too proud. I took on Kim. Who was over here on a year's sabbatical.'

'But Kim was good. You said so!'

'Yes, but young. And only temporary. A very young Aussie who was going back home in time, and that suited me because . . . well, because I wanted to be the elder statesman to her. Like Hugh had been to me. But you know, in time, even Kim realised I was missing things. Five years younger than me,' he said bitterly. 'But she knew. She was too loyal to say, but before she went back, she kept hinting that if she wasn't sure about something, she sent patients straight round to Harley Street for a second opinion – which she didn't much, incidentally. Kept saying it. Kept looking me in the eye and saying it. Trying to tell me something.'

'Which is what you do a lot,' I whispered. My hair felt damp on the back of my neck. 'You *do* do that.'

'Yes. I do. Pretending to the world that it's because I'm a cautious, conscientious chap. But actually . . . covering my back. And it's worked. Mostly. I've muddled through. Because you see' – he turned back and looked at me beseechingly – 'I'm not a bad doctor, Annie. I'm just – not a very good one.'

I put my arm around his neck, holding him close. 'Oh my darling.'

He rested his head on my shoulder and, to my distress, sobbed again. I held on, very tight. After a while, he recovered. Composed himself.

'Sorry,' he muttered, turning away. He tugged a hanky from his pocket and blew his nose noisily. Moved over to the fireplace. He placed his feet apart and shoved his hands in his pockets. Gazed into the grate. 'Can't think what's come over me. Blubbing like a baby.'

'Don't be silly, you need a good cry,' I said staunchly. 'Golly, we all need a good cry sometimes. I know I do.'

He didn't seem to hear me, though. Seemed miles away. Staring into the empty fireplace. Finally he took a deep breath, and let it out slowly, shakily. It seemed to me his whole body shuddered.

'Anyway,' he said quietly, 'Hugo's got all sorts of ideas up his sleeve. He's had years of experience with this sort of thing.'

'Because everyone makes mistakes,' I said firmly. 'Of course they do.'

'Yes, everyone makes mistakes. But it's a bit more serious when you're a doctor. If you make a mistake, Annie, if you write a terrible chapter, your book isn't published. If Michael makes a mistake, the share prices plummet; if Clare makes a mistake, an important client gets irate. I make a mistake, and . . . well.'

I crossed the room and put my arms around him from behind. Laid my head on his back and squeezed hard.

'It's all going to be fine,' I said firmly. 'You'll see. Hugo will find a way. That's what these expensive lawyers are for.'

'Yes, and so I wriggle again. And meanwhile there's a wife with no husband, and three children with no father.'

I froze. Gazed into his pink shirt, at a loss to know what to say. We were quiet for a moment.

'I should go,' he said suddenly. I felt his back muscles tense. 'Hugo said he'd see me at his office tomorrow. Said he'd run through some things with me.' He turned.

'Go in the morning,' I urged. 'Early. Not now. You're too upset to drive now, David. Sleep on it and go tomorrow.'

'No, I—'

'Please, darling, don't go now.'

In the event, I persuaded him to stay. That night, in bed, he held me very close.

'I don't know what I'd do without you, Annie,' he said into my shoulder. 'Really don't know. I think I'd go to pieces.'

'Nonsense.' I laughed softly, stroking the back of his neck.

'I need you, Annie. I really do.'

'And I need you too,' I murmured, but there was a desperation in his voice that unnerved me.

'I want to make love to you tonight. Please.'

'Of course. I do too,' I assured him, wishing he hadn't said please.

His love-making was intense, desperate even, with a ferocity about it which alarmed me. I tried to come up with some kind of reciprocity of scale, gripping him tightly, trying not to gasp in pain as he pinned my arms to the bed, but found after a while that he was almost oblivious of me anyway. He was in a world of his own, or trying to be. Losing himself in me. All the bedclothes were on the floor as he wrapped himself around me, engulfing me, possessing me, making noises that sounded almost primeval. I was terrified Flora, next door, or even Matt upstairs would hear.

Eventually, he flopped round on his back, sated; exhausted; his body heaving. I lay quietly beside him. I was worried that he'd lie awake for hours, but after a moment, I saw him lean across to the bedside table and take a pill. Something else I'd never seen. He lay back without a word, and after a while, I heard deep, rhythmic breathing as he sank into a heavy sleep.

I, meanwhile, for the second night in succession, lay awake for hours, eyes wide and raw in the darkness, listening to the waves lapping gently in the creek and the wind rustling the treetops. My mind was racing. So much I didn't know. I didn't know Hugo had had to keep him out of court. I hadn't even heard of Hugo. I didn't know he'd repeatedly failed exams – not that it mattered a jot – but why hadn't he told me? In conversation? Just as I'd told him I was hopeless at school? The old lady in Battersea I had known about; I remembered his white face as he'd come home from work one day, told me she'd died and that it could have been prevented if he'd got her to hospital, acted sooner. I didn't know of Gertrude's misgivings. Of course I didn't, she was loyal, and anyway, he'd been a doctor for years before he met

me, why would it come up? Round and round went
my mind, my thought processes spinning, until,
eventually, Morpheus rescued me, and I fell into a
fitful sleep.

The following morning, I awoke to find the bed
empty beside me. David had gone. On the duvet was
a note, folded in half. I snatched it up.

> My darling,
>   I'm so sorry for all the histrionics last night.
> You were right, things do look better in the
> morning. I'm sure all will be well. I love you.
>   David

I sighed and lay back on my pillows for a moment.
Then, with a mammoth effort, swung my legs
around and pulled on my dressing gown. I put the
note in my pocket and went to the bathroom. When
I'd brushed my teeth, I leaned the heels of my hands
heavily on the basin, gazing at my reflection in the
mirror. My eyes looked pinched and tight through
lack of sleep, and my long dark curls flat and lank. I
ran a hand through them listlessly. Raised my chin.

'All will be well,' I murmured, repeating the line in
David's note. 'All . . .' I assured myself, 'will be well.'
My dark eyes gazed back, slightly wider, but with no
real conviction.

The house was full of sleep as I crept downstairs.
Certainly Flora's door was shut as I passed, and Tod
wasn't around. I made myself a cup of coffee, and

leaned back against the yellow Formica work-top, cradling my mug, and wondering what to do with myself. My eyes unaccountably filled with tears. Still tired, I reasoned, swallowing hard. Lack of sleep. What I needed was to work. Needed the single-minded focus that writing afforded, so that whilst my body took refuge in the discipline of tapping a keyboard, my mind took refuge in someone else's fictitious life. I remembered Adam asking me once why I wrote, as I scribbled away furiously in an exercise book, lying on our bed in London. I'd replied, without thinking, that it had always been a safe place to go. I'd glanced up and caught the surprise in his eyes. The guilt. It pained me now to think that I was going to the summer house for the same reason. I didn't want to be happy only in dreams. I wanted still the bright anticipation of yesterday. But, for the moment, it had gone.

I made a fresh cup of coffee and took it out into the garden. As I passed the study window, I saw that Matt, head down, had had the same idea. His window was open and, as I went by, he glanced up.

'Everything OK?'

Not 'morning', or 'hi', or even just a grunt to indicate he'd registered but was busy, but: 'Everything OK?' Quietly. Solicitously. In that soft, melodious accent.

I nodded, gave a weak smile, and passed on.

Tears were welling again, and I couldn't speak. Mustn't speak. Mustn't even think. He would, of course, have noticed that something was wrong last night. Would have noticed when he and Tod returned from the beach. Glancing into the sitting room, he'd tactfully ushered Tod and Flora out into the garden to eat the pasties they'd bought on the way home, claiming food always tasted better in the fresh air, even if it was a bit windy. And all the while David and I had sat huddled inside, talking in tense whispers, me clutching his hands, trying to soothe him, trying to shake some confidence into him and banish the demons. Matt would have noticed, too, the repeated calls back and forth to Hugo, the dining-room door opening and shutting, and the fact that neither of us had any supper and went early to bed. Nice of him to shield Flora for me, I thought. To feed her, and take her off later with Tod to look for cormorants on the cliffs with binoculars.

I shut the summer-house door behind me and sat down. As I switched on my computer a sea of words filled the screen, but I stared, almost unseeing, feeling sick inside for poor David, but also so horribly, horribly confused.

'Everything OK?'

He could have chosen tactfully to ignore me, but instead the blue eyes had flashed up, soft, concerned, over his glasses. I raised my own eyes to the ceiling, knowing they were full and mustn't spill over. Swallowing hard, I pulled myself together. Right. Now. Lucinda. My heroine. I had to get a move on with this wretched book, or my editor would be wondering what the hell was going on. And Lucinda hadn't even got her kit off yet. She was still wandering around her empty house, Justin's invitation clutched to her heaving bosom, eyes shining, her heart full. Oh no, I thought, rereading the last paragraph in panic, that wouldn't do at all! I quickly erased a few lines. She wasn't supposed to fall in love, for heaven's sake, not with Justin Reynolds! That way madness lay. I tapped away furiously.

Lucinda stalked into the drawing room and cast the invitation ruthlessly aside, pushing it behind a stack of similarly embossed cards on the mantelpiece. She regarded herself sternly in the mirror above it. Certainly her husband's faithlessness had to be avenged, certainly a dalliance of some sort was in order, but allowing another man into her heart could only lead to more pain. Terence, on the other hand, was an entirely different proposition. Her heart would slumber peacefully whilst her body did all the work. Even now she could hear his heavy tread in the kitchen as he came to collect the dogs for their afternoon walk. She flew to intercept him. Flashing him a winning smile, she dangled the tartan leads from her finger.

'Have a nice walk, Terence,' she purred.

'Aye, I will,' he said, surprised by her change of mood. He took the leads. 'Thanks.'

'And I wondered, would you like to do something tonight? Only my husband's still away and I thought . . . we could go out.'

'Aye, we could.' He brightened. 'We could get a bite to eat, like. That'd be grand.'

He rubbed the doorframe feverishly with his fingertip, eyeing her speculatively. Lucinda fought her instinct to remove his grubby hand from her paintwork, and pinned on a smile instead.

'Yes, that would be . . . grand.'

Later that evening, in a shimmering, low-cut Ungaro gown, she swept into the eatery on his arm.

''Ave you ever been to an 'Arvester before?' he enquired, proudly pulling her chair out for her.

'No, never.'

'Only I wouldn't want you to be spotted, like.'

Lucinda gazed around at the simple polyester-clad folk, who appeared to be helping themselves at something called a salad bar.

'I don't think there's any danger of that,' she murmured.

The evening grew even more novel as Lucinda was encouraged to wander around, join queues and use tongs. As she returned to her seat to toy listlessly with a lettuce leaf, Terence sat down opposite her, aghast.

'Is that all you want, lass?'

Lucinda blinked at the tottering pagoda of sausage, beans, chips, eggs, beans and more beans on Terence's plate.

'By 'eck, you can 'ave as much as you like! It's all the same price.'

'Thank you, Terence. This is sufficient.'

As she sipped her mineral water, she wondered nervously what such a colossal helping of fibre would do to his performance later? Would the duvet literally hover?

As it transpired however, her fears were groundless. Once she'd led him to the suite of her choice at the Savoy and shut the door firmly behind them, although unnerved that Terence insisted on removing her Ungaro gown over her head – 'Arms up, luv!' – instead of letting it drop gracefully to the floor, when he dropped his trousers all was forgiven.

He advanced towards her, staggeringly priapic, and spectacularly hirsute, too, Lucinda thought, marvelling. He turned for a moment to toss his socks on a chair and Lucinda's eyes popped in astonishment. Why, even his backside bristled, like Neanderthal man! Playfully she reached out and grasped his furry—

'Mum!'

I jumped, hands flying, and knocked my coffee cup for six.

'Shit!'

Desperately mopping the keyboard with the bottom of my T-shirt, I turned to find Flora's astonished face in the doorway behind me. I shielded the screen, at the same time trying frantically to wipe up.

'What?' I yelled.

'Clare's on the phone, that's all. Why are you so jumpy?'

'I'm not!' I bellowed. 'I'm just trying to work, that's all. Can't anyone leave me in peace just for five minutes? God, *cons*tant interruption!'

'Sor*ry*,' she said sarcastically, letting the door slam. Then 'Stressy or what?' I heard as she went up the garden path.

I hesitated for a moment, then flicked off the computer and flew after her.

'Sorry, darling,' I panted as I caught up with her. 'I was just a bit – you know. Into it, that's all.'

She flashed me a smile. ''S all right. Thought maybe you were in the middle of a steamy sex scene or something.'

'Ha!' I attempted a hollow laugh. 'As if I'd know about that.'

'Well, I should jolly well hope you do,' she retorted as she wandered back in the direction of the garage to resume her table-tennis game with Tod. 'Or something's going badly wrong,' she called over her shoulder with a grin.

I watched her go, pausing for a moment on the back step to bite my thumbnail. It was getting a lot of

attention these days. Then I went through to the hall
and picked up the phone.

'Hello,' I said absently.

'Oh Annie, sorry. I know Flora said you were
working, but I just wondered . . . only she mentioned
you'd seen Theo at Tintagel and—'

'Oh, yes! No, you're fine, Clare. In the clear.'

'You mean—'

'I did talk to him, and no, you didn't sleep with
him. You did throw up over him, though.'

'I didn't!' she gasped, as I simultaneously heard a
small cough behind me. I swung around. Matt's door
was ajar. I cringed. Damn.

'You did,' I hissed, turning back, 'but listen, have
you spoken to Michael?'

'No, but I'm about to write to him. What d'you
think?' she asked anxiously. 'Thought I could – you
know – express myself better on paper. Grovel more.
Any tips?'

'Not really, but for heaven's sake be sure to mention that nothing went on between you and Theo.
Believe me, it'll make a big difference. Husbands are
funny about their wives' fidelity. For all Michael's
posturing about you being a pain in the tubes to live
with and it being the straw that broke the camel's
back, de-da, de-da, take it from me, this is all about
whether or not you bonked Theo Todd.'

There was a pause.

'You're getting awfully perceptive in your old age.'

'It's this writing lark.' I sighed. 'Makes me think

far too clearly. And, Clare, if you don't mind I'll ring you later for a chat, I was in the middle of it when you rang.'

'Sorry, yes, you go. We'll speak later. And Mum sends her love.'

As I put the phone down I could have kicked myself. Damn. I *could* have had a quick word with Mum, since she was clearly sitting close by, waiting to have the receiver passed on. It was just . . . if I didn't get back to Lucinda, I'd start thinking about my own life again, and that would be fatal. The phone rang again. I snatched it up, guilt making me irritated.

'Hello?' I barked. There was a pause.

'Oh, uh, can I speak with Matt, please?' It was a girl's voice. American. 'It's Louise.'

'Oh. Er, yes, just a minute.' Embarrassed, I went to Matt's door. Knocked, then pushed through. Empty. He'd obviously decided to vacate while I was on the phone. I went to the back door.

'Matt!' I yelled down the garden. No response. I went back to the phone.

'He doesn't seem to be about, can I take a message?'

'Yes, would you tell him I called, and have Tod please call his mom?'

'Have Tod call his mom. Mum. OK.'

'Only it's kind of complicated . . .' She hesitated.

'Oh! Oh no, it's OK, I know all about that,' I assured her quickly. 'About Tod not being with you, and being here instead.'

'You do?' She sounded surprised. 'Oh, OK. Well, Madeleine called a moment ago, and I told her he'd gone for a bike ride with my son, but that he'd call her right back, so . . .'

'Yes, no, I see. I'll pass that message on,' I assured her.

'Thank you.' She sounded relieved.

She sounded nice, too, I thought as I hung up. Louise. Matt's cousin, married to Tom the doctor. I wondered what the rest of the family was like. Parents; brothers and sisters. What sort of a house they all grew up in. And at a time when I should have been consumed with worry about my fiancé's career, I found myself wondering about her, too. Madeleine. I had a terrible urge to go into Matt's study and look for a picture. Rifle through the jacket hanging on the back of his chair and see if I could find an ancient family snap hidden in his wallet. Happily though, the moment passed and, turning on my heel, I went doggedly back to work.

chapter twenty

That evening, Flora and Tod were clamouring for a fishing trip and a campfire on the beach again. Matt and I exchanged the briefest of glances. Almost by tacit consent we'd avoided each other for most of the day, but now he was at the kitchen table reading the newspaper, and I was at the sink, washing up pans that seemed to have accumulated again. Tod and Flora were eating crisps on the back step.

'Come on, Dad, let's go down and get a fire going.'

'I don't think so, guys,' he said quietly, not looking up from his paper.

'No,' I muttered. 'Not tonight.'

Definitely not tonight, I thought as I scrubbed the living daylights out of a saucepan. Not a cosy beach barbecue. I didn't want to be alone with him under the stars, gazing into the embers when the children had gone to bed. Interesting that he should feel that way too.

'Oh Mum, come on, it was fun last time!'

'No, Flora, we'll eat here, at the house,' I said firmly.

'Well, let's at least have a barbecue out in the garden,' said Tod.

I busied myself in the sink. Didn't look at Matt.

'Sure,' he said lightly. 'We can do that. I'll go get some steaks.' He reached over my head to the shelf where his car keys hung on a hook. The sleeve of his jumper inadvertently brushed my hair. I carried on scrubbing as if my life depended on it.

In the event though, that plan seemed to strike the right chord. We sat, just outside the back door, plates on our laps, the children's music playing loudly through the open French windows, in a friendly, relaxed way, but without a hint of atmosphere. And then later on, I told myself, when the children had gone to bed, I'd give a big yawn, stand up and mutter something about having an early night, bid Matt a breezy goodnight, and skip up the stairs after them. Matt seemed equally keen to keep things light and convivial; he joked around with Flora and Tod as we let them cook for us, complaining we'd be dead soon if they didn't feed us. Finally, with a fanfare, the food arrived.

'I've got half a cow here,' I observed, picking up an enormous T-bone steak in two hands.

'No point lighting the thing for a few chipolatas and a potato like a bullet.'

'Ah. You've been to a few English barbecues then.'

He grinned and perched on the back step, balancing his plate on his knees. 'My cousin's husband, Tom, likes to look mean in the garden with prongs and meths. Hell of a nice guy, but boy, does he go to some lengths to produce a burnt chicken leg. I reckon I've been closer to salmonella in his back yard than anywhere else.'

'Tom who's married to Louise?' I asked, even though I knew. 'The one I spoke to earlier?'

'That's it.'

'She sounded nice.'

'She is.' He wiped his mouth with a finger. 'Known her for ever. Grew up with her in the same neighbourhood, just a couple of blocks away. Our moms are sisters. Real close.'

'And she married an Englishman?'

'She married an Englishman. Who'd gone out to the States to get a research fellowship. Louise was his lab technician. He took her back home along with his fellowship. Our loss, his gain. That was fifteen years ago. Now they have four kids, and a wonderful beach house right here on these cliffs, around the coast at Trebarwith. You'd love it.'

'Which is,' I said, glancing at Tod who was out of earshot, turning some peppers on the barbecue with Flora, 'where Tod is supposed to be now?'

'Exactly.'

'How much longer have you got him for then?'

'Just a couple more days. Louise is coming to get him on Thursday. He'll have a day with her boys, then back to Cambridge.'

'And Madeleine will be none the wiser?'

'Nope.' He stabbed a forkful of salad viciously.

'You'll miss him,' I said at length. 'I mean, having spent all this time with him. Having him around.'

He glanced up. 'I miss him, period.'

'Of course,' I said quickly. 'Course you do.' Stupid, Annie. A silence ensued. I looked at Tod, small and blond, joking with Flora as they pretended to joust with kebab sticks.

Tod caught my eye and brandished a kebab. 'More peppers?'

I smiled. 'No thanks, but your dad will eat them, I'm sure.'

'Pile them on,' said Matt, holding up his hands. 'Oh, OK, six of 'em, and a stack of mushrooms too. I'll do my best.'

I waited until Tod was out of earshot again.

'And that's where you met Gertrude? At Tom and Louise's?'

'That's it. Two summers ago, when she was down. Tom and Louise had her come over. Tom had known her late husband pretty well, he'd done some work experience with him as a medical student at Oxford, before he decided to go into research. A brilliant man by all accounts.'

'Tom? Or Hugh?'

'Well, both, but I meant Hugh.'

'Yes. Yes, he was,' I mused. 'Which may be . . . half the problem,' I said sadly.

He looked at me. The children had finished their steaks and were busy burning bananas in tin foil.

'Whose problem?'

I shook my head. Swallowed. 'Nothing. I shouldn't have said that.'

Matt laid his plate aside and narrowed his eyes into the setting sun. It burnt a full half-circle on the horizon, like a giant red eye above the trees, out at sea.

'Annie, I couldn't help noticing David left in one hell of a hurry this morning. You want to tell me about that?'

'Yes, he . . . had things to do. In London. He, um—'

'Because if not, don't bother. You see I can already detect a half-baked lie forming on your lips and I gotta tell you, I can spot it a mile off.'

I smiled, despite myself. 'You know me too well already.'

He didn't reply to that. In the event, I broke the silence.

'Well, OK. David misdiagnosed a patient who ended up having a heart attack and dying.'

Matt calmly wiped some bread around his plate. 'He's not the first doctor to do that, and he sure as hell won't be the last.'

'No, but there have been others. Other mistakes.'

'Lots of others?'

I put my plate on the grass. Found myself flushing. 'Not . . . lots, but enough for him to be worried. Very worried. And, Matt' – I turned to face him – 'that's what bothered me more than anything about last night. His reaction. I really couldn't care less if he loses his job, but he took it so badly. And David's usually so cool, so collected. He completely went to pieces. Really broke down.'

'Cried?'

'Well . . .' I hesitated. Felt disloyal. 'Yes, actually.'

He shrugged. 'For some calm, collected people that acts as a release. We all do it, it's just you're not used to seeing it in David.'

'Yes,' I agreed quickly, relieved. 'Yes, you're right. I'm sure that's it.'

'Are you sure,' he said carefully, 'it wasn't your reaction that bothered you? How it felt to see him like that?'

I lowered my eyes, ashamed. 'Yes, that too. It unnerved me. But the awful thing is that even before it happened, before his solicitor rang with the news last night, I was unsettled by my feelings towards him in so many ways. I . . . can't explain, really.'

I pulled savagely at some dandelions growing by my chair, tugging them up by the roots. I felt awful. It was so treacherous sitting here discussing David, yet, in another way, it seemed Matt was the only person I could do it with.

'How were you when you met David?' Matt asked, watching as Tod and Flora started a sword fight with barbecue tongs. 'Steady, guys.'

I glanced up. 'How was I?'

'Yeah. I mean, how did it happen?'

'Oh. He saved me from sudden death.' I grinned. 'Pushed me out of the way of some falling glass. But not just that. He saved me from myself, too. I was a mess when I met David. Exhausted, underslept – frankly in an abject state. Still grieving for Adam. I mean really grieving. Not eating properly, getting sick, going under, almost at rock bottom, basically.'

'And now you're better.'

'Well, yes,' I said uncomfortably. 'Thanks to David. He saved both of us. Me and Flora. And now he needs me,' I said determinedly. 'And I'm going to be there for him.'

'Just at a time when perhaps you were ready to move on.'

'No. Of course not!'

'Annie, sick people need to be saved sometimes, but savers often need to do the saving. They need to be those people who rehabilitate others. As doctors we have to walk around ourselves very carefully, scrutinise ourselves from every angle and examine our motives. Would we be happy, for example, if Jesus Christ strolled through a ward and cured everyone? Or pissed off 'cos we had no one left to heal?'

I laughed nervously. 'Are you suggesting that that's what attracted him to me? The fact that I was a wreck? A bit of a basket-case? That's balls.'

He shrugged. 'Vulnerability can be awfully attractive. To some people. Not to others.' He looked at me steadily. 'For some people it's a turn-off.'

'You mean me.' I reddened. 'It's not that I find him unattractive now that he's down,' I said angrily. 'That's awful. An awful thing to say!'

"Night, Mum.' I jumped. Flora was at my elbow, bending to kiss me. I hadn't heard her come up behind me. Sensing an atmosphere, she glanced from me to Matt, unsure.

"Night darling,' I said quickly, recovering. 'You're going up early.'

She looked at my watch. 'I know, but I'm bushed. So's Tod. And anyway, we might get up early tomorrow to go water-skiing. The boat leaves the jetty at nine.'

'OK, darling.'

I kissed her and felt angry tears welling. I turned away from Matt to hide them, pretending I was watching Flora go into the house. After a moment Tod followed suit, and we heard his footsteps echoing up to the attic, then his door closing.

'I'm not saying you find him unattractive because he's down,' Matt said in a low voice. 'I'm sure that's not the case. I'm saying you're a different person now than when you first met him.'

I fought hard with this, but it was undeniable. I had changed. I was stronger, happier, but surely that was because of him? Because of David?

'Is this you with your psychiatrist's hat on?' I asked, forcing a smile.

'No, it's my Matt Malone hat. The one that fits me best.'

I reached down and tugged at some more dandelions, knowing he was stumping me with common logic.

'Annie' – he cleared his throat – 'I was badly hurt too, like you were with Adam. And I didn't find a saviour like you did, although I had a few kind offers. A couple of them I took up, too. One was a female registrar with great legs; another, a cute neighbour two blocks down with a shy smile and a cat that jumped on the bed at inopportune moments. But both of them purely transitory. Both on a ships-in-the-night basis. Nothing platonic, you understand, but nothing emotional either. A physical healing, sure, but I never let my heart get involved. It wasn't ready. Wasn't fit for action.'

'Wasn't?' I made myself look up from the grass. 'You mean it is now?'

'Oh, sure.' His eyes collided with mine. Blue, focused, and very frank. 'Road-tested and everything.'

The blood stormed into my cheeks and the silence that ensued was alive with intensity, crackling with electric current. I held his gaze.

'Annie, I think there's something going on here that both of us are denying. Some subject we're skirting politely around, which has nothing to do with David's reasons for entering the medical profession or embarking on a relationship with you, but more to do with something the two of us have thrown into the equation.'

All of a sudden the garden seemed oddly still. Unnaturally quiet. The CD had come to an end inside, but I knew that was immaterial. No amount of teenage music and bright lights and jolly banter on the terrace could blanket this moment. It was out there suddenly, in the open, like a shining sea creature coming up out of the water through the murky weed and plankton. The rising up of a truth. And it would have happened whatever, and wherever; it was naïve of me to pretend otherwise. On top of a bus, in a crowded room, in a little blue rowing boat out at sea, under the stars by a campfire. He was right. This was something undeniable, and of our making.

I stood up quickly and stooped to pick up the children's plates from the grass, hoping to break the intimacy of the moment. I made a stack of crockery on the table, but was aware that he was standing behind me, and that my hands were trembling. I gazed down at the bits of steak and lettuce stuck to the plates, numb with a mixture of horror and longing.

'Annie.'

I turned and, in that instant, when he looked at me, I was in pieces. He folded me in his arms, and the world as I knew it burst like a bubble. His lips found mine, warm and responsive; his hands held me close. He smelled of the sea, grass and fresh air as I kissed him. This man, this stranger, whom I'd known all of six days, who'd strolled into my life and rocked my world. Who'd opened up a room in my heart I hadn't known existed, or if I'd suspected, had kept firmly locked. As one long kiss unfurled after another, it seemed to me I was going deeper and deeper into this forbidden place. As we paused for air, I simultaneously came to my senses.

'We're right under Flora's bedroom!' I breathed.

'So we'll go inside,' he reasoned, hands in my hair, lips softly touching mine again. 'God, you're lovely, Annie.'

And the thing was, I felt lovely in his arms. And so we went in, making it just through the French windows, where his hands cupped my face again, kissing my neck, tasting me, savouring me, inside my shirt, my shoulder.

'We can't!' I gasped. 'The children – upstairs.'

'Of course we can't,' he agreed. 'But I can kiss you, can't I?'

'Oh yes,' I panted. 'You can kiss me.'

And so he did, until a ring on the doorbell had me flying from his arms and shooting across the other side of the room.

'What was that!' I gasped.

He shrugged. 'Doorbell, I guess. Strange time to call.'

I flew to the little bay window that overlooked the porch, wiping my mouth in horror, tugging down my shirt, convinced it was David. My heart was racing. I peered around.

'It's Adam,' I breathed in relief.

'Oh, OK.' Matt was clearly relieved too. He scratched his head. 'Boy, you sure have a full quota of admirers. I never know which Romeo's gonna show up next.'

I turned to him anxiously. 'What shall I do?'

'I guess show him in, Annie.' He went into the kitchen and started to fill the kettle. 'Be hospitable, get the cookies out. Or maybe he's a gin-and-quails'-eggs man, you tell me. But either way, if you leave him standing out there any longer he'll stroll right round the side of the house thinking we can't hear the bell 'cos we're in the garden, and come in anyway, so— Ah, Adam. Welcome!' Matt stuck out his hand and beamed widely as Adam appeared through the French windows.

Adam shook the proffered hand, nonplussed. 'Hi.' He frowned. 'Sounds suspiciously like you were expecting me.'

'No, no, not expecting, but certainly a pleasant and delightful surprise. Always a pleasure to welcome friends to our little abode. Just making coffee: will you have some?'

'Sure, why not.' Adam ran his hand through his curls, taken aback. 'Blimey, I'd forgotten you were still here, actually. Forgot you two have this weird kind of modus vivendi.'

'Oh, not weird,' said Matt, shooting him a blow-torch grin. 'Not when we have so many unexpected visitors keeping us sane and normal. Not when we're overflowing with guests to iron out our troubles with and keep us from feeling blue. Pretty much open house here in the summer season, eh Annie? Party's never over. Coffee for you too?'

'Please.' I suppressed my amusement. Suddenly

felt brave. If he was going to brazen this out, then I could too. I folded my arms and watched as Adam strolled speculatively around the sitting room, hands in pockets. It was a controlling, territorial tactic, and one he'd employed a lot in my London house. As he stopped to stare up at a print of a gull above the fireplace, it struck me that he was really quite a small man. And going a bit thin on the back of his head. Why had I never noticed that?'

'Never been inside before,' he mused, glancing round at me. 'Bit dark, isn't it?'

'That's because we haven't treated you to the light show yet,' said Matt, reaching under a standard lamp and switching it on with a flourish. 'Da-dah! White-man magic.'

Adam smiled good-naturedly and fished in his pocket. 'Here.' He handed me Flora's watch. 'She left it behind. I was passing, so I thought I'd drop it in. Thought she might need it.'

'No one "passes" this place, Adam,' I said, placing the watch in an ashtray. 'It's pretty much off the beaten track.'

'No, well, I . . .' He looked almost uncomfortable. 'I wanted to see you. Have a word.'

There was a pause.

'Oh, Lord, don't mind me.' Matt threw up his hands in mock horror. 'I'll check out the sunset.'

He placed a tray of coffee in front of us, flashed Adam another smile, then took his own mug and sauntered out into the garden. I watched him go. My eyes were shining. Yes, I thought. Yes, this was the way with Adam. Mocking, deprecating, cocky. Why had I never cultivated this particular distancing technique before? I turned to look at my ex-husband and felt a miraculous, almost airborne quality. I perched on the edge of a table.

'So. What was so urgent that it couldn't wait until morning?'

He slipped into the sofa, cradling his mug. 'Well, not urgent, as such. I just . . .' He stopped. Scratched his chin ruefully. 'You know Annie, this isn't quite how I envisaged this little tête-à-tête. I mean, you perched up there and that guy hovering down the garden. Come sit by me.' He patted the sofa, grinning slyly. 'And let's turn the light show off.'

I smiled. 'No, thanks. Come on, Adam, spit it out.'

He looked surprised. Licked his lips. 'Right. Look, Annie, maybe over supper tomorrow. Maybe we could have a chat. I gather the Bistro's not too busy over at Padstow. What d'you say? Just the two of us.'

I set my coffee aside. Sighed. 'Adam, if you've come here to say what I think you have, that things aren't going too well with Cozzy, that you've realised the error of your philandering ways, that you're sorry you let our marriage slide and couldn't go the distance, but that was then and this is now and you're no longer emotionally immature and pretty sure you've got your shit together and let's have another stab at it and – oh yeah' – I held up my finger – 'you miss waking up beside me in the mornings, my head on the pillow, et cetera et cetera, then I have to tell you you've picked a bad moment.' I stood up and went to the sink. 'I was just washing up the supper things and, as you know, I can't abide an untidy house. So unless you'd like to dry up?'

I turned and threw a tea towel at him. It landed on his head. He regarded me in astonishment.

'Well, stone me,' he said finally. 'I seem to be about as irresistible as a greasy plate.'

'Oh don't take it personally.' I ran the taps hard. 'It's just I've heard it all before.' I pushed up my sleeves and began rinsing crockery with fiendish efficiency. 'I heard it when I found you'd been shagging Shirley in our bed-sit in Clarendon Road; I heard it when you slipped away with Antonia after *Love's Labour's Lost* in Cardiff; heard it when I found Sally's sex letters to you in the bedside table in Brighton, and if I said: Yippee! now, grabbed my coat and slipped into the passenger seat of your convertible outside, I'd no doubt hear it in six months' time too. And the thing is, Adam, I *know* that right now you really, really mean it. You do want me to come back, and sincerely believe it'll be for ever, but you just can't help it, can you? The fact is that some people are born with honour, and some aren't.'

He blinked. 'What?'

'It's true. You either have it, or you don't – like good health or an Irish accent or blond hair or an artistic eye. It's a natural force and, actually, one of the strongest, and most incommunicable. Sadly, you don't have it. But never mind, it's not your fault.' I turned. Gave him a bright smile. 'Come on, Adam, dry these plates up for me, there's a good chap. There's something terribly attractive about a man at the draining board, and you never know' – I twinkled at him – 'I might change my mind. Might forget all about that integrity nonsense for a moment and give you a quick one on the sofa anyway. Just for old times' sake.'

He stared at me, slack-jawed. Poleaxed. Then he snatched the tea towel from his head, threw it down huffily and stood up.

'Right. Well, if that's the way you want to play it, Annie, taking the piss out of all our years together, the sanctity of our marriage vows, our—'

'Ooh, I think you'll find there's only one person who took the piss out of those, Adam.'

'And won't even consider the happiness of our daughter, our child, the saddest casualty in all of this mess—'

'And the only person I've *ever* really considered. Look.' I threw the dishcloth angrily in the sink with a splash and strode to the back door, hands dripping. I flung it wide. 'I'm sorry you've fallen out with Cozzy, and I'm sorry this Cornish holiday isn't working out for you, but it's working out for me. So please take your sentimental heart and your bullying ways and your pathetic bowl of self-pity elsewhere, and dump it all on someone else's doorstep!'

Something flashed in Adam's eyes. I'd slipped up,

and he knew it. He got up and sauntered towards me, hands in pockets, a smile playing on his lips.

'Ah, so it's working out for you, is it? Yes, well, clearly. You're not clutching the furniture like you usually do in my presence. Not blushing and running your hands through your dishevelled hair like some timid little creature, trying to look at me with loathing when any fool can see the longing in your eyes as I brush past you while you shakily spoon the tea leaves into the pot. In your own home, and even with your boyfriend present.' He was standing very close to me now. He reached up and stroked my cheek. Then he let his hand fall gently to my breast.

I slapped it away angrily. 'Piss off!'

He raised his eyebrows, still smiling. 'Hm, interesting. Not even a frisson. I'm impressed. Tell me,' he drawled, cocking his head down the garden in Matt's direction, 'does the good doctor know about this?'

He winked at me. Then, whistling softly, he strolled out of the back door, and around the garden to his car. I stood and watched him go for a moment, then slammed the door hard. It rattled in its frame. I stared at the wooden panels, fists balled to my sides. Suddenly I put them to my eyes, burst into tears, and ran up to my room, slamming the door behind me.

chapter twenty-one

I tossed and turned that night, and finally heard Matt come up at about midnight. His door closed softly above me. Thereafter, I slept fitfully, dimly conscious of my dreams billowing around, of even a few pertinent images. I woke again, suddenly, at five, eyes wide open. I lay there, staring into the darkness, waiting to be filled by tears and terrible regret, or by relief – whichever it might be. I waited and waited, but all I felt was a ghastly, mind-numbing confusion.

And then, I knew. I got up, woozy with lack of sleep, but heady with resolve as I seized my dressing gown and tottered to the bathroom.

It was still early, only seven o'clock, when, already dressed, I stole into Flora's room next door.

'Flora darling, wake up.' I shook her shoulder gently.

'Hmm? Wha'?' She rolled over, her arm draped above her head. She peered at me through bleary eyes. 'Wha's going on?'

'I thought we might go to Granny's today, sweet-heart. You know, we said we'd go and see her while we were down here, and we haven't yet. Come on, get dressed.'

She turned her head and peered at her clock in astonishment. 'Why so early?'

'Because it takes an hour and a half to get there, and I want to miss the traffic and go while it's cool, that's why. Now come on, buck up.'

'God, Mum, we're supposed to be on holiday!'

'*Now*, Flora,' I hissed abruptly. 'Please.'

Something in my tone brought her up short. Perhaps it was also in my face, with the underslept, shadowed eyes, the wild hair and the grey pallor, and perhaps it reminded her of a mother she thought she'd seen the back of, but either way, muttering darkly, she dragged herself out of bed.

'Oh, all *right*,' she grumbled, hauling herself off to the bathroom.

I, meanwhile, tiptoed downstairs to make her some toast. Yes, this was a good idea, I thought as I manically buttered away, my hands shaking slightly. I needed to get away; needed to think; Mum's was the perfect place. I needed to consider so many things, like what I was doing letting a man I hardly knew kiss me like that, so passionately, when I was getting married in five weeks. I dropped the knife with a clatter. Put a hand to my cheek in horror.

Rallying, I made a piece of toast for myself, but then couldn't face it – felt sick at the sight of it, actually – so I put two on Flora's plate and took it up to her, mounting the stairs two at a time, adrenalin making me agile.

'Here darling, some brekkie,' I said with forced jollity as I breezed in and intercepted her in the bathroom. She had her head in the basin, brushing her teeth. 'I'll put it on your bedside table, shall I?' I hovered. 'There's a cup of tea, too. You can eat it as you get dressed.'

She turned from the basin, mouth full of froth, and gave me an incredulous glare. 'Wha's the 'ush?' I interpreted, but I ignored her and slipped away to pack.

Yes, to pack. An overnight bag, definitely, but actually, secretly, enough clothes for a few days. I'd sneak some in for Flora too, without her seeing. No point alerting her to the length of our stay. But a protracted stay was definitely in order, because the thing was, I figured, hands trembling as I packed, the reason last night had happened, the reason we'd ended up in such a – a compromising position, was all to do with proximity. Yes, that was it. Heavens, it was well documented. When people of the opposite sex were cooped up together for any length of time, emotions were unnaturally heightened and things . . . well, things that wouldn't normally happen happened. Take office affairs, for instance. It was the convenience factor: no effort required, just stroll over to the photocopier and Bob's your uncle – or your brand-new lover. Holiday romances too. And that was all last night had been, I decided firmly, throwing shoes, trousers, T-shirts in a bag: a holiday romance. Where all the senses are heightened by the sun and the sea and romantic fishing trips and beach picnics, and where no proper work or routine intrudes. And a few drinks helped, of course. Except that I hadn't had much to drink, I thought in dismay. Just a couple of glasses.

Anyway – I shook my head dismissively – the point was this would never have happened had I not been sharing this wretched house. If only I'd listened to David, I thought miserably, dropping my toothbrush in. Oh, my poor David! I *should* have listened to him. Should have gone up the road to the Complete Angler, but I hadn't wanted to. Not just because of this gorgeous house, but ... because of the gorgeous man in it. I froze as I admitted it to myself. Yes. Yes, he was gorgeous. *Damn.*

But I would book it, I thought frantically, chucking a handful of underwear in the bag, the Complete Angler, the moment I got back, or – or – maybe somewhere even further away? More far flung? Eastbourne perhaps. Or Bournemouth? Or were they full of old ladies? Old ladies. Perfect. Just what I needed. Just so long as there weren't any red-blooded American psychiatrists prowling around too.

I paused for a moment in my packing to gaze out of the window at the familiar view beyond: the farmland on the opposite side of the creek, the gulls

circling the recently mown hay, looking for rich pick-
ings. Oh God, what had I done? Well, I'd kissed a
man, that's all, I reasoned soberly, picking up a huge
bottle of shampoo and pouring some into a smaller
bottle. Golly, hardly a heinous crime; hardly even a
leg-over situation. But it was made worse, somehow,
by the fact that it had felt so right. So good. I gazed at
the haystacks. His hands in my hair, his breath on my
face, close up and – oh! Damn. Shampoo on my
pants.

Hurriedly I scooped it up, scraped some more off
the bedcover, and then, deliberately leaving my bag
on the bed, crept downstairs. It was still very early
and there was no one about as I tiptoed down the
dew-soaked lawn to the summer house. Better take
my laptop with me, I decided, pushing open the
blistered green door. I could come back for everything else later.

I felt so sad unplugging it, stashing it away in its
case, knowing I wouldn't be sitting here ever again,
tapping away and occasionally glancing over the
treetops to the little boats bobbing about on the
creek. Swallowing hard, I tucked it under my arm
and headed back up the daisy-strewn lawn. David
had threatened to mow it while he'd been here, but
Matt and I had groaned, protesting that we liked the
daisies and the dandelions, that it felt as if the lawn
were taking a holiday too . . .

Breathing deeply and willing myself to think hard
about the Euro debate, or even the Chancellor of the

Exchequer himself, anything other than Matt and me sitting out here, laughing amongst the buttercups, I hurried into the kitchen where Flora was pouring her tea down the sink.

'It's cold. I'm going to make another one,' she announced, flicking on the kettle.

'Oh! No, darling, have some orange juice, look.' I reached into the fridge and hurriedly poured her a glass from the carton, sloshing juice everywhere. 'Nice orange juice. And take it with you in the car,' I urged, pressing it into her hands. 'Come on, we must go!'

'God, what are you on?' she said incredulously as I bullied her out of the back door clutching her glass. I hastened her around the drive to the car. 'I haven't even had a pee.'

'You'll live,' I muttered, opening the passenger door for her. 'I'll stop at a service station later. Go on, get in, I'm just nipping back for, er . . . a couple of things.'

'So can't I nip back for a pee?'

'No!'

Gazing at me in wonder but, luckily, still half-asleep and therefore unusually compliant, she flopped into the front seat with a face like thunder. I threw the laptop on the back seat, slammed the door on her, then, glancing fearfully up at the attic windows in case he'd heard the door, fled back to the house. Taking the stairs at a canter, I snatched up the bag from my bed, then nipped next door into Flora's room. Rummaging hurriedly through her drawers and feeling a bit like Burglar Bill on speed, I crammed some of her shorts and T-shirts into my bag. Then I zipped it up, and hurried down the passage and back downstairs with my booty. As I got to the bottom step and turned to flee through the kitchen and make my escape out of the back door, I ran slap into Matt, coming out of the study.

'AARRRGHH!' I dropped my bag in fright.

He eyed it. 'Going somewhere?'

'God.' I clutched my heart. 'Um, yes. To Mum's.'

'Ah.'

'I didn't know you were up,' I breathed, heart pounding.

'Couldn't sleep. Got up at about five and worked in the study.'

Oh no so he'd been in there all that time; he must have seen me racing down the lawn like a lunatic, heard me bullying Flora in the kitchen.

I picked the bag up hastily and made to move past him, eyes down. I wouldn't look at him. Wouldn't. He put his hand on my arm. Forced me to look up. His eyes, when I met them, were gentle, sad, and very blue.

'Is this wise, Annie?'

I gulped. Looked away. 'Yes,' I muttered. 'It is. Very wise.' And so saying I pushed past him and hurried, head down, to the car, aware that tears were taking their chance now and fleeing down my face. I threw the bag in the boot and got in, wiping my cheeks furiously with the back of my hand.

'What's up?' Flora looked at me in surprise.

'Hay fever,' I muttered.

'You don't get hay fever.'

'WELL, I'VE GOT IT THIS MORNING!' I bellowed. 'Must be the pollen count,' I added, less forcefully.

'Oh.' She blinked, startled. Then: 'What did you just put in the boot?' she asked as I performed an extremely fast and furious three-point turn in the drive, gravel flying everywhere. 'Blimey, steady, Mum!'

'Just some coats. In case it's cold.'

'Cold? It's going to be twenty-eight today!'

But I wasn't listening. I was watching Matt, who was standing at the sitting-room window, watching me. His eyes steady, hands in pockets. Very still.

Flora saw him and waved. 'Bye!' she yelled.

He raised his hand slowly as we sped off down the drive. Flora twisted round in her seat, still waving.

'We'll be back by tonight, though, won't we? Tod goes soon. I wouldn't mind a bit more time with him.'

I licked my lips carefully. 'Well, I thought we might stay. One night. Granny would be thrilled, and then . . . we'll see.'

She swung back to face me. 'We're staying the night? You didn't say. I haven't got my things.'

'I've got them,' I said as we flew along the country lanes, all the time putting distance between us and that house, I thought grimly as I gripped the wheel.

'Right,' she said in surprise. 'Does Granny know?'

'She does. I rang her this morning.'

This much was true. I'd called her at six-thirty as she was having her breakfast. Five minutes late, by her standards.

'Of course you can come, love,' she'd said in surprise. 'I'll make up the beds. This is very sudden, isn't it?'

'Not really, Mum,' I'd breathed down the phone. 'I just felt the need to see you.'

There was a pause. 'Funny that. Clare felt the need to see me a couple of days ago.'

I'd shut my eyes tight. Swallowed. No flies on Mum. 'Well, I'll see you in an hour or two, then.'

'Righto, love.'

Flora eyed me now as I rifled through the glove compartment, searching for my sunglasses. I found them and shoved them on.

'Seems like you've thought of everything, then,' she remarked drily.

I pretended I hadn't heard her and was intent on reading the road signs, aware that her gaze was upon me.

'What were you and Matt arguing about last night?' she said suddenly. 'When I came to say goodnight to you?'

'We weren't arguing,' I said quietly. 'We were discussing.'

'Oh.' She was silent for a moment. 'But you like him, don't you?'

'Of course I like him,' I said lightly, reaching across her to the cassette box and popping in some Chopin. Joyful piano music filled the car. 'What is there not to like?'

When we arrived at Mum's an hour or so later, I felt heady with relief. After we'd slowly inched our way down the familiar track full of potholes, dodged the big ones, avoided the craters, and rounded the bend into the farmyard, I turned off the engine and leaned gratefully on the wheel. An ancient stone farmhouse with two small gables sat before us, and in the yard, encircled by a low, dry-stone wall, the chickens and bantams poked and strutted around. A delicious silence enveloped us.

'Clare's here,' said Flora in surprise as she spotted her car in the drive.

'Yes, she . . . had some work to do. Needed some peace and quiet, but didn't want to traipse all the way back to London.' Amazing the lies that tripped off my tongue these days.

'Oh, look! One of the bantams has had chicks. It's Madame Blanche.' She got out excitedly as the pure white French Silky with elaborate pantaloon legs fussed over her chicks by the edge of the pond, urging them to drink, but not to follow the duck's example and take to the water.

In the Dutch barn to the left of the yard I spotted Ted Philpot, the neighbouring farmer to whom Mum rented the land and sold the stock when Dad died, and who also had use of the outbuildings. He was pitchforking hay into a trailer – no doubt inexpertly, since, according to Mum, no one forked, or furrowed, or sprayed, or dipped and dagged, or for that matter did any manner of farm work or animal husbandry half as well as Dad had, but particularly poor Mr Philpot. She had her beady eye on him day and night, muttering under her breath and bossing him around. He raised his hand when he saw me, and I waved back.

As I walked towards the house Mum appeared in the doorway. The last time I'd seen her I'd been quietly alarmed at how thin she was getting, the bones at the base of her throat sticking out, but I was relieved to see she looked a bit plumper. She was wearing a blue summer dress with a tea towel slung over one shoulder.

'Madame Blanche's had chicks, Granny!' Flora called, dispensing with any formal greeting to her grandmother.

'I know, love. I thought that would please you, but she's that fussy with them.'

'That's because the fox got them all last year. She remembers.' Flora abandoned the chicks for a moment to kiss her granny, and I followed suit.

'Hello, Annabel, love. Everything all right?' Her sharp grey eyes scanned my face anxiously.

'Fine.' I smiled. 'Just woke up this morning and felt like coming to see you, that's all. You look much better, Mum, you've put on a bit of weight.' It was true, her face had recovered its bloom and her eyes were brighter. Dad had died four years ago now, but it had really knocked her for six.

She chuckled. 'Eating too much, probably. So used to baking for a family, I do it out of force of habit, then eat it all myself.'

There was something sad about her doing that, I thought: making enough scones for the four of us when there was no one to eat them with, but she looked happy enough. 'And with all the exercise I'm getting, I should be pounds thinner,' she went on, ushering us in. 'The sheep got out the other week and I was all over the county roundin' them up. Right over to Tom Toper's land at Fenstorm they went.'

'Mr Philpot not fencing them in properly, then?' I teased, ducking my head as I followed her through the low doorway.

'Oh, he's not doin' too badly. It was his idiot boy. Left the gate open.'

'Oh, right,' I said, surprised not to get the usual tirade about how he only banged in post and rails and didn't use the more traditional dry-stone walling, but perhaps she was getting more tolerant in her old age. And of course she was getting older too, I thought anxiously. Perhaps Clare was right, perhaps she shouldn't really be all on her own down here in such a remote spot, but there was no shifting her. This was her country and she loved it; she'd been born and raised at a farm across the valley which *she* still called home. It wasn't up for discussion; as far as she was concerned, she'd die here.

Inside, the kitchen gleamed. The waxed terracotta floor shone up at the solid fuel black Rayburn that Mum still filled and stoked by hand, which sparkled at the blue and white delft china on the pine dresser on the opposite wall. The kitchen hadn't changed since Mum, who'd inherited it from Gran, had given it what she regarded as a radical facelift in the seventies. She claimed she was still getting used to the tiled work surfaces and the 'jazzy' yellow curtains at the window. Ralph, the border collie, was snoozing peaceably by the Rayburn, thumping his tail on the floor by way of apology for being too old to get up and greet us properly. All was exactly as it should be: home. I sank gratefully into the Windsor chair by the Rayburn with its faded gingham cushion, and Flora bent to make a fuss of Ralph.

'No Clare?' My eyes drifted to the open window where the green hills rolled away into the distance, dotted with sheep; similar to the Cornish landscape we'd passed through but, to the connoisseur's eye, much lusher and gentler, more forgiving.

'She's upstairs tryin' some clothes on. We went into Exeter yesterday and she went mad.'

I smiled. Mum wouldn't be used to Clare's style of shopping: panic-buying everything in sight while she had an hour away from her desk or her children.

'Any other babies, Granny?' asked Flora, still

crouched on her haunches, stroking Ralph's grey muzzle.

'Yes, love, there are ducklin's out back, an' if you go right into the far corner of the barn you might find Cinders with yet another litter of kittens. She can't keep away from that tom up the lane, the little hussy. Must get her spayed.'

Flora slipped off eagerly, persuading Ralph to accompany her.

'So how is she?' I asked as Mum poured boiling water into the old brown pot waiting on the stove.

'Cinders? Or the other little hussy?'

I grinned. 'The other. Clare.'

'She's fine,' she said shortly. 'Now. She wasn't though, when she came. She was beside herself for a bit. Haven't seen her like that since she got a low mark in her geography mocks on account of flu. And I haven't had her open up to me, neither.'

'She did that?'

'Not entirely. But a bit. Well, she said she'd had an altercation with Michael, and you know Clare. That's shorthand for he's left me.'

I looked up. 'She told you that?'

'No, but I guessed as much.' She settled down opposite me in the other Windsor chair and let the pot sit on the Rayburn between us for a bit. 'All that walkin' she's been doing since she got here, been goin' for miles, she has, an' you know Clare, she never walked further than the library. An' she's not herself, either: not tellin' me what to do and where to

live and what to eat. Been better company, actually,'
she said thoughtfully, getting up to pour the tea.

I smiled. Mum told it like it was.

'And as I say, shoppin' like her life depended on it
yesterday. Like a thing possessed. Treated me to a
bite to eat, though. At the Regal.' She handed me a
cup and saucer.

'Oh, lovely.'

Mum regarded the Regal in Exeter as the ultimate
in sophistication.

'But always tryin' to cover up, you know? Chitter-
chatter chitter-chatter over the crème caramel, an' her
eyes much too bright and tense. Holdin' herself
together.'

'Oh.' No, well, clearly she hadn't opened up that
much, and I'd hoped she would, to Mum.

'But then again this morning, well, I don't know,'
she pondered, taking a moment. 'She seems a bit
perkier. More relaxed, somehow.' She paused to sip
her tea.

'Perhaps country air and home cooking is finally
working its magic?'

'Oh yes, it'll do her the power of good, but it won't
mend hearts.' She eyed me beadily. 'How's David,
love? Knows you're here, does he?'

I breathed in sharply at his name. 'Um, no. Not yet.
I'll ring him.'

'I should.' She reached out and passed me the
phone from the side. 'Or he'll worry.'

I stared at it in my lap. 'Yes. Yes, he will.'

'Only I know you've got your mobiles an' that, but if he rings that house in Cornwall an' finds it empty . . .'

'Well except it's not empty, there's someone else – someone else staying there,' I faltered.

'Oh yes. Clare said.'

She sipped her tea quietly, watching me. I could feel my face burning. I took a deep breath and tapped out David's direct line under her steely gaze. Thank God. The answer machine. I didn't have to speak to him and feel even more duplicitous than I already did. I cleared my throat.

'Um, David, hi, it's me. Just to let you know I'm staying at Mum's for a few days, so you can reach me here. I'll speak to you later. Bye!'

'A few days?' said Mum in surprise when I'd hung up.

'Well, I'll . . . see how it goes.'

'Ah. That's just what Clare said. Said she'd— Ooh, look, talk of the devil.'

The door opened and Clare appeared in the doorway, looking as if she were going to Ascot. She was wearing a shocking pink suit, black stilettoes and a huge black hat. 'Da-daa!' She struck a pose, then nearly tottered off her heels when she saw me. 'You're here! Blimey, you're early.' She laughed. 'You weren't supposed to see this!'

I boggled. 'What have you come as?'

'I've come as the sister of the bride,' she declared, giving a twirl. 'Like it?' She struck another pose, hands on hips, head thrown right back, supermodel style. 'It's for your wedding.'

'Oh!' I spilled my tea in the saucer.

'Mum and I went into Exeter yesterday and we went completely berserk. I have to say I had no idea the shops down here were so terrific. Almost as good as London. Has this just been made?' She took the lid off the pot and peered in suspiciously.

'Just this minute, love.'

'And you should see what Mum bought,' she said, helping herself to a cup. 'Honestly, Annie, I've never seen her look so smart, it's stunning. And a bag too, and shoes to match – and a hat!'

I turned to Mum, feeling the colour drain from my face. 'But I thought you'd decided . . . since it was Claridge's . . .'

'Oh, that was just nerves talkin'.' She brushed some crumbs briskly from her lap. 'No, I put down that phone and said to myself: Marjorie Hooper, what a ninny you are. Of course you won't miss your daughter's weddin' on account of it being in London and havin' nothin' to wear, and Ted said the same.'

'Ted?'

'Philpot,' put in Clare, giving me a look.

'No, I wouldn't miss it for the world, love,' went on Mum smoothly, 'and I apologise if I gave the impression otherwise. It's all decided now. I'm stayin' with Clare for two nights an' I'm all set outfit-wise, too. Clare's seen to that.'

'Honestly, Annie, Claridge's!' Clare said incredulously. 'I nearly fell over when Mum told me. It's so un-you.'

'Thanks.'

'No, but you know what I mean. *So* smart.'

'It was David's idea,' I muttered, sinking into my tea.

'Well, obviously. Now come on, Mum, show her your things,' Clare urged.

'Later, love,' Mum demurred.

'Oh no, go on, now! Tell you what, I'll get them. Don't move!'

She teetered out of the kitchen and off up the stairs on her heels. We heard her clip-clipping across the landing above us. I stared dumbly into my tea. A moment later she was back, holding a dove-grey suit from a hanger, a hat box, and a pair of blue shoes. Mum stood up and Clare held the suit against her.

'What d'you think?' Mum asked shyly, taking the hanger.

'Oh, and the hat. The hat makes it.' Clare got it out and placed it carefully on her head. Adjusted it, then stood back to admire.

I forced a smile at Mum; my mum, standing proudly before me, with her mother-of-the-bride outfit.

'Lovely,' I gulped. 'Mum, you look gorgeous.'

She bent her head and stroked the cloth reverently. 'It's silk,' she said in wonder. 'Never had anythin' like it in my life, not even when I married your dad.

But Clare insisted, so I took out some savings an' your sister chipped in half.'

'Cost a fortune,' affirmed Clare blithely, whipping the hat off her head and putting it back in its box. 'But as I told Mum, it's an investment. It'll never date.'

I nodded. Couldn't speak.

'And you did cheat us out of a wedding the first time round,' Clare warned. 'Oh, and we saw a lovely dress for Flora, didn't we, Mum?'

'What's that?' Flora came in breathless, being pulled along by Ralph who'd clearly got his second wind. 'Oh Clare, look at you! You look like Cruella de Vil!' She giggled.

'It's for your mum's wedding,' Clare said proudly, giving another twirl. 'And actually, if Mummy says it's OK, I'll take you into Exeter and see if you like this dress I saw. It's a floaty Ghost number, not twee at all. I think you'll love it.'

'Oh, cool! Can I, Mum?'

'Yes, of course,' I breathed. My throat felt inexplicably dry, constricted.

'I was wondering what I was going to wear,' said Flora. 'Do I have to have a hat?'

'I wouldn't have thought so, love,' said Mum, 'but, Annabel, you ought to ring that girl who's makin' your outfit. See if it's finished. You've only got a few weeks to go now.'

'Yes, you should have a fitting,' agreed Clare. 'You might have lost a bit of weight; most brides do. She's somewhere in the Fulham Road, isn't she?'

'Yes, somewhere there.'

'And what are you having exactly? Ivory silk?'

'Yes. It's . . . a shift dress.' I stood up, ostensibly to pour some more tea, but actually to turn my back to them. My hands were trembling. The window was open but it felt airless in here. I moved to throw open the back door.

'With pearl buttons?' Clare was prattling on.

'Yes. Down the back.' I gazed out of the back door at the hills rising in the distance. I wanted to be out there now, on top of the furthest one. Biggen Tor, the one I'd always taken Ralph's mother Pippa to, clambering right to the top, flopping down for a rest in the rough grass, Pippa racing round me in circles, barking with excitement, then running down together, the wind in our hair.

'Flora, love,' Mum was saying, 'come and help me get your bags from the car an' I'll show you your room. It's the usual one, up in the rafters, with the wood pigeons for company. Lunch isn't for an hour, you two,' she warned. 'Clare, put those in the bottom oven for me, would you?' She nodded at the quiches on the Rayburn as she went out with Flora in tow.

Clare pushed up her pink sleeves and gingerly picked up the brimming pastry cases. She giggled. 'I feel like Fanny Craddock, dressed like this.'

I watched her, and felt my heartbeat come down slightly, now that Mum had left the room.

'You're chipper,' I remarked, sitting down again.

'Much more chipper than when I last saw you.'

'Oh.' She blushed. Shut the oven door. 'Yes. Well, Michael got my letter. He called first thing this morning, as soon as it arrived.'

'And?'

'And . . . nothing earth-shattering, but he did agree to talk.'

'Did you tell him about Theo?'

'I did.'

'And what did he say?'

'He said: "Ah, just a fumble. That makes us even."'

I smiled. 'Told you.'

'Yes. But he also . . . laid down a few conditions.'

'Such as?'

'Such as I give up work.'

'Clare!'

'But I'd already decided to do that anyway,' she said quickly.

I blinked. 'Really?'

'Well, this job, anyway. And no, before you suggest it, I can't just cut down my hours, it's not that sort of job. It's all or nothing. But I'll do something else. Something part-time.'

'But you love that job!'

She looked at me squarely, eyes wide and frank. 'I love my husband more. And my children. And that hasn't come to me in a blinding flash; I've always known it, Annie. And I can't have both. Don't want to have both. Not if it means going at it

all half-cocked, half-crazy with tiredness and not
enjoying any of it, which was what I was doing. I'm
going to take a break, and then . . . well, then we'll
see.' She grinned. 'Maybe I'll enjoy being a mum at
home. I always envied you doing that, and it's not
as if we need the money. Michael's doing brilliantly.
And he wants me to help. You know, entertain his
clients, give dinner parties, that sort of thing.'

I blinked. Entertain her husband's clients. The very
vocabulary would ordinarily have had Clare retching
into her briefcase, but she looked calm. Happy.

'We're a team, Annie, or should be. Not two
breakaway factions trying to compete with separate
bank accounts. If I bothered to go to the opera with
his clients more, got tarted up, had my hair done, I
could be a real asset to him.'

'Golly, Clare. The corporate wife.'

She laughed. 'Trophy wife even, and why the hell
not? I've worked bloody hard; I deserve a break.
Deserve to go to Wimbledon and Glyndebourne. Let
him bust his balls. Anyway,' she mused, 'this is all
hypothetical. We're still at pre-negotiating stage, but
I thought, if I put my cards on the table, it may help?
Help him take me back?' she asked anxiously.

'Ye-es, except he may not want to lose total sight of
the girl he married. You've got a lot to offer, Clare,
intellectually. I'm not convinced you'll flourish at the
hairdresser's or making vol-au-vents like some fifties
housewife. Some middle ground might well be what
he wants. What you both want.'

'Well, exactly, something part-time, but I'm certainly taking a year off first. I tell you, just a couple of days here with Mum and no husband and kids has made me realise this is the first proper holiday I've had in years. Even though my marriage may be breaking up, this is the first time I've felt – well, like me. Not someone's wife, or mother, or boss.'

'Doesn't sound as if your marriage is breaking up.'

'Well, we'll see. We're having dinner tonight, in Exeter,' she said shyly.

'Oh Clare, I'm so pleased,' I said, relieved. 'He wouldn't have agreed to that unless he was reconsidering, surely?'

She shrugged. 'Either that or he's going to issue me with divorce proceedings over the prawn cocktail, but he did say the kids were missing me. He also said that they were breaking all the rules: putting milk bottles on the table and throwing leftovers away without covering them in cling film and putting them in the fridge.' She grinned.

I smiled. At least she could laugh at herself. 'And, Clare' – I took a deep breath – 'if it does work out, don't go back to the kids all guns blazing and—'

'I know,' she interrupted quickly. 'You don't have to tell me. Not so full on. Turn it down. Less beach volley-ball. Let them all chill. Let them lie on the floor picking their noses with their feet up the walls. I *know*, Annie. What d'you think I've been doing on these windy hilltops these past two days, apart from reassessing my life? I tell you, all this fresh air is very good for the soul; I highly recommend it. It's forced me to confront some very uncomfortable home truths.' She went to the sink to rinse the teapot out, then turned back to eye me carefully. 'Although I wasn't aware that you were in need of this place's healing properties.'

I glanced quickly down at my tea. Aware of her gaze still on me.

'What brings you down to the re-hab clinic then? What made you hurtle down to Exeter's answer to The Priory at such short notice, hm?'

chapter twenty-two

Luckily Mum and Flora came back at that moment, and I didn't have to answer; I could get out of the beam of her enquiring stare and back to ordinary things, like making a salad and laying the table for lunch.

The day drifted on; Clare washed her hair and lay in the sun to dry it and top up her tan like a girl on her first date, then she painted her nails, all in preparation for her dinner that evening with Michael – the first they'd had alone, she confided to me guiltily, since their wedding anniversary three years ago. She'd been away on business for the last two. I lay beside her on an ancient, creaking sun lounger in the back garden, breathing in Mum's carefully tended stocks and lupins, and asked her about Ted Philpot.

She shrugged. 'Mum's said nothing. All I know is her attitude's changed towards him. She says his farming methods are different from Dad's, more modern, but that that's no bad thing, and that now he's on his own, she asks him in for lunch most Sundays. Says a man can't be expected to fend for himself all the time, and that it's only neighbourly.'

'He's on his own?'

She waved her nails in the air to dry them. 'His wife died last year. Didn't you know that?'

I didn't.

I gazed thoughtfully into the valley beyond; long shafts of light filtered through the copse at the bottom of the garden where a squirrel jumped from tree to tree, then leaped headlong to the ground. I was aware that behind me in the kitchen Mum was baking a cake with Flora and keeping a watchful eye on her daughters through the window. However much I was considering her, she was considering me more. It occurred to me too that this was the first time the women of the family, indeed the only surviving members, had been alone together since Dad had collapsed with a heart attack in the hay barn four years ago.

Naturally Clare and I had dropped everything then – she having more to drop than me – and driven at breakneck speed together from London, staying on a week to help with the funeral. Clare, despite her sadness, or perhaps because of it and all the other complicated emotions that had made up her relationship with Dad, had gone into overdrive. She'd taken charge and whirled like a dervish, informing the vicar of his duties, instructing the undertakers, putting notices in the papers, delegating me to organise the flowers, whilst Mum, helpless with grief, had retired to her bedroom and left us to get on with it. It was on that day that I'd felt the dynamics of the family change; Dad had gone, so naturally we all felt eviscerated in the way that people do when others die suddenly, when they seem to scoop themselves out of you, but I also felt a more subtle shift: I felt the surviving parent become the child and the children the carers, and, to some extent, that relationship had continued ever since.

Mum was on her own now, and isolated, so naturally we worried; we rang her religiously – daily, in Clare's case – whereas before we'd call if we missed her, or needed something; never dutifully. But lately I'd wondered if Mum had grown tired of Clare's vigilance. Had been glad of it at first, but would now like to retire from her scrutiny. Timely, perhaps, that another shift was now taking place. That as recently as a few days ago, the pendulum had swung the other way, and both her daughters had tugged on the umbilical cord and rushed precipitously to her farmhouse. Although Mum would not wish any grief on her children, it seemed to me she'd reached instinctively – and almost gratefully – for the reins again.

Later that afternoon, I fed the ducks with Flora by the pond in the yard. Ted Philpot was unloading ewes from a trailer in the birthing pens, and made a point, I felt, of pausing in his work to come over and chat to us. He was a tall, gentle man with rheumy hazel eyes, and a shy habit of twisting his cap in his hands and looking beyond one into the distance. Anyone more different from Dad – who'd been wiry, spry and alert, and whose sharp eyes had pinned you to the wall – you couldn't imagine, but nice, I thought. I said as much to Clare when I went back inside. She was at the sink peeling carrots.

'I agree,' she said, surprising me. 'I mean, he's not going to set the world on fire, but he's pleasant enough company and he's kind. He mended all the plumbing, you know, when the pipes froze solid this winter, and he chops all the logs for her.'

'So . . . is there something?'

'You tell me. You know Mum, she wouldn't say, but her attitude has certainly softened towards him. She was there, you know, when his wife died.'

'What, not literally?'

'No, but he came running over when she collapsed. Asthma, apparently. Mum called the ambulance. Helped Ted cope. And then she and his sister helped him with the funeral.'

I sighed. 'Convenient, I suppose. Both losing their partners and living at neighbouring farms . . .'

She shrugged. 'Nothing wrong with convenience. Look how many happy marriages are born of it. Mum only married Dad because their parents were best friends, and again, had neighbouring farms, and how many people meet someone at work or on holiday? I met Michael on holiday and— Why are you going all pink?'

'I'm not,' I said, hiding my face as I bent spuriously

to tie the laces of my deck shoes. 'Anyway, Mum will make up her own mind. Nothing we think or say will make any difference, happily.'

'Exactly.'

Later that day, as I drifted aimlessly about, wandering from the house to the garden and back again, Mum shooed me out for a walk.

'Go on, love,' she said shaking a tea towel at me kindly. 'And take Ralph with you. The air will do you good.'

And I did go. I walked all the way to Biggen Tor, waiting for Ralph occasionally, whose spirit was willing even if the flesh wasn't entirely – which was my problem in reverse, I reckoned, as I bounded up the steep track which wound its way around rocks and boulders. Fizzing with nervous energy, my flesh was raring to go, but the spirit desperately wanted to be elsewhere.

I went right up to the very top, where only a few intrepid sheep grazed, and then stood panting, holding my sides and gazing down at the glorious view before me. Devon was at its most biscuit-tin-like at this time of year: green and lush and gentle, with only a few grey farms sprinkled in the folds of the valleys. The wind was in my hair and the light moved in great curtains across the land which seemed sunk in afternoon sleep. This should have been my moment. I breathed in, willing it, knowing it could happen; knowing I could lose myself in this special place and find peace, had always done so, but it failed to work its magic. Still Matt's face, his gentle blue eyes, his voice, the touch of his hands last night came to me. There was no escape.

Give it time, I told myself grimly, walking back down, as troubled as when I'd gone up. I swiped savagely at grass heads with my hand along the way. Give it time. You've only been away a few hours. All will be well.

When I got back, Mum was just putting down the phone in the kitchen.

'Oh, you've just missed him.'

'Who?' I said stupidly, my heart pounding.

'David. That was him callin' you back, but he said not to ring just now, as he was dashin' off for a game of squash with Jamie after work. He said he'd call you later.'

'Oh.'

That was good. A good sign. He only played squash when he was feeling up and buoyant, and it occurred to me he used to play a lot with Jamie, an old university mate, but hadn't recently. Hopefully he'd got things more in perspective.

'How did he sound?'

'On good form. We had a lovely chat 'cos I haven't spoken to him in a while, and he seemed pleased you were here, love. Told me you could do with some home cookin'. Needed feedin' up a bit an' havin' a bit of spoilin', and told me to persuade you to stay on a bit.'

I smiled. 'Yes, he would. And I think I probably will. D'you mind, Mum?'

'Not a bit. I'd be delighted.'

I had to get round Flora, of course, I thought, going slowly upstairs to my room, biting my nail. I paused at the landing window and gazed down at her on the lawn, chatting to Clare, pinching her aunt's nail varnish and painting her toes. But actually, she seemed perfectly happy now that she was here, with the chicks and the kittens and the prospect of a shopping trip in Exeter. She'd adapted quickly as she always did, and she'd always loved the farm. No, Flora wasn't the problem. It was me.

That night, knowing I wouldn't sleep, I stayed up late when Mum and Flora had gone to bed and Clare had gone to meet Michael. I pretended to watch a late-night film, but lost the plot in minutes. When the final credits rolled I climbed the stairs, dreading the night ahead. In my old room, where I'd grown up, everything was as it had always been. The books were still where I'd left them in the shelves, and in the gloom, even with eyes shut, I could still put my hand on Noel Streatfeild, Josephine Pullein-Thompson, and E. Nesbit. The faded rose wallpaper, the dressing table with its floral skirt behind which I'd hidden all manner of secrets including letters from Adam, the ivy creeping round the window, the stain on the carpet where I'd dropped a mug of coffee, the cigarette burn on the bedside table: all were exactly as I'd left them. I remembered causing that burn when I was about fourteen, hurriedly stubbing out a cigarette and missing the ashtray as Dad, detecting smoke, came into my room. In one of his rare moments of intuition, he'd sat beside me on the bed, calmly got out his packet of Players, and lit one for each of us, insisting I smoke one with him, and deliberately making me feel so sick and uncomfortable I'd never smoked again.

I turned on my side in the little single bed, feeling wretched with the exhaustion of willing myself to think about anything, *any*thing other than what was really on my mind, and saw my laptop sitting on the dressing table where Mum and Flora had left it.

Of course, I thought impulsively, flinging aside the duvet, which had wound itself around me like a coil, I could work. All night if needs be. Lose myself in pulp fiction.

I set a chair at the dressing table, plugged myself in, and waited for it to boot up. I'd received an email from Sebastian Cooper yesterday, enquiring as to the progress of the novel, and ending: *Incidentally, Sapphic fiction all the rage now. How about slipping some in? Love and stuff, Sebastian.*

I'd frowned as I'd read it. Sapphic fiction? I'd thought it was eighties sex and shopping he was after? Was Lucinda expected to have a lesbian scene in Gucci, perhaps? Proposition the sales assistant over the Hermès scarves? And 'love and stuff'? Golly. Quite familiar. But no, no. Cool, actually, and I was so *un*-cool, as Flora kept reminding me.

I sighed as the words flickered up. The problem was that in my present frame of mind, casual sex –

gay or otherwise – felt so wrong, and Lucinda's meaningless fling with Terence at the Savoy even more wrong. Ghastly, in fact. On an impulse, and even though I knew Mr Cooper would strongly disapprove, I erased almost the entire chapter and certainly the last two lurid paragraphs. (Oh that life were that simple.) Instead, I had Terence deliver Lucinda safely back to her front door, which she shut firmly in his face, ignoring his plaintive plea for coffee.

Lucinda glanced at her Cartier watch. The night was still young. Terence had booked the table for high tea at the Harvester, so it was only ten o'clock, and Lucinda had coffee with someone else on her mind. Coffee, but no more. This was to be a meeting of minds.

Tottering on her Jimmy Choos, she ran to the kitchen window and gazed up. Justin's studio light was still on. Trembling at her own temerity, she opened the back door and flew down the path to the gate in the wall which conveniently connected the two properties, a dear little Spode jug in one hand, her Marlboro Lights in another. To her astonishment, when she lifted the latch and pushed it open, Justin was on the other side, his eyes ablaze, jaw chiselled, a sugar bowl in hand.

'Oh!' he exclaimed, startled. 'I'd run out of sugar for my coffee, and I just wondered—'

'How extraordinary!' she interjected. 'I'd run out of milk.'

Their eyes kindled with recognition of their secret intent. Justin took the jug. 'I'll fill this up,' he promised, giving her a hot look, 'and be over in a jiffy.'

True to his word, moments later he was striding into her kitchen with the milk and a sketch pad. Lucinda took the jug and put the kettle on with a shaking hand.

'I must admit, the coffee was a bit of a ruse,' he murmured, moving closer. 'You see, what I really want is to draw you. Naked.'

The little Spode jug flew from Lucinda's hand and smashed to smithereens on the floor. She kicked the pieces hastily under the dishwasher with her stilettoes.

'Where . . . would you like me?' she breathed timorously.

'In here,' he commanded, taking her arm and leading her purposefully into the darkened drawing room, all thoughts of Nescafé forgotten. He indicated a goatskin rug by the fire.

'Recline here, my beauty,' he purred, 'while I put a match to the fire. I'll draw you by its tender light.'

Lucinda's limbs twitched ecstatically as with trembling fingers she discarded her clothing. She didn't like to tell him the fire was only gas effect and the twigs in the rush basket merely for show, as he piled them on and set light to them. The room filled with smoke but, undeterred, Justin settled on a chair before her, his eyes roving over her nakedness. Lucinda instinctively raised her arms above her head. Breastfeeding had taken its toll, and she didn't want a little thing like gravity to spoil her portrait – then realised she hadn't shaved her pits and clamped them hastily back down again. She fervently hoped the children were sound asleep upstairs. This would take some explaining, particularly to Orlando who, at twelve, had been locking the bathroom door rather a lot recently. She watched as Justin's hand moved skilfully over the parchment. Oh that it would move as skilfully over her!

'Perhaps the fire was a mistake,' he spluttered eventually, eyes streaming.

'Not at all,' coughed Lucinda seductively. 'You can light my fire any time you— Damn. The doorbell.'

Seizing the goatskin rug, she wrapped it around her and hurried to answer it.

'Yes?' she barked irritably, peering around the crack. It was Terence.

'You, um, left yer 'andbag behind, like. In my Vespa.'

'Keep it!' she hissed, slamming the door firmly. If only the world would go away! She must remember to sack him tomorrow.

She hastened eagerly back to the drawing room where she stopped and caught her breath. Justin had abandoned his chair and was lying, naked but for a black thong, in the position she'd recently vacated by the fire.

Lucinda blinked at his muscular figure, his taut thighs, his broad shoulders, his enviable waist. Slowly, hypnotically, he knelt up and held out his arms. Shamelessly Lucinda ran to him. He clasped her tightly and her senses swam. She had to get him upstairs, she couldn't breathe in this terrible fug, but his hands were already exploring her territories.

'Come!' she commanded suddenly, and then, seeing his startled face, wished she hadn't. 'To my boudoir,' she added quickly.

'Ah. Yes!' he ejaculated joyfully.

Hand in hand they stole upstairs, the light from the moon streaming through the landing window and gleaming on Lucinda's pearly buttocks and Justin's thong. She couldn't quite work out why he got to keep that on when she was so flagrantly undone, but soon found out when she tore it aside with her teeth in her toile de jouy bedroom.

She blinked. 'Oh!'

'It is small,' he agreed, 'but very, very active.'

And so it proved to be. Three hours later, Lucinda lay back, spent and exhausted on her Yves Delorme pillows. 'No more!' she croaked.

And indeed there was no more, as my fingers too slipped exhausted from the keys. Well, Sebastian would be thrilled after all, I thought bitterly as I crawled wearily back to bed. I'd fully intended to provoke that meeting of minds with Justin, to instigate a meaningful encounter and maybe even a cosy discussion on Kierkegaard and the merits of existentialism, but the muse, it seemed, had had other ideas. Oh well, I thought, lying back drained and exhausted but hopefully unburdened. I'd always found it best to go with the flow and if it was too racy, I could always erase it in the morning and restore Lucinda's virtue intact. For the moment though, it felt good. Very good.

My head hit the pillows and I fell instantly and dreamlessly asleep. I would have slept on – on and on, perhaps until noon – if Mum hadn't woken me sometime later that morning. She had hold of my shoulder and was shaking me vigorously awake.

'Annabel. Annabel, wake up!'

I remember opening my eyes blearily, and seeing the sun pouring through the thin yellow curtain behind her. I saw her anxious face silhouetted against it as she leaned over me. My eyes flickered quickly to my screen. In my comatose state I'd failed to turn it off last night, and the blue light shone out like a beacon, white letters gleaming accusingly. I groaned.

'Oh Mum, you haven't been . . . you didn't—'

'Listen, love, Gertrude's been on the phone. She's just rung.'

'Gertrude?'

I raised myself up on to my elbows. Stared into her worried face. 'Why? What's happened?'

'Annabel, I'm so sorry.' Her eyes filled with tears. She put a hand to her mouth. 'It's David. He's taken an overdose.'

chapter twenty-three

I stared at her, horrified. 'An overdose!' My heart stopped. 'Is he dead?'

'No! No, he's not dead, he's been taken to hospital. He's alive, but they're pumping his stomach.'

For a moment I could only gaze at her in frozen horror. Then I snapped to, flinging back the bed-clothes and swinging my legs out. 'Is Gertrude still on the phone?'

'No, she had to go, she's at the hospital. But, Annabel love, she said David didn't want you to know.'

'What?' I paused to snatch up my jeans. Felt disoriented. Hearing but not hearing.

'Said he'd begged Gertrude not to tell you, but she felt that you should know.'

'Of course I bloody should!' I cried, flying across the room to grab a T-shirt and some shoes. 'Where is he?'

'He's at the Chelsea and Westminster, I've written it down, it's in Chelsea I think she said, but . . . Oh

my love, why on earth would he do such a thing?'
Mum wrung her hands, distraught. 'Such a terrible,
terrible thing!'

'I don't know,' I muttered, diving into my clothes
and knowing full well that I did know but . . . God,
not to this extent, surely? I hadn't known it had
affected him *so* deeply.

'David.' I paused to clutch my mouth in shock,
and gave a muffled moan. I shook my head. I should
have gone back with him, I thought suddenly, of
course I should. It came to me in a flash. This would
never have happened if I'd gone back to London
with him, never.

'But he's getting married in a few weeks,' wailed
Mum, still clasping and unclasping her hands. 'Why
would a young man with a weddin' coming up, with
his whole life ahead of him—'

'It's not to do with me.' I swung around suddenly
and gripped her shoulders. 'At least . . . I don't think
it is.' I let her go. 'It's to do with work, Mum.
Something at work. He . . . made a mistake, you see.
Someone died. It upset him terribly.'

'Oh!' She sat down abruptly on a chair. 'Oh, I see.
Poor David.'

'Yes. Poor David.' I ran my hands through my hair
despairingly. 'And I should have been there for him,
Mum,' I choked.

Suddenly my knees gave way and I sank down on
the side of the bed. I put my head in my hands and
burst into tears. She flew to sit by my side.

'There now, don't take on so,' she murmured, her arm firmly around my shoulders, squeezing hard. 'How could you have known? There's nothing to blame yourself for, you weren't to know this could happen, were you? And more likely as not he told you not to break short your holiday.'

'Yes.' I nodded miserably. 'Yes, he did. Told me to stay, that I couldn't be any help to him—'

'Well, then,' she said consolingly.

'But, Mum . . .' I looked up at her beseechingly, my face wet with tears. 'If things had been different, I *would* have gone, whatever he'd said. I would have gone automatically, wouldn't I?'

'What things, love?' Her anxious eyes searched my face, uncomprehending. 'I don't know what you mean.'

If it had been Matt, was what I meant, I thought horrified. If it had been Matt in trouble, would I have gone? Yes, like a shot. Terrified by my own feelings, I got to my feet.

'I must go,' I muttered, heading for the door. 'Must go to him. Now.'

'Of course you must, an' he'll be fine, don't worry.' She hastened out after me, across the landing and down the stairs. 'Let's face it, he must have called an ambulance, must have come to his senses to some extent to be in hospital in the first place, so no doubt he can put it all behind him. All will be well, you'll see. It's you I'm worried about,' she said as we reached the hall.

419

I turned quickly. 'Why?'

'Well, first off, I don't want you drivin' all that way all upset like this. You'll have an accident. Have a cup of tea an' put somethin' in your stomach before you go. Calm down a bit.'

'Oh. Yes, you're right.' I followed her numbly into the kitchen and sat down at the table as if in a dream. Watched as she poured from a pot already brewed. I glanced at the clock. Nine o'clock. She would have been up for hours when Gertrude called.

'Where's Clare?' I glanced nervously about.

'Still asleep. It went well with Michael. I heard her come in; she came in and sat on my bed and told me. Flora's asleep, too.'

'Good.' I licked my lips. Swallowed hard. 'Mum, don't tell them, will you?' I looked at her pleadingly as she put a cup and saucer in front of me. 'I mean, I'm sure you're right and he'll be fine, and so – so there's no reason for anyone to know really, is there?'

She fixed me with her grey eyes. 'No. No reason.'

I thought of the shame he'd feel if Flora knew . . . Clare, Michael. Rosie and Dan . . . I bent my head and clutched my hair, pulling hard at the roots. Oh David, why did you do it?

'Why did he do it?' I whispered aloud to the table.

'He didn't,' Mum said firmly, bustling around the kitchen, opening the bread bin and taking out a loaf. 'He's still alive. It's what's known as a cry for help.' She reached into the fridge for the ham, and I watched numbly as she quickly sliced the bread, buttered it and cut the sandwiches into triangles before packing them neatly in the foil. 'A cry for help,' she repeated carefully, setting the package on the table in front of me, 'that only he can answer.'

I wasn't sure what she meant by that. Felt dazed by the whole thing, actually. I gazed at the glittering tin foil.

'I can't eat,' I muttered.

'I know, love, that's why I've packed it. Eat some on the way. It's a long drive.'

I nodded, then got up. 'I'd better go. You'll look after Flora for me?'

'Of course.' She followed me to the door.

'Say I had to go to London to . . . Well. Just say David's ill or something. Bad flu. Or – or a problem with the wedding arrangements.'

'I'll think of something.'

As I kissed her floury cheek on the doorstep, she put a hand on my arm. 'Think very carefully, my love,' she said. 'Really carefully. Nobody wants you to be a martyr.'

'What d'you mean?'

'What I say. One in the family's quite enough. An' you're very like me, Annabel. Too like me. Nothin' like Clare or your father. Very biddable. Malleable. Like me.'

I held her eyes, and it seemed to me all her years with Dad rolled back before me. I wondered how much she'd suffered in silence. Felt profoundly shocked. Clare had certainly been bludgeoned with education, but . . .

She smiled, reading my mind. 'Oh no, love, nothin' terrible. Your dad and I rubbed along quite happily as it happens, an' I never let him think otherwise. Companionship gets a very bad press these days, yet sometimes it's worth fightin' for. But you, Annabel, you've got more choice than I had. An' I don't think you're lookin' for companionship. Although if you did choose it, no doubt you'd make as good a fist of it as I did.'

Companionship. I stared at her, wanting her to say more, but she was patting my arm, walking me to the car.

'Mum.' I licked my lips, knowing this moment might not come again. 'Mum, with Ted, is that companionship, or . . .'

She stopped in the yard. Looked ahead. 'I've known Ted all my life,' she said quietly. 'Longer even than I knew your dad. Went to school with him. But Shirley set her cap at him, an' Ted was an easy-goin' young man, easily flattered, so he married her. And I married your dad. And very happy we all were too, on our neighbourin' farms.' She walked on and opened the car door for me.

'But you always loved him?' I stared at her back, horrified. 'Ted? Is that what you're saying? That you loved him all that time?' She stayed silent. Looked up at the hills. 'But, Mum, you were always criticising him, always needling him. Told us his methods were all wrong, that Dad's were much better, and—'

'We must shield the heart somehow, mustn't we, love?' she said softly. She turned and gave me a look of perspicacity.

I stared at her for a long moment. 'So – so then why didn't you . . . I mean, Dad's been dead four years now, why didn't you—'

'An' Shirley's not been dead a year,' she said quietly.

'Oh,' I breathed. 'Yes, I see,' I said, our eyes still locked.

'Now come on,' she said brightly, breaking the moment, 'be off with you. An' as I say, whichever way you go, whichever way the wind takes you, all will be well. You'll be as happy as I was. It's in your nature to make the best of things, just as it is in mine. All I'm saying is, never forget you have a choice.' She waited for me to get in the car, then shut the door firmly behind me. I wound down the window.

'I'm getting married in five weeks.'

She regarded me for a long moment. 'Course you are, my duck. Course you are.'

As I turned the car around in the yard, she walked back to the open front door. I saw her in my rear-view mirror, standing framed in the doorway, the green architrave freshly repainted that spring as it had been every third spring for the past thirty-five years, the well-tended bedding plants nodding in tubs beside her, soon to be replaced with autumn pansies. She'd recognised her desires, but recognised

423

her duties too. Contained her passion. She raised her hand, trying not to look anxious as she waved me off.

As I bumped off down the potholes I gripped the wheel hard, feeling sick to my stomach. Oh David, why, why? I pleaded as I flew down the lanes. But I knew why. Knew why he'd done it. Knew how much his reputation meant to him, what he'd seen in his mind's eye. 'Doctor in negligence scandal!' screamed the tabloid headlines, the cameras catching him in a blinding flash as he walked, head down, from the Royal Courts of Justice, his solicitor beside him, shielding him. Oh, I knew what being dragged through the courts would do to him – would do to anyone – but particularly a man for whom – I stopped. Was I going to say for whom appearance was all? Was that true? *Was* it all? Surely there was more substance to David than that? I mean, certainly the letters after his name, the surgery in Belgravia, the house in SW6 all mattered, but what about me? What about Flora, Gertrude . . . had he really been about to leave us? Surely we mattered more than anything else?

I tried not to, but couldn't help imagining him: pale, shaking, sweating, his fair hair falling over his face as he sat on the side of the bed – our bed perhaps – opened his briefcase and took out the packets of pills so readily available to him. Swallowing handful after handful, gulping them down with water, and then lying back, wide-eyed, on the bed. I was horrified to find anger welling up inside me as well as pity. How could he have decided life wasn't worth living when I was still in it? And what if he had died, wasn't that such a coward's way out? Where was his strength of character, to leave a bride, weeks before she was due to walk down the aisle, except ... I breathed deeply and clutched the wheel harder. Realised that in all conscience I couldn't pursue that line of thought. Because ... what if David had had an inkling about my feelings for Matt? What if that had tipped the balance?

I'm sorry, I'm so sorry, I breathed at the windscreen, tears burning my eyes. I'll make it up to you, I swear I will, we'll put this all behind us!

We'll move, I thought determinedly as I raced up the motorway, joining it at full throttle, my heart revving madly too. Get married and then move away, that was it. We'd go ... well, maybe to Yorkshire, or somewhere quite remote, where no one knew us. David could join a little country practice, and we could buy a lovely stone farmhouse on the – what were they, the moors? Or the Dales? Anyway, James Herriot country, with winding lanes and sheep-flecked hillsides, and I'd bake and have hundreds of children and Flora would play with all the village children and we'd be terribly, *terribly* happy. I had a feeling I was deep in Sunday night telly land now, complete with flower-print dresses and 1950s hairdos, and I also seemed to recall the TV wife became rather disillusioned with her domestic lot, stamped her foot and tore off her pinny before fleeing to London, but I put that from my mind. 'We'll be fine,' I repeated to myself like a mantra as I tore along the M5. 'David and I. We'll be absolutely fine.'

When I got to London, some hours later, I wove my way through the busy streets to the Fulham Road and parked behind the hospital, in the underground car park. I ran up the ramp and then, not wanting to look too desperate, made myself walk along the bustling pavement, through the jostling crowds, to the main entrance. Taking a deep breath, I pushed through the plate-glass doors and went into the cool, marble, minimalist interior.

I'd been here before on a couple of occasions to pick David up on our way out to dinner, usually when he'd popped in after surgery to see how one of his patients was doing. He'd often done that, I thought with an aching heart. Followed up his patients after they'd been admitted to hospital. He didn't have to, but he was so caring. Of course, I thought with a pang, he was well known here. Well known by the medical staff.

When I asked the girl on reception, she looked at me in surprise.

'Dr Palmer?'

'Yes, he's – a patient.'

'Oh. Yes, of course.' She flushed with recognition, embarrassed. 'He's in the Parthenon ward, fifth floor.'

The lift took for ever to come, so I ran up the

escalator and then down the shiny linoleum corridors flanked by vast floor-to-ceiling windows. I arrived panting at another desk. Clutched it.

'Could you tell me, I'm looking for Dr . . . Oh. No, don't bother.'

A tall figure rose from a chair at the far end of the corridor. Gertrude was coming slowly towards me, her usually erect figure slightly stooped, dressed in a midnight-blue velvet cloak, a lace hanky clutched in one hand. I ran to her.

'Gertrude!'

We embraced.

'Annabel, my dear,' she said softly. 'I'm so sorry.'

'Is he all right?' I gasped.

'Asleep,' she said, motioning her head to a room behind us. 'We won't disturb him. Come. Sit by me.'

She took my arm and led me wearily back to a line of grey plastic chairs outside his door, sat down and patted the one beside her.

I stood though, staring through the round glass pane in his door. I saw his face, a face I loved, pale on the pillow, turned to one side, his eyes shut, mouth slightly open. His shoulders in the white hospital gown looked narrow and vulnerable, his hands limp and sensitive on the white blanket. How he must hate to be here.

'Oh David,' I moaned, my hand shooting involuntarily to my mouth.

'Come,' Gertrude repeated gently, standing up and

taking my arm. This time I went. Sat beside her. Numb. Horrified.

'I blame myself,' I whispered, realising I did. I really did. This was all my fault.

'Don't be ridiculous,' she said crisply. 'This has nothing whatever to do with you.'

Her words stung, almost like an insult. I turned. She laid a hand on my arm. 'And everything,' she went on more gently, 'to do with David being David. So much of which he should have told you.'

'Oh but he did, Gertrude, he did!' I insisted. 'He told me about the patient dying, about the possible court case, the family suing him – I know all about that. And he told me all about Hugh, too, his reservations about David becoming a doctor, David's own worries about not being good enough. I know all of that.'

She nodded. 'And you think that could be enough to tip him over the edge like this?' She regarded me keenly. I blanched.

'Well . . . no. I didn't really think so, to be honest. I'm surprised. Which is why I thought maybe it was me . . .' I trailed off.

'No, Annabel, it's not you. It goes further back than that.' She sighed, rearranging her cloak around her. She was silent for a moment. I waited.

'You know I brought him up, of course. So I know him well, hm?'

'Of course. Of course you do.'

'And you know, too, that I inherited a little

428

eight-year-old boy who'd lost his parents. A very bewildered, frightened child.'

'Yes, I know that. They died in a boating accident. Gertrude, I know that must have been awful for him, but—'

'One died in a boating accident,' she interrupted quietly. 'His mother. She dived off a boat far out in the middle of the Camel estuary one evening. Never came back.'

'The Camel—' I stared. 'But I thought . . . David said it was abroad. At least I thought it was. Or someone said . . .'

'Well, he never really says, if you think about it. Never talks about it. And if you ask directly, he says they drowned at sea on holiday, then clams up and you don't ask any more, but you're right, one assumes a ship somewhere, overseas. He deliberately keeps it vague. And I do too, for him. For his sake. But I should have told you where it happened when you came to see me to ask about the house. Nearly did, as a matter of fact, as we were standing there looking at that painting in the dining room. But he'd expressly asked me not to.'

'So . . . Taplow House? It happened there?'

'On a family holiday. David was on the boat with his parents one evening; they had a little dinghy which they kept in the creek. His mother was swimming from it, and David and his father were fishing. Pammy obviously got into difficulties, and they didn't notice. She was a strong swimmer, and she'd said she was going to swim out to a rock. Had done it before, apparently. Well, David caught something, and Angus, his father, was helping him reel it in. When they turned round, she'd gone. There was no sign of her, just empty sea. Angus dived in and swam around desperately, and finally he found her, floating amongst a mass of driftwood and seaweed, face down. Somehow he managed to haul her back on board, and then rowed like crazy back to the shore.'

'Was she alive?'

'Just, apparently. Angus tried to resuscitate her on the shore but failed, so he carried her up to the house, up to their bedroom, sobbing, panicking completely, demented with grief, trailed by David. He laid her on the bed, still desperately trying to resuscitate her, shutting David out of the room when he tried to come in. He should have been calling the emergency services, but he was still clinging to her as the life drained out of her, grief-stricken. She was his whole life, you see. A strong, beautiful vibrant woman, and he of course was a brilliant man. Brilliant doctor. But he couldn't save her. It was David who finally dialled nine nine nine, downstairs on his own, trembling, terrified.'

'Oh God . . . how awful!'

'But then when the ambulance came, ten minutes later, the sirens wailing up the lane, which Angus must have heard, there was a loud bang from upstairs. David ran up, and found his father lying in a pool of blood. He'd shot himself. Propped his shotgun up against a cupboard door, and used his foot as a lever to shoot himself in the mouth.'

'Oh dear God!' I shot out of my chair. Flew to the window opposite and gripped the handrail hard.

'David was there for a few minutes on his own with them before the ambulance men arrived.'

I swung around, appalled. 'Gertrude, how awful! He never told me. I never knew!'

'I know, and he should have done. Of course he should. Except . . .'

'Except what?'

She hesitated. 'Well, if you had known, at the beginning, might it not have put you off? Might you not have thought: Golly, he must be a thoroughly mixed-up individual, and then watched for every sign? Every irrational move he made, every surface he obsessively wiped, every time he raised his voice, might you not have thought: Ah ha, traumatic childhood, when in fact it could be a perfectly normal character trait? David hated the idea of that. The idea that every move he made could be traced back to that seminal moment in his childhood. It revolted him, so he kept quiet.'

'I don't blame him for that,' I murmured. 'I think it's brave of him not to use it as an excuse. Some people would. Do. Take no responsibility for their own actions and hang everything on a hook in their past, but . . . surely later, Gertrude, when he asked me to marry him. Surely then, when we were committing our lives to each other?'

Gertrude sighed. Shrugged her shoulders wearily. 'Should we own people so completely? Know every single detail, if they're to be ours?'

I considered this. 'It's not a detail, Gertrude.'

She nodded. 'I know. It's a fundamental truth about him, and I agree, one he should have shared with you, ultimately. But who's to say it's still the genesis of all of this?' She waved her jewelled hand despairingly at the door behind which David lay. 'We're now surmising, or at least I am, that because he was at that house again, it triggered all this off.'

'But why *go* to the house?' I said, baffled. 'Why encourage me to take it – which he did, Gertrude, he really did – when presumably he hadn't been back there since . . .'

'No, you're right, only once, since it happened. Hugh and I took him one year, hoping for the best, but it was a disaster, so after that, we always took him to France, and used Taplow House when he was at boarding school.' She sighed. 'Perhaps we should have sold it, but we loved it there. Felt guilty that we *did* love it after all that had happened, but we didn't blame the house, you see. Still don't. And yes, I *was* astounded when David rang me and said you wanted it for the summer, but you know, my dear, I think he wanted the day of reckoning.' She turned to look at me. 'Wanted to face up to the demons. Banish them. Because I don't think he ever has entirely faced them, and he knew it. He certainly never talked to me, or Hugh, about the manner of his parents' death,

432

and although we tried – gently at the time, when he was young – he always clammed up. Wouldn't speak of it. And of course in those days there wasn't the counselling there is now. Wasn't the emphasis, and we somehow felt, well, poor little scrap, he's been through enough. Let's leave him be. My fault, perhaps.' Her strong face crumpled. I took her hand as she pressed a hanky to her eyes with the other. She suddenly looked terribly old and tired.

'Nonsense,' I said quietly. 'Not your fault. All you did was take him into your house and love him and treat him as your own son. It's no one's fault, Gertrude. We're both trying to blame ourselves, and it's . . . well. It's life. Tragic and raw.'

I thought back to that little boy, standing over the bodies of his parents at that scene of horror. Suddenly my mouth dried. I swung around to her.

'Gertrude, where – which bedroom was it in?'

'The main one, with the big picture window, looking out over the bay.' She regarded me squarely. 'We always slept there, Annabel, Hugh and I. It's the best room. We redecorated it completely of course, changed all the furniture, but it's not the house. Never was. I had no qualms about knowing you were sleeping in that room, although I did wonder at David . . .'

'Yes,' I breathed, remembering our two nights in there together. How must he have felt? I remembered his bout of passionate love-making. Was that banishing the demons? I shivered.

'I think I shall sell it now, however,' said Gertrude, straightening up in her chair. 'I'm getting too old. And after all this . . .'

We were silent for a while. Each staring bleakly out of the window at the rooftops of London beyond. The sun hung in a misty haze over them. I felt my own mood, too, suspended, floating. After a while, I stood up.

'I'm going in now, Gertrude. Going to see him.'

She nodded. 'And I'm going home for a bit. I'm exhausted.'

'You must be.'

I went to the door and stared through the circle of glass at his sleeping profile. Took a deep breath.

'Remember,' Gertrude cautioned, coming up behind me, 'he didn't want me to tell you. Felt it was too shaming. He doesn't know you're here.'

'I know.'

I turned and squeezed both her hands. She squeezed mine back and we traded brave smiles, both with watery eyes. Then I reached for the handle and went in.

chapter twenty-four

As I shut the door softly behind me, David's eyes flickered. He was lying on his back, his head slightly elevated by the bed-head. It took him a moment to wake up and register, but then he groaned.

'Oh God.'

'I know,' I said, crossing the room and slipping quickly into a chair by his bed. 'Gertrude said you'd told her not to tell me, but she had to, David, you must see that.' I took his hand, lying limp on the blanket.

'Why?' he said harshly, turning his head away.

'Because . . .' I faltered, then tried again. 'Well, because if I don't know, I can't help you. Oh my darling, how are you?' So inadequate, but what else?

'How am I? I'd have thought it was perfectly obvious to even the most casual observer that I'm recovering from a little bout of stomach irrigation. I'm feeling the effects of an internal explosion having tampered with the self-destruct button.' His voice was almost militant in its detachment.

'But – but why, David? Why did you do it?' I squeezed his hand. 'Was it just the court case?'

'*Just* the court case?' he said with heavy emphasis. He turned his head back to me. 'My professional reputation dragged through the mud? My good name in tatters? My practising certificate taken away from me, unable to work as a doctor again, everything I've worked for – *just* the court case?'

'I – I know,' I stammered. 'Awful. But it hasn't happened yet, David. They've only threatened legal action, haven't they? And you're innocent until proven guilty, and they may not even find you guilty!'

'They will,' he said flatly, turning away again. 'But it wasn't just that,' he added bitterly. 'Since you ask. It was everything.'

I felt scared. Licked my lips. Tried again.

'David, Gertrude told me about your parents. I'm so sorry. So sad and sorry for you.'

He didn't bring his head back this time. Stared resolutely at the opposite wall. 'But, you see, that's not what I want,' he said quietly. 'Your sympathy.'

'N-no, I – I'm just saying.' I swallowed, hunting for the words. Everything I said sounded wrong or trivial. 'I'm just saying I couldn't come in here and pretend I didn't know.'

'Why not? I did. For years. Why does everything have to be put out and aired on an emotional washing line? Examined for stains, held up for general inspection?'

I inhaled sharply. Everything about his demeanour was hard and knowing. He was so composed, despite his evident physical weakness. I squeezed his hand. Tried a different tack.

'I'm so glad you didn't do it, David,' I said warmly. 'So glad you called an ambulance.'

He turned to face me. 'I didn't. My neighbour in Islington found me. She'd taken delivery of a registered parcel. She's a key-holder, and because I'm never there, always at your place, she used her key to let herself in and put it on my kitchen table. She walked past me lying on the sofa. Dropped the parcel and screamed the place down, apparently. Then called an ambulance.'

I stared at him, horrified. 'You were going to do it?'

'Oh yes. I was.'

'And . . .' I tried to scramble my thoughts together. 'N-no note, or anything?' I stammered. 'I mean – what about me?'

Awful. He'd wanted to end his life, and all I could think was: What about me? It hung in the air, suspended. I couldn't take it back.

He kept the expressionless mask in place as he stared at the ceiling. Suddenly it buckled. 'That's what I said,' he gasped, 'when it happened to me. What I said when my father did it. What about me!'

Tears began to flood sideways out of his eyes, streaming down on to the pillow. He covered his face with his hands. I swooped to hold him, cradling his head in my arms as he sobbed.

'Don't, David, shush!' I rocked him.

'I'm so sorry, Annie,' he choked. 'So sorry!'

'Don't. Don't!'

He sobbed on and on, and we stayed like that, me holding his head tightly, like a rugby ball, as he cried into my shoulder. At length, he recovered. Nodded to show me he was fine. I unclasped him. Took his hand as he rested his head back on the pillow.

'And I'm sorry I didn't tell you,' he said, wiping his face roughly with his forearm. 'I wanted to, so many times. Wanted to go to the house with you, tell you there. Tell you what had happened there so long ago. Wanted to get over the past once and for all, and I thought I could do it with you beside me, you see. Thought I could draw strength from you, because I loved you so much. And I thought I loved you more than I loved them, my parents, so it would work. That one love would triumph over another. But . . . I discovered it's not necessarily the ones you love the most that have the most effect on you. I didn't know that.' He was quiet for a moment. 'And anyway,' he added bitterly, 'how was I to know I was comparing one delusion with another?'

I felt stricken. A delusion. They hadn't loved him enough to stay, and I hadn't loved him enough to . . . But how could I protest?

'And that's why you did it?' I whispered. 'Tried to kill yourself?'

'Yes, because I realised I'd never overcome the pain. Never. I'd held out for that moment you see, for being in that house, and then when it didn't work, I felt such an overwhelming sense of defeat. It was so frightening. When I got back here, to London, I felt this wave of terror literally sweep from my head to my toes. Because I knew that having faced it and failed, I was hollow. Knew that *not* facing it was the only way I'd contained it all these years. It had given me strength, and now I'd lost it.'

'And I was no help. No help at all.'

'But you didn't know. Weren't to know.' He sat up a bit and reached for a box of tissues by the bed. Blew his nose noisily. Then he turned his head again and stared out of the window. We were silent for a while and I digested what he'd said. After a while, a nurse popped her head around the door.

'Everything all right?'

David didn't answer. Continued staring out of the window.

'Yes, we're fine, thank you,' I said swiftly.

She came in and glanced at the chart on the end of his bed.

'Right . . .' she murmured. She glanced at David coldly, nodded curtly at me, and then went away again.

I took his hand. 'Are they nice to you in here?' I asked anxiously.

'Not particularly,' he said wryly. 'Suicide cases are always treated with disdain, to dissuade them from trying it again. And a doctor who tries it, who wastes their time when they've got genuinely sick people to care for ... well, I don't exactly get tea and sympathy.'

I took a deep breath. Let it out shakily. Oh David. My poor, dignified, dapper Dr David Palmer, striding in here as he usually did in his Jermyn Street suit, briefcase in hand, nodding and smiling at nurses on his way up to see a patient ...

'Anyway. I won't be here for long. I can discharge myself tomorrow.'

'Exactly.' I raised a smile. 'And then you'll be back around the corner in Sloane Street again, where you belong. When you've had a bit of time off.'

He gave a thin smile. 'Oh no, I'm not going back to the surgery. I'm taking a long time off.'

My heart lurched. 'You're not ... giving up? No, David, they can't make you do that, they surely can't.'

'I'm not sure what they can and can't do, but I'm going anyway. A long way away.' He turned to look at me. 'I'm going to Nicaragua, Annie.'

'Nicaragua!' I was startled. 'Why?'

'Because there's a terrible famine unfolding over there, and the Red Cross are desperate for qualified doctors. I think I could be of some help.'

I stared. He looked back at me. Composed. Implacable.

'Right.' I swallowed. Golly. He thought he could be of some help. Did he mean him, or all of us? I thought of the three of us out there, crowded into a little mud hut in the jungle – or was it the desert? My mind spun. Nicaragua. Heavens, where was it? Africa, somewhere? I saw myself frenziedly slapping suncream on Flora's fair skin, squirting mosquito spray all round the hut, getting water from the well – or the river, even – holding hands with all those poor children with pot bellies, feeding them rice perhaps, or – or no, not just feeding them. No, I'd have to join in. My stomach lurched. Have to – you know – nurse. There'd be blood, and – and worse, and . . . Oh God. I felt faint.

David was watching me. He smiled. A proper, gentle smile, for the first time since I'd been in that room. 'No, you were right the first time, Annie. It's what *I'm* going to do, not what *we're* going to do.'

'You mean . . . on your own?'

He held my gaze. 'Do you want to come?'

I stared. 'Well, I . . .'

'Do you love me, Annie?'

I opened my mouth to speak. His eyes were challenging. Not hostile, but challenging. I glanced down.

'I . . . Well. Of course I—'

'Hey,' he interrupted softly. Squeezed my hand. 'That's enough. Let's not go there. We both know the truth. I love you to pieces, to distraction, always have done. But somehow I knew that once you'd recovered from your shattered marriage and your pit of despair about Adam, you might fly. Leave me. And you have. You're streets ahead of me already, Annie. You've met someone else.'

I glanced up in terror.

'I know,' he said gently. 'I could tell. In Cornwall. And it's all right, my darling, I promise. Yes, I'm sad, but it wasn't the catalyst for all of this. Didn't help, naturally.' He looked beyond me. Took a deep breath. 'When love is withdrawn, you don't just feel its absence, you feel . . .'

'Demeaned?' I put in. I knew. Had had it withdrawn from me.

'Yes.' He nodded. 'But now, because another phase of my life is unfolding, and because it's all going to be so different, I can face it alone. I couldn't in all conscience take you and Flora on this journey halfway across the world, and it is something I've always wanted to do. You know that.'

I bent my head. Rested my forehead on his hand in shame.

'Oh David, I'm so sorry,' I whispered. 'I'm so ashamed!'

'Don't be. You can't help your feelings. You can't help falling in love. Passion is the only true motivation; it's what it's all about. And anyway' – he turned his head away – 'I think I always knew someone proper might come along.'

'Proper?' I raised my head.

'You met me when you were so low, Annie. I was just what you needed at the time. Necessary ballast to keep you afloat. Keep you safe. And I badly wanted to keep you. Thought marriage, babies – lots of babies, quickly – would do the trick. Bind you to me. But I see now how hopeless it was.'

'You mean, that sort of control?'

'It wasn't about control. It was about survival. My survival strategy.'

He gave a wry smile. 'This may sound ridiculous, but I'm actually glad I took an overdose. Glad I was rescued too. By doing something so terrible, so drastic, I've drawn a line in the sand. I've stared rock bottom in the face, recognised it, and now I can only go up. I've changed the course of my life completely. It's made me realise what I *have* got, and what I *can* do. And I do want to live. I'm so glad I didn't die. I panicked, you see. Thought I was losing everything, but actually, there are some things I've gained. As soon as the court case is over, which Hugo now says will be short and sharp with possibly an out-of-court settlement, I'll be off. Jamie – you know, my mate from Oxford – has a brother in charge of the Red Cross out there, and I know he'll find me something, whatever the outcome of the trial.'

'And you'll be brilliant at it, David,' I said warmly. He would. Because despite everything, he was dauntless. And also . . . incredibly good in the purest sense. I could see him now, bronzed from the sun, in a white coat, running a clinic in a tent; a row of mothers in turbans with their babies on their knees waiting to see him; other like-minded medics around him, maybe even a pretty nurse . . .

David looked at me enquiringly. 'Where are you, Annie?'

'Hm?'

'Please tell me you're not in a Red Cross tent.'

'Sorry?'

'You know, with me in a white coat, all sort of God-like, syringe in hand, orderly ranks of Nicaraguan folk before me in fun, ethnic dress, awaiting their serum from handsome Dr Palmer and his assistant, attractive Nurse Dewy-Eye who's gazing up at him adoringly? Please tell me you're not there?'

I flushed. 'Well . . .'

'It won't be like that,' he said softly. He took my hand. 'Believe me. It's a famine, Annie. The pictures on the six o'clock news, the awful ones with pro-cessions of emaciated bodies traipsing hopelessly across the desert, close-ups of babies, their mouths besieged by flies, staring children with huge, swim-ming eyes, their tummies bloated with air, gazing blankly at the cameras: those are the sanitised ones. The ones they feel we can stomach in our sitting rooms. The ones they feel they can show the Hampshire housewife who's watching it on the little kitchen telly, stirring the gravy, awaiting her husband's return on the six-twenty-two. But the ones they can't show are far, far worse. Please don't think you could have come and sent Flora to the village school, washed your clothes in the river and dried them on a line from the roof of your dear little rush hut. It won't be like that.'

I hung my head.

'But I'm delighted you considered it,' he

whispered, lifting my chin so I had to look at him. 'Thank you. You're so selfless, Annie. I almost think you would have done it. Married someone you didn't love so as not to rock the boat. So as not to upset the wedding apple cart. I mean, after all, the reception's organised, everyone's bought presents, outfits . . .'

'Except it wouldn't have been selfless, would it?'

'Not in the end, no. You'd have ended up resenting me, and trying to hide it, but I'd have known. And we'd have had a miserable time. No, this is the right way, Annie. I can't say I'm letting you go with joy jumping in my heart, because I love you so much, but this is the only way.'

I gazed at him, silent. Marvelling at him.

'What shall I tell Flora?' I whispered eventually.

'The truth. You'd be amazed at how much straight-talking kids can take, and she may not be all that surprised, either.' He swallowed. 'It . . . goes without saying that I'm very fond of Flora, Annie. And I'd hate never to . . .' He tipped his head back, inhaled deeply.

'Oh, we'll see you often!' I cried. 'Stay the best of friends, write to you, keep in touch—' I broke off, horrified. Keep in touch! The man I'd loved, who so recently had been the core of my universe, the pivot in my world, who I'd been due to marry in a matter of weeks?

Suddenly I lost control. I was overcome with tears which seized their chance and fled hot and salty down my face. David held out his arms and I clung to him as we mourned what we'd nearly had.

After a while though, after much nose-blowing and reassuring nods at each other and exchanging of shaky smiles, he patted my hand. I knew it was my signal to go. I stuffed my hanky up my sleeve, sniffing. Clinging on.

'But where will you go?' I whispered. 'I mean, after here?'

'I'll go to Gertrude's for a bit. She'll love having me to fuss over, to look after. And I'll sell the flat and go abroad as soon as I can. I'm looking forward to it. Really, Annie.' He smiled.

And actually, I sensed that he was. That beyond all of this, like hills rising beyond hills, there was a kind of optimism, which, given the right conditions, would spark out of the darkness of such desperate events. And although I felt stricken that he'd felt he'd reached the end of all hope, had succumbed to total despair and was lying here now, I felt relieved too. Because a new life *would* course through him, unlike any previous life. I hoped it would enable him to embrace whatever was current and possible, and not to grieve for what had passed. Be his true survival strategy. I squeezed his hand.

'Go on,' he whispered. 'Before I change my mind. Before I beg you to stay and marry me and have babies with me. Before I chain you to me with rows of nappies and tiny hands clutching at your skirt. Go on. Get out of here.' He smiled. It was an anointing smile.

I managed a watery one back. Then I leaned across, kissed his forehead very gently, hovered for a moment, and left.

chapter twenty-five

I sat in my car in the hospital car park for a long while, my head resting on the wheel. It was tempting to wallow in emotion, in profound regret for what we'd lost, David and I, and I sat there, waiting for it to happen, waiting to feel bereft. Instead, as I lifted my head at last, something else flooded through me: something that felt profoundly like relief – albeit guilty relief – yet it was there, as assuredly as if the dam gates were bursting and the water gushing out. In fact, the knowledge that I'd done completely the right thing back there came to me with such resounding clarity that I was faintly shocked. Not that *I'd* actually done anything, I realised with another guilty pang as I switched on the engine. It was David; all David's doing. Letting me go, cutting the ropes, giving me an out – and he'd been right, timorous creature that I was, I might not have gone of my own accord; might have shuffled along, sheep-like, with all the arrangements if he hadn't taken the whip hand. Anything to keep the peace.

Except – I swung out into the busy main road – except no. No, I wouldn't have, actually. In my heart I knew I couldn't have gone through with it. Would have put a stop to it eventually, but probably right at the last minute, much too late, of course. At the altar, no doubt: nice and dramatic, running back down the aisle, veil flying, tossing my posy, making things far, far worse. And the reason I couldn't have gone through with it – this, again, came to me with all the subtlety of the Rank gong – was because the force driving Matt and me together was already far too strong. We were already too deeply in . . . what? Was it love? I nearly drove off the road. Yes. Yes, that was it. I'd fallen in love.

Swallowing hard but feeling horribly euphoric, I beetled off down the Fulham Road towards the M4. Towards the sun. If any sense at all prevailed, every-thing told me that after a four-hour drive from Devon I shouldn't even be contemplating doing the same again plus another hour to Cornwall, and should be heading for my home around the corner to spend the night before setting off the next morning. I dithered for a moment at the junction to my road. OK. I'd pop home and collect the post, I decided, but that was all. There'd be no sensible overnight stay. I hadn't fallen slowly and judiciously in love with Matt, I'd fallen headlong and impulsively, and in the same manner did I joyously swing the wheel to flit – only very briefly – home.

The familiar road was dry and dusty, suffering in

the late July heat, and on my doorstep the geraniums and petunias wilted forlornly in the sun. As I went in, the mustiness closed around me like a shawl: the fug of a forgotten townhouse in summer. It all looked so small, so dingy. Familiar, but in a long ago, regretful sort of way. It made me feel sad. I stooped on the mat to collect the sea of post, then went down the passage into the kitchen. A coffee cup David had used was in the sink, and I gulped when I saw one of his cashmere sweaters hanging over the back of a chair. It seemed to me the arm waved reproachfully at me. No doubt he would come in and pick up his things when I was away, I thought. Yes. Much easier. A clean break, no fuss. I clenched my fists. So clinical after all we'd . . . No. Not down that sentimental path, Annie. That way nostalgia lay, not my heart.

I had a quick glass of water then headed purposefully back outside, double locking the front door behind me and walking to the car. Another great wave of relief washed over me. Made me stop still in the street, actually. Because it was true, I was secretly pleased it would all be cleared out while I was away. Pleased that I'd come back to find all trace of him gone. How callous was that? Except the thought of being there on my own again filled me with another sort of dread. Would I, though? Would I be on my own? Surely not. Or was I imagining more with Matt than there really was?

My mobile rang as I drove off down the road, cutting into my thoughts.

'How is he, love?'

It was Mum.

'He's . . . fine, Mum. Fine. Recovering.'

'And you?'

'Yes, I'm OK, too. We've sorted everything out. There . . .' I faltered. Licked my lips and started again. 'There isn't going to be a wedding.'

She paused. 'I thought not.'

We were silent a moment. She knew. Didn't have to ask. The details would come later. If necessary.

'And how do you feel?'

'Well, the awful thing is, I feel rather relieved.'

'Not awful,' she said slowly. 'The only awful thing is realisin' how quietly influenced you've been. Not maliciously, in David's case, but influenced, none the less. But you don't realise that until they've gone. Then you feel . . . liberated.'

'Yes. Yes, that's just what I feel,' I said, surprised.

We were silent another moment, each considering the other's life. I felt suddenly still and soothed. Something deep inside me relaxed.

'How's Flora?' I asked at length.

'Well, that's what I was ringin' to tell you, love. She went off with Clare, back to Rock. Clare had a lovely night out with Michael by all accounts last night, very starry-eyed she was at the breakfast table this mornin', very unlike Clare. I don't know what their bust-up was about, but it's done them the world of good. Anyway, she couldn't wait to get back this mornin', and she took Flora with her to stay with the cousins. We didn't know how long you'd be, love, and Flora seemed keen enough, and we weren't sure what to do for the best. An' I thought: Well, if you was heading back to Cornwall, silly to make a detour here. Flora's got your bags an' that, so you'll need to pick her up first . . .' She sounded anxious.

'No no, quite right, Mum. You were right. I would have been going back there. I need to . . . sort some things out.'

'I thought as much,' she said. 'Well. Good luck. I hope he's worth it. Hope you've got it right this time.'

I stared into the receiver. My mum. My wise old mum.

'He is,' I breathed. 'Yes, I have got it right, Mum.'

It was a long drive but I didn't mind. In fact I felt quite energised, and concentrated on driving well and fast, and overtaking a lot instead of sitting lazily in the middle lane as I usually did. I was certainly tired – I'd driven miles already that morning – but there's a kind of tired you can get that has its own energy. Its own momentum. I was hungry too, and suddenly glad of the sandwiches and coffee Mum had packed and which I hadn't been able to face on the way up, but polished off now with alacrity. Finally, just as the evening sun was setting and the sky turning a dusty pink, I rounded a bend in a country lane, and there was the sea, stretching out in a huge expanse before me.

When I got to Clare's house in Trebetherick, all

was quiet. In the peaceful cul-de-sac on the hill overlooking the beach, the little white bungalow – one of so many in a grid, which every year packed families in, Tardis-like – was empty. The back door was open though, so I went in and almost tripped over. Buckets and spades littered the sandy kitchen floor, and surfboards and wet towels were draped decoratively on the table. Through in the sitting room, wetsuits lay strewn across the floor like headless black corpses in the aftermath of some terrible uprising, and all the beds were unmade, I noticed, as I wandered from room to room, stepping over piles of dirty washing. I was impressed. In all the time Clare had been taking this house I'd never seen it submerged in such glorious two fingers existence, and yet Clare had beaten me back here: I could see her overnight bag dumped on her bed. She'd had time to clear up. Progress, I thought with a wry smile as I went out into the garden through the open French windows. Definitely progress.

I sauntered down the lawn. It was a beautiful evening, and I knew they wouldn't be far away. I opened the back gate and went down the lane towards the beach, passing the little shop selling postcards and buckets and spades and children's windmills, spinning in the breeze. As I walked across the dunes, shading my eyes against the sun which was sinking low and pink over the water, I saw two familiar figures huddled by a rock, gazing out to sea, while the children made sandcastles nearby. Dan had

453

his arm around Rosie's shoulders, which, for some reason, brought a lump to my throat as I approached.

'Hello, young lovers,' I said, settling down in the sand beside them, hugging my knees. 'Admiring the sunset and counting your blessings?'

Dan looked round with a smile. 'Spot on, actually. And to our surprise, we find we have more than we thought.'

'Where've you been then?' asked Rosie, peering around Dan to look at me carefully.

'Oh, here and there,' I said lightly. She caught my eye and I had a feeling she knew. 'So come on then,' I went on quickly, 'what are they, these blessings?'

'Dan's been offered a job,' said Rosie excitedly, forgetting about quizzing me.

'Oh Dan, that's marvellous.' I put an arm round his neck and gave it a squeeze. 'Congratulations! When did you hear?'

'Well, it's been in the offing for a day or two now,' he said going a bit pink, 'but they rang at lunchtime today, to confirm.'

'Terrific! Back in the square mile? Dusting off your pin-stripes and flogging insurance?'

'No, in a white coat flogging shellfish, actually.'

'*Shell*fish?'

'Well, oysters, primarily. But I'm happy to turn my hand to all manner of crustacean. Cockles and mussels, Molly Malone style. You name it, I'll throw it on my barrow. Splendid aphrodisiacs, incidentally, oysters.'

'But . . . Hang on, where? Billingsgate market or something?'

'Wadebridge, actually,' put in Rosie helpfully. 'On the industrial estate. Not the most salubrious of locations, but jolly convenient.'

'Convenient!' I stared. 'Well, hardly. Only about a four-hundred-mile commute. Are you two on drugs or something?'

Rosie grinned. 'Oh no, something much more intoxicating.' She leaned forward excitedly. 'Remember that supper we had the other night at Rick Stein's? When we went out with Michael's friends, you know, the estate agent and his wife?'

'Er, yes.'

'Well, the estate agent's uncle, who joined us later for a drink, runs this seafood business down here, only he wants to retire. He's got a fantastic supplier and sells all over the country, but mostly to all the fancy London restaurants – you know, the Ivy, the Savoy – everywhere. They've bought from him for years because he guarantees the quality.'

'What – so you're taking over or something?'

'Exactly. He's looking for someone to run the business.'

'But you can't do that from London!'

'Oh no, we'd have to move down here.'

'Down here!'

'Annie, you're doing that really annoying thing of repeating every last thing I say.'

'Sorry, but—'

455

'Yes, move. Sell Fulham for a fortune – hopefully – and buy ourselves a lovely old cottage – or a farmhouse even, property's so much cheaper here – and then Dan can drive to work instead of sitting on a sweaty tube.'

'But . . .' I blustered. 'Hang on. Won't you miss London?' I knew as I said it they wouldn't, but I felt desperate. Horrified to lose her.

'Not a bit. Except for friends, but even then only a few. Most have moved out. The only person I'll really miss is you.'

A great lump came to my throat. I couldn't speak. I knew she was right, that they should do it, but the idea of London without Rosie appalled me.

'We were at our wits' end, Annie,' Rosie said softly. 'Really desperate. We were sinking in London. Ploughing into savings and going under the waterline. Dan's been out of work over a year now, and the City's in turmoil, so even if he got back in, what security would he have?'

'I'd be constantly watching my back, knowing that when heads started to roll again, mine would be first. Last in, first out, that's the rule. And that's not nice, Annie. Not a nice feeling, when every time the internal phone rings you wonder if someone's PA is going to ask you to step this way to the top floor. And when it happens, you straighten your tie with a shaky hand, and you go up in that lift, heart pounding, palms sweating, to be told by someone from Personnel who you've never seen in your life before that they're terribly sorry, and it's nothing personal. Of course it's bloody personal. Then ten minutes later you're clearing your desk in front of embarrassed colleagues, and off home to tell the wife and kids, feeling sick to your stomach. Well, I'm never going through that again, Annie. Never. I'm going to run my own show and be my own boss, and I don't care how hard I'll have to work to do it. To get rid of that gut-wrenching insecurity is worth all the overtime in the world. No one can ever sack me again.'

'And the children?'

'They can go to the local church school, which these guys the other night say is terrific. He lost his job, incidentally, before he started the estate agency business. No school fees will save us a fortune, and we'll all have a much better quality of life. I mean, look at it, Annie.' He swung his arm along the coastline, taking in the dunes, the shore, the sunset. 'This is where I grew up. Where I'd love my children to grow up. But I'd never, ever, considered it a possibility. Can you beat it?'

I stared into the setting sun as it drifted over the horizon, the huge rock in the bay silhouetted against a hazy pink sky. A lone seagull hovered overhead. Dan, the West Country doubter, had surely been down the road to Damascus and out the other side, and he was right. On a day like this, you couldn't beat it. But in winter? Quite isolated. Quite cut off, and Rosie . . . I turned to her.

'What about you?'

'Oh, this isn't just about Dan. We're going to run this thing together. Go into partnership, so some days I'll be with the kids, and some days Dan will. And we'll be up in London a lot too, not always down here. All over the country, in fact, because that's the sort of personal service these fancy restaurants demand. You know, with our vintage van in its smart green livery, the pair of us in matching long white aprons – despite the fact we've roared up the motorway in a white Transit van and transferred the produce to the cutesy antique one parked in London – but you know the sort of crap townies like. And that's why this guy's done so well.'

'Well, not that well,' cautioned Dan. 'It's only shellfish, not Euro bonds, but well enough to bring up his family and retire on the proceeds. And we'll do the same. We'll never be millionaires, but we don't want that.'

They looked at each other and exchanged smiles. And I smiled too. Forgot my selfishness and how much I'd miss them, because I knew they were right. It would be hard work, and possibly lonely, but they were gritty and determined and devoted, and not idealistic. They'd survive. They had to. They'd been offered a chance, and they were bloody well going to grasp it in both hands.

And actually, they would thrive down here, I thought. I could just see Rosie lovingly transforming a neglected old house, just as she had in London, but where she'd got so frustrated by its size. She'd pains-takingly restored it down to the last doorknob, and then looked around helplessly for more to do. She needed a project like this.

'And you could always do B & B,' I put in help-fully. 'Just while you're starting up.'

'I could, and we thought of that, but I don't want to be changing other people's linen, thank you. No, this will work, you'll see.'

'And to get the kids out of that brat race,' added Dan. 'Not to worry about whether they need to play another instrument, or have extra maths to get into another school we can't afford, to just let them swim and surf . . .'

'Heaven,' I agreed. I followed their eyes out to the horizon. I was pretty sure the kids would still want ballet and riding lessons and they'd just have to drive further to get them there, and I knew too that there would be tough times ahead; it wouldn't be a doddle financially. But they were at that lovely, euphoric, plan-making stage and I wasn't going to tread on their dreams. I knew too that love conquers all. Believed that. I dredged up a great sigh of longing.

'And you?' said Rosie, softly.

'Hm . . . ?'

I gazed across the bay, imagining Rosie in a pretty coastal cottage garden, picking the roses around the door, waiting for Dan to come home from Wadebridge, laying a table for supper in a little cobbled courtyard . . .

'Annie, Clare told us. About David.'

'Oh.'

I was brought back to earth with a jolt. Back from
the land of gingham tablecloths laid under apple
trees and posies in jam jars to the hospital with staff
stuffing tubes down his throat, turning on the suc-
tion pump. So. Mum had told Clare after all. Perhaps
it was just as well.

'Annie, I'm so sorry.' Rosie laid a hand on my arm.
'Is he OK?'

'He's fine,' I said shortly. 'Feels a bit foolish, I
think. A little sheepish, and he can't wait to get out of
that hospital, but he's fine.'

'And the two of you . . . ?'

I heaved up another great sigh. Seemed to have a
surfeit of them these days. 'He's . . . very kindly let
me go, as I believe they say in the city, Dan.'

He smiled down at the sand.

'Very unselfishly, and very magnanimously, and in
a very David-like fashion.'

'Ah. I hoped he would,' Rosie said.

'You're not surprised?' I turned to her, astonished.
'You were very fond of David.'

'Still am. I like him enormously, but I wasn't
marrying him, you were. And he was . . . not right
for you, Annie. I can't say I'm desperately surprised,
no. And neither will Clare be.'

I felt quietly shocked. How little I knew. My best
friend and my sister were in agreement. Had they

discussed it, I wondered? Discussed my fiancé's unsuitability? Or mine perhaps?

'We were worried about your lack of enthusiasm,' she said gently. 'Lack of . . . I don't know, wedding mania, *joie de vivre*, excitement. God, you hardly even told me what you were going to wear, for heaven's sake, I'm not sure I even knew. You hadn't bothered with the flowers, hadn't even booked a reception, left it all to David. And he's not stupid. He would have spotted that. You weren't exactly flicking through *Brides* magazine, dithering between gypsophila or a tiara. I know it's your second time around, but even so.'

'And I don't know many blushing brides,' put in Dan quietly, 'who could happily spend the entire summer apart from their fiancé, in self-enforced isolation. Unless of course they're Hindu and living in Nepal with strict religious customs, and incidentally, if that's the case and you've changed denomination, I'll gladly bathe you in ass's milk and take a few conjugal rights reserved for the best friend's husband. I'm sure that tradition still holds.'

I hung my head. 'He was supposed to come down for weekends,' I said defensively.

'Weekends,' scoffed Rosie. 'God, if you were mad about someone, you'd be driving all over the country to see them. Wouldn't want to waste a moment out of their sight. Come dashing back to see them rather like you've just done today,' she added craftily. 'Driven how many hundred miles in one day,

461

Annie?' She eyed me beadily. 'What's the rush?'

I flushed.

'And I haven't even met this guy. Clare's certainly beaten me to it on that score. Says he's something of a dish.'

I caught my breath. 'You mean you both suspected?'

'Oh, we suspected all right. What, all those quiet suppers and little fishing trips and the general lack of your company around this neck of the woods? I don't think I've seen you more than twice since we've been here.'

'Didn't realise it was that obvious,' I muttered.

'Only to the initiated. Dan didn't twig but then he's only a fishmonger. I, on the other hand, am the fishwife.'

I smiled. 'He'll stink, you realise that?'

Dan waggled his eyebrows. 'Some women find it very alluring.'

'And stop changing the subject,' put in Rosie. 'Oh look, here's Clare, she'll pin you down.'

I turned as Clare, arm in arm with Michael, came strolling across the sand, for all the world like love's young dream. Suddenly she threw back her dark head and laughed uproariously at something he said. I hadn't seen her do that for ages. Years. God, all these happy loving couples – suddenly I didn't want to be here. Felt sick. I wanted to leave and find my own other half. I felt my heart pounding.

'Where's Flora?' I called, when she was in earshot.

'Oh, I took her back to Taplow House!' She

stopped short in the sand. Then walked towards me quickly. 'Sorry, I thought that was where you were going. Only I rang Mum, and she said you were on your way back, and you know what Flora's like, she got funny about staying the night here.'

'Oh! Did she?' I got up anxiously.

'Said she'd rather go back and wait for you there. I left her with Matt and Tod. I hope that's OK?'

'Yes, fine. But I'll get back if she's a bit jumpy.' I made to go.

'Annie.' Clare stopped me, resting her hands on my shoulders for a moment. She looked me in the eye. 'I'm so sorry. Mum told me about David.'

I lowered my eyes to the sand. Nodded. 'Yes. Well, he's going to be fine.'

'And . . . she told me everything else, too. About the wedding.'

I glanced up. 'She told you it's off?'

She nodded. 'Thought it would be easier coming from her.'

I swallowed. 'And I gather from Rosie it doesn't come as a huge surprise to anyone.'

She shrugged. 'We were all . . . well, very concerned. About certain aspects. The frenetic baby-making, for instance.'

'I know,' I said softly, looking down again. I sighed. Watched as a tiny little crab scuttled over my foot. I glanced up. 'Anyway. Good to see you two back in one piece.' I slid a grin in Michael's direction. He smiled back and hugged Clare's shoulders.

'As I said to you on the phone, Annie, best thing that ever happened to us. But now for different reasons.'

'Knocked some sense into her is what he means,' said Clare drily.

'I'll second that,' I said, giving them all a backward salute as I moved away, on up the beach, towards the car.

I was aware that they were all watching me go and would probably all settle down to talk about me now. Hunker down in the sand and discuss me in worried tones; wonder if I knew what I was about, if I was doing the right thing, going straight from the frying pan into the fire?

'I mean, it's all very well,' I could hear my sister say, 'but she's only known this guy for a week or so and he may be gorgeous, but who the hell is he? It's classic rebound stuff, isn't it?'

And Rosie would quickly stick up for me, saying I knew my own mind better than Clare thought I did, and Michael would agree, and so it would go on. They'd happily chew the cud for an hour or so in the setting sun, both couples bathed in a rosy optimistic glow: Dan and Rosie excited by the prospect of the new world ahead of them, and Clare and Michael relishing their new-found togetherness. And whilst they certainly wouldn't be relishing the fact that I hadn't quite achieved their own state of nirvana, they'd find, nevertheless, that their own happiness was vicariously heightened by the uncertainty of mine.

And I was desperate to get away from them.

Longing to see Matt. To have my own joyful reunion. To have my own deeply romantic happy-ever-after experience. I hastened to my car, but as luck would have it, when I hit the road I got stuck behind the slowest tractor in the West Country. As I crawled along behind it, down the narrow, winding lanes, the floral banks rearing up mockingly on either side of me, cow parsley nodding teasingly, I banged my fist on the wheel in frustration.

'Oh, come on. Come on!'

But time, for this farmer, was not of the essence, and every time I tried to overtake, a car sped towards me. Finally I gave up and sank back in my seat, sometimes achieving twenty miles an hour, and willing myself to be patient.

With nothing else to do, I opened my post from London. I gathered it all from the passenger seat, and piled it into my lap. It was bills, mostly, and plenty of freebie magazines, but there was also a thick creamy envelope, recognisable from the in-house stamp as being from my publishers. My publishers. My heart did a foolish flip at the proprietorial nature of that sentence, at the use of the personal pronoun. I tore it open and propped it up on the steering wheel as I drove.

Dear Mrs O'Harran,

It has recently come to our attention that a temporary member of staff has been commissioning manuscripts when he had no authority

465

to do so. Sebastian Cooper, nephew of our chairman, Anthony Cooper, was doing work experience here in his gap year. His task was to read unsolicited manuscripts and pass on anything of interest to a more experienced member of staff. Unfortunately, it seems he took it upon himself to write personally to prospective authors, encouraging them with offers of potential advances. We are also deeply embarrassed to learn that these prospective authors – all female – were encouraged to write as salaciously as possible. We understand you are of their number, and would like to offer our sincere and profound apologies. An experienced editor has since read your synopsis, and I'm afraid we will be unable to publish your manuscript. Mr Cooper has left our employ, and is continuing his education at Swansea university. Once again, we offer our deepest apologies.

Yours sincerely,

Emma Tarrant (Head of fiction)

I stared. Read it again. Then my jaw dropped. Bloody hell. Bloody *hell*! God, the little toerag was a ruddy schoolboy! Just out of sixth form and getting cheap thrills from urging frustrated housewives to pen their sexual fantasies! I nearly went up the back of the tractor I was so livid. How dare he? My blood boiled as I imagined some gauche, spotty, loose-limbed youth behind a pile of manuscripts in a dusty, forgotten office at the top of a publishing house, glasses steaming up as lurid sex scenes unfolded before his eyes, mouth open, tongue hanging out – and heaven knows what else under the desk – as he devoured them. And playing on women like me, I thought with a jolt. Women desperate to be published, desperate to go to any lengths to see their work in print. Well, we'll soon see about that, I seethed, hot with indignation and shame. I'd – I'd sue, that's what I'd do. I wouldn't take *this* lying down, oh no!

I put my foot down and sped, with an alarming lack of thought, past the tractor. I missed an oncoming car by inches and, as it swept past me, horn beeping angrily, I flushed hotly. All that work, I seethed. Wasted! But narrowly avoiding a head-on collision had sobered me up a bit. I chewed my nail.

Perhaps it was for the best, I reasoned bitterly. I mean, had I, in all conscience, felt very comfortable with my work recently? Had it sat easily? Oh, it had flowed all right, like an oozing wound, but perhaps it *had* just been the sexually frustrated outpourings of a woman engaged to the wrong man, and not actually something I'd be proud to see in print? Let alone for anyone else to see. Flora, for instance. Or Mum. Mum! My hands leaped off the wheel in terror and the car lurched towards a ditch. I swung it hastily back on the road. And how explicit would I have got, I wondered uncomfortably, with encouragement? How erotic a tapestry would I have woven? How depraved a cast of characters, how many members would I have crammed in – so to speak.

No, I decided hastily. No, this was a blessing in disguise. Thank goodness for Emma Tarrant. Thank goodness she'd nipped it all in the bud before heaven knows what had gushed from my gaudy pen. Lordy, Sebastian might even have got his three in a bed with goat scene, as one of his recent emails had suggested. 'Go for it, Annie!' he'd urged. 'Animals are very big at the moment. Maybe a pig, too?' Oooh . . . I gripped the wheel.

I felt sad though, as I turned into the narrow lane that led to Taplow House. Sad that my secret dream of becoming a novelist was in tatters. There'd been real ambition there; the executing of a private desire that concerned me and no one else. A decision to stick my head above the parapet, and either have it knocked off or, if not laurelled, at least encouraged. But maybe I should try again? Write not romantic fiction, but something that truly fired my imagination? Something that came from the heart? Something I really wanted to write?

I sighed as I pulled into the drive and crunched slowly up the gravel. I was surprised to see an ancient blue Volvo already sitting in pole position, so I swerved and parked alongside it. I frowned. Then it came to me. Of course, it was Thursday, so

Tod was due to be collected by his aunt. By Louise. No wonder Flora had been keen to get here before he went, to say goodbye.

As I got out and walked past the car, I noticed a pile of boys' football boots in the back. Tod's cousins', no doubt. The green front door under the little wooden porch was ajar in the sunshine, lobelia nodding from the hanging baskets, blowing in the breeze. I ducked underneath the blue petals, and felt a sudden rush of relief as I pushed through the door. Nothing mattered. Not really. Not David, not the book. I was back, you see. Back where I belonged in this heavenly house, where not even a spotty seventeen-year-old getting his rocks off courtesy of my scribbles could impinge on my joy at being here. This was where I wanted to be, and it felt good.

'Flora?' I called as I went into the dim, flagstone hall, the Cornish slate cool beneath my feet. It smelled churchy somehow, of wax polish and flowers. 'Matt? I'm back.'

My heart leaped ridiculously as I said that. As if I were home, and he were a part of it.

As my eyes adjusted to the gloom of the timbered sitting room, I saw someone hunched over a newspaper, silhouetted in the bay window. A pretty, dark-haired girl with merry brown eyes glanced up at me. Smiled. 'Hi.'

'Oh, hi.' I smiled and dumped my bag on a chair. 'You must be Louise.'

469

She stood up slowly, the smile fading slightly. She licked her lips.

'Uh, no,' she said hesitantly. 'No, actually. I'm Madeleine. Madeleine Malone?'

chapter twenty-six

I stared at her. Couldn't speak for a moment. Then I found my voice. 'Oh! You mean—' I broke off, astonished. 'Matt's wife.'

As I said it, the implication horrified me. My God. Tod.

'Ex-wife, actually, but yes.'

My mouth went dry. I walked quickly across to the window on the opposite side of the room on the pretext of opening it, to give myself time. I flung it wide and clutched the sill, my heart pounding. I felt the sea wind sharp in my face. Matt's wife. And where the hell was Matt? Tod? I turned back from the window.

'I . . . thought you lived miles away,' I said, managing a nervous smile. 'In Cambridge.'

'I do, and I've just driven all the way down from there. Might I ask who you are?' she said a trifle impatiently.

'Oh, I'm Annie. Annie O'Harran.'

'Well, nice to meet you, Annie O'Harran, but I'm

none the wiser.' She gazed at me steadily. 'Where exactly do you fit in? You see, I'm somewhat nonplussed by what's going on around here. Could you enlighten me? I'm looking for my son.'

I looked back at her. Her eyes were very unusual: amber, intent and focused. She wasn't a bit like I'd imagined. Not a bit. Very pretty, but in a petite, fragile sort of way; with chestnut curls and a pale, heart-shaped face, not slick and blonde and stylish at all. She was wearing a baggy checked flannel shirt, loose over jeans and trainers.

'Only I have to tell you, I'm going slightly out of my mind with worry.' She gave a nervous laugh. Ran a hand through her hair. 'Wondering if he's – I don't know – drowned in the ocean, or gone wandering off someplace.'

I licked my lips. 'I'm afraid I've just arrived back from London. I don't know where he is.'

'But he is here? I mean – living here?'

I took a deep breath. Walked over to the heaving bookcase and stared at the dusty spines. I ran a finger down one of them. Oh dear God. Where are you, Matt?

'Mrs O'Harran, do you have any children?' The voice, when it came, seemed to come from far away.

'Yes. Yes, I do,' I admitted into the ranks of books.

'Then perhaps you'll appreciate how I felt when I called Tod's cousins in Bodmin this morning in order to speak to Tod, and was informed by the housekeeper that no one of that name was staying. No Tod.

Oh, but hang on, this woman said, last week, there had been a boy. A cousin, she thought, American, but only for one night. He'd gone the next day. And no, ma'am, he certainly hadn't been back since.'

I swallowed, staring down at my feet, listening as her voice continued behind me.

'Louise? I asked in panic, fear rising within me like a high-speed elevator. Where was Louise? Oh, out visiting friends in Exeter with the boys, she said, and Tom, her husband, was at work. When I asked who'd picked up the boy, the American boy, she said a man had. A tall man, with a similar accent, who she'd guessed was the father. Well, I tell you, Annie O'Harran, my blood ran cold.'

I turned sharply. 'Why? Is that so terrible? For a father to want to spend time with his son? To collect him for a holiday?'

'You bet your life it is.' She raised her chin in an effort to control her emotion, but I could hear it in her voice. She took a crumpled pack of cigarettes from her jeans pocket, lit one with shaking fingers and blew the smoke out quickly.

'So. Down I came, hitting ninety on the freeway, breaking every damn rule in the book, and arrived at the house in Bodmin a little after four, out of my mind with worry. The house looked deserted. No cars were in the drive, and so I took it Tom and Louise were still out, but happily, the housekeeper was there. I saw her face at the window as I drew up, and as she bobbed behind the drapes, I guessed she'd realised she'd made a mistake. She opened the door just a crack when I rang, and didn't want to let me in. She had to, though, because I pushed her pretty roughly out of the way. It's fair to say I was in quite a state by then.'

She took a swift drag on her cigarette. Walked to the open window, one arm clamped fiercely around her stomach, her back to me.

'So then I set about trying to find Tod. Crazy really, 'cos she'd already told me he wasn't there, but still I went from room to room, shouting like a maniac, running up to the bedrooms, flinging open doors and closets, but sure enough: no trace of him. No clothes, no books, no nothing, and yet I'd driven him to that very house barely a week ago. Had coffee with Louise in the garden, admired the house, seen the room Tod was all set to share with his cousin.'

I continued staring at my shoes. In my peripheral vision, I saw her turn back from the window and regard me carefully, gauging my reaction. She tilted her head down, the better to see my face.

'Awful, huh?' she said softly, finding my eyes. 'When you come to think of it? Think about it properly, Annie. Think how *you'd* feel if you'd left your child in someone else's care and they betrayed your trust. It's treacherous, isn't it? Appalling.'

I raised my head, but didn't respond.

'So, finally,' she went on, 'I went back to the kitchen and made for Louise's desk. The housekeeper's wringing her hands as I rifle through her papers, protesting like the chorus from some Greek tragedy, but I'm oblivious. I'm like – possessed. I went through Louise's diary real thoroughly, her address book – *any*thing just to give me a clue to his whereabouts. And d'you know what I found in the address book under Matt Malone?'

I glanced up.

'Why, sure you do. I found his Boston address, naturally, and then underneath, in pencil, Taplow House, and this telephone number. At first I couldn't think where in the hell Taplow House could be, but you know, as I racked my brains, I remembered . . . remembered about two years ago, when Matt and I were still together and staying at Louise and Tom's on a trip over here, we met this eccentric old English lady. She had a quaint old house on a creek by all accounts, which Matt thought sounded so cute and was real keen to rent. But then I thought: No. No, it can't be true. Matt's in the States. He can't be over here. He wouldn't be so duplicitous. *Couldn't* be. So I reached for the phone and I dialled the Boston University Hospital. I spoke to his secretary – a new one, who doesn't know my voice – who assured me that yes, Matt was definitely on vacation. In Europe for sure, and possibly England. Well, my heart was pounding like you wouldn't believe as I put that phone down. At first I didn't believe it, didn't believe he'd be capable of such a thing, but then I thought: Jesus, Madeleine Malone, you'd better believe it. And you'd better get yourself over to that quaint old house right away.'

She tipped back her head and blew smoke out in a shaky blue line at the ceiling.

'So, my mind racing, I got back in the car, and I drove the distance over here. No real address mind, just a village and a house, but there aren't many houses at the end of a creek, and sure enough, after quizzing a few locals, I found it. Empty. Deserted. But that's OK because, running frantically around it, I find a room, right at the very top, that's clearly Tod's, with all his stuff in it. And you know what? I sat down on that bed and I clutched his sweatshirt to me and I burst into tears I was so damn grateful.'

I took a deep breath. Let it out shakily. I felt her eyes on me as she took another quick drag of her cigarette.

'And then, as I moved around this kooky old house, it got stranger and stranger. Matt's clearly living here. I figure that out because I find his stuff in a room upstairs. But there's a woman too. Not with him, in his bed, but down a floor. And another child, a girl.'

'I can explain that,' I said quickly. 'Matt rented this house, but there was a misunderstanding because I also—'

'Oh, please' – she held up her hands – 'spare me. Matt's domestic arrangements became a matter of complete indifference to me a long time ago.' She flicked her cigarette ash sharply into an ashtray.

'So then I find this note, fixed to the fridge in the kitchen, which is so damn cute, and, I guess, addressed to you.' She reached into the back pocket of her jeans and handed me a piece of paper.

I read it: *Gone fishin'. Got cabin boy, and Girl Friday too. Wish you were here. Matt.* My heart leaped ridiculously. Couldn't help it. I glanced up. She narrowed her eyes at me as she exhaled a long stream of smoke.

'Touching, isn't it? And clearly you are touched, although I think you should know what you're dealing with here.'

'What I'm—' I started. 'Look, I don't know what you're implying about Matt, but—'

'So then,' she went on, cutting me off brusquely in mid-sentence, 'then I go into the study. I mean, I could just sit tight because by now it's dawned on me that Louise and Matt have pulled a fast one and I'm the dupe, but at least Tod's here and that's all that matters. But you know, something makes me want to keep looking around. I just have this feeling, this hunch there may be more. And how right I am. Because in his study – which I know is his because it's so chaotic – I search through the drawers, and find these.'

She dipped into her handbag and pulled out an envelope. Handed it to me.

'Open it.'

I did. Slowly. Stared at the two pieces of paper in my hands.

'Two tickets to JFK from Heathrow for tomorrow afternoon,' she said, carefully. 'One way.'

I swallowed.

'Now. Who d'you suppose those are for?' she drawled softly, head tilted to one side. 'You and Matt?' She reached out and took them from me. 'No. I don't think so. I don't think you're going anywhere with him, honey.'

I licked my lips. I'd already read them. Mr M. Malone, and Mr T. Malone. I sat down slowly on the arm of the sofa.

'Matt and Tod,' I said softly.

'Exactly. Matt and Tod. So what we have here is not just a little vacation with his daddy, which any-one who didn't know Matt's full history of abuse might say was only fair since he hadn't seen his kid in over a year, but a deliberate, calculated plot to abduct my son from under my nose and take him out of the country and back to the States, which I doubt even Tod knew about.'

I stared at her. Her face was white, bloodless.

'Abuse?' I whispered. 'What d'you mean? Matt wouldn't . . . he wouldn't . . .'

'Wouldn't do this?' She quickly unbuttoned her shirt and revealed a scar, livid and red, the stitches still raised and puckered, running from the base of her throat right down to her breast. I gasped, horrified.

'Pretty, isn't it?'

'Yes, but he told me about that,' I said quickly,

averting my eyes. 'About the glass table smashing, about it flying up at you—'

'And you believed him?' She shook her shirt open and my eyes were drawn back like magnets. 'Look at it, Annie. This is no flying glass scratch. Take a real close look.'

'Of course I believed him,' I faltered at last. 'Of course I did, I—'

'Even though a jury in a court of law, two police officers, a judge and a probation officer didn't?'

I met her steady gaze. Her eyes were peculiar. Almost yellow. Like a cat's.

'Yes,' I whispered. 'I believed him.'

She buttoned up her shirt. 'More fool you. The judge called him a dangerous man. A danger to children. A danger to his own child. Said he was removing Tod from his father for his own good.' She took a step closer to me, her face inches from mine now. 'Tell me, Annie, how many fathers in this country are not allowed access to their own children? No visitation rights at all? It's pretty unusual, wouldn't you say? Not even chaperoned? At weekends?'

Her eyes bored into mine, like burning gold. I felt my mouth go dry.

'He's not well, Annie. Really not well. And he's out there now, somewhere, with my boy, planning on skipping the country. And at the moment, he's got your daughter – who I take it is Girl Friday – with him too.'

I stood up quickly. She'd deliberately phrased it

479

like that to frighten me. Ridiculous. None the less, anxiety accumulated in my chest, one grain at a time. Where were they? Which boat had they taken, I wondered? The little blue one, *Pandora*, or – or something bigger? Nonsensical thoughts spun around my head like a kaleidoscope, about them heading out to sea, up Taplow Creek and beyond, towards Ireland perhaps: crazy, irrational thoughts that made my head whirl, but that was how this strange, beautiful, amber-eyed woman was making me feel. That Matt was capable of anything. I had to get away from her. I got up, stumbling in my haste, almost thinking she might pull me back, and made quickly for the kitchen, for the back door. Wrenching it open, I hastened across the terrace and down the garden towards the creek, my heart thumping somewhere high up around the base of my throat.

At the end of the lawn I plunged straight into the woodland, ignoring the path and taking the shortest route straight down as the crow flies. I shielded my face from branches with my arms, but was almost oblivious of the boughs and brambles, my mind racing. Could it be true? A whole courtroom of people, a jury, and that appalling scar. I'd no idea it would be like that, so huge, so disfiguring, and yet—
'Oh!'

As I crashed through a bush, I ran slap into Matt coming up the main path, his tall frame taking the force of our collision.

'Hey, steady!' He laughed, catching my arm.

'No!' I pulled away roughly. Our eyes met in that terrible moment. His, bewildered. Mine, fearful.

'Flora!' I panted, looking frantically around. 'Where's Flora? I—'

'Here,' she said, as she rounded the same bend, carrying a bucket of water and sloshing fish, jeans rolled up, feet bare, with Tod beside her.

'Oh, darling!'

'What's up, Mum?' She too looked bewildered.

'Matt, I'm sorry, I—'

I turned back, but the damage had been done. I saw it in his face. I saw him stiffen too, as he suddenly looked beyond me over my shoulder. He'd glimpsed Madeleine, standing at the top of the garden, high up on the terrace steps, her brown curls blowing in the breeze. His eyes hardened.

'Tod,' he said softly, keeping his eyes on her. 'Tod, listen.' He reached a hand back to grasp his son's arm, but Tod had already seen her.

'Oh shit,' he breathed, backing away.

Matt turned to him urgently. 'Tod, you can do this.'

'I can't!' he gasped, pulling away.

'Sure you can.' Matt reached out his other hand and, in one swift movement, grabbed Tod's shoulder and pulled the boy to him with not a little force. 'And you know what?' he said, his arm tight around his son, his face close but his eyes back on Madeleine. 'We should have done this a long time ago. This isn't the way, Tod. Sneaking around like this, hiding. We need to face her, OK?'

'She'll make me go back,' he whimpered.

I'd never seen him so small, so scared.

'Not if you stand up to her. Come on. It's time.'

'I can't, Dad, you know I can't.'

Flora and I watched in astonishment as this normally cheerful, albeit shy boy shrivelled before our eyes. We followed at a distance as father and son walked up the path, Matt's arm round Tod's shoulder, then up the lawn towards her. As they got closer, Madeleine suddenly flew down the terrace steps, ran down the garden and scooped Tod up in her arms. She lifted his feet off the grass for a second, as if he were a small child. I saw the tears in her eyes.

'Oh baby. My baby!'

Tod seemed to go limp in her arms. Then she let him go and stood back, holding him at arm's length, her eyes scanning his face anxiously. 'You OK, honey? He hasn't hurt you or anything?'

Tod shook his head.

She shook his shoulders impatiently. 'You're sure?'

'Sure,' he muttered.

'OK then,' she breathed in relief, clasping him briefly to her again. 'Let's go. I've packed all of your stuff up from your room, got your backpack and everything and put it all in the car. Let's get going and we'll ring Walter on the way. He's out of his mind with worry. We'll call him on the way back and tell him you're safe and we're on our way home.'

I watched in disbelief as Tod, without a backward glance at his father, or me or Flora, let himself be led up the garden, his shoulders encircled by his mother's arm, up the terrace steps and towards the car in the drive. I swung around to Matt.

'Matt, surely . . .'

Matt followed but didn't attempt to stop them. He seemed to have lost all colour in his face.

'Tod . . .' he called softly. His son didn't turn. 'Madeleine, wait, please.'

'For what?' She spun round abruptly, spitting the words out, her eyes no longer wet, but bright and furious. She reached into her bag, pulled out the airline tickets, and tossed them angrily in the air. They fluttered to the ground. 'For you to abduct my son?' Her voice rose shrilly. 'For you to take him away from me? What are you, some kind of animal, Matt, that you'd take him out of the country without even telling me? Away from his mother, his family. What were you thinking of!'

'I bought those tickets over a month ago,' Matt said carefully. 'Because Tod asked me to. Emailed me. Asked me to come over and get him. Said he couldn't take it any longer and was desperate to come home. It wasn't supposed to be as furtive as that, but we knew of no other way. He's not a child any more, Madeleine. He'll be thirteen in the fall, old enough to decide, with or without the court's blessing, who he chooses to live with. And he chooses to live with me.'

'How dare you!' she breathed. She was trembling with emotion and her grip tightened on her son's shoulder as Tod continued to stare at the ground. 'How dare you tell such flagrant lies in front of him, put words into his mouth, when you know he adores me, would do anything for me. My God, Matt, I'm well aware of your capacity for emotional blackmail, and I'm quite sure you persuaded him to spend time with you because you pulled every heart-rending string in the book, but to lie and suggest it was his idea—' She broke off and gazed down at her son's bent head. Brushed the fair hair out of his eyes. 'Tod? Honey, you want to come home now, don't you?' She gave his shoulder a little squeeze. 'Home with Mom?'

There was a silence. We waited.

'Tod?'

He nodded. 'Sure,' he whispered.

'Don't do this to him, Madeleine,' said Matt in a low, dangerous voice. 'Don't play this card. He came here of his own volition, because he wanted to. He stays with me.'

'The hell he does!'

'He's staying here.' Matt took a step towards her.

Her hand flew into her shoulder bag and she pulled out her mobile. 'You take one more step towards me, Matt, just one step, and I'll call the police.' She flicked it on. 'I swear to God I will.'

'Dad, please,' whimpered Tod. 'I'll go. Please, just let me go.'

Matt looked at his son's white face. Madeleine raised her chin in triumph.

'OK, son.' Matt nodded. 'Sure. I understand.'

'But he wants to stay here!' cried Flora suddenly, shrilly. She came out from behind me and took a step towards him. 'I know he does, we've talked about it loads of times and he's told me. Tell her, Tod. Tell her where you want to be!'

She gazed at him incredulously, but Tod's eyes were blank. Expressionless. He looked beyond her to the woods, to some abstraction in the fields on the other side of the creek. Then, abruptly and rather absently, he bent down and began mechanically to tie the laces of his trainers, which were wet and trailing from the boat. As he straightened up, he carefully pushed his glasses up the bridge of his nose. Then, wordlessly, he set about picking up a book from the table where he'd been sitting on the terrace, a CD, his Walkman.

'Ready, honey?' murmured his mother.

'Ready,' he said flatly.

Without another look at his father, he allowed himself to be guided down the terrace steps, around the side of the house, towards the car. Madeleine still had her arm around his shoulders and when they got to the car, she opened the passenger door for him and helped him in, protecting his head with her hand, rather as one would for an elderly person. After she'd shut the door, she quickly ran around to the other side, got in, and snapped her belt on. Without a backward look, she started the engine and drove off down the drive in a cloud of dust. Flora and I stood and watched in astonishment. When the car had disappeared from sight, I turned.

'Matt, I don't understand. Why—'

But he'd gone. I just caught a flash of his faded blue T-shirt as he disappeared around the side of the house. I hurried after him but he was moving fast. I was just in time to see him walk quickly down the garden towards the woods, heading for the creek.

And then he was gone.

chapter twenty-seven

'Mum, I don't understand.'

Flora turned huge eyes on me. 'What's going on? Why has he gone with her?'

'I don't know.' I stared through the gap in the trees where Matt had disappeared. Then I swung round to her.

'What's he told you?'

'Tod?'

'Yes, Tod!'

'Well, that he's scared of her. That's she's manipulative, controlling.'

'That he hates her?'

She thought carefully. 'No,' she said slowly. 'No, not that.'

I nodded. 'Wait here,' I muttered. 'I'll be back.'

I set off quickly, following Matt's tracks down the garden, through the woods and to the creek. He'd walked fast though, and despite plunging pell-mell down the path through the trees, when I emerged out into the dusk on the other side, I found no trace of him. The tide was low, and the creek one long stretch of grey wet sand, with only the gulls and cormorants poised, one-legged, heads tucked under wings, on sandy mounds waiting for night. Further out, the main estuary swelled with a turning tide and as I swung about desperately, narrowing my eyes in the gloom, I thought for an awful moment he'd kept on walking, right out there into the dark water. Then all of a sudden I saw him sitting on some rocks at the farthest point of the creek, arms locked around his knees. I started quickly towards him, running clumsily through the claggy sand, then scrambling over rocks, slipping and tearing my espadrilles on the barnacles to reach him. I was almost there – when something made me stop short. I steadied myself, wobbling precariously on the slippery rocks.

'Matt?'

He must have heard me, but stayed motionless, head turned resolutely out to sea. I felt my heart lurch in my throat. I'd doubted him, you see. Pulled away from him in the wood. I was about to turn back, misery rising within me, when he said my name.

'Annie.' Softly.

Relieved, I turned back. I picked my way over the rock pools and sat quietly beside him, following his eyes out to the horizon, sensing he was fighting with emotion and didn't want me to look at him. The sun had gone behind the water now, and an evening wind began to stir, swelling the silent estuary and the sea it flowed into. The green hills opposite were losing their colour, turning to iron grey in the twilight, seeming to swallow the little stone church in their soft folds. The warm fragrance of midsummer still hovered though; gentle, like the touch of a hand. Eventually, Matt broke the silence.

'So. It's over.'

I fought to comprehend. 'But . . . why, Matt? I don't understand. Why did he go? When it's so perfectly obvious to even the most ignorant bystander that he wants to be here, with you. Why does he go when she snaps her fingers?'

'It's not as simple as that,' he said slowly. 'You're assuming he hates his mother. For taking him away from me, for forcing him to live in England, but he doesn't. He loves her. She's his mom. The only one he's got, and, for all her faults, he won't hurt her.'

'But Flora says she's manipulative, that she scares him. He's told her that!'

'And so she does, sometimes. But he deals with it. Has to. And *she's* frightened too, you know, of what she's done. And Tod knows that. Pities her. Feels sorry for her.' He struggled to explain. 'You can't just reject your parents, Annie, because they're not perfect, because they don't match up. You darn well get on with what you've been allocated. It's a question of allegiances.'

'Yes, I agree, but he does have a choice. He has you!'

He shrugged. 'Just as Flora has Adam. And even

though he's a womaniser and a fly-by-night, he's the only dad she's got, so she sticks with him.'

'Yes, but the point is she wouldn't choose to live with him!'

He turned to look at me. 'Did you ask her?'

I faltered. 'Well . . . no. But then I'm—'

'Her mother. Exactly. And that's how it works. That's how the world turns, socially and biologically.' He smiled ruefully. 'I never had the advantage of the umbilical cord. A child's attachment to its mother is a universal force, and pretty well indestructible. Something has to go seriously wrong for it to break.'

'Yes, but something *has* gone seriously wrong, and now he'd rather live with you!'

'But he won't tell her that,' he said patiently. 'Won't hurt her to that extent. He's too . . . kind. He's all she's got, you see, and he knows that.' He sighed. 'And to be fair, she did bring him up. I worked too hard – for them, of course, always the father's sad plea – but long hours and weekends, and they were alone a lot. The bond between them is very strong, even though he sometimes hates her. He was the only child she could have, and she loves him with a passion. Too much, probably. We both love him too much. And children can't cope with that sort of spotlight,' he added soberly.

There was a silence as we listened to the rhythm of the sea.

'Flora's said that too,' I reflected sadly. 'That

sometimes I overdid it. That she longed for a brother or a sister to take the heat off her.' I glanced down and picked at a shiny black mussel on a rock. It stuck resolutely. 'Says she looks longingly at families with three or four children, where the love and expectation is more spread out, less concentrated.'

'Of course she does. These solitary kids, they're aware of the microscope upon them. Aware that every picture they bring home from school is a potential masterpiece, every sack race an Olympic achievement, and it's hard for us as parents not to overreact like that.'

'But not good for them.'

'Hell no. Not that sort of pressure.'

I sighed. Rested my chin on my knees. 'It was one of the reasons I agreed to have more children with David,' I said. 'Even though I secretly knew my body wasn't up to it and I was only shoring up more grief for myself. I desperately wanted some company for Flora.' I smiled wanly into the sunset. 'Although I realise a twelve-year age gap isn't exactly what she had in mind.

He smiled. 'No. I'm not sure the little guy in the diaper would be up to chucking a frisbee with her, or sharing her first illicit cigarette.'

'Well, quite.' I picked sadly at the mussel again. And then of course my mind flew insanely, ridiculously, to Tod. Tod, who would be up to it. I saw the pair of them tussling and laughing together in boats, on the lawn, at the table-tennis table, almost as if they *were* brother and sister, and then my mind cut loose from its moorings entirely and I imagined them bowling up to school together. A co-ed school – not the smart all-girls establishment she disliked so much in London – a much more relaxed environment, with Tod in the year below, and Flora saying casually to girls in her class: Oh, yeah, that's my step-brother. To have a companion to seek out at lunchtime if her days were rough and friendless, to have someone to go home on the bus with, to discuss homework with, to— Oh no, Annie, *no*. I gasped almost audibly at my audacity. Too much. Far too much. There weren't going to be any fairy-tale endings here, nothing so neat. Real life wasn't like that.

'But' – I tried a different tack – 'you say Tod wouldn't leave her, wouldn't leave Madeleine, but he did go to elaborate lengths to see you. And wasn't it his idea to buy the air tickets? What was that all about?'

He sighed. 'That was madness. I see that now. Tod and I emailed each other constantly, it was our private lifeline, and often he wrote saying how much he missed me, longed to be home, things that broke my heart. But one day, after a particularly bad row with his mother, he wrote: "Please Dad, please take me home. I can't bear it here. I'm sinking." '

'Oh God.'

'Well, impulsively, I went straight on the Internet and bought those tickets, to coincide with the end of my stay here. I kept them in my wallet for weeks, knowing we'd probably never do it, that Tod wouldn't be able to hurt her like that, and just disappear from her life. I wasn't convinced I was up to it either, but boy, it felt good. To have them there, in my jacket, next to my heart. Like – I don't know – an insurance policy. I'd get them out and look at them from time to time; be having lunch in the hospital canteen, open my wallet to pay, and stare at them. It was like having him there with me. It kept me going.'

'And did he know?'

'That I'd bought them? No, because I thought it was too much pressure.' He gave a wry smile. 'He knows now, of course. Madeleine saw to that.' He shifted position on the rock. 'And you know, for all I know, his email could just have been a whim. On a bad day. We all do things like that, for Chrissake, and he's only a kid.'

'But you've talked?' I persisted. 'I mean, since you've been here together, fishing and surfing, when hopefully Flora's given you a moment's peace?'

'Oh sure, we've talked, and I know he'd prefer to be with me, Annie. I've always known that.' He turned to look at me properly. 'But when he's *ready* to leave his mom, not with me prising him away like one of these goddamned barnacles. And one day, he will come to me. Maybe – I don't know – maybe before he goes to college or something, maybe he'll call one day and say: "Dad, can I crash in your apartment in Boston for a year or so?" And I'll be delighted. Thrilled to bits. But . . . not yet. He's not ready. I have to be patient.'

I thought back to Tod's white face as his parents faced one another defiantly on the lawn; Madeleine had been trembling with emotion, her fists clenched. And Tod had withdrawn. I remembered his face as he'd left; closed, expressionless. He'd retreated somewhere where no one could reach him. Suddenly I remembered something. I had to ask.

'Matt, that scar. She showed me. It's horrific.'

'I know. Appalling. And I've wondered about that too. When I saw it in court, when she was asked by the judge to unbutton her blouse, when the huge colour photographs were passed around the jury, I almost passed out. I saw the disgust on those twelve faces. Felt disgust myself. Felt sick to my stomach that I could have inflicted that on her with one thump of a fist on a table. I crumpled. Clutched the chair in front of me, I remember, my knuckles white. And in that moment, I caved in and stopped fighting for Tod. I was never prepared to put him in the witness box – even though my attorney insisted it was the only way to win – but when I saw those pictures . . . oh man. That's when I really threw in the towel. What sort of a person does that, I thought? What sort of a maniac *are* you, Matt Malone?' He licked his lips. Paused reflectively. 'But then later, you know, I got to thinking. And I sort of knew that I hadn't. Hadn't done it. That it wasn't possible. A shard of glass flying at whatever velocity through the air wouldn't have inflicted such damage, or caused such a long deep cut. So I asked a pathologist friend of mine at the hospital, and we went to see some forensic guys, guys who specialise in this sort of thing. Showed them the pictures. I even went so far as to put my fist through a couple of glass tables, and no. It couldn't have happened.'

I stared at him, horrified. 'You mean . . . you think *she* did it?'

'Made it worse.'

'Oh God.' I looked down quickly. Felt sick again.

'Because she was desperate,' insisted Matt. 'Don't judge her so, Annie. She was desperate to get Tod.'

'Yes, but—'

'And she knew I might get him.'

'Why?' I looked up. 'I mean, she's the mother after all, and, as you say, the courts tend to lean in that direction, so—'

'She is the mother, sure, but she was also a patient of mine. A psychiatric patient. That's how we met.'

'A patient!'

'Yes. Not entirely ethical, but not unusual in psychiatry circles. Although not something, frankly, that the courts would have looked kindly on from either point of view. Particularly hers.'

'Well, obviously! She's clearly completely unhinged! I would have thought that was your trump card!'

He gave a short bark of mirthless laughter.

'Doesn't say much for my prowess as a doctor, does it?'

I gazed at him.

'Mental illness is treatable, Annie,' he said patiently. 'Curable, even. If someone had pneumonia, say, but recovered, you wouldn't say: Oh well, she's had pneumonia, must be incapable of looking after a child. Would you?'

'No,' I said slowly. 'But . . .'

'But popular perception of mental illness is different, sure, I agree. The majority of people think: Once a nutter always a nutter. I know that. Madeleine knows that too, which is why she went to such elaborate lengths to get Tod.'

'Cut herself.'

'I think so. Know so, almost.'

I struggled with the idea. Felt out of my depth. 'And . . . had she ever done anything like that before? I mean, when she came to see you as a patient?'

'No, never. This was a calculated, and quite clever, deliberate act. One that actually someone with no history of mental illness, someone like you or me, say, might even have done.'

I stared at him. 'No way!'

'Really? If Adam was poised to take Flora from you in court on the grounds that you were unstable? Wouldn't you use any measure available to you, to prove that he was more so?'

I thought about it. Knew there was a grain of truth in what he said. That I would do anything. *Any*thing.

I stared out to the middle of the estuary, a gun-metal grey now, cold and bleak. The surface of the water shivered in the wind.

'What did she have? I mean, what was her illness?'

'Acute paranoiac depression.'

'Oh.' I swallowed. Out of my depth.

'Eminently treatable, and hugely successfully, in most cases. Including hers.'

'And you fell for her . . . what, straight away? When she first came to see you?'

My chest felt absurdly knotted with jealousy. I imagined her in his consulting rooms, slim, petite, with those huge eyes, sitting down hesitantly perhaps, but brave enough to come. And I saw Matt behind his desk, at the peak of his career, commanding, handsome, caring, his broad shoulders encased in a blue Brooks Brothers shirt with a silk tie. I saw him glance up from some papers, ask her to sit down, noticing – professionally – her pallor, a slight tremor in her hand, but also those haunting amber eyes in that heart-shaped face, those fine bones, the mop of chestnut curls.

'Not straight away, no,' he admitted. 'I noticed she was beautiful, naturally. You'd have to be blind not to see that. No, it was later on . . . when I started treating her on a regular basis. I felt such admiration for her. At how she'd coped with her illness, hidden it. Carried on working. She's a doctor herself, you know.'

'I know. You said.'

'And she was... so beguiling. Enchanting.' His eyes swam as he gazed into the distance.

I swallowed. Cleared my throat. 'And that's when you started seeing her? You know, romantically?'

'Oh no, not actually from the consulting couch, that really would have been unethical. Later, when she was better. When I'd discharged her. I asked her out then.'

My heart felt heavy, like a colossal lead weight inside me. I had an awful, awful feeling he still loved her. 'Beguiling.' 'Enchanting.' I curled my legs around and tucked my size seven feet firmly under me. Nothing beguiling about them. I snuck a sideways glance at him in the dusk. He was gazing, almost hypnotised, out to sea. Seemed miles away. With her, no doubt. In the days before it all went wrong. Before she left him. Took his son. Broke his heart. I felt a lump about the size of the one I was sitting on lodge in my throat.

'And, Annie, I apologise for my behaviour the other night,' he went on in a low voice. 'I was out of order. Forgive me.'

He did look at me when he said that, but distractedly. Through me. As if he'd remembered to apologise, but his mind was elsewhere. And why apologise? For what? For that glorious, endless kiss? That heavenly embrace? Surely we were ready to embark on more of the same, and then who knows what of a more permanent nature? But to *apologise*... My stomach flipped in fear.

Of course, he was desperately sad about Tod, I reasoned, my heart pounding, but in his heart he'd known Tod would go back to his mother, at least for the foreseeable future, and although now certainly wasn't the moment to rekindle our love affair – golly, I wasn't that insensitive – surely some sweet gesture, some squeeze of the hand, some hot, suggestive look to imply more . . . ? But to admit he was sorry it had ever happened . . . I felt as if I'd been kicked in the teeth. Wondered if I'd ever get over it, actually. But I wasn't even allowed the luxury of wallowing in my misery, because suddenly a shrill whistle rang out from above.

Recognising the summons, I swung around quickly. Back down at the other end of the creek and high above us, at the bottom of the garden behind the treetops, stood Flora. She took her fingers out of the corners of her mouth, cupped it with her hands, and yelled, 'Matt! Someone called Louise is here!'

Matt stared at her, then: 'Coming!' He got quickly to his feet.

I watched numbly as he crossed the rocks in his deck shoes, leaping from rock to rock, until he reached the sand. He crossed the flatland at a trot, dodging the pools of water, and headed for the path through the woods. As I saw his back disappearing through the trees, it occurred to me that he was about to disappear from my life as abruptly as he'd entered it. That in a very short while, in a matter of hours perhaps, he'd return to America and I'd never see him again. I stood up slowly and followed at a distance. Suddenly I felt very small. Very stupid. How could I have got it so wrong? How could I have imagined anything could come of us? He lived in America. I lived in England. He was still mourning the loss of a beautiful, tragic woman who'd walked out on him when he still loved her, not to mention a son. Why would I even come close to compensating for that loss? I breathed deeply to stop myself from crying as I reached the sand; then quickened my pace as I followed his path through the wood.

And so what if he'd advised me against marrying David? So what? There was nothing self-seeking in that, it had been a simple kindness; a concern for my wellbeing, as any friend, seeing a woman about to attach herself to the wrong man, would feel. Nothing more. And I'd been mad to think it was. I'd lost touch with reality. Thought that because I felt a certain way, he was feeling the same way, too.

You fool, Annie, I thought bitterly, tears stinging my eyes as I climbed through the wood after him. You stupid little fool. It was a holiday romance after all, no more no less, and one that hadn't even properly got under way, either.

As I reached the top of the hill, a pretty blonde girl with long, perfect legs coming out of khaki shorts came running from the terrace steps down the garden towards Matt, her hair flying.

'Oh Matt, I'm so sorry.' Her voice broke. 'This is all my fault. I'm so sorry!'

Her hand went to her mouth in a strangled sob as he swooped to embrace her, to reassure her. Again, I felt an unbearable wave of jealousy crash over me as he gave her a hug. Why couldn't I have one of those? Oh, for heaven's sake, they're cousins, I told myself sternly. Cousins, that's all. But why were all these American women so tiny? So resolutely size six? Where the hell were their bottoms? I gazed at her knees. They were the size of my knuckles.

'It's not your fault, Louise.'

'But it is! I feel dreadful!' She pulled back. 'I just hadn't told Bernie, our help, you see, because I hadn't seen any need to involve her. But it was so stupid of me. I might have known Madeleine would call and ask for Tod when I wasn't there, I might have known! Why didn't I think?'

'You weren't to know,' he insisted. 'And, frankly, it doesn't matter.' He held her by her shoulders at arm's length. 'Listen, Louise, Tod and I had our time together and we had a great time. And I wouldn't have spirited him back to the States on those tickets.'

'You wouldn't?' She searched his face, still distraught.

'No. I wouldn't. Couldn't have. So our time would have come to an end at this point anyway. It just . . . wasn't quite how I'd figured on saying goodbye to him, that's all. This is Annie, by the way.'

'Hi.' She flashed me a lovely smile before turning anxiously back to Matt.

'Hi,' I muttered, feeling distinctly peripheral.

'Well, as long as you're sure,' she went on uncertainly, jangling her car keys nervously in her hand. 'I just feel such a fool slipping up like that. I left the boys with Bernie and flew right over when I heard.'

'You needn't have. Listen, I'll get you a drink. You look like you need one, and I sure as hell do. Come on.'

'Thanks,' she said gratefully and she let him lead her, an arm around her shoulders, back up the garden, then up the steps to the terrace. He found her a deck chair and she sank into it. As Matt disappeared inside to get a bottle, she put her head in her hands and ran her fingers through her hair, clearly shaken. I pulled up a chair and perched opposite. She raised her head and looked at me hard.

'Bitch,' she muttered.

I started, then realised she must mean Madeleine.

'Is she?' I said hopefully.

'Oh, totally. First class. She had her claws into Matt from day one. No one could understand why he married her. She totally took him in with that vulnerable little-girl-lost bit, and now she's got her claws into that poor boy.'

I could tell I was going to like Louise.

'But he obviously still adores her?' I ventured, heart in mouth. 'I mean, she is very beautiful. I met her.'

She got out a packet of cigarettes. 'She is also completely barking mad. However much Matt protects her and maintains she isn't.'

'Oh!' Splendid.

'And Walter's such a creep. How she could ever, *ever* leave Matt for that man just beats me.' She shook her head incredulously.

'Really?'

'Well, I thought so.' She leaned forward conspiratorially. 'He's one of those arrogant, tweedy, dandruff-ridden English types. No offence . . .'

'None taken,' I assured her quickly.

'So full of himself and his pompous Cambridge ways, forever looking down his nose at anything from across the pond – and to think Matt took him into his house, made him welcome, showed him round Boston. Ooh.' She shuddered eloquently. 'Makes my blood boil.' She put her cigarette in her mouth and dug a lighter out of her shorts pocket. 'Actually, I shouldn't have said that,' she said, removing the unlit cigarette from her mouth. 'She's not a bitch, she's just a rather beautiful nutcase. And you know men when it comes to weak, defenceless women: can't get enough of them. But I still say she injured herself on purpose. Tom says it was as clear as day from that scar, and he should know, he deals with that kind of thing all the time. I just *wish* Matt could have brought himself to expose her in court, but he couldn't, he's too darned nice. He couldn't bring himself to tell everyone his wife was a raving lunatic, and he wouldn't let Tod listen to that, either.' She paused. 'And of course he was her psychiatrist as well as her husband, he'd thought he could sort her out, so I guess a certain amount of professional pride was involved.' She sighed. 'And he wouldn't let Tod testify either. Wouldn't let him get involved.' She straightened her back. 'Jeez, I wish someone had asked me. Wish I'd been invited into that box for two minutes. Just *two minutes*, that's all it would have taken.' Finally she lit the cigarette and took a quick drag. She exhaled with feeling.

'So you were all there? In court?'

'Oh sure, we were all there,' she said bitterly. 'Sitting on our hands and listening in horror while this lovely, gentle man, his head bowed, a man who wouldn't hurt a fly, was branded in front of everyone – including his son – as some kind of madman, unfit to look after a child. It made me spit!' She stubbed the cigarette out fiercely. '*Damn*,' she muttered with feeling. 'Gave that filthy habit up months ago.'

'And yet you'd once been friends?' I ventured. 'You and Madeleine?'

She glanced up. 'Oh sure, once. I accepted her for Matt. And to be fair, Matt kept her on an even keel. She was OK before she met this Walter guy. I just wish—' She broke off suddenly. Stared beyond me, transfixed. For a moment I thought she was still musing on what might have been, if the past had been played out differently, if Madeleine hadn't met Walter. Then, as the silence grew, I realised that whatever was gripping her was being played out right behind me.

I swung around. At the same time, a car door

slammed in the drive. It was the old blue Volvo, back in position. And coming around the side of the house was Tod. He was walking, his head held high, way in front of his mother, who, as she felt her way slowly around the car, hands clutching the bonnet, looked very pale. Her hair was mussed over her forehead, which even at this distance I could see was damp with beads of sweat. She looked ill.

At that moment, Matt stepped out of the back door with a bottle of wine and some glasses. He saw Madeleine, and stopped still on the steps. Their eyes met across the garden and the gravel drive, and in that moment, something unspoken went on. Something that meant a lot to them, and very little to the rest of us.

chapter twenty-eight

She let her hands fall loosely at her sides. I noticed they were red and raw, her nails bitten down to the quick. Her shoulders drooped in her oversized plaid shirt.

'You've won,' she said flatly.

'It's not a question of winning,' said Matt quietly.

She raised her head. 'It is to me.'

She looked terrible. Grey. All in. Matt held out a chair for her. 'Sit,' he commanded gently.

She shook her head, lips taut. Then reached out quickly and held on to the back of it for support. She took deep breaths to steady herself.

'What happened?' asked Matt.

She swallowed. 'We got as far as Launceston. Then Tod got out of the car at some lights. Started walking back. Not running, and he didn't say a word before he got out, just started walking in the opposite direction. I parked the car and ran after him. He wouldn't speak to me, but eventually I made him talk. He said he couldn't live with me any more.' She caught her breath, her voice shaking. 'Said he missed you too much and was only really happy when he was with you. Said he wanted to live with you.' Her face crumpled. 'I've lost him. I went through all that, the court case, the agony of it all, and now I've lost him after all.'

She hung on to the chair with one hand and covered her face with the other as she wept. Her shoulders shook. I waited for Matt to fly to comfort her. He didn't. He turned to Tod.

'Tod? Is this how you really feel? Or just an over-reaction because you've had another bust-up with your mom?'

'You know it's how I feel, Dad,' Tod said in a low, almost angry voice. 'You don't have to ask. Don't have to test me. It's just ... I've never been brave enough to say it before. Just gone along with what everyone says I should do.'

'It's nothing to do with bravery,' Matt said more gently. He glanced across at Madeleine. 'More to do with compassion.'

'And it's not you, Mom,' Tod said in a high voice, looking at her directly. 'It's my whole new life, which I don't want and never asked for and never liked. It's that creepy dark house in Cambridge; Walter, who looks at me as if I'm some kind of amoeba that's crept out from under a stone; his sons who call me a Yank and take the piss out of my accent. It's the school, the stupid uniform; it's everything. It's not you, Mom, you know that, don't you?' he said urgently. 'I never wanted to choose. Just wanted to go on living with my mom and dad, together, at home, as a family. You made me choose by getting it to the point where I couldn't bear it any longer. The thought of another day in that redbrick Victorian pile with Walter playing his opera all day and barking at everyone to be quiet just made me feel ill. When we were driving back just now – I simply had to get out. I can't explain why. I felt . . . suffocated. Like I was – I don't know – driving back to die or something. I love you, Mom. You know that, don't you? I just can't live in that house with you.'

His voice was level now, implausibly rational. Dispassionate, almost. He was stating facts. He looked older, too. Taller, as he looked her in the eye. I saw Flora regard him with admiration and wondered if he noticed. Madeleine seemed to crumple with every blow he calmly delivered. This was what Matt had been waiting for, I thought. One day he knew this would happen. Well, one day had come, earlier than expected.

Madeleine licked her lips. They were pale and bloodless. She held on tight to the back of the chair. Then, with an effort, she turned to Matt. Gave a strange, twisted smile.

'And, of course, it's much too late to do what Tod really wants?'

'Which is?' Matt asked, surprised.

'For you and me to be together. As a family. So he never has to choose. For me to come home.'

I caught my breath at the audacity. Saw Matt almost wince. I couldn't believe she was asking him that question, and in front of me, Louise, Flora . . . I caught Louise's eye.

'Much too late,' said Matt firmly.

She nodded. Accepting the answer for what it was. Defeat. It had been an heroic, selfless, last-ditch attempt to save her son, and suddenly, in spite of myself, my heart went out to her. She was that desperate. And she'd tried everything now. She'd lied in court, disfigured herself, and now grovelled and humbled herself in front of her son and an audience. But that was what love did to you. Particularly the maternal kind. And as Matt had said, what if it were Flora?

'When will you go back?' she said, raising her chin, collecting herself. 'To the States. Tomorrow? Will you use those tickets?'

'I don't know,' admitted Matt. 'I haven't thought. Don't know what we'll do. Tod?' He turned to his son, but Tod had felt the full force and pathos of his mother's last desperate plea, and was staring miserably at the ground, his courage momentarily deserting him. Matt sensed it ebbing away and put a hand on his shoulder.

'Say goodbye to your mom, Tod.' He gave him a little push and Tod went over. I had to turn away. I couldn't bear it.

'Come on, Flora,' I muttered, and we went into the house.

I headed for the kitchen where, strangely, I often found myself in times of emotional crisis, and more particularly the sink, which naturally was full of washing up. Turning the taps on full blast and squirting liquid over the greasy pans, I silently handed Flora a tea towel. Out of the corner of my eye, through the window over the sink, I saw Tod and his mother hug each other hard. Heard her weeping loudly, her head on Tod's shoulder, then Louise's sensible voice.

'She can't possibly drive all the way back to Cambridge now. She can come back with me. Spend the night, and then go home tomorrow. She's all in.'

'That would be kind, Lou,' said Matt, discussing his ex-wife over her head as if she wasn't there.

I wondered if it had always been so in that marriage. If he'd always looked after her, guided her, arranged things for her, because that was the nature of his role when they'd met; he'd been her doctor, her protector, just as David had been mine, I realised with a start. Had Matt recognised the parallel, I wondered? When he'd advised me to break the link myself? Recognised the similarly paternal ground he and David occupied?

After a while, when I'd scrubbed the living daylights out of those pans, I realised the garden had gone quiet. Glancing out of the window, I saw that Louise and Madeleine had gone, and, in the distance, heard the crunch of gravel as two cars purred away in tandem. It was almost dark now, but down at the bottom of the garden, silhouetted against the trees, Tod's hunched figure was walking fast, heading for the gap that led to the creek. I turned to look at Flora drying up beside me, but she was already putting her cloth down. The next minute, she was walking slowly down the garden, biting her thumbnail. She turned and caught my eye through the window. I shrugged uncertainly. I don't know, darling. I really don't. She hesitated, then carried on walking, letting me know with one eloquently raised hand that she knew he needed to be alone, but that perhaps he wouldn't mind someone hovering in the shadows, should he need to talk eventually?

Quite grown up, I decided. Much more so than me. Because frankly, I felt like picking one of these coffee cups out of the sink, hurling it at the wall, and bursting into tears, which was, of course, monumentally selfish, because I should be so happy for Matt and Tod. So happy that they could carry on fishing and surfing and being a father and son team back home in Massachusetts, with Tod going back to his old school and skateboarding in the street with his friends. How selfish would it be of me not to want it to be so? Of course I wanted it.

Miserably, I pulled the plug in the sink and felt a strand of something revolting wrap itself around my little finger in the depths. I shook it off and wiped my hands. Suddenly I didn't want to be alone in this house. I needed the night air as much as anyone else who was fighting with their emotions around here. I pushed open the back door and walked outside, gulping back the tears as I went. There was no sign of Matt, and my heart ached for him in a way that it had never ached for anyone, I realised; neither Adam nor David. And up until a few minutes ago, I'd never actually considered his going, but of course he would now. Now he'd got what he wanted, what he'd come for. What was there to keep him?

I headed down the lawn past the summer house, the scene of yet another recently fostered dream that had come to nothing. The lady novelist. A deep and profound melancholy rose within me. So strange, I reflected, when only weeks ago I'd been so happy. A woman on the brink of getting married, writing her book, about to become a doctor's wife, a large house in Hurlingham, more babies planned: all gone. And even though I knew it was right that it had gone, the fact that there was nothing to put in its place was hard. Real tough, as Matt would say in his dark brown accent. A ball of tears scuttled up my throat at the memory of his voice and I swallowed it down, walking quickly down the sandy path through the woods.

When I reached the river bed there was no sign of Tod or Flora. They must have gone on around the headland. I walked along the bank, and stood in the spot where Matt and I had sat that night, around the dying embers of the campfire, tingling with longing for each other – or so I'd thought – love and firelight racing in every vein. I raised my face to the heavens; they were clear, dark and relentlessly deep, and now with a smattering of stars. I had a horrid feeling I was really going to howl now, shed hot tears of self-pity, and that with Tod and Flora lurking around somewhere, either separately or together, this wasn't the place to do it. Instead, I turned a sharp right and headed uphill for the cliff path. The wind was strong now, buffeting my face, which was strangely comforting, and, as I went up, I had to reach out and hold on to tufts of rough grass to support me as I climbed. The light was very dim too, so that when the track finally plateaued out at the top and I came across a tall figure blocking my path, I shrieked.

It was Matt, leaning back against a tree, one leg propped up. He glanced round at my cry and hurriedly stuffed some bits of paper into his pocket. The moonlight just caught them though. It was the airline tickets, being tucked furtively away. And suddenly I was enraged. The brimming tears of self-pity turned to ones of fury and sprang from my eyes.

'Going to use them?' I cried bitterly. 'Tomorrow, isn't it?'

'Sorry?' He blinked in my face.

I wiped the tears unceremoniously from my cheeks with the back of my hand.

'Well, that's when they're for, isn't it? Tomorrow afternoon, Heathrow to JFK. I'll pop you up there if you like. Give you a lift to the airport. Wave you off, even.'

'What d'you mean?' He straightened up from the tree. 'I'm not going anywhere tomorrow. I was looking at those tickets thinking: How extraordinary. All this time they've represented Tod for me, and now they've actually become a reality. But I'm not going anywhere.'

'But you will, won't you?' I said brokenly. I was horrified at myself, but I couldn't help it. My voice cracked. 'You'll go back to America, and Flora and I will become something that happened on a cute little English fishing holiday, a diversion while you got custody of Tod. My God, you even apologised for *kiss*ing me back there, as if that was completely abhorrent, a complete aberration. Well, I have no such regrets, Matt.' I was shaking now, possibly even slightly out of control. 'I enjoyed every minute of it, and was looking forward to more of the same, maybe even something of a more permanent nature, but then I haven't had the luxury of a string of affairs like you have since the end of my marriage. Add me to your list, why don't you? Pop me down as number three, straight after the radiologist with the great legs and the neighbour with the inconvenient cat: the eccentric Englishwoman! The divorcee who threw her clothes away and wrote cheap books, with the screwed-up child with obsessive behavioural problems. The one who threw in her chance to administer to famine victims in – in war-torn Africa, in a war-torn tent in a Red Cross uniform—'

He blinked. 'Red Cross?'

'Yes, why not!' I shrieked. 'Christ, I could be rivalling Florence sodding Nightingale, making the world a better place! I could be handing out rice, digging wells—'

'Wells? Where?'

'In the ground!' I yelled. 'For the starving millions!'

'What, in a long white dress?'

I stared. 'What?' I panted to a standstill.

'You'll be digging wells in a long white dress?'

I shook my head, rubbing my wet nose with my fist. 'What dress?'

'The one you're getting married in in five weeks' time. The one that's being specially made for you in London. You're gonna sink wells in that? After the reception at Claridge's? With your mother and sister in grey and pink respectively, both with new shoes and bags purchased from Bowman's of Exeter?' He shook his head. 'Get real dirty.'

I stared, flummoxed. 'Wha— What d'you mean?'

'I called the farm this morning. I wanted to check you were OK. You took off so suddenly yesterday, like a bat out of hell. I spoke to Clare, who'd just woken up. She said there was no sign of you, but she yelled downstairs to your mom who said you'd gone to London to see David. "Ah," said Clare, back down the phone to me. "A little romantic tryst. Honestly, Matt, in a few weeks' time that girl's gonna be with that guy for the rest of her life, but she still drives four hours to see him for ten minutes. Can't keep her hands off him!" How we chuckled. And then I got the whole low-down on the wedding, right down to the colour of Flora's bridesmaid dress and the ushers' buttonholes. Oh and, incidentally, your ma's shoes and bag *are* from Bowman's, but the suit itself is from an exclusive little boutique round the corner. She's gonna be in dove-grey silk.'

'But – but I'm not!' I said, horrified.

'Not in silk?' He scratched his head dubiously. 'A mistake, I fear. It's very *à la mode* for brides this season.'

'No! I mean I'm not getting married! It *was* all organised like that, just as you've said, all planned without me by David, but – but, Matt, the engagement's off! I split up with David today in London. He's going away, to Nicaragua. We're not getting married.'

There was a silence. 'You're not . . . getting married?'

'No. I'm not.' I squinted in the dusk. Looked at him incredulously. 'You didn't *know* that?' I whispered.

'Do I look, or sound, like a man that knows that? No. As a matter of fact, I didn't. How could I have known it, Annie, when you neglected to tell me?'

My mind spun. *Had* I? Had I neglected to tell him? 'So – so all the time, when you were wriggling and apologising and—'

'Trying to behave like a gentleman and do the right thing because I realised you were still getting hitched and hadn't changed your plans on account of me, and that the evening we'd shared together had clearly meant precisely nothing to you – yeah. Yeah, that's what I was doing.' He scratched his head. 'Felt a bit of a heel, as a matter of fact, for trying to talk you out of your big day. It occurred to me you might actually love this guy, and there I was, selfishly trying to turn things to my advantage, and all because . . .'

'Yes?' I hung on.

'Well, all because . . . I wanted you.'

'Oh!'

There was a silence. We gazed at one another. He went on in a low voice.

'I love you, Annie, you must know that. And I want us to be together, you, me, Tod and Flora. But I had an awful surge of guilt there that I was prising you away from another life you'd planned and wanted for a long time, and that even though I could see it was wrong, that *he* was wrong, you couldn't. You see, I've done that masterful role before, Annie, the one David was doing, and it's a mistake. You don't need anyone to look after you. You need someone to look you in the eye.'

'I know,' I whispered, moving closer, holding his eye. 'I know that now, and, Matt, I love you too, so much. I just don't know how on earth we're going to . . . well . . .' I hesitated.

'What?'

'I mean, you live in America and I live here, and this isn't even our house! We're just playing at living in it and—'

'Details,' he murmured, pushing his fingers up through my hair and stopping my lips with a kiss. 'Let's worry about the details later.'

A second later I was in his arms and he was kissing the life out of me. And he was right. Nothing mattered. Nothing, except that here I was, right where I wanted to be, his lips on mine, his hands strong and warm on my back, the wind in my hair and my feet – well, was it my imagination or were my feet just slightly off the ground? And with a glorious, glorious feeling flooding through every vein that if this moment were to go on for ever and nothing practical were ever sorted out, well, then that would be fine too. I wouldn't object. And perhaps it would have done, if a startled voice behind us hadn't said quite clearly and shrilly:

'Mum!'

We parted, panting. Swung around breathlessly. A few feet away, Tod and Flora were staring at us.

'Oh! Darling.' I hurriedly smoothed down my hair, flushing madly. 'There you are. Matt and I were just . . .'

'Your mother and I were getting some details sorted out,' said Matt as the children continued to boggle, their eyes and mouths wide. Matt took my hand. 'And, as it happens, we're not through yet; we have way more to discuss. Way more. Like who gets to take the garbage out and who does the dishes and – oh boy, all manner of things. So, here.' He reached into his back pocket and drew out a wad of tenners. 'You guys eaten yet?'

'Er, no,' muttered Flora, dazed.

'Tod.' He turned to his son. 'Take Flora over to Padstow on the ferry, and have yourselves a pizza. Then take yourselves off around the town and spend the rest on mindless junk like CDs and T-shirts, and anything overpriced with a logo on it.'

'Cool!' Tod's eyes lit up as he took the money. 'What's the catch?'

Matt put his arm around my shoulder and led me away, walking me firmly down the cliff path and away from them, towards the house.

'The catch is,' he called back over his shoulder, 'that you're back at ten o'clock, and not a moment before. I don't want to see your horrible inquisitive little faces back here until precisely then, when you creep straight to your bedrooms. Deal?'

We couldn't see their faces as we marched away from them, grinning like children, but we could hear the glee in their voices.

'Deal!'

chapter twenty-nine

'Call that rowing?' I murmured, leaning back in the bows of the boat and letting the sun play on my eyelids as it flickered lacily through the dappled shade of the trees. 'I've had better galley slaves.'

'Oh, I don't doubt it,' Matt said, pulling hard on the oars in his dark suit, his white rose bobbing in his lapel. 'And one of the first things we're going to address, Mrs Malone, is the question of slaves. I sure as hell ain't cleaning the bath tub every day, and knowing you as I now do, I'm pretty sure *you* aren't going to either, so my mind flies naturally to housekeepers.'

'Housekeepers?' I opened one eye.

'To keep some kind of order around the place while I'm away in Exeter curing the sick and you're penning your Emily Dickinson biography. Believe me, honey, the dust will gather.'

I sat up a bit. 'You know what Quentin Crisp said? After the first four years, the dust doesn't get any thicker.' I giggled.

Matt grimaced. 'Happily, I'm not sharing a house with the self-appointed last-of-the-stately-homos, and frankly the detritus two kids make – not to mention one very shaggy dog we seem to have acquired – is more than mere dust.'

I half closed my eyes into the sun, letting my fingers drift languidly in the cold, clear water, being careful not to let the scalloped edge of my lace sleeve get wet.

'I have to admit the whole idea of staff has always made me rather nervous,' I murmured. 'I'm too middle class to know how to deal with them; I haven't the natural authority to tell them to plump the cushions and get right in those corners, and would probably let them shake a duster around ineffectually before sitting down at the kitchen table to eat me out of chocolate biscuits. But if that's what you want, I'll happily go along with it.' I slipped a satin shoe off and put my foot in his lap. 'Frankly, my darling, today I'll go along with anything.' I wiggled my toes, watching his face.

Matt let the oars go limp in their rowlocks for a moment. He leaned forward on them, regarding me. 'Well, we sure aren't going to make it back before the guests drive round inland if you carry on like that,' he said softly, his mouth twitching. 'As a matter of fact, I'm tempted to undo all those pearl buttons which I noticed in church go right the way down the back of that dress, and let it fall in a heap in the bottom of the boat, along with that shoe.'

There was silence for a moment, while our eyes feasted and we rashly considered this option. I sat up hastily.

'If you think I'm arriving at my reception looking like a girl who's just been ravished in the bottom of a boat, you're wrong. Row on, my man.'

He grinned and picked up the oars. 'Who said anything about ravishing? Just wanted to see you in a rowing boat in your smalls. And incidentally, why can't I use the outboard motor on this thing? Get us there a whole lot quicker.'

'Ah, but it wouldn't be romantic, would it? No no, the idea is that you row me from the church across the creek like something out of a Milk Tray advert, while I languish in the bows like this.' I threw my head back dramatically and let my hair fall Pre-Raphaelite style over the side.

He laughed. Shook his head. 'Just so long as everything's going according to plan, Mrs Malone.'

'Oh it's going perfectly, Mr Malone,' I beamed, sitting up again. 'Just perfectly.'

I twisted around in the boat and gazed wistfully back at the little stone church we'd just left on the opposite shore. Its cool grey façade and slate roof glinted in the sunlight as it nestled in the soft green lea of the land.

'It *was* pretty though, wasn't it, Matt?' I breathed. 'Everyone said so, and everyone said how heavenly it looked inside, full of harebells and cow parsley and red campion . . . You know Rosie and I were up at dawn collecting all those flowers? They wouldn't have lasted overnight.'

'So I gather, although most brides would have let a florist do all that work, with proper hot-house flowers, but not my bride. Oh no, hot-house flowers weren't good enough for her. She wanted the church to look like an extension of the hedgerow, without a carnation in sight.' He shook his head ruefully. 'I had no idea you had such firm views on wedding etiquette.'

I leaned forward eagerly. 'But I knew exactly how everything should be today. Right down to the provençal tablecloths in the marquee and the chocolate sponge inside the wedding cake and the jars of poppies on the tables – which I hope Clare remembered to bring.'

He regarded me a moment. Smiled. 'Good. I'm glad. That's how it should be. Oh, and the *other* reason I knew about those darn wild flowers was because you woke me at dawn to tell me you were off to collect them. Remember? And I grunted and swore about being woken so damn early?'

I smiled. 'Sorry. Just thought I'd better tell you in case you woke up and thought I'd done a bunk.'

'Now that,' he admitted with an eyebrow cocked, 'didn't even occur to me. Too arrogant, you see. No, I just woke up and thought: My, what a lucky girl that Annie O'Harran is, to be marrying a— Oof.' He doubled up in mock agony as I aimed a gentle toe in his groin.

'Sorry, honey,' he gasped. 'I'll just row a little faster, shall I? Keep to your tight schedule?'

'We're nearly there,' I said excitedly, sitting up straight as the little blue boat drifted towards the shore. 'Oh Matt, this is *so* special, isn't it? And look, Tod and Flora have even decorated the beach!'

He turned round to glimpse the buttercups and poppies strewn across the shore. Grinned. 'I wondered what those two were up to this morning. How's the banner up close?'

I gazed up at Taplow House, the roof of which was just visible behind the trees, and across which Tod and Flora had strung a banner – climbing through an attic window to do it whilst Matt and I, horrified, had yelled from the garden below, 'Come down NOW!' – which read: 'Congratulations Matt and Annie.'

I smiled. 'It's brilliant.' I gazed above it to the cloudless blue sky, feeling the breeze in my hair. 'And the weather held, didn't it? And everyone said September could be so dodgy—'

'And that the heavens could quite conceivably open and drown us in our cross-channel voyage, but not my dear wife, who had the day planned to such a tee, that I for one sent a silent prayer up to the Almighty to keep those rain clouds at bay and not spoil her big day.'

'Our big day,' I breathed. 'We're here.'

Matt hoisted in the oars, taking care not to crush the flowers and streamers I'd decorated the boat with that morning, and we drifted into the clear, glassy shallows.

Happiness and excitement bubbling up within me, I held on to the sides as Matt, looking ludicrously handsome in his morning coat, trousers rolled up to the knees, jumped out and waded the last few feet, pulling us up the beach. He held out his hand to me as I stood up and our eyes locked for a second.

'I'm not sure whether I've mentioned this,' he said, 'but you're looking rather lovely today.'

'Thank you.' I smoothed down the vintage cream dress shyly. Glanced up. 'You hadn't peeked and seen it, had you?'

'I most certainly had not.' He helped me out. 'Flora told me it was in the closet in her bedroom along with the rather fetching grey number she's wearing today, but that if I so much as set foot in her room I'd be on the first ship back to the colonies.'

'I found it in an antique shop in Helston.'

'Of course you did. No spanking new designer labels for my wife. Only the best bit of tatty old lace.'

'Less of the tatty or you'll definitely be on that ship— Oh, listen, Matt. I can hear them!'

We paused for a moment as we tied up the boat and listened to the muffled voices above us. The rest of the wedding party had gone on in a procession of cars inland, whilst we'd rowed across alone, seen off from the shore by only Flora and Tod, who'd waved and jumped up and down before beetling back to the cars, determined to beat us.

We held hands as we walked along the beach and then up through the wood, following the familiar, winding sandy path to the top. As we emerged through the trees into the sunshine, I saw that someone had thoughtfully raised the sides of the tiny candy-striped marquee by the terrace, revealing the legs of the guests inside, who, for a small clutch of people, were making a great deal of excited chatter. There were children all over the lawn, scampering about with our newly acquired hairy dog, and as Giles, my nephew, spotted us and darted inside the marquee to report, I felt a knot of excitement grow in my stomach. A great cheer went up as everyone came out to greet us: champagne glasses were raised high as we approached, and then the throng parted and they roared us in. Blinking and laughing foolishly, I kissed Rosie and Dan, who were at the front, then Clare and Michael, who were whooping and clapping loudly behind, then more friends – some down from London who were staying in bed and breakfasts – and our windsurfing vicar, who'd astonished Matt and me a few weeks ago after our banns had been read by changing into a wetsuit and surfing home. I spotted Mum at the back, raising her glass and blinking madly, and remembered how in church she'd been unashamedly dabbing away with her hanky as Matt and I had taken our vows. I blew her a kiss. Matt's parents were here too, over from the States and staying with Louise and Tom. Everyone wanted to pump Matt's hand and kiss my cheek as we came through.

Matt's father, an extremely tall, rather distingu-ished-looking academic who still lectured occasion-ally at Princeton, was the first to claim me, whisking me away while Matt went to see my mum.

'So, congratulations are in order on all sorts of fronts, I gather,' he said, twinkling down at me from his very great height. 'Firstly for looking like the most handsome couple I've seen in a long time, but also for becoming people of property. I understand from Gertrude over there that a little transaction is about to take place?'

I smiled over in Gertrude's direction, where, elegant in a long biscuit linen coat, with dramatic feathers looping from a tiny hat perched on the back of her head, she chatted to Flora.

'Well, she's been wanting to sell it for some time. She feels she's too old to hang on to it any longer, and since Matt's been offered the head of psychiatry at Exeter – well, we've got to have somewhere to live and frankly we can't think of anywhere nicer.'

'Oh sure, it's a peach of a place. But all year round? Winter too?' He gave me a quizzical gleam as he regarded me over his half-moon glasses. 'Matt grew up on the ocean so I don't doubt his enthusiasm, or Tod's for that matter, but I have to tell you, January will be pretty bleak when the storm clouds gather and the wind whips around this place.'

'Oh, but I can't wait! The bleaker the better. I can't wait to see this house out of season, when the waves are beating against the rocks down there and the spray comes right up to the windows. I love that feeling of being safe and warm inside while the sea whips up to a frenzy outside.'

He smiled. 'I'm with you there. Given the choice it's how I'd live all year. There's nothing quite like waking up to the sound of the sea breaking on the shore in the morning.'

'And I won't be remote and lonely at all, because Rosie and Dan are just around the corner, and Louise and Tom too.'

'Whose boys, I gather, are something of a hit with your daughter?'

I laughed. 'Well, the middle one's certainly made an impression.' I turned to look as Flora chatted animatedly to a lanky blond fourteen-year-old, who was scratching his leg shyly and blushing.

'And of course they're all going to be at the same school,' said Louise, overhearing and coming up to offer her congratulations. She kissed my cheek. 'My boys can't wait till next term to swagger into class with Flora.'

'Well, I can assure you the feeling's mutual. It's a dream come true for her, really. Not only to be going to a mixed school but to have Tod and the cousins there too.'

'And Tod's happy?' she asked. 'I mean, to be staying here?'

'Oh definitely. He was desperate to get away from Cambridge, but quite content not to go back home for a bit. He wants to go to university in the States, but he's happy to have a few years at school in England first. As long as he's with his father and by the sea, he's fine.'

'And you, my dear, you're happy?' Gertrude drifted up as Louise moved away. She kissed me, and her grey eyes were kind and quizzical. 'You certainly look it.'

'Oh I am, and I can't thank you enough for coming, Gertrude. It means so much to me, it really does. I thought, well, after David . . .'

'That I'd never speak to you again?' She pulled a face. 'I'm too fond of you and Flora for that, and we all know you did the right thing. David too. He wrote to me recently, incidentally, to say he's inoculated over two thousand children against measles already and they're awaiting more vaccines. The infant mortality rate from the disease and the malnutrition out there is appalling apparently.'

'Golly.' I gulped. 'How awful. Sort of . . . puts everything into perspective, doesn't it? This all seems a bit inconsequential and trivial compared to that.' I gazed around sheepishly at all my friends and family, laughing and drinking.

'Nonsense,' she said, patting my arm. 'I didn't mean to dampen your day, this has its own importance. And David needed a cause. Some people do, you know. And now he's found one. Just be glad it's not you.'

She gave me a mischievous smile and moved on,

picking her way around a group of children on the lawn who were throwing a frisbee about. As Rosie's eldest leaped up to catch it, he missed, and it sailed over to the herbaceous border where Mum was chatting to Matt's mother in a patch of sunlight. Mum ducked as it looked about to take her hat off, then squealed thankfully as a man's hand shot out to grab it. She fell laughing on his arm. He threw it back to the children, caught my eye, and sauntered over.

'Adam.'

'Congratulations, my love.' He leaned in and kissed my cheek. 'You did the right thing in the end and married the right man. Bastard.'

I grinned. 'Thanks.'

'And thank you, for the invitation.'

I gave a wry smile. 'Well, I have to tell you, I deliberated long and hard.'

He laughed. 'I bet you did. And Matt, presumably, couldn't care less?

'Oh, Matt couldn't give a monkey's. The more the merrier was his attitude.'

'There's confidence for you. And yours was?'

'Sorry?'

'Your attitude?'

'Oh, that it would be nice for Flora. And it is.' We both turned to look across at her, still chatting to Tod's cousin, her cheeks glowing as she flicked her hair back from her shoulder, looking really rather stunning in her long grey dress.

'We're going to have to keep an eye on her,' said

Adam as the same thought crossed his mind. 'Rather too many predatory male adolescents trailing her this afternoon for my liking. They'll have to be handy with their fists. I'm not having any old Tom, Dick or Harry taking her out.'

I smiled. 'I'm sure she'll use her father's discretion.'

He raised an eyebrow. 'And what's that supposed to mean? I'll have you know I'm a changed man since I heard about your engagement. Quite laid me low, as a matter of fact, and I haven't so much as laid a finger on— Ooh, I say. What have we here?' He stood aside to accommodate a rather voluptuous blonde in a very short skirt and plunging neckline, who was muscling through to congratulate me.

'I know you're busy chattin' an' that, but I gotta kiss the bride at some point, en I!'

I grinned as she left half of Max Factor on my cheek. 'Of course you have. Adam, this is Lorraine, Matt's new private secretary at Exeter Hospital. Lorraine, this is my ex-husband Adam.'

She turned to him, grinning coquettishly, and dug him hard in the ribs with an elbow. 'Oh yeah, I heard all about you from Flora. Bit of a ladykiller, by all accounts!'

Adam puffed out his chest. 'Well, I wouldn't say *kill*er exactly. No maiden, to my knowledge, has actually been fatally slain on account of my charms, but perhaps felled at the knees would be a better analogy?'

She chortled. 'Funny, ent ya? And my auntie saw

you in rep in Truro. Said it was worth goin' just to see you in tights. Said you fairly blocked out the sun!' She roared loudly.

Adam was cheering up considerably now. 'Well, your auntie sounds like a woman of taste,' he murmured. 'Tell me, um, Lorraine. Can I get you a drink? Only you seem to be bereft.'

'Be-what? Oh, yeah. Well they've only got champagne see, an' I get really really bladdered on that, so better not.'

Adam smouldered professionally. 'Surely just a little glass wouldn't hurt? After all, this is a celebration, and we can mix it with a dash of peach juice if you wish? Have a Bellini?'

'Have a what? Ooh, you saucy—! Yeah, orright, go on then.'

'Come,' said Adam, gently guiding her by the elbow towards the drinks table under the apple tree, a smile playing on his lips, a familiar light in his eyes. 'Come and admire the ripening Coxes. I might even pluck you one.'

'Might you indeed.'

I smiled at their departing backs and drifted on, nodding and thanking as, all around me, tides of greeting and congratulations flowed; travelling light, the scent of lavender and old-fashioned roses filling my lungs, and always feeling Matt's presence, glimpsing him occasionally through the throng.

Clare and Rosie were talking energetically by the huge chocolate cake, and Rosie broke off as I approached, her face alight.

'I was just saying, my only reservation about moving down here was not knowing a soul, but now I've got my best friend round the corner!'

'I know.' I hugged her hard.

'Except of course I'll be the one left in London.' Clare pulled a sour face. 'I'll be no-mates Clare.'

'Oh Clare, you've got loads of mates,' I rallied, managing to avoid catching Rosie's eye. 'And think how often you can come down now that you're not working? You can come and stay for weeks in the summer with the children.'

'That's true,' she conceded. 'And lovely for Mum to have you so close by. Now she's getting older.'

'Lovely for me too,' I said hugging her as she approached, resplendent in her grey silk suit. 'Church all right, Mum? Meet with your approval?'

'Ooh yes, love, everything I dreamed of. And you look a picture too, doesn't she, Ted?'

'Aye. That you do.' Ted beamed, pink and burly at her side, and looking as if he might go pop at any minute in his ancient, tight-fitting tweed suit.

'Your dad would have been *so* proud,' Mum went on. 'I don't know what he'd have said about this hat, though.' She put an anxious hand to her head. 'Flora made me stick this feather in the side, said it made it, but I'm not so sure myself. And I can just hear your father, Annie. "Marjorie, you look like a chicken."'

'Then I'm a lucky man,' said Matt, coming up beside her. 'Not many men can boast a spring chicken for a mother-in-law, and a glamorous one at that,' he added gallantly, making her blush delightedly. 'But now I fear I must break up the party. Michael and Tom are ready for us, honey.'

Matt took my hand and I wondered if I'd ever stop getting a thrill up and down my spine every time he called me that. I looked up at him, tall and broad beside me as we moved on air to the top table, where Tom, Matt's best man, and Michael, who'd given me away, were waiting. Michael raised his glass as we stopped beside him, a huge grin on his face.

'Ladies and gentlemen,' he boomed. 'I give you . . . the bride and groom!'

Glasses were raised and a chorus of voices soared right up to the top of the marquee.

'THE BRIDE AND GROOM!'

A Married Man

Catherine Alliott

When Lucy Fellowes is offered a dream house in the country she leaps at the chance. It's hard enough living in London on an uncertain income, but when you're widowed with two small boys it's even harder. And anyway, a rural retreat will bring her closer to Charlie. Charlie? The only man in four years to make her heart beat faster. Perfect. Or it would be. If only he didn't belong to someone else . . .

A wickedly witty new novel about how complicated relationships get when you grow up, from the best-selling author of *Rosie Meadows regrets* . . . and *Olivia's Luck*.

'Alliott's skilled handling of such delicate, difficult and deep material marvellously counterpoints the Cotswolds comic archetypes and provides psychological depth and shadow to the sparky surface action. Sensitive, funny and wonderfully well-written.' Wendy Holden, *Daily Express*

0 7472 6722 7

headline

Rosie Meadows regrets . . .

Catherine Alliott

Well, what could I say? If he was smitten then I could be too, and I sank back into the whole cosy relationship with a monumental sigh of relief. I didn't have to try too hard, didn't have to be too witty, too amusing, too beautiful . . . It was like landing on a feather mattress after all those years of being Out There.

Three years down the line, however, Rosie's beginning to think that 'cosy' isn't all it's cracked up to be. Bridge parties have never really been her thing, and it would be nice to feel beautiful just once in a while. Enough is enough. It's time to get her life back.

'Alliott's *joie de vivre* is irresistible' *Daily Mail*

'Hilarious and full of surprises' *Daily Telegraph*

'A joy . . . you're in for a treat' *Express*

0 7472 5786 8

headline